CONFESSIONS ON THE 7:45

Also by Lisa Unger

THE STRANGER INSIDE
UNDER MY SKIN
THE RED HUNTER
INK AND BONE
THE WHISPERING HOLLOWS (novella)
CRAZY LOVE YOU
IN THE BLOOD
HEARTBROKEN
DARKNESS, MY OLD FRIEND
FRAGILE
DIE FOR YOU
BLACK OUT
SLIVER OF TRUTH
BEAUTIFUL LIES
SMOKE
TWICE
THE DARKNESS GATHERS
ANGEL FIRE

CONFESSIONS ON THE 7:45

LISA UNGER

ISBN-13: 978-0-7783-1015-0

Confessions on the 7:45

This edition published by arrangement with Harlequin Books S.A.

Park Row Books
22 Adelaide St. West, 40th Floor
Toronto, Ontario M5H 4E3, Canada
ParkRowBooks.com
BookClubbish.com

Printed in U.S.A.

For Jeffrey.
Because after twenty years and counting,
you are first, last and always.

CONFESSIONS ON THE

"If you want to keep a secret, you must also hide it from yourself."

—George Orwell, *1984*

PART 1

ALL OUR LITTLE SECRETS

PROLOGUE

SHE WATCHED. THAT was her gift. To disappear into the black, sink into the shadows behind and between. That's where you really saw things for what they were, when people revealed their true natures. Everyone was on broadcast these days, thrusting out versions of themselves, cropped and filtered for public consumption. Everyone putting on the "show of me." It was when people were alone, unobserved, that the mask came off.

She'd been watching him for a while. The mask he wore was slipping.

He, too, stood in the shadows of the street, a hulking darkness. She'd followed him as he drove, circling like a predator, then finding a place for his car under the trees. He'd parked, then sat as the night wound on and inside lights went out, one by one. Finally, he'd stepped out of his vehicle, closed the door quietly, and slipped across the street. Now he waited. What was he doing?

Since she'd been following him the last few weeks, she'd seen him push his children on the swings in the park, visit a strip club in the middle of the day, drink himself stupid with his buddies viewing a game at a sports bar. She'd watched as he'd helped a young mother with a toddler and baby in a carriage carry her groceries from her car into her house.

Once, he'd picked up a woman in a local bar. Then, out in the parking lot, they romped like animals in his car. Later, he went to the grocery store and picked up food for his family, his cart piled high with ice cream and Goldfish crackers, things his kids liked.

What was he up to now?

The observer only sees, never interferes. Still, tonight she felt the tingle of bad possibilities. She waited in the cool night, patient and still.

The clicking of heels echoed, a brisk staccato up the deserted street. She felt a little pulse of dread. Was there no one else around? No one else glancing out their window? No. She was the only one. Sometimes didn't it seem like people didn't see *anymore? They didn't look* out. *They looked* down, *at that device in their hands. Or* in, *mesmerized by the movie of past and future, desires and fears, always playing on the screen in their minds.*

The figure of the young woman was slim, erect, confident. She marched up the street, sure-footed, hands in her pockets, tote over her shoulder. When he moved out of the shadows and blocked her path, the young woman stopped short, backed up a step or two. He reached for her, as if to take her hand, but she wrapped her arms around her middle.

There were words she couldn't hear, an exchange. Sharp at first, then softer. On the air, far away, they sounded like calling birds. What was he doing? Fear was a cold finger up her spine.

He moved to embrace the girl, and she shrank away. But he moved in anyway. In the night, he was just a looming specter. His bulk swallowed her tiny form, and together in a kind of dance they moved toward the door, at first jerking, awkward. Then, she seemed to give in, soften into him. She let them both inside. And then the street was silent again.

She stood frozen, unsure of what she'd seen. Later, when she realized what he'd done, who he truly was under the mask, she'd hate herself for staying rooted, hiding in the shadows, only watching. She'd tell herself that she didn't know then. She didn't know that beneath the mask, he was a monster.

ONE
Selena

SELENA LOVED THE liminal spaces. Those precious slivers of time between the roles she played in her life.

She missed the 5:40 train because her client meeting ran long, knowing before she even left the conference room table that there was no way she would be home in time for dinner with her husband Graham and their two maniac boys, Stephen and Oliver. The wild hours afterward—showers, pajamas, random horseplay, vicious but brief sibling battles, television maybe if either of them could sit still a minute—that concluded in story time would have to unfold without her. Selena didn't often work late; she made a point to be home on time. Chaotic as their evenings often were, that was the best part of her day.

But when she *did* miss the train that night—she didn't even bother trying to get to the station—it created a space that hadn't been there before. Just a little over two hours between the 5:40, which she normally took, and the 7:45, which she intended to catch after finishing up a few things at the office.

In that gap, she could feel herself expand. She wasn't working. She wasn't mothering. She just was. She could think. And truth be told, Selena did have some things she needed to think about. These things were a white noise in the back of her mind.

She slipped out of the cab she'd taken back to the office, into the cool autumn evening. The noise of the city washed over her, the manic rush of people on their way home after a long day. Then she stepped into the hush of the quiet lobby, with its marble floors and gleaming walls. Selena nodded to the doorman who knew her, then swiped her card through the gates. Up the elevator alone.

Here her heart started thumping, mouth going dry. Her bag was too heavy, the tote pulling down on her tight shoulder muscles. She hadn't missed the train on purpose; she really hadn't wanted to cut the client off as he went on and on.

But.

The office was empty. The literary agency had a small staff; most of them people with families. Many of the parents left before school pickup, then worked at home in the afternoons. Beth, her boss, also her lifelong best friend, had things set up like that so that people could work well and take care of their families—imagine that. It was the rare humane workplace.

She didn't bother flipping on the light in her office, enjoying the glittering downtown view through her big window. A rush of heat to her cheeks as she dropped her bag. She shifted off her jacket and sat in front of the computer and took a deep breath before opening the lid on her laptop.

It was after 6:15 now. The boys would have had their dinner. If Selena knew their nanny, Geneva, and the efficiency with which she ran the show, Oliver and Stephen would also be showered and in jammies. She probably had them settled in front of the television already.

Selena leaned back in her ergonomic chair, felt its pleasant tilt.

She hadn't hidden the camera, precisely. Geneva had been made aware of cameras in the home—one upstairs, one down.

Selena had simply moved the one from the boys' bedroom, and told neither Graham nor Geneva about it.

She paused another second. Her desk was cluttered with framed pictures of the boys and Graham, drawings from school, a ceramic owl Oliver had made at art camp. She picked up the glazed misshapen thing; he'd carved his name in the clay bottom. She touched the ridges of the wobbly *O*, the backward *e*. Somewhere she heard a vacuum cleaner running.

Her wedding picture—where her smile beamed, and Graham was dashing in his classic tux. He'd whispered to her while the photographer snapped away—dirty things, funny things. Then: *This is the best day of my life.* His breath in her ear, his arms around her. Her whole body tingled with joy, with desire. Nearly ten years ago now. God, it was a heartbeat, a blink, a single breath drawn and released.

She put the photo down. Then, she clicked on the app that would allow her to watch on her laptop the video feed from the camera she had placed in the boys' playroom.

It took a moment for the image to load.

When it did, she was not surprised by what she saw.

Graham, her husband, was fucking Geneva, her nanny, on the activity rug that Selena and Graham had carefully selected together at IKEA.

The volume was down, so she was spared their grunting and moaning.

When had she started to suspect? About two weeks ago. She happened to catch a glance between Graham and Geneva. Something that small, a millisecond, a microexpression.

No, she'd thought. *Surely not.*

But she'd moved the bedroom camera to the playroom.

This was the second time she'd watched them. A weird calm came over her, a kind of apathetic distance from the whole thing.

Geneva wasn't *that hot*, Selena thought, as she watched the young woman who had shiny, wheat-colored hair, and flushed cheeks. Selena leaned closer to the screen, to see the girl more clearly. Attractive, certainly. But not *much* more so than Selena.

Okay. The other woman was a bit younger—but only by a few years. Maybe there was a softness to her that Selena lacked, a freshness. But she was nothing special. In fact, Geneva's just-slightly-above-average looks were a point that Selena had taken into consideration when hiring her as a nanny. Geneva was a reasonably attractive, smart, personable career childcare professional with a long list of glowing references. She was no bombshell. No blushing twentysomething with glossed lips and inappropriately placed tattoos she would later regret. Most women, Selena included, knew better than to bring some nubile hottie into her home on a regular basis. It just wasn't good business.

Besides, Geneva was *known* to Selena—coveted, in fact. They'd met on the playground during Selena's first year home with the boys. Work, the commute, the race to pick up from preschool, the balancing act that never quite balanced. It had worn her to a nub. She and her husband Graham decided that she should stay home for a time—indefinitely. They could afford that—Graham made good money. There wouldn't be Range Rovers and trips to Tahoe every spring break. But they would be fine.

Selena had *loved* the way Geneva was with the Tucker boys, Ryan and Chad. She was sweet but firm, prepared but not anal. The boys listened to her. *Eyes on me*, she'd say brightly, and so it was. Geneva wasn't like the other nannies Selena observed at the park—millennials staring at their phones while their charges ran amok or stared at devices of their own. Geneva chased, pushed swings, played hide-and-seek.

And, you know, she was not *that* hot.

Lovely features—a button nose and full lips, dark, heavily lashed doe eyes, buxom but just the tiniest bit—pleasantly—plump. Broad in the beam, as her father used to say. In a nice way, the way of strong women built for physical labor. Selena was long and slim, a genetic boon for which she was grateful because god knows she didn't have the time anymore to work for it.

Now, she turned up the volume a little, listened to them groaning. Did it sound—forced?

Selena remembered how she and Geneva had chatted almost daily. Selena's boys—Oliver and Stephen—loved her. *Is Geneva going to be there?* Oliver, her older, sometimes asked as they were headed to the park. *Probably*, Selena would answer, wishing that she had someone like Geneva, even just part-time. Someone with whom she felt good about leaving her children. But she was happy enough to be home. She didn't miss her publicity job. She'd never had that *drive to accomplish* that so many of her friends seemed to have. She just wasn't wired that way. She liked working—the independence of it, the comradery, the satisfaction of doing something well. The money. But it had never defined her.

Graham: "Oh, yeah. That's so good."

She bumped the volume down again. Picked up one of the framed pictures of the boys, holding it up so that it blocked the screen, and gazed into their flushed, joyful faces.

Motherhood defined Selena in a way that work hadn't, the idea that she was there for her children—that she cooked their meals and kept their house, their schedules, their doctor appointments and haircuts. That she was there on car line, at parent-teacher conferences, school Halloween parties. It wasn't sexy. It wasn't always easy. There wasn't a ton of cultural praise for the role, not really. But she found a level of satisfaction in it that she hadn't found elsewhere.

Then Graham unexpectedly—well, did anyone ever expect it?—lost his job. Not his fault, really. Publishing was shrinking, and his big salary was hard to justify in a flailing self-help imprint. That very same week, over cocktails, Selena's good friend Beth serendipitously offered her a huge job—a licensing director position at Beth's literary agency. Selena's salary would be more than Graham's, plus bonuses. Of course, there would have to be a nanny. Because Graham, well, he wasn't exactly hardwired for caregiving. *And finding a job is a full-time job, babe.*

So, it felt like kismet when during a chat at the park—the very next day, when Selena was grappling for solutions to their problem—Geneva told Selena that she was about to lose *her* job. Mrs. Tucker wanted to be home for a couple of years, she said.

When things were easy like that, it meant you were *in the flow*, didn't it? Isn't that what they said these days? It made it easy for Selena to go back to work. It wasn't necessarily what she wanted. But you did what you had to do, right? Graham would find another job. It wasn't forever—though the money was nice.

The way the camera was positioned, Selena had the best view of Geneva—who apparently liked to be on top. Was it Selena's imagination? Geneva didn't seem that into it. Though from the look on her face and the movement of her lips, she was surely making all the appropriate noises.

On the other video feed from the downstairs camera, the boys were slack-jawed in front of *Trollhunters*. They were both scrubbed clean, fed, and in their jammies, waiting for Selena.

Geneva was faultless on that count, which was odd to note in a moment like this. But Selena had really appreciated that Geneva wasn't one of those nannies that tried to be the mommy. As soon as Selena returned home in the evenings, Geneva took her proper place, eagerly leaving as soon as she could, sometimes before Selena even came back downstairs from changing. The house was always clean, the boys were usually calm-ish—as calm as boys five and seven could ever be. But they weren't wild like they were when Graham was at the helm. On the rare occasions when Graham had the kids for the day, they'd be filthy, overstimulated, out of routine—desperate for order and a way to calm themselves. Graham thought he was one of them, acted more like a corrupting older sibling than a parent.

Like now. As he boned the nanny in the playroom while his young sons watched television downstairs.

Why wasn't she angrier about this?

It had been a buzz in the back of her head since the first time she'd watched them three days ago. A barely audible thrum, something she pushed away and pushed back, down, down, down. Why wasn't she weeping with anger, the sting of betrayal, jealousy? Why hadn't she raced home after the first discovery, raging, and tossed him out, fired Geneva? That's what anyone would do.

But Selena was only aware of a kind of numbness that had settled after the first time, a mean, heartless apathy. But no. Beneath that numb layer inside was something else.

Now, Geneva had her head back in pleasure. Graham wore that helpless look he had right before he was about to climax; he kind of lifted his eyebrows a little, lids closed the way violin players did sometimes when they were rapt in their music. Selena realized she was clutching the arms of her chair so tightly that her hands ached.

She was distantly aware of another feeling, one she deeply pressed down for a good long time, long before this. At some point after the birth of their second child, Selena had started to dislike her husband. Not all the time. But with shocking intensity—the way he interrupted her when she was talking, hovered over her in the kitchen micromanaging, the way he claimed to share the housework when he didn't. At all. Surely it was true of all couples who had been together for a long time. Then he lost his job—sort of gleefully, it must be said.

Oh, well, I was looking for a change. And you said you were missing work.

Had she said that? She didn't think so, since she hadn't been missing work.

At some point after that, when she'd come home to find him in the same athletic pants two days in a row, or when she checked the browser history on the computer and couldn't find a shred of evidence that he'd been looking for a job at all, she started to hate him a little. Then more. That svelte and charming man in the tux, the one who made her laugh and shiver with pleasure, he seemed like someone from a dream she could barely remember.

Now, as she leaned in to turn up the volume again and heard him moan beneath Geneva, the depth and scope of her hatred was primal. She understood for the first time in her life how people might kill each other—married people who once loved with passion and devotion, who once cried happy tears at the altar, and went on a magnificent honeymoon, conceived beautiful children, built a lovely life.

That thing lurking inside her, it was pounding to get out. She could hear it. But she couldn't quite *feel* it.

She'd been on autopilot with Graham, going through the motions, rebuffing his advances. If he'd noticed her distance, he hadn't said anything. The truth was, it wasn't the first time he'd cheated. But she thought they'd moved past it. There'd been counseling, tearful promises. She'd—foolishly it seemed—forgiven him and allowed herself to trust him again.

"Graham."

The voice startled Selena, snapped her back to the present moment.

Geneva had climbed off Selena's husband, already pulled her skirt down. Both times there had been hasty dressing afterward, averted eyes and frowning faces. At least they had the decency not to lie around after sex, not to *luxuriate* on the playroom floor.

"This has to stop," said Geneva. Selena heard the notes of shame, regret. Good. Good for you, Geneva!

Graham had pulled up his pants, sat on the couch and dropped his head into his hands.

"I know," he said, voice muffled.

"You have a nice family. A beautiful life. And this is—fucked," Geneva said, her face flushed.

Oh, Geneva, thought Selena crazily, *please don't quit.*

"I think I should give notice," said Geneva.

Graham looked up, stricken. "God, no," he said. "Don't do that."

Selena laughed out loud. No, it wasn't love. He wasn't afraid of losing the lovely young Geneva. He was *terrified* that he would have to be the primary caregiver for Stephen and Oliver while he "looked for another job."

"Selena relies on you," he said. "She appreciates you *so much*."

Geneva let out a little laugh, which made Selena smile, too, before she caught herself. How could Selena still *like* the woman who she'd just watched fuck her husband? She must be losing her grip. That's what working motherhood did to you; it robbed you of your sanity.

"I doubt very much that she'd appreciate *this*," Geneva said.

"No," said Graham. He was pale with shame, rubbing at his jaw. He looked up and, with a strange rush of relief, for a second Selena saw him—her husband, her best friend, the father of her children. He was still there. He wasn't a fiction she'd created.

"Then, look," said Geneva. She wrapped her arms around her middle, started moving toward the door. "You need to be around less. You need to find a job."

"Okay," he said. His hair was wild; it looked like he hadn't shaved in days.

What did Geneva see in him? Truly? At least he and Selena had a history; their love affair had been epic, their travels full of adventure, their home life quite lovely. His infidelities, prior to this one, had been relatively minor. That's what she'd told herself anyway—not affairs exactly. He'd been a decent husband until recently, a provider. He was her best friend, the person she wanted to share everything with first. Funny. Charming. Smart. Even now, in this ugly moment, she wished she could call him to talk about her monstrous husband who was fucking the nanny. He'd certainly know what to do.

"It's not a good idea for men to be home," Geneva went on. "I've seen it a lot in recent years. It's just—a bad idea usually."

"Yeah," he said again, sounding ever more dejected. Poor Geneva. She didn't know she would have to be Graham's nanny, too.

Selena slammed the lid on her laptop closed with more force than she'd intended, slipped it into the case, stuffed the case into her bag. She shouldered on her dark wool jacket, feeling a churning in her stomach.

She *was* angry, hurt, betrayed—she knew that. But it was dormant, lava churning in a deep chasm within her, pressure building. She'd always been this way, the surface calm, the depths rumbling. She pressed things down, away—until she couldn't. The eruptions were epic.

By the time she'd reached the street, a pall had settled over her again. The gray numbness. The city was a crush. She pushed her way through the crowded streets to the subway, then through the bustling station to the platform, just catching her commuter train home.

She walked through the cars as the train hissed, seemed about to pull from the station, then stopped.

There. A seat beside a young woman, who, for a moment, looked almost familiar. She had straight black hair, mocha eyes, a slight smile on red lips. Svelte, stylish—even from a distance Selena instantly liked her. Seeing Selena move toward her, the other woman lifted her tote to make room. And Selena sank into the space beside her issuing what must have been a telling sigh. She clutched her *People* magazine in her hand. All she wanted to do was lose herself in those fluffy, glossy pages for the next forty minutes, a blessed escape from her problems.

"Rough day?" asked the stranger. Her expression—a half smile on full lips, a glint in her dark eyes—said that she knew it all. That she had been there. That she was in on the joke, whatever it was.

Selena half laughed. "You have no idea."

TWO

Anne

IT HAD BEEN a mistake from the beginning and Anne certainly knew that. You don't sleep with your boss. It's really one of the things mothers should teach their daughters. Chew your food carefully. Look both ways before you cross the street. Don't fuck your direct supervisor no matter how hot, rich, or charming he may happen to be. Not that Anne's mother had taught her a single useful thing.

Anyway, here she was. Again. Taking it from behind, over the couch in her boss's corner office with those expansive city views. The world was a field of lights spread wide around them. She tried to enjoy it. But, as was often the case, she just kind of floated above herself. She made all the right noises, though. She knew how to fake it.

"Oh my god, Anne. You're so hot."

He pressed himself in deep, moaning.

When he'd first come on to her, she thought he was kidding—or not thinking clearly. They'd flown together to DC to take an important client who was considering leaving the investment firm out to dinner. In the cab on the way back to the hotel—while Hugh was *on the phone* with his wife—he put his hand on Anne's leg. He wasn't even looking at Anne when he did it, so for a moment she wondered if it was just absentmindedness. He was like that sometimes, a little loopy. Overly affectionate, familiar. Forgetful.

His hand moved up her thigh. Anne sat very still. Like a prey animal. Hugh ended the call and she expected him to jerk his hand back.

Oh! I'm so sorry, Anne, she thought he'd say, aghast at his careless behavior.

But no. His hand moved higher.

"Am I misreading signals?" he said, voice low.

Stop. What most people would be thinking: *Poor Anne! Afraid for her job, she submits to this predator.*

What Anne was thinking: *How can I use this to my advantage?* She really *had been* just trying to do her job well, sort of. But it seemed that Pop was right, as he had been about so many things. If you weren't running a game, someone was running one on you.

Had she subconsciously been putting out signals? Possibly. Yes. Maybe Pop was right about that, too. You don't get to stop being what you are, even when you try.

They made out like prom dates in the cab, comported themselves appropriately as they walked through the lobby of the Ritz. He pressed against her at the door to her hotel room. She was glad she was wearing sexy underwear, had shaved her legs.

She'd given Hugh—with his salt-and-pepper hair, sinewy muscles, flat abs—the ride of his life that night. And many nights since. He liked her on top. He was a considerate lover, always asking: *Is this good? Are you okay?* Confessional: *Kate and I—we've been married a long time. We both have—appetites*. She couldn't care less about his marriage.

Anne didn't actually believe in the things other people seemed to value so highly. Fidelity—really? Were you supposed to just want one person your whole life? Marriage. Was there ever anything more set up to fail, to disappoint, to erode? Come on. They were animals. Every last one of them rutting, feral beasts. Men. Women. All of society was held together by gossamer-thin, totally arbitrary laws and mores that were always shifting and changing no matter how people clung. They were all just barely in line.

Anne neither expected nor encouraged Hugh to fall in love. In fact, she spoke very little. She listened, made all the right affirming noises. If he noticed that she had told him almost nothing about herself, it didn't come up. But fall in love with Anne he did. And things were getting complicated.

Now, finished and holding her around the waist, Hugh was crying a little. His body weight was pinning her down. He often got emotional after they made love. She didn't mind him most of the time. But the whole crying thing—it was such a turnoff. She pushed against him and he let her up. She tugged down her skirt, and he pulled her into an embrace.

She held him for a while, then wiped his eyes, kissed his tears away. Because she knew that's what he wanted. She had a special gift for that, knowing what people wanted—really wanted deep down—and giving them that thing for a while. And that was why Hugh—why anyone—fell in love. Because he loved getting the thing he wanted, even if he didn't know what that was.

When he moved away finally, she stared at her ghostly reflection in the dark window, wiped at her smeared lipstick.

"I'm going to leave her," Hugh said. He flung himself on one of the plush sofas. He was long and elegant; his clothes impeccable, bespoke, made from the finest fabrics. Tonight, his silk tie was loose, pressed cotton shirt was wilted, black wool suit pants still looking crisp. Garments, all garments—even just his tennis whites—hung beautifully on his fit body.

She smiled, moved to sit beside him. He kissed her, salty and sweet.

"It's time. I can't do this anymore," he went on.

This wasn't the first time he'd said this. Last time, when she'd tried to discourage him, he'd held her wrists too hard when she tried to leave. There had been something bright and hard in his eyes—desperation. She didn't want him to get clingy tonight. Emotional.

"Okay," she said, running her fingers through his hair. "Yeah."

Because that's what he wanted to hear, needed to hear. If you didn't give people what they wanted, they became angry. Or they pulled away. And then the game was harder or lost altogether.

"We'll go away," he said, tracing a finger along her jaw. Because of course they'd both lose their jobs. Hugh's wife, Kate, owned and ran the investment firm, had inherited the company from her legendary father. Her brothers were on the board. They'd never liked Hugh (this was one of his favorite pillow talk tirades, how Kate's brothers didn't respect him). "We'll take a long trip abroad and figure out what comes next. Clean slate for both of us. Would you like that?"

"Of course," she said. "That would be wonderful."

Anne liked her job; when she'd applied and interviewed, she honestly wanted to work at the firm. Numbers made a kind of sense to her, investment a kind of union of logic and magic. Client work was a bit of a game, wasn't it—convincing people to part with their cash on the promise that you could make them more? She also respected and admired her boss—her lover's wife—Kate. A powerful, intelligent woman.

Maybe Anne should have thought about all of that before she submitted to Hugh's advances. He wasn't the power player; she'd miscalculated, or not run the numbers at all. She made mistakes like that sometimes, let the game run *her.* Pop thought it was a form of self-sabotage. *Sometimes, sweetie, I think your heart's not quite in it.* Maybe he was right.

"Ugh," said Hugh, pulling away, glancing at his watch. "I'm late. I have to change and meet Kate at the fundraiser."

She rose and walked the expanse of his office, got his tux from the closet, and laid it across the back of the couch. Another stunning item, heavy and silken. She ran her fingers lovingly along the lapel. He rose, and she helped him dress, hanging his other clothes, putting them back in the closet. She did his tie. In his heart, he was a little boy. He wanted to be attended to, cared for. Maybe everyone wanted that.

"You look wonderful," she said, kissing him. "Have fun tonight."

He looked at her long, eyes filling again.

"Soon," he said, "this charade can end."

She put a gentle hand to his cheek, smiled as sweetly as she could muster and started to move from the room.

"Anne," he said, grabbing for her hand. "I love you."

She'd never said it back. She'd said things like *me, too* or she'd send him the heart-eyed emoji in response to a text. Sometimes she just blew him a kiss. He hadn't seemed to notice, or his pride was too enormous to ask her why she never said it, or if she loved him. But mainly, she thought it was because Hugh only saw and heard what he wanted to.

She unlaced her fingers and blew him a kiss. "Good night, Hugh."

His phone rang, and he watched her as he answered.

"I'm coming, darling," he said, averting his eyes, moving away. "Just had to finish up with a client."

She left him, his voice following her down the hall.

In her office, she gathered her things, a strange knot in the pit of her stomach. She sensed that her luck was about to run out here. She couldn't say why. Just a feeling that things were unsustainable—that it wasn't going to be as easy to leave Kate as he thought, that on some level he didn't really want to, that once things reached critical mass, she'd be out of a job. Of course, it wouldn't be a total loss. She'd make sure of that.

There was a loneliness, a hollow feeling that took hold at the end. She wished she could call Pop, that he could talk her through it. Instead her phone pinged. The message there annoyed her.

This is wrong, it said. I don't want to do this anymore.

Just stay the course, she wrote back. It's too late to back out now.

Funny how that worked. At the critical moment, she had to give the advice she needed herself. The student becomes the teacher. No doubt, Pop would be pleased.

Anne glanced at the phone. The little dots pulsed, then disappeared. The girl, younger, greener, would do what she was told. She always had. So far.

Anne looked at her watch, imbued with a bit of energy. If she hustled, she could just make it.

THREE

Selena

AS SELENA WAS settling into her seat next to the other woman, the train just died on the track, emitting a defeated groan. The lights went dark, then came back up. She waited.

Please, she thought.

If the train left the station now, she could still make it home to see the boys before they were asleep. She glanced at her seatmate, who was staring out the window. All she could see was the curtain of her glossy black hair, the edge of her elegant profile. Did they know each other? she wondered again.

Selena texted Graham, the cheating bastard:

Train delayed!

Ugh, he wrote back. Nanny gone. I'll start bedtime. Boys waiting for you. Love you!

She loved how he didn't use Geneva's name. Hadn't she read

something about that? Distancing. Like: I never had sexual relations with *that woman.*

His text sounded repentant, didn't it? It was the exclamation mark, a thing he rarely used. All editors hate the exclamation point; it's a cheat. The dialogue should speak for itself. But, in texting, it communicated warmth, enthusiasm, brightness—something. If he'd resorted to it, he must feel like a monster. He *was* a monster.

Love you, she texted back reluctantly. No exclamation point.

But she did. Always had, all their years together. He made her laugh. He knew just how to rub her shoulders. He was strong; he handled the business of their lives, chopped firewood, did the landscaping. He had been, in many ways, a good husband. And she did love him. Odd. Because she also hated him with equal passion. That rumble inside. That volcanic mix of sadness, anger, love. Villages would be reduced to ash when it finally erupted.

Selena looked out the window.

Black.

All she could see was the faint reflection of the other woman's face in the glass. There were only a few other people in the car now. Many had gotten up and left to find alternative transport, she guessed. Selena could have moved to another seat, so that they each had a section to themselves. But was that rude?

Her face.

What was it?

The other woman's cheekbones were high and pronounced. Her dark eyes an abyss. There was a sensual shape to her mouth, something almost sweetly crooked. She was about to make polite conversation when the other woman spoke. A whisper, something Selena didn't hear at first. When she later would look back on this first encounter, she tried to find reasons for what happened next.

Maybe it was just one of those strange, deep connections that take you by surprise like falling in love. Or was it that delay, the darkened car, the powerlessness of waiting?

Sometimes it just happened that way with women, an instant intimacy. Selena had experienced it a number of times. You just look at each other—and you *know.* The journey from girlhood to womanhood, the hopes and dreams they all share, how life rarely delivers, and, even if it does, how it's never quite what you expected. There's no glass slipper, no Prince Charming. That princess updo, it hurts after a while, your hair pulled too taut, the pins too sharp. The disappointments, the dawning of reality. And, yes, all the good things too—real love, true friendship, the birth of children. You just look into her eyes, and you know the path, the journey, all the hills and valleys, the cosmic joke of it.

The other woman spoke again.

"Did you ever do something you really regretted?"

It was almost a whisper. Maybe she was just talking to herself—which Selena did all the time. Whole conversations in the shower.

Who were you talking to? Oliver, her oldest, the curious one, wanted to know the other night.

Myself, she told him.

That's weird.

At least she could be sure someone was listening, engaged. Often, she had excellent advice for herself in the shower, as if there was a little therapist in her head, one who had all the answers.

"Yes," Selena said now. "Of course."

Oh, there were so many things, stretching back as far as childhood. She regretted not inviting Marty Jasper to her fifth-grade birthday party; Marty was an odd kid, not always nice, and everyone avoided her. They weren't friends, but Selena should have invited her to be kind. She regretted losing her virginity on a dare, then losing her best friend because of it. There were some one-night stands in college that were risky, almost dangerous.

She had regrets (lots) about her ex-boyfriend Will, the one everyone thought she would marry. She should have tried harder to breastfeed; now her kids were finicky eaters because of that probably. Or maybe not. Who knew? There were other things. She could fill a book with her lists of regrets.

"I'm sleeping with my boss," said the other woman.

"Oh," said Selena, surprised but somehow not. "That one."

Just last year her good friend Leona had slept with *her* boss—both of them married; what a mess.

"If I break up with him," the other woman went on, "I think it could get very ugly. He wants to leave his wife for me."

"Oh," said Selena, leaning in. She felt a kind of salacious glee, a delightful escape from her own drama.

"His wife owns the company," she said. "Where we both work."

"Hmm," said Selena, nodding. She wasn't sure what else to say. It happened sometimes, didn't it? You just needed to confess? It was all too much to hold in; you couldn't tell the people closest to you for a million reasons. That's why people spilled their guts to the bartender, the hairdresser, right?

Sometimes a stranger was the safest place in your life.

The other woman turned to look at her in the dim of the broken-down car. She lifted a hand to her mouth, her eyes going wide.

"I'm sorry!" she said. "Why did I just tell you that?"

"Obviously," said Selena, feeling motherly and knowing, "you needed to talk."

Selena knew how that felt. She hadn't told a single soul about Graham. Not her mother, not her sister, not Beth. It was a stone in her gut, an acidic ache in her throat. What a relief it would be to release it. But how could she tell anyone? Her marriage—*Graham and Selena*—it was the fairy tale, the love-at-first-sight, happily-ever-after. It was the envy of—everyone. Now, they were just like everyone else—pitifully flawed, broken—possibly beyond repair.

The train sat, and Selena felt the crush of despair, the dark outside deepening, the stillness of the train expanding.

"I'm Martha," said the other woman, offering her hand.

"Selena," she said, taking it. Martha's hand was cool, delicate, but her grip firm.

Martha started rifling through her bag, retrieving two minibar-sized bottles of vodka. She handed one to Selena, who took it with a smile. It reminded her of her best friend and boss, Beth, who hoarded mini-bottles of everything—booze, shampoo, moisturizer, hand sanitizer, mouthwash. She'd load up at hotels, stashing the take in her suitcase, her tote. Chances were if you needed anything, needle and thread, a comb, mouthwash, lotion, Beth had it somewhere in the giant bag she hauled with her everywhere.

Martha cracked open the tiny bottle and, after a moment of hesitation, Selena did the same.

"To making a shitty day a little better," said Martha. They clinked bottles, Selena looking out for a conductor. You weren't supposed to drink on the train, were you? She felt the little tingle of glee she always felt when she was breaking a rule.

"Cheers," she said.

The vodka was warm, a slick down her throat, heat on her cheeks. Another sip and she felt a welcome lightness. The train stayed still and dark. Some of the other passengers were talking quietly on their phones. The man across from them was sleeping, his head resting on his rolled-up jacket.

Selena felt her phone ring in her pocket and fished it out. FaceTime.

"I have to get this," she said. Martha nodded, reached for the bottle, and Selena handed it to her to hold.

She answered the call to see her boys crowding to get both

their faces on the screen. She lowered the volume, rose and walked to the space between the bathrooms.

"Mom," said Oliver. "Where are you?"

"I'm stuck on the train, buddy," she said, voice low. "So sorry. Did you guys read a story?"

"Dad read *The Boy with Too Many Toys*," he said.

"Again," chimed in Stephen.

Graham was not the preferred story time parent. He didn't read with the requisite enthusiasm, only read one book, which *he* chose, no negotiation. Whereas Selena was in there for an hour, letting each boy pick a book, then often lying on the floor a while as they drifted off. Sometimes she fell asleep in there, too, and Graham had to retrieve her.

"I'll come in and give you guys a kiss as soon as I get home," she said. "I hope it won't be much longer."

She looked around again for a sign of the conductor, or someone to ask. But there was no one. What *was* the fucking hold up?

Stephen, blond, two front teeth missing, started talking about how a boy in school cut his own bangs with scissors and had to go home he was crying so hard. Oliver hadn't liked his snack, and could he have raisins tomorrow. Finally, Graham cut in.

"Okay, guys," he said. "Time for bed."

He took the phone as the boys protested, then yelled in unison: "Love you, Mom!"

"Love you, boys!" she said. "Be home soon."

"What about me?" said Graham. Now it was his face on the phone. Dark eyes, stubble, his crooked nose (broken in a football game, never healed quite right), hair tousled. That smile, devilish, rakish. "Do you love *me*?"

"I do," she said, trying to sound light. "You know I do."

She tried to block out the image of Geneva on top of him, but it came unbidden. It was, in fact, on an ugly loop in her brain, a television on in another room, a song she heard through the wall. There was an unpleasant squeeze on her heart. He must have seen it on her face.

He frowned. "What is it?"

"I should go," she said.

"Okay," he answered, rubbing his eyes, then looking back at her. "Keep me posted."

He was oblivious, no idea what she'd witnessed. And what was more, if she hadn't seen it, there was nothing in his demeanor that would suggest anything off. He was exactly as he always was—tone, expression, body language. What did that mean? That it was nothing to him; that he'd forgotten all about it? Or that he was such an accomplished liar and cheater that he was able to bury any feeling of guilt or regret. For a moment, on the screen, he looked like a stranger.

"Graham."

"Yeah?"

"If there's laundry in the washing machine, will you put it in the dryer?"

He rolled his eyes like it was the most gargantuan task in the world. "Yeah. Okay."

She ended the call without another word, his face freezing on the screen, then disappearing into nothing.

Selena returned to her seat, sitting heavily, and Martha handed her back her little bottle. She took another big swig.

"Sounds like you have a nice family," said Martha. She lifted a palm. "I didn't mean to eavesdrop."

"I'm very lucky," said Selena.

Because that's what you were supposed to say, right? *We're so blessed. I'm filled with gratitude.*

It was true; she did think that most days. Until she moved the nanny cam.

Her mother had warned Selena—carefully, gently, as was her way—after the Vegas incident: *He'll do it again, honey. Cheaters keep cheating.*

But Selena hadn't listened. Graham was *nothing* like her father, she reasoned, who'd had affair after affair. Her mother, Cora, had stayed in the marriage, enduring, she said, for the sake of Selena and her sister, Marisol.

But that was her *parents*. Selena's situation with Graham was different; the first incident wasn't an affair—exactly. They'd had therapy. It was just—not the same. That's what she'd told herself then, anyway.

"So, what are you going to do?" asked Selena, eager for the distraction from her own life. "About your boss."

Martha shrugged, shifted back so that they could see each other better, weren't just sitting side by side staring at the back of the seat in front of them. Her eyes—heavily lashed, lightly shadowed, almost almond-shaped—were searing, hypnotic.

"Don't you ever just wish your problems would take care of themselves?" Martha said with a sigh.

"Wouldn't that be nice?" asked Selena. She glanced at her bottle to find that it was almost empty. That had gone down fast. She felt looser, her shoulders less tense.

"Like maybe he'd just lose interest in me, you know?" she said. "Meet someone else."

Something about the words hit Selena the wrong way, and she felt all the sadness she'd tamped down rise up. When the tears came, she couldn't stop them. The nanny, of all people! What a cliché!

"Oh, no," said Martha, looking stricken. "What did I say?"

"I'm sorry," Selena managed, fishing tissues out of her bag and wiping at her eyes.

"Tell me," said Martha. "Since we're playing true confessions."

And, without thinking it through, she did. She told this stranger on the train how she *suspected* that her husband was sleeping with the nanny, while she was working late to support their family. She omitted how she'd watched the video—TMI.

Because wasn't that too weird, that she'd watched? Twice. And still hadn't done anything about it.

"I'm sorry," Selena said again when she was done. "Why did I just tell you that?"

"Obviously," said Martha with the same kind smile Selena had tried to offer her earlier, "you needed to tell *someone.*"

Martha produced another little bottle of Grey Goose. Her manicure, bloodred, was perfect—her fingers slender and white, no rings. As Selena cracked the bottle open and took a sip, she noticed the other woman staring at her diamond engagement ring. (Women often did. It was huge.) It felt good to let it all out. She'd put the weight of it down for a while.

"But you don't know for sure?" asked Martha.

Selena shook her head.

"Do you have reason to doubt him?" she asked.

"No," said Selena. "It's just a feeling."

"Well," Martha lifted her little bottle and they clinked again. "I hope you're wrong. And if you're not, I hope he gets what he deserves."

She offered the final sentence with a devilish smile, but something inside Selena went a little cold. What did he deserve? What did anyone deserve?

"Men," said Martha when Selena stayed silent. "They're so flawed, so broken, aren't they? They've screwed up the whole world."

The other woman's tone had gone dark, her eyes a bit distant. "All they do is create damage."

Selena felt the bizarre impulse to defend all men, even Graham. After all, she had two boys of her own. But it died in her throat. It was true, wasn't it? In some sense—war, climate change, genocide, cults, pedophilia, rape, murder, most crime in general—men were responsible for a good portion of the world's ills. They'd been running amok for millennia.

"Don't you ever just wish your problems would take care of themselves?" Martha asked again. "No effort on your part?"

But problems didn't solve themselves. And suddenly it occurred to Selena that Martha was *the other woman*, sleeping with someone's husband. A woman who owned the company where Martha worked, who was probably as trusting of her husband and her employee as Selena had been. Earning a living, supporting her family, while her husband fucked the first pretty girl to come along.

"How would *your* problem be solved?" asked Selena, dabbing at her eyes.

"Today I was thinking it would be great if he just—died," she said with a wicked smile. "Car accident, heart attack, random street crime. Then I could just keep my job, no one the wiser."

Martha laughed a little, a sweet, girlish sound, then took another delicate sip from her little bottle. She was just kidding, of course. Wasn't she? Selena shifted away slightly, clutching her bag to her middle.

"And I'd never be so stupid again," Martha went on. "I wouldn't be so afraid for my job that I'd submit to some predator's advances."

Was that how Geneva felt? Selena wondered. Had Graham come on to her, and she'd submitted because she was afraid to lose her job? It definitely didn't seem that way. But there were always layers, weren't there? Graham *was* in a power position. Selena knew that Geneva *did* struggle to make ends meet, couldn't afford not to work, even for a short time.

The lights flickered and the train jerked forward. Selena felt a surge of hope. But then nothing.

"There was a blockage on the track," came the conductor's voice, carrying over the speaker system. The man beside them jerked awake and looked around, confused, sat up and checked his phone. "It's been cleared, and we should be on our way shortly. We apologize for the inconvenience."

The man gathered his case and walked to the other car.

"And how would *your* problem be solved?" asked Martha. Her stare was intense, and Selena felt almost pinned by it.

She tried for a wry smile.

Single women, they just didn't get it yet, all the complicated layers of a marriage, of a life with children, all the sacrifices and compromises you made daily so that everything worked.

My problem can't be solved, thought Selena.

Divorce her husband, become a single mother with the kids gone every other weekend and holiday? Or stick it out? Fire Geneva, a girl the boys both loved, and try to find a reason that was palatable to them, that didn't shame Selena and ruin her husband in the eyes of their kids? Then quit her job and live off savings until Graham found another position and went back to work. Confront him, couples' counseling, maybe find a new way forward. There was no solution that didn't introduce a whole host of new problems. Problems she frankly just didn't have the energy to solve.

"Maybe she'll *disappear*," said Martha. "And you can just pretend it never happened."

Her voice, it slithered like a snake, was a whisper in the dark.

When Selena looked into Martha's eyes, it was like staring into space, cold and distant, empty. The vodka was making Selena feel a little sick.

What *if* Geneva just didn't turn up for work one day? Disappeared. Graham would pick up the pace on his job hunt big time, Selena bet, if he was full-on with the kids. Maybe Selena *could* just pretend it never happened. It would be so much easier. For a second, it seemed possible. Her mother, after all, had done it for decades to keep her family intact.

But no. She couldn't. She couldn't unsee what she'd seen, unknow what she now knew about her husband. She wasn't like her mother. She couldn't just stand by for the sake of the children. Could she?

The train came to life then, lights coming on, lurching forward. Nauseated, heart racing a little, Selena started to gather her things.

"Yeah," Selena said, managing a thin laugh. "I don't think I could get that lucky."

"You never know." Martha twisted a strand of her dark, silky hair. "Bad things happen all the time."

Selena moved over to the seat on the other side of the aisle.

"I'll spread out," she said as Martha watched with a polite smile. "Give you some space."

Martha nodded, pulled her tote up off the ground.

"Thanks for the drink," Selena said when she'd settled. "And for listening."

"Thank *you*," said Martha. "I feel better. I think I know what to do."

"Sometimes we just need an ear."

"And a little push in the right direction."

What did she mean by that? Selena didn't really want to know. Something about the conversation, the other woman's tone, the vodka, had her feeling uneasy, and very much wanting the conversation to end. Why had she told this stranger about herself? Something so personal?

She opened her magazine and started flipping through the glossy pages of impossibly slim bodies, flawless faces, enviable lives. When she looked over at Martha again, she seemed to have nodded off. As the train neared her station, Selena gathered her things, but the other woman didn't stir. She slipped off as quietly as she could, not saying goodbye, not looking back, hoping that they wouldn't meet again.

FOUR

Geneva

GENEVA STACKED CRATE and Barrel plates in the dishwasher, then wiped down the gleaming quartz countertop, listening to the boys bouncing around upstairs while Graham tried to read a story and get them settled for the night. Jumping off the beds by the sound of it, a heavy thud that caused glasses in the cabinets to rattle slightly. Something neither Selena nor Geneva would ever tolerate. Story time was for winding down, not winding *up*.

She put away the leftover food from dinner, leaving a plate wrapped in the fridge for Selena, even though she'd probably already eaten.

"I'm sorry," she whispered as she closed the refrigerator door. She *was* sorry. She liked Selena, respected her. She would never have chosen to hurt and betray her in this way. In the worst way one woman could betray another.

She was used to it. That hot feeling of shame. Its familiarity was almost a comfort. The heat started in her center, then radiated up to her face in a rush. Finally, there was a bottoming out that left her with a gaping hollow in her center.

Why? Why would she do this? Again and again. She didn't want to.

There was only one reason. And this was the very last time. She'd been putting money away. There was almost enough now to break free.

She sat at the table and wrote a list for Selena.

"Oliver needs a new uniform shirt, order from the school office; Stephen's teacher—" who seemed like a bit of a tight-ass to Geneva "—said at pickup that he was a chatterbox lately, distracting his friends, and not paying attention."

In fact, Stephen *was* a chatterbox—but he was lovely and creative and sweet. Anyway, Selena would know what to say to Stephen, and to his teacher. Luckily, Geneva's job was only to report the problem; she didn't have to *handle* it. That was the joy of being a nanny and not a mommy. You got to go home.

The pen felt heavy in her hand.

She could still taste Graham on her lips.

When she met him, during her interview with Selena and the boys, she thought he was the handyman, someone Selena had hired to do the jobs her high-powered husband didn't have the time to do himself. He'd been struggling with stones in the low wall that surrounded their expansive backyard.

During the all-important recon, she'd seen him in pictures on social media. Once, she'd seen him on the train from the city as he commuted home from work. At that time, he'd been dressed in a well-made suit, good shoes. He'd been clean-shaven, put together. When she saw him at the house, she didn't recognize him at first.

"Oh, there's Graham," said Selena, who'd just shown Geneva around the gargantuan kitchen. "He'll be around some. But mainly he'll be out interviewing, I'd think."

Selena misread the confused look on Geneva's face.

"My husband," she clarified.

"Oh, right," said Geneva. "Of course."

Geneva had watched him a minute as he lifted the rocks, stacking them. There was something virile about him, even though—or maybe because—he was sweating from physical labor. Jeans, T-shirt, work boots. He'd gained weight since she'd last seen him, but his arms were muscular, shoulders broad. There was an appealing strength to his physicality. The stubble on his jaw was not unattractive.

Still. When Geneva looked at Selena—slim, dark, with fine, proud features and unblemished skin. She must know, right, that her husband was not her equal in any way? Why did so many women do that? Not just a stunner, Selena was also smart, personable, a good mom. One of those Wonder Woman types this culture was so good at producing.

And Graham, well, anyone could see—or maybe it was just her because she was good at reading people. Like, psychic good. He was a man baby. The world handed to him like a rattle he smashed on the floor when he didn't get what he wanted. Geneva had known so many men like him in her line of work. Too many.

It was definitely time to consider a career change. She wasn't cut out for this game, its consequences. The kids were okay; that part she enjoyed. It was the adults that were the problem. The men especially.

Geneva finished her note to Selena. The banging upstairs had ceased. She could hear Stephen and Oliver talking, laughing, the rumble of Graham's voice. Maybe, she thought, she shouldn't come back tomorrow. She gave the counter one last wipe down, moving aside the big toy robot, with all its funny gears and big red eyes. *Danger! Danger!* it said, among other things. It was one of those annoying, frenetic toys that kids loved and parents hated. She'd confiscated it from the boys when they were fighting over it. She thought about running it up to the playroom, but she didn't want to go back there. The scene of the crime. She left it by the stove.

Geneva packed up her bag, the portion of the dinner she'd made for herself stored in the Pyrex container she'd brought from home—meals were part of the arrangement. She let herself out quietly, locked the door behind her.

It was only a couple of days after she started working for the Murphy family before Graham started hovering while the boys were at school—Stephen still just a half day at kindergarten and lunch bunch, Oliver in first grade until 2:30. She ran Selena's errands, did the chores, and whatever Selena needed before Stephen's pickup at 12:30.

Graham would be there suddenly in the laundry room, talking about this or that—how he'd played football in college, might have gone pro if not for a knee injury. Sure. How he'd had a job offer but he'd turned it down because it "just didn't feel right." He had that faux-pompous aura that certain types of men had, putting it on to cover a deep feeling of inadequacy. She tried to communicate that she wasn't interested. No eye contact. Polite, one-word responses. A quick: *Oh, I gotta run and do an errand before I get the boys.* Your boys, she didn't say. While your wife works to support you all. And you're doing *what* exactly?

She almost quit before it was too late. Sometimes, you know, these things just don't go down the way you expect them to and you have to pull the plug.

But Selena was so grateful, so complimentary. The boys—well-attended to, loved—were so sweet, such nice kids. The house was beautiful, calming. Geneva enjoyed her time there, pretending when she was alone that it was *her* beautiful house. She'd go through Selena's drawers sometimes—look at her makeup, her perfume, her pretty underwear. She never took anything. She looked.

It happened in the laundry room the first time, knocking up against the dryer.

It happened just like it was always going to happen. What was it?

She knew that she was just slightly better than average-looking. Maybe it was the caregiving thing. She really had a knack for that, for taking care of other people. She *wanted* to do it, to give in that way that comforted others. Children. The elderly. Animals. She just wanted to be kind to others, and to help them. Maybe that was why she could never say no—even when she wanted to.

The light was still on in the boys' room as she crossed the street in the cool night, and climbed into her Toyota. Graham wasn't the worst father she'd ever met, not even the worst husband. That particular award might go to her own father, a total stranger who she wouldn't be able to pick out of a lineup.

Shivering in the transition from the warmth of the house to the chill of outside, she pressed the start button on her new car, a consolation prize from her last disaster. The engine hummed to life, the dashboard glowing. It was a good thing people didn't talk anymore. In this Instagram world, everyone wanted to broadcast filtered versions of their best moments, and bury everything else. All the dull, shameful things, all the flawed, failed ventures and endeavors, hidden. Where did people put those things?

She drove, the air slowly warming, her body relaxing. No music, her smartphone stowed. Her place wasn't far, just over the railroad tracks—away from the big houses and manicured parks, past the supermarket and the cemetery. Her building was a low, neat structure facing a manmade lake with a fountain in its center. There were trees and benches, a playground, a family of ducks that returned year after year. Not fancy, but not run down and sad like other places she'd lived.

She parked her car in the spot reserved for her unit, climbed the outside stairs to the second floor, and walked down the exposed landing. As she went, she shed layers of herself—the smiling nanny, the accommodating millennial, the laundry room lay—all things that were her and weren't really.

Her place wasn't much, a small one-bedroom with a nice-sized kitchen and dining area, a sitting room she'd made cozy. It was fine. It was hers. And when she closed the door, she was alone, could breathe a sigh of relief. She would never live with the family in her care like an au pair. She always needed her own space.

Her phone chimed and it filled her with dread. Surely, not another text.

Please. I'm desperate. I can't stop thinking about you.

She didn't answer, had turned off her read receipt, so he wouldn't know if she'd gotten it or not. She should block him, that would be the smart thing to do.

Why won't you answer me?

I trashed my whole life for you.

This was the usual pattern. Something casual—that had come earlier. Just thinking about you. Hope you're doing okay. Then something pleading. Then more aggressive. Then nasty.

The least you can do is answer me.

Nothing to do but ignore it.

Geneva changed into sweats, put her hair up, then ate her food without bothering to reheat it. Sitting at the kitchen table, she stared absently out of the window into the park where she watched two slim teenage girls on the playground. It was late for kids to be out alone, wasn't it? Maybe not, just after seven. But it was dark. One of them stared at a phone. The other pushed herself languidly on a swing, her head tilted against the chain.

The phone again: You know what? Fine. You're ghosting me? You just make a mess, then disappear.

The two girls on the playground reminded her of another self, another life, one so long ago that it was faded and seemed as unreal as a dream, or an episode of a bad television drama that she'd watched without really seeing.

Two girls. One who wanted everything. And one who wanted nothing more than to disappear. She wondered if either one of them would ever get what they were after.

Another chime: One of these days this shit is going to catch up with you.

She reached over to block his number, but he got a final shot in before she did:

Whore.

The word burned a hole through her. She dropped the phone like it was hot. Her stomached knotted.

We reap what we sow, her mother used to say.

There was that rise of shame again. Was that true? Surely not. Because bad things happened to good people and good things happened to bad. Her sister was fond of saying how there was no justice beyond what you delivered yourself.

Geneva walked to the window, but the girls were gone, the playground dim and abandoned.

That's when she saw his car. Windows black, headlights off. Just sitting.

Had he watched her come in?

She would call the police. But how could she?

Was *he* the criminal, the one to fear? Or was she?

She stood there watching the dark car, staying to the side of the window until finally the vehicle came to life and drifted away.

FIVE

Pearl

PEARL LISTENED, THAT was her superpower. She had a gift for making herself invisible in a room so that people forgot that she was there. Slim and dark, plainly dressed, she wore thick-framed glasses that mostly hid her face. She made sure her voice was always soft, that a small half smile always played on her lips. She blended into her surroundings and most people didn't mind her company.

At school, she was neither bullied, nor did she have any true friends. She made a point of being distantly agreeable.

"Pearl's an easy child to like, a good student, highly intelligent, and helpful to others. Should we talk about her quietude, though? Her shyness? I wonder if she spends too much time on the sidelines. Though she always knows the answers when called, she rarely raises her hand." A gentle query from her English teacher on Pearl's stellar report card, at which her mother had glanced quickly, knowing that Pearl would have straight As.

"Shyness?" her mother, Stella, had mused, looking at Pearl with those watery blue eyes. There were layers and layers there.

Pearl could almost get a glimpse of all the things her mother had been before she was Pearl's mother—a neglected child, a stripper working her way through community college, a trophy wife cast aside for trophy wife number two, a single mother, a drunk, a bookseller with a struggling shop. Those eyes, they looked right into Pearl, knowing every cell of who she was. Stella, for all her failings as a mother, knew Pearl better than anyone.

"The last thing you are is shy."

True. That's the last thing Pearl was.

Tonight, fifteen-year-old Pearl was watching Charlie. He'd been an object of fascination for her since he'd wandered into her mother's life a few weeks earlier. Not Mom's usual type. He was quiet, bookish, a regular guy. But not. There was something behind his eyes, a flicker, a slither, a slipping darkness. There was a laughter there, too—not the nice kind.

One day he was the new clerk at her mother's bookstore, unpacking boxes in the back, stocking shelves, ringing up customers. Pearl wondered how Stella could afford to bring on a new employee. The store was on the brink of going out of business. She knew better than to ask.

Then the following week, Charlie was driving her mother home at night. Pearl had watched from the window as they lingered in the black car that looked like a shark. Its engine rumbled, body gleaming in the streetlight.

Tonight, he was in their kitchen, cooking. He hummed, the kitchen alive with light and wonderful aromas.

The others—and there were many—were not like this guy. Mainly big, loud men. Tattoos, fake smiles, empty eyes. Dumb. They were generally not her mother's equal in terms of intelligence. Her mother would be giddy at first, all breathless smiles, and fluttering hands. Then, quickly, she would shift to annoyed or angry, let down or bored. There might be fights, yelling—usually her mother doing the yelling, the men cowering, or leaving abruptly, never to return. Or sometimes they just disappeared—there one day, gone the next with no explanation.

Pearl had learned to pay them little mind. They ran together in her memory. She came to think of them as versions of the same man. Harmless; they never bothered her. Useless, one of Stella's favorite critiques. Ultimately not good enough, lacking in some way. Pearl had collected an array of gifts—from Tom a bracelet with a real diamond chip, from Christian an iPod, a stuffed unicorn from…what was his name?

Her mother was willowy and bottle blonde with sea-glass eyes. She was fire. She was ice. *Bewitching*, one of them had called her. Your mother, she casts a spell on men. We dance.

Pearl didn't see it.

Her mother just seemed tired, ground down by the consequences of her bad choices. If Stella could cast a spell, Pearl thought, surely she'd have done better than to conjure herself a bookstore teetering on bankruptcy, their run-down two-bedroom ranch house, a string of loser boyfriends, and the thankless life of a single, working mother.

Tonight, Pearl had set the table. She'd filled a pitcher with filtered water and placed it on the table. Then she settled into a chair, opened her notebook.

Charlie moved with ease around the kitchen, as if he lived there. He seemed to know where things were without asking. Pearl doubted that even her mother would be so at home in their cabinets. She couldn't even remember the last time Stella had cooked anything other than scrambled eggs and toast on Sundays when she was feeling jovial for any reason.

"What are you reading these days, Pearl?" Charlie asked, startling Pearl, who had drifted into thought.

On the stove, chicken sizzled in some kind of sauce, there was bread baking in the oven. A colorful salad sat tossed in a bowl she didn't even know they had. Pearl's stomach was rumbling; she hadn't eaten all day.

"Jane Eyre," she said.

None of the men her mother knew had ever asked such a thing.

"For school?"

"No. In school we're reading *The Giver.*"

"Very different books," he said, moving the chicken around the pan. "Any common themes?"

What a question. Something fired off in Pearl's brain, the kind of joy she could only achieve when thinking about fiction—the words of others, or the stories that she herself wove, alone in her bed at night. Stories about herself, about who she could become, about the father she didn't know, people she would meet and places she would go.

She thought about it, doodling in the notebook she had open in front of her. Classic literature versus modern dystopian young adult. She hadn't considered making comparisons between the two. But there were similarities if you dug for them. She glanced up at Charlie, whose glasses were as thick as her own. Was he hiding behind those big frames, too?

"Both characters are asked to believe something about themselves that turns out not to be true," she said.

He raised his eyebrows at her, smiled, ground some pepper into the pan. "Expound."

She felt a strange thrill deep in her center. It was the thrill of being seen. Of inquiry.

"Jane is raised to believe that she's worthless, a burden, less than the other members of the family," she said. "And in *The Giver,* Jonas is raised in a society that has eliminated all the pain and strife of human history. Neither of them understands themselves until they've struck out on their own."

Charlie nodded thoughtfully. There was a stillness to his face, an intensity to his gaze. She'd walked over and stood by the counter without realizing it.

"That's a deep observation," he said. "They're both coming-of-age stories. Worlds apart, more than a century. And yet, the story of the young person breaking from the strictures of family and society to forge his or her own path is a timeless one. Why do you think that is?"

He dropped her gaze, moved with fluidity—whisking the bread from the oven, dressing the salad. It was as if he'd always been there.

"Because we all have to find our own way," said Pearl.

"Exactly," he said. "Society doesn't always know what's right. Our families tell us stories about ourselves that often aren't true. Sometimes we have to follow our hearts."

He handed her the salad bowl and she carried it to the table.

"Mom should be pulling in the driveway any minute," he said.

Mom. Not *your mom.* Something intimate, possessive about the turn of phrase, wasn't there? And so it was. The glow from the headlights slid across the back wall.

"Stella said you were smart," said Charlie, handing her the warm basket of bread. "I wonder if she knows how smart. Sometimes we don't see what's right in front of us."

Pearl didn't know what to say, felt her cheeks go hot. This was not the kind of conversation she was used to having with anyone but her English teacher.

And then her mom was there, blustering about the store—so busy today!

"That coupon you ran, Charlie, amazing. And twenty-five people bought tickets for that open mic night. You're a genius."

"It was your idea, Stella," he said. "I just nudged you to make it happen."

She swept off her coat, dropped all her bags, gave Pearl a quick squeeze.

"And dinner!" she gushed. "Thank you."

Stella kissed him on the cheek and Pearl watched his hand linger on the small of her back. And Pearl disappeared. When

Stella was in the room, she filled it—with her beauty, with her scent, with the volume of her being.

Pearl didn't mind. She liked the shadows. That's where you got to see all the things that other people missed.

At the table, they ate the meal Charlie had prepared, and talked about Stella's plan for surviving as a small brick-and-mortar bookseller. It was one of her high-energy nights, when she had Big Plans. She was going to build the newsletter list, the online sales, invite book groups to use the space if they bought the book at the store. She was going to attend the regional book fair, invite authors to visit. Charlie made all the right noises, nodding his head and encouraging with an enthusiastic "Yes!" or "That's great, Stella!"

Stella was all smiles, touching Charlie's hand, leaning her body toward his. After dinner, most nights, Pearl would go up to her room and finish her homework, read until she fell asleep. Charlie and her mother would disappear into Stella's room. She wouldn't hear another peep from them. He likely wouldn't be there when she got up for school in the morning. But right now, as they all ate, she watched.

There was something different about Charlie. All the other men who'd shared this table were in Stella's thrall, hanging on her every word, rapt by her—beauty? Was it beauty? No, it was more than that, something that radiated from inside, a kind of magnetism. But the energy between Charlie and Stella—it was like she was the dancer, and he was the approving observer.

"Tell us about school today, Pearl," said Charlie.

Stella seemed surprised, as if she'd forgotten Pearl was there. Pearl was surprised, too.

"I dissected a frog in science class," she said. "We removed its heart."

They all looked down at their plates. "Really, Pearl?" said Stella, disgusted.

"Ah," said Charlie. "Did you learn anything that surprised you?"

"Well," said Pearl. "I wasn't too enthusiastic about the lab. But it wasn't as revolting as I thought. In fact, it was kind of fascinating. How things work under the skin. You don't think about your organs too much, you know?"

Charlie's grin was wide and knowing as Stella pushed away from the table. Pearl had been looking for a reaction and she got one. And Charlie saw it all.

"Well, there goes my appetite," said Stella, rising.

"Sit down," Charlie said.

Pearl startled a little, glanced at her mother. His voice was gentle, coaxing. But Stella did not like it when the attention of a conversation turned away from her. And she did not like to be told what to do—especially by any man. Would she rage? Would she storm off? Pearl braced herself for what came next.

"I think Pearl's just trying to shock us," said Charlie, still grinning. The energy in the room cooled.

Stella surprised Pearl by sitting back down, scooting her chair back toward the table. She gave Pearl a look—half amused, half annoyed. Pearl pushed the chicken around her plate.

"Sorry," she said.

"I emptied the mousetrap in the store room today," said Stella. "It was every bit as disgusting as I imagined it would be. How's that for shocking?"

Charlie put a hand on Stella's. "You don't have to do things like that, Stella," he said. "I'm here now—to help."

"Thank you, Charlie," she said. Her voice was soft and sincere.

This one was definitely different.

Pearl helped Charlie clean the dishes while Stella went into the study to balance the books. As Pearl moved around the kitchen, she felt Charlie's eyes on her.

"You're a funny kid, Pearl," he said, when she lifted her gaze to his. He tapped his temple. "Clever."

Pearl had grown used to being invisible. She didn't even know until that moment how nice it was to be seen.

SIX
Selena

HER HOUSE DIDN'T look like her house as she pulled into the drive and sat, car running. It was a shimmering facsimile, a pretty place that didn't belong to her. It was exactly the kind of home she'd dreamed of as a girl—a big two-story, with expansive rooms, high ceilings, with shutters and shingles, big leafy shade trees, careful landscaping. She changed the perennials out every season, weeded meticulously in the summer, decorated elaborately for Halloween and Christmas. Her mother always said: *Your home is the heart of your life.* Her heart was broken. And her home, her life, would likely follow.

The boys' lights were out; she could just make out the orange glow of their night-light through the drawn shades. She was sorry that she had missed kissing them good-night, but she was glad she didn't have to put on a happy face.

Since her encounter on the train, she'd been buzzing—something about the stranger, her voice, her words. She wasn't going to be able to sit with this. She couldn't pretend, not for another day.

She killed the engine, leaving the car in the drive with enough room for Graham to get his car out. If she opened the garage door, she risked waking the boys and she didn't want that.

Entering the warmth and light of the foyer, she dropped her bags by the door and walked down the hall to the kitchen and waited.

When Graham pushed in through the door, she could see that he'd showered. Of course. Washing away the scent of what he'd done. But he looked good, smelled good.

"Hey," she said. "We need to talk."

They met on a rainy evening in the East Village. She was on her way to a book party for a famous mixologist at a tiny venue near Avenue A. Selena, running late, jogged down the street under a helter-skelter umbrella that had twisted in the wind and was essentially useless, broke a heel and went tumbling to the sidewalk. The contents of her bag rolled onto the concrete, phone flying into the street with an unpleasant crack.

"Oh my god! Are you okay?"

She was more stunned than anything, though she'd scraped her knee pretty badly. A hunky guy with dark hair, a stylish bomber jacket over slim pants, chased after her phone, her lipstick, her wallet. He helped her to her feet. The umbrella was a tangled mess on the ground. The rain kept falling. They were both getting soaked.

"It's okay," she said with an embarrassed laugh. "I'm a klutz. I'm used to falling."

She *was* clumsy, and always wearing some kind of impractical shoe. The city sidewalks conspired to take you down; she seemed always to be running late, was rarely mindful.

"You're bleeding."

"Ugh," she said, looking down. "Gross."

Blood ran down her calf, a single rivulet from her knee to her ankle. She dug a tissue out of her bag while they stood there in the drizzle. She could barely look at him, she was so embarrassed. He took it from her before she could stop him, bent down and wiped at her leg.

When he looked up at her and smiled—rakish and knowing—she was in love.

"I'm Graham," he said.

"Selena."

"Are we going to tell our kids about this night?" Graham asked when he rose, tossing the tissue in a nearby bin.

She almost started to cry; it had been an awful day—overslept, missed her train, fouled up royally at the office, earning a talking-to from the boss who already seemed perpetually underwhelmed by her performance. But it turned out to be the best day of her life. That day.

Poor Will. They were living together at the time. She broke up with Will before she started dating Graham; she wouldn't even kiss him until she'd moved out into her own place. It was a politely painful split, where they tried to hold on to their friendship. *Are you sure about this guy?* Will had asked a few months later over coffee. *More sure than I've been about anything.* Which, looking back, was an insensitive thing to say to your ex.

A glorious courtship—dinner at Eleven Madison Park, ziplining in Costa Rica, a surprise trip to Paris. A glittering diamond presented at Wollman Rink in Central Park. Big (stupidly big) wedding at her father's country club, honeymoon in Hawaii, a new house. Picture perfect.

Are you sure about this guy?

The first time she caught Graham cheating—well, not really cheating as he saw it—he was sexting with an ex-girlfriend. Selena happened to see his phone, discovering the X-rated chain complete with dirty pictures. There was a screaming blowout. She went to stay with Beth in the city for a few weeks—this was before the kids. He begged her forgiveness. There was counseling.

Graham had issues with self-worth, and admitted an addiction to porn (this sext affair was really just an extension of that, wasn't it), fear of intimacy—all this from the male therapist. They worked on it, moved on. Then there was Oliver. A babymoon period followed where they were in love with their child, their new life as parents.

Then, the boys' weekend in Vegas. Strippers. A prostitute; the details even now were vague. She thought it was best to keep it that way. She didn't need a visual; she already had sexting pictures seared into her imagination. Graham and their friend Brad got arrested in Vegas that weekend. She had to leave Oliver with her mother, fly there to bail them out. More counseling. The stress of new fatherhood, this time, according to the therapist, who was frankly starting to sound like an apologist. Poor Graham was struggling with the responsibility, the crushing effort of working and parenting and being a husband. God, it was just all so hard. More counseling.

"Think of him as an addict," said her new therapist in one of Selena's individual sessions. This doctor had fewer excuses for Graham. "His behavior is something outside of you that you don't control and can't fix. Don't hang your worthiness on his failings. But now you have to decide where your boundaries are, what you will and will not tolerate. Every marriage is a negotiation. Both parties have to obey the terms."

After Stephen, Graham changed, or really seemed to. Stephen was his soul mate. Something about that child's arrival caused Graham to calm down completely. Graham plugged in to their family, focused on work with a new zeal, weekends he was home. There were no more boys' nights—it helped that his two most corrupting friends had both settled down.

There was a night when both boys were down, and they stood together over Stephen and watched him sleep.

"Thank you," he'd whispered to her. "Thank you for waiting for me to become a better man. I'll never let you down again. I swear to god."

She believed him. She had to, wanted to. She loved him so much—wild, deep, mad love, even when she hated him, wanted to kill him, railed against his stupidity and selfishness. There was something raw and primal beneath it. He was hers. And she was his. A fiery, blind devotion.

That's what she thought.

Now this.

It hurt even worse because she had believed in him, in them.

"I saw her on top of you, Graham. In the boys' playroom." No point in beating around the bush.

The look on his face. It was almost comical. It shifted from stunned, to a practiced look of innocence, then to despair.

"The nanny?" she went on into the leaden silence. "Really, Graham?"

She didn't want to cry; she promised herself she wouldn't. She needed a steel resolve for what would come next. But she did cry, a tear trailing down her face.

He started stammering. "I— It-it-it was a *mistake*, a moment, it just happened," he said. "I've been—depressed, I think. You know with losing my job and everything. She came on to me and I just—*reacted*."

Really? He was going to make it sound as if Geneva came on *to him*? What a sad play. She truly couldn't see it.

"Twice," she said quietly. "I saw you do it *twice*."

He got up and started moving toward her. She walked away, putting the kitchen island between them. The weird thing was that there was a part of her that wanted him to take her in his arms, to comfort her. She wanted to believe that he loved her, in spite of his flagrant infidelity. If she could take a pill to make herself unsee what she had seen, to make it all go away, she would have.

Wouldn't it be nice if your problems just went away?

But problems don't go away, not by themselves. When things are wrong, you have to fix them with your own mind and spirit.

"Don't come any closer to me, Graham," she said, her voice tight. "Just leave. I need time to think things through."

"Selena."

She moved a few steps back, and he kept coming toward her.

"Baby," he said, his voice buttery soft. She saw the sadness, the desperation on his face. She'd seen it before. There were always big soulful eyes, heartfelt begging; she'd forgiven too many times.

"Please," he said. "Listen."

She tried for cool, but her voice just sounded small and sad. "I can't imagine what you think you might say this time."

He wasn't listening, though; he just kept moving closer until she was backed into the corner, no place else to go.

She didn't like that feeling, of not having any options. Anger flared. Fear.

And she didn't like the look on his face. She'd seen it before, when fights got ugly. He'd never hit her, but his rage could be frightening. And she knew, maybe she was the only one who knew, what he was capable of when he was angry.

Graham reached for her, and when she screamed, her voice felt like an explosion.

"Get away from me, Graham!"

Her voice rang out loud, and her last thought before she reached behind her and found Stephen's toy robot—a big heavy thing with lots of hard edges—was that she hoped she hadn't woken the boys.

SEVEN
Anne

WAS IT HER imagination? The air felt electric with bad energy as Anne walked into the office. She sensed it right away, even before Evie, the receptionist who had never once even bothered to hide her naked contempt for Anne, looked up and smiled.

"Kate wants to see you," Evie said, a little crinkle to her nose, a glint in her eyes. Malicious glee.

Evie's teeth were a dazzling white, a contrast to her olive skin. Her eyes were the same deep black as her hair. Evie's Instagram feed was ridiculous—a catalog of selfies or posed shots of herself in various locations where she was heavily made-up, provocatively dressed, filtered into cartoonish beauty. Evie pressed out her lips, her cleavage, preened—daily—for her few Instagram followers to a smattering of likes and heart-eyed emojis. What did someone like Evie want? She wanted what everyone wanted these days, to be a star, someone wealthy and lauded for no good reason. She wanted to be perfect. No. She wanted to appear perfect to others.

But nothing was ever perfect. Nothing real. So it was a losing battle that left her feeling perpetually empty.

Anne could see all the layers of Evie. And she didn't like any of them.

"Okay," Anne said lightly. "Thanks!"

She also didn't like the way Evie looked at *her.* As if she could see what no one else saw. Maybe she did. There were those people. The people who *saw,* or felt. The seers—cops often, private detectives. The feelers, sensitive types, empaths who picked up energies, creatives—artists, writers, photographers.

There's something about you. When I look into your eyes, I feel like I'm floating into nothing, her first boyfriend had whispered to her one night. This was when she still thought maybe she could love someone.

But mainly, people were so wrapped up in their own inner hurricane that they never saw anything outside the storm of themselves.

"Have a nice day," Evie called after her. But when Anne glanced back the other woman's eyes were sending another message. Something was definitely off.

Things are not always within your control. That was something to learn early on. There was a cultural misconception, a particularly American idea, that the individual was the master of her own destiny. Positive thinking, creative visualization, manifestation, vision boards, asking the universe to fulfill your desires. If you can dream it, you can do it. Anne believed this to a certain extent. The idea had taken her far, given her the confidence to achieve things and go places where others might hesitate.

But there was often a wild card, one element you didn't expect. Usually it was human frailty. People were totally unpredictable. That was one of the first things Pop had taught her.

She passed Hugh's office, but he wasn't at his desk—which wasn't unusual. He generally strolled in around 9:45. Kate was always here before anyone else. She rose at 5:00, Hugh had told her, met with her trainer for an hour, had a green smoothie and triple shot of espresso, and was at her desk by 7:30 latest. Fear. People who drove themselves that hard were usually afraid of something. What did people like that want? They wanted to be the best, to have the most. Because being the best meant that they were safe from harm.

But no one was ever safe from harm. Not really.

Anne sat at her desk, unpacked her bag. Her Moleskine, her pens. Her sack lunch. Slowly. She wouldn't go running into Kate's office before she'd collected herself, assessed the situation. She mentally reviewed her evening with Hugh last night. She thought about texting him, but decided against it.

The buzzer on her phone rang. She answered.

"Yes."

"Hey, Anne." Brent, Kate's assistant. "Kate would like to see you."

"On my way," she said brightly.

She let five more minutes pass. Delaying, making people wait, was a power play.

When the phone buzzed again, she didn't bother to answer. She rose and walked down the hallway to Kate's office, a big corner space with plush couches and floor-to-ceiling bookshelves, an enormous desk.

Anne had imagined herself there one day, before she realized what the balance of power really was at this firm: Kate at the helm, Hugh there but by her good graces. Hugh acted like the boss, and Kate let him, because clearly he needed that. A good marriage was the ultimate long game, everyone happy as long as everyone is getting what he wants.

Brent was not at his desk, so she walked over the plush carpet to Kate's office, where the other woman sat at her desk. Anne tried to read the room before she entered.

Kate sat cool and composed at her desk, her body stiff, eyes alert. Once again, Anne had to admire her beauty. Patrician, slim, blond hair cropped close, Kate had all the money necessary to maintain her considerable physical assets, her dewy skin, her tall, toned body. She didn't wear her usual kind, open smile.

Her expression was grim. That was bad. Even worse, Hugh slumped on her couch. He looked like he had food poisoning, greenish, dark circles under his eyes. He glanced over at Anne, and he gave her a nod. A nod.

"Good morning," Anne said brightly.

"Good morning, Anne," said Kate. "Have a seat."

Anne sat, pulling herself up in the chair that seemed small and distant from the desk. She was a child in the principal's office. A prisoner before the parole board. A suspect in the interrogation room.

Brent closed the office door, and all the air seemed to leave the room.

This could be about a number of things.

Hugh. That was the most likely, of course. Anne had been sleeping with Hugh for months. He was in love with her, or so he'd said, intended to leave Kate so that they could be together. Not that she wanted him to love her, or to leave his wife. Not that she loved him, or had any intention of staying with him.

Or it could be about the money. Anne had found a way to discreetly siphon funds from various of the firm's accounts into one of her own. Tiny amounts that were adding up nicely.

Possibly this was about the client. A has-been pro basketball player who'd been fobbed off on Anne. He'd made a pass last week, and she'd rejected him. He hadn't taken it well. She wasn't too worried about that one.

She kept her face open, innocent, a wondering smile on her lips. It was an expression Pop had helped her to perfect. *They don't know what you're thinking or what you're feeling. Keep it off your face, whatever it is.*

"So," said Kate, her eyes clear, posture straight. "I'll get straight to the point. Hugh and I have been married a long time, twenty-five years."

Kate folded her hands on the desk in front of her, then went on.

"You're a young woman, so I don't expect you understand the nature of such a long relationship. There are good times and bad. There are phases when you're in love and moments when you're not. Hugh and I—we've both made mistakes, hurt each other."

Anne nodded, kept her face open but wrinkled her eyes in a kind of mild confusion as if she couldn't imagine why Kate would confide such a thing in her.

"Friendship and the willingness to forgive, that's the foundation of all long marriages."

Better to stay quiet. Always better to say nothing.

"So," said Kate with a breath. "Hugh and I had a big row last night, about something else completely, but it led him to confide in me that you two have been having an affair."

Anne marveled at the other woman's calm. It didn't seem put on at all. There were no tells of a quivering inside—no foot tapping, lip biting, hand wringing. Her gaze was steely.

"These things happen. You're a beautiful woman. And, men—" She cast a glance over at her husband with mild annoyance. "Well."

Anne hung her head, an imitation of shame, regret, which she did not feel. It seemed like the right body language, though. Kate kept her eyes levelly on Anne.

What was going to happen here? The whole "Me Too" thing was really going to work in her favor. They couldn't exactly fire her; she could claim harassment and would, as loudly as possible. Kate would not want that kind of embarrassment. If it were Anne in Kate's shoes? She'd fire Hugh, kick him out on his ass, and move on. That wasn't going to happen, of course. Anne was going to be the one holding the fuzzy end of the lollipop.

Shit.

Anne rather liked her job, the office, the money, the travel. She'd really fouled this one up. She would have been better off having an affair with Kate.

She remained quiet and Kate went on.

"I don't imagine that you're in love with Hugh. And—in spite of what he's told you—I assure you that he's not in love with you."

Kate looked back and forth between Anne and Hugh. What did the older woman see? Anne wondered. Was Anne just some tramp, an inconvenience in an otherwise very orderly existence? And Hugh? What was he to her, a possession? A showpiece? Did she truly love him? And, if so, *why*? These questions, they fascinated her. Why did people do the things they did?

Hugh wouldn't even look in their direction, a sullen boy deprived of his plaything. He rested his head in his hand, put a foot up on the coffee table. Cleared his throat. The silence expanded, swelled to fill the room. Anne could even hear the very faintest sound of a siren, through the thick glass, far away. She thought about denying the whole thing. But instead she just stayed quiet. Pop always said: *It's better to say nothing. Silence is golden.*

Anne dropped her forehead into her hand, as though she was in a state of despair.

"If you are." Kate's voice was oddly gentle, almost compassionate. "The two of you. Madly, deeply, can't go on without each other. Feel free to go now. I won't stand in the way of true love."

Anne wondered, would he leap up? Declare his love, take her hand and storm the two of them out. Even though she hadn't wanted that, *didn't* want it, she wished he would, just so that she could see what Kate's reaction might be. But no. He shifted in his seat, crossed the leg that had lagged on the coffee table over the other and looked out the window.

Coward.

Pop always said it and it was true: *Cash is king.* Kate wore the crown very well.

"So, the question is, Anne," Kate went on into the quiet, her voice now firm, practical. "What do you want?"

That was an interesting thing to ask. It really did cut through all the bullshit. There would be no emotion here, just as it was in the boardroom. Kate was famous for saying, *Let's cut through it, can we? We're burning daylight.*

Anne looked up at Kate now, and felt a hard, familiar twist of envy. No, it was darker than that, whatever the feeling was. It was the feeling that made her want to key beautiful cars, or slash priceless art, or make happy people cry.

Their eyes met. Anne felt nothing. Not fear, not anger, not regret, not disappointment, not even shame. All things that might be appropriate here, that other people might feel. It was Kate who looked away first. They always did.

"What do you want," Kate said to her folded hands, "to walk away from your job, whatever it is you were doing with my husband, and to sign a nondisclosure agreement for this incident and its resolution?"

The room shimmered a little and Anne had this feeling she'd had before. As if she'd lifted out of her body, was floating above and looking down at herself, at the imperious Kate, and the defeated and slouching Hugh. She wondered how the scene had played out last night. Not that it mattered. He was never going to leave his wife, his cushy job, their children, the world of wealthy friends and successful colleagues he inhabited.

Well. Let's cut through it, can we?

It was that easy. She named her price. It was a high one, but there was no negotiation. She was given the business card of their lawyer, told that there was an appointment tomorrow at 9:00, that she should not miss it under any circumstances.

"And that concludes our business," said Kate. "Allow me to show you out."

Anne took the long walk back down the hall, feeling eyes on her, and packed her things; just what she'd carried in that morning in her bag. She'd never had any personal items on her desk—no framed pictures, or pretty knickknacks.

Hugh stayed in Kate's office, as Kate discreetly escorted Anne from the building.

On the street, in the unforgiving light of the bright winter sun, Anne could see the fine lines on the older woman's face. The skin on her neck was crepey. Anne observed just the very slightest shake in her hands. So, she was human. Not like Anne, who still felt nothing except some vague satisfaction. It wasn't quite the payout for which she'd hoped. But it would do.

"Let's never see each other again," said Kate, still holding the door handle. She couldn't step away from the fortress, could she? In a street fight, she could never best Anne and they both knew it.

Anne nodded, tried to look chastened but couldn't keep the corner of her mouth from turning up in a smile. The other woman had already disappeared back into the lobby, the darkness swallowing her thin frame.

It was true. Kate would never see Anne again. Because when she came, she'd come from behind. And Kate? She would never know what hit her.

During the long train ride home, Anne dissected the job—what she'd done right, what she'd done wrong. By the time she got in the car that she had parked at the isolated station, she had a clear list of mistakes, and areas for improvement. Her biggest errors were poor planning—she'd actually started the job wanting to work. She'd fallen into the other thing. So, there hadn't been enough recon. Then, she'd let things drag on too long. The truth was that she enjoyed Hugh, the luxuries of being his mistress. She'd lost control of the situation. Still, the score was good. A bit messy. But Pop would be happy enough with the outcome.

She drove, out into the woods, down the long winding drive

that led to the house. The sky was a bruised purple-gray, the trees winter-black, some snow still clinging to the ground, to the branches. She hated winter, the quiet of it, the emptiness, the waiting of it. Hugh had promised her sunshine and cocktails, a tropical escape. She could feel the warm salt water on her skin, taste the tang of a fruity drink. She'd have let him take her away. It was all part of it, let it ride until it ran out.

The house sat low and dark, nestled into the trees, as she brought the car to a stop and killed the engine. She sat in the gloaming, let all traces of Anne fall away. Then she exited the vehicle and walked up the stairs to the porch, unlocking and pushing in the front door.

"I'm home," she said as she stepped through the front door. The wood floor creaked beneath her feet.

"You're early. What happened?"

"Things didn't go as planned."

"Oh?"

"Don't worry, Pop," she said, shedding her coat, dropping her bag. "It was a decent score. And I already have something else going."

"I never worry about you, kitten. It's the other guy who'd better be watching his back."

"You know me better than anyone."

"That's true. That's very true."

Her phone pinged and, when she saw who it was, she felt an intense wave of annoyance. The missives that came through were typically whiny, panicky.

I don't want to do this anymore.

It's wrong.

Don't you ever get tired?

I think things have gone south here. I want to leave.

She didn't even bother answering, just went upstairs and changed out of her work clothes into more comfortable attire—jeans, a soft long-sleeved T-shirt, her leather jacket, boots.

"You seem angry," said Pop when she came back down. He was sitting on the couch, the back of his balding head to her. "It's never a good idea to act out of anger. That's when we make mistakes."

"I'm not angry," she said.

Don't you ever get tired?

She did. Sometimes she got very tired.

EIGHT

Geneva

GENEVA HATED THE way winter afternoons started to darken around three. As the light leaked out of the sky, a kind of heaviness descended on her spirit. She turned on the lights in the kitchen, and loaded the dishwasher. The boys, sitting at the table with their snacks, were always a little cranky after school, but more so today. Stephen was sulking. Oliver, as usual, was bent over his book. Something about the energy of the house was just—off.

When she'd arrived that morning, the Murphy family was already gone. She'd used her keys to get in, found a note in the kitchen.

"We all had to leave early this morning," it read in a scrawling hand—Selena's or Graham's, she couldn't tell. "Please pick up the boys at the usual time."

The house had been a mess, with breakfast dishes still on the table, the boys' beds unmade. Not the usual state of affairs. Usually, the boys were eating their eggs and toast at the kitchen table when she arrived. She'd find them dressed in their uniforms, hair brushed, bags and lunch sacks waiting neatly by the door.

Selena liked to do all of those things before work; Geneva knew it made her feel like she'd taken care of things before she headed out for the day. She put notes in the boys' lunchboxes, special treats sometimes—not too sugary. She was plugged in during the day, always calling right as the boys got home. Available if they wanted her.

It was the complete opposite at the Tuckers'—the kids ran wild, no limits on devices, neither parent wanted to be bothered during the day unless it was an emergency. The Tucker boys would still be in pajamas, hopped up on some sugary cereal when Geneva arrived in the morning.

She didn't feel as bad about what had happened at the Tuckers'.

But Selena Murphy was a loving, present mom. A faithful wife. A fair and kind employer. She didn't deserve what was going on behind her back.

Geneva immediately got to cleaning—making the beds, throwing in a load of wash, then the kitchen. It was intimate, wasn't it, this position? Handling people's clothes, tucking in their sheets, clearing the plates from which they'd eaten. She thought about that, as she wiped down the counter, how close she was, and yet—not. A paid employee; someone who might be fired at will. As intimate in some ways as family, but in no way as permanent. Expendable.

That word was in her head when she'd noticed a brown dot on the counter. She walked over to work on it. What was it? It was only when it came up on the cloth that she realized.

It was blood.

There was another spot over the by the stove. She cleaned them both, feeling an odd tingling of dread.

Now, the boys ate their snacks at the kitchen table while she unpacked their lunchboxes.

"My teacher hates me," Stephen said startling her back to the present. He rested a chubby pink cheek in hand.

"No, she doesn't," said Geneva, starting the wash cycle.

There had been another chat at pickup. Stephen was acting out, said his uptight teacher. Apparently, he'd pushed another little boy down on the playground. "She knows that you're a nice boy who can behave better with others."

"She *does* hate you," said Oliver unhelpfully. He was in a mood, too, though Geneva wasn't sure why. He wasn't a talker. Stephen would tell all, but Oliver held it in. "She hates you because you're a *brat* and a *baby*."

"Shut up!" yelled Stephen, reddening and near tears.

"Oliver," said Geneva easily. "Apologize."

"Sorry," said Oliver, sounding not sorry at all.

They were eighteen months apart, acted more like rival gang members than brothers most of the time. But there was a closeness there, too, some rare moments of tenderness. Sibling relationships were so complicated. When Oliver left the room, Stephen followed. They both cleared their plates on the way out. Geneva rinsed them in the sink, thinking of her older sister a moment, that textured mingle of affection and competition, of admiration and resentment. But she pushed the thoughts away as she finished cleaning up.

A few minutes later, she heard the boys running up the stairs. They'd been making videos of each other, recording on their iPads. This activity seemed to keep them goofily getting along, so she didn't hassle them about too much time on their devices. It was creative at least, making and editing silly videos.

In the living room, she tidied—folded the blanket, fluffed the pillows. She caught sight of her reflection in the screen when she turned off the television. Hair up, outfit slouchy—baggy shirt and jeans too big. Her boobs—they looked huge, not in a good way. Men were *so* into it. But she just thought her large bust made her look fatter than she was—and she was no skinny waif. Today, she wasn't even wearing makeup. She looked like the worst cliché of a housewife. One without a house and who wasn't a wife.

Again, thoughts of her sister—her perfect sister who was a flawless beauty, never made mistakes, was always in control of every enterprise—surfaced, unwanted.

Are you even dating? she'd asked recently. She had nothing but disapproving things to say about Geneva, her life choices, her work. Geneva shouldn't want her approval so badly, but she did.

The washing machine chimed that it was ready. She was about to go change it to the dryer when she heard the garage door open.

Shit.

Graham.

Her palms got all sweaty. But he'd leave her alone, right? The boys were up. Since it was Friday, Selena could come home at any time. She went to the laundry room, changed the wash. She'd make a hasty exit. Selena could pay her on Monday.

Then, after a few minutes, she heard Selena's voice.

"I'm home early!" she called. Thunder on the stairs a moment later as the boys came down, yelling for her. *Mom! Mahhhm! Mommy!*

How nice that must be, thought Geneva, feeling a twinge she sometimes felt. The twinge of the voyeur, the interloper, the outsider on the inside.

When is your life going to start, Geneva? Her sister again, that silvery voice heavy with mock kindness. *There's more to you, isn't there? I'm just worried about you. You're like a case of arrested development.*

Arrested development. When a person stops maturing at a point of trauma, grief, or at a place in her life when she felt the profound and total loss of love from a primary caregiver. Maybe it was an accurate diagnosis. No one ever accused her sister of being stupid.

She finished folding the wash, headed downstairs.

In the kitchen, the kids had attached themselves to Selena's body, and she with an arm around each. She was tall and slim. Oliver shared her dark good looks, Stephen favoring his lighter, thicker father. Selena extracted herself, giving each boy another hug and kiss, then offered Geneva a tight smile. When their eyes met, Geneva's stomach clenched. There was a distance to the other woman's gaze, a coldness.

She knew.

"Lucky you," said Selena. "You get to start your weekend a bit early, too."

"Great," Geneva said, smiling.

"Of course, I'll pay you for the full day," Selena said kindly.

"Thank you."

She didn't *seem* angry. If she knew—how could she stand the sight of Geneva? If she knew—how could she have gone to work? Pretend like nothing was wrong? She thought about that drop of blood she'd wiped away.

She started gathering up her things.

I'm sorry, Geneva wanted to say. I don't even *like* him. There are reasons, deep and twisted, why I did it—according to my shrink. If you only knew the things that have happened to me, you might understand why I make so many bad choices. And then there's my sister, what she asks of me, what I do for her. I'm tangled in my life. I can't free myself.

But she didn't say any of those things.

"Where's Dad?" asked Oliver.

"He's away this weekend," said Selena. "You remember."

Oliver shook his head, offered a confused frown. "No."

"Boys' weekend," she said. "He went fishing with Uncle Joe."

"Like a playdate?" asked Stephen, eyes wide with innocence.

"Exactly like a playdate," said Selena with a playful roll of her eyes. Geneva tried to share a smile with her, but Selena wouldn't meet her gaze.

"He didn't say goodbye," said Oliver, looking toward the door as if he expected Graham to walk back through.

"He did," said Selena. "In the early, early morning. You woke up, remember?"

"No," said Oliver stubbornly. "He didn't."

Selena touched his head, gave him a loving smile.

"You just don't remember, sleepyhead."

"I remember," said Stephen, presenting himself for Selena's approval. "He whispered."

"That's right," said Selena, dropping a hand on Stephen's shoulder. Stephen shot Oliver a victorious look, but the other boy was still frowning, unconvinced.

"Is he going to call at bedtime?" Oliver wanted to know.

"If they have service," said Selena, voice neutral. "I haven't heard from your dad today. So I wouldn't get my hopes up."

If Selena was annoyed about Graham's trip, if there was any more to it, it certainly didn't show in front of the boys. The rag Geneva had used to clean up the small amount of blood had come away dark and red. There was still the faintest tinge of pink on the counter that wouldn't come up. They said you could never really clean away all traces of blood. The hemoglobin always stayed behind, sank into porous surfaces, clung to fibers. She'd put the rag through the wash twice with bleach, stuffed it in the back of the cabinet with the other rags.

"I'm just going to quickly change," she said. "Do you mind getting them settled?"

"Not at all," said Geneva. "And if you need an hour to yourself this weekend, just drop me a text."

"I might take you up on that," Selena said. Still, she glanced away, and then she disappeared up the stairs.

Geneva got the boys in front of the television, agreeing on *Trollhunters*, which they were watching for about the millionth time. She kissed them each on the forehead, telling them to be good for their mom this weekend.

Then she gathered her things, including the check Selena left on the quartz counter. It was exactly what she was owed; usually Selena rounded up or put a little extra.

People communicated in the little things. Most people didn't even realize how the smallest details spoke volumes. Geneva stared at the check, Selena's flowery signature, the careful way she wrote the date.

I'd better put my résumé together. Her sister was not going to be happy. But doubtless she'd have a plan.

At the bottom of the stairs, she called up. "Boys are all set! I'm heading out."

"Thank you," called Selena, her voice muffled from down the hall.

Usually Selena would linger with Geneva, chatting about the boys or about work or the neighbors. But a wall had come down.

The other woman was biding her time, wasn't she? Figuring out her plan before she acted. She was a cool customer; she'd known people like that before. They didn't react right away, kept it all inside. Action, when it was taken, was quick and decisive.

She didn't look back at the boys, at the house. Time to go.

Geneva stepped out into the dim late afternoon, the sound of the television disappearing behind her as she closed the door. Sometimes when the air was frigid like this, she wondered if spring would ever come. Late January, all the fun of the holidays past, just the gray ceiling of the northern winter sky, a waiting for brighter days. A kind of hollow would open inside of her, an emptiness that felt as if it could never be filled. Her footfalls echoed down the walk.

Athens. Venice. Barcelona. Anywhere. She could go anywhere really. She didn't have as much money saved as she wanted. But she had enough to get by for a while, until she found another situation. Nannies. A good one was always in demand.

She liked the Murphy family, and she was sorry for whatever role she might have played in what was happening now. But, to be honest, the fractures were already there. They always were, little cracks that would widen and deepen, threaten the whole structure when pressure was applied. If the structure was sound, nothing ever would have happened. She'd been in homes where the husband didn't even look at her, let alone touch. Men who were in love with their wives, engaged with their kids, happy. Those men—and they did exist—left her be.

Just before Selena's family, there was the Tuckers. As a couple, the Tuckers were already unhappy when Geneva came—two jobs, two kids, a huge mortgage, two leased cars—a Lexus for her and a shiny BMW for him—a country club membership. The kids were wild—largely ignored by parents obsessed with work, their devices, their social lives. It was chaos. Erik Tucker had been handsome and charming; and something else. There was a darkness there. It was obvious now.

Geneva was a serial homewrecker. She didn't mean to be. She and her therapist talked about it at length without talking about all the layers, all the reasons. There were things she couldn't share about her life. About the real reason why she found herself in these situations.

When the same thing happens again and again, we have to look at that. We have to unpack it and figure out why we cause ourselves and others pain.

At the curb, she paused. Should she go back?

Should she try to talk to Selena? Maybe she could be honest with someone for once. Maybe this was one of those moments when you did something different, and something different happened.

No, that was the first rule: always pretend that nothing was wrong.

People—especially women—werc racked with self-doubt. They looked around at others for cues, ways to orient themselves to a situation, the way passengers on a turbulent aircraft might look at the faces of the flight attendants. Just keep smiling, keep moving. Walk, don't run.

But maybe if she came clean with Selena, the other woman would help her. She was that kind of person, one who would seek to help even someone who had hurt her.

Geneva, though, just kept walking away from the house.

The neighborhood was quiet, the street shaded beneath towering oaks. She never saw anyone out in their front yards. Kids rarely played in the street, or rode bikes. There were no sidewalks. The large homes were set back far from the street, seemed remote from each other somehow though the lots weren't huge. But that was the world now, everyone in their little silo, broadcasting versions of their lives from a screen, onto the screens of others. In the stillness, her footfalls echoed off the pavement. Her breath came out in clouds.

She was just about to get into her vehicle when she heard the sound of a car door opening and closing. She felt the sound in every one of her nerve endings.

Then, there was a dark figure on the street, moving toward her. Geneva looked back at the house, the warm interior lights glowing orange in the blue of early evening. The other houses were dark.

She dug into her purse for her keys, the figure moving closer.

Geneva's heart raced a bit as she searched for and didn't find those keys. Why was her purse such a mess? But as she approached her car, the doors unlocked automatically. She kept forgetting about that. How in the new car, the key was just a fob.

Something stopped her from climbing inside; she turned around instead.

As the form grew closer, Geneva squinted into the dim.

Who was it? When she finally saw, she felt the shock of surprise and dread.

"Oh," she managed. "It's you."

NINE
Pearl

"YOU SHOULDN'T DO THAT, should you?"

Charlie had walked into the bookshop back room to find Pearl digging through her mother's leather tote.

"She doesn't care," said Pearl.

She inspected a small notepad shaped like a heart on which nothing was written.

Pearl loved her mother's purse, which Stella carelessly left all over the place. On the passenger seat of the car, the kitchen counter. She'd leave it in the shopping cart, walk away from it to look for this or that, as if daring someone to take it.

It was a magic pouch, filled with mysteries. Pearl, whenever she got a chance, dug through it shamelessly. Lipsticks, all shades, matches from restaurants and bars Pearl had no idea when Stella had visited. A lighter shaped like the body of a woman. Whatever book she was reading—it might be Kafka, or some obscure foreign writer, or the latest romance bestseller. Literary, romance, thriller, classic, science fiction, fantasy, women's fiction—her mother did not discriminate.

Story is story, Stella said. It's a portal you walk through into another world. And this world—which usually sucks—just disappears.

A package of condoms. Mom slept around; just as with her reading, she was not particularly discriminating when it came to men—whoever struck her fancy, construction worker, doctor, businessman, store clerk.

Candy. There was always candy. Swedish Fish, Tic Tacs, Mars Bars—Junior Mints were her favorite. Wadded up bills—why could Stella not put the money in her wallet? Because that would delay its spending, quipped Stella. Don't even bother trying to hold on to it; it's gone as quick as it comes. Phone numbers on scraps of papers. Sometimes cigarettes. Once a joint. Floss. Stella was meticulous about her dental hygiene.

"Your mother's a mystery, isn't she?" asked Charlie.

"Not really," said Pearl. As far as Pearl was concerned, her mother was an open book.

"All women are mysteries."

"Only men think that," said Pearl. "Largely because they're not paying attention."

Charlie was at her mother's desk, doing something at her computer. Apparently, according to Stella, he was managing the accounting now. He'd been an increasingly large part of their lives for the last couple of months. Certainly, he was around more and for longer than anyone else had been. He was often in the kitchen now when Pearl came down before school, making breakfast. Last week, he'd proofread her English essay and they'd spent a long time talking about it. Pearl liked Charlie, but she wasn't going to let herself get attached. She knew Stella too well. She'd tire of him eventually.

"The only thing more mysterious than women are teenage girls."

She was aware of his eyes. He was always watching her. And she was always watching him. Trying to figure him out. He was polite, intelligent. He was always on time. Good with the customers. Good, according to Stella, with the books. He was well-read. He hand-sold, getting to know patrons and recommending books they might like. He's a throwback, said Stella. A real bookseller, in an industry that had stopped caring about story and only cared about numbers.

But. But. But.

There was something else. Pearl was a watcher. She hid in the stacks, observing. Still, she couldn't figure him out. Handsome, in a geeky way. Too skinny. Always impeccable—pressed button-down shirts, crisp khakis, sensible shoes. His socks always matched his pants.

"Can you stock some books this afternoon?" he asked. "We just got a big shipment, the new Karin Slaughter."

He nodded toward some boxes stacked by the door.

"Sure," said Pearl.

"Not too much homework?"

"No," she said. "I'm good. Where's Mom?"

Charlie shrugged. "Like I said. Mysterious."

"Her purse is here," said Pearl. She took a piece of Black Jack gum from its wrapper and stuffed it in her mouth.

Charlie frowned, considering.

"I'm pretty sure she had her wallet and her phone. Her keys," he said finally.

The bell rang outside, and they watched a group of kids enter the store from the monitor that hung on the wall. Charlie got up to greet them, giving her a smile as he left the room.

Their voices carried back to Pearl, laughter bubbling. They'd put out some fliers at her school, and now kids were coming to study in the afternoons. It had been Charlie's idea, one of many good ones.

Pearl grabbed the box cutter, carefully slicing open the first carton. She loved unpacking—the smell of new paper, the shiny or matte jackets, the raised letters beneath her fingertips, the weight of a real book in her hands, the whisper of paper. She loved hardcovers, and floppy trade paperbacks, the blocky mass markets—each with their own place in the store.

The store outside had grown quiet, the kids who came to study were actually studying. She recognized one of the girls, but not the other two. Pearl's school was a sprawling concrete monster that looked like a prison. She didn't know everyone. She didn't know anyone really. She might sit with the other nerds at lunch; they were nice enough to her. But she mainly kept to herself, her nose in a book.

A few more kids trickled in, headed for the donuts, then grabbed a space on one of the couches. They, too, settled in, took out notebooks and laptops. This was the most people she had seen here on a weekday afternoon. If it wasn't for online sales, and the money that came from renting out the space for parties, meetings, book groups, Stella's Pages would have gone out of business long ago. Charlie was good for the store. Good, it seemed, for Stella. And Pearl didn't mind him either.

She wouldn't let herself get attached.

The afternoon wound on. Pearl stocked the books on the front table reserved for big bestsellers. Then, she walked around with the feather duster—from literature to science fiction, from young adult to picture books. After she was done, she flopped into the overstuffed chair by the storefront window and worked on her homework.

Finally, it was growing dark and time to close up. Stella had not returned.

"I guess we'll just meet her at home," said Charlie, frowning at his phone. She'd watched him text a couple of times, then stare at his screen. She felt bad for him; this was probably the beginning. Stella was probably getting tired of him. Pearl knew the signs.

"We'll carry in dinner," he said.

They cashed out, locked up. Pearl took Stella's tote along with her own bags and rode home in Charlie's GTO. He was quiet, thoughtful. They stopped for burgers.

The lights were on upstairs as they pulled into the driveway. The smell of hamburgers and fries filled the interior of the car. Pearl saw a shadow in the window. Then her mother's silhouette joined the form in an embrace. A new boyfriend, Pearl guessed.

Had Charlie seen it, too?

"You know," he said, pushing up his glasses. He kept his eyes straight ahead. "Maybe just have your mom call me. If she wants."

Pearl wasn't sure what to say.

"Take the burgers," he said quietly. "Make sure you both eat."

He was pale in the streetlight, a muscle clenching in his jaw.

"I'm sorry," said Pearl, exiting with her bags, her mom's, the food. She took a hamburger from the sack and handed it to Charlie. When he reached for it, their eyes locked and he smiled; she smiled back. It was the closest she had ever come to feeling something for someone. Which she knew, distantly, was weird. But you can only be who you are.

She wanted to say something else, but he just waved her inside.

In the foyer, she heard music, her mother's laughter wafting down the hall. Then, the rumble of a man's voice. She looked back before shutting the front door. Charlie still idled in his car in front of the house. What was he doing? Just making sure she got inside safely.

She ate at the kitchen table alone, reading. The music from her mother's room grew louder. After dinner, she cleaned up—loading the dirty breakfast dishes in the dishwasher, wiping down the counter. More laughter. An odd thudding.

She went up to her room, to finish her homework where it was quieter. Then the house grew silent again.

She was glad she hadn't let herself get attached to Charlie.

But when she looked out her bedroom window just before turning out her lights to sleep, his car was still there.

TEN
Selena

STEPHEN AND OLIVER argued through dinner, fought as they all watched a movie, finally quieted down for a story, and took some parting shots at each other while they lay in their beds, Selena lying on the floor between them.

"Boys, be nice to each other," she whispered in the night-light-dim room. On the ceiling, stars glowed green. She remembered sticking them up there with Graham. It took forever, both of them with aching arms and backs the next day. "Love each other."

"Ew," said Oliver.

"Shut up," said Stephen.

"I'm one second from leaving this room," warned Selena. They both quieted down at that, Oliver with a huff, turning his back. She felt the heat of Stephen's stare. When he was smaller, he would watch her until his eyes closed finally for sleep.

The hard floor felt good on her aching back. The day had been brutal. It required herculean effort to pretend that everything was okay when your whole life was about to fall apart.

The energy that it took to smile, to talk with clients, to put on the mask of normal; she was drained, cored out from the effort. Her networking lunch—all idle chatter and polite laughter and immobile botox faces, and designer handbags worn like shields—just about did her in. She'd left with a pounding headache.

"You okay?" asked Beth in the cab afterward.

Did she not seem okay? She really thought she was putting on a good front.

"Fine," she lied. "Great."

Selena hadn't been sure what it would be like when one of your best friends was also your boss; but it worked. Mutual respect, compassion, teamwork, lots of laughs. Wasn't it only men who implied that women couldn't work well together? She'd never had a problem with female colleagues. In fact, quite the opposite. Any leg up she'd ever had professionally had been due to female mentors and friends.

"Just allergies," Selena conceded. "My head is killing me."

She and Beth had been friends a long time. They were publicists together in their twenties at a small publishing house, been through it all—boyfriends, breakups, the death of a parent, meeting the right guy, weddings, pregnancy, the birth of children, Beth's divorce, and Michaela, the friend they'd lost to a sudden heart attack.

Beth nodded and offered a sympathetic smile, a squeeze of her hand. Her gaze lingered a moment, and then she went back to the email on her phone. Her nails were perfect candy-pink squares, glittering like the diamond in the ring that she bought herself after her divorce. Their tapping was hypnotic.

"Let me know if you want to talk about it," Beth said easily. Translation: *It's okay if you don't want to tell me what's really going on. But I'm here.*

"I'm fine," Selena said. "Really."

"How's Graham's job hunt going?" Translation: *When is your loser husband going back to work?*

"It's going."

Another quick glance, then back to the phone. Beth didn't like Graham. She'd never said so, but Selena could tell. There was a way she leaned on his name, a certain expression she wore when they all got together. But they didn't need to love each other's spouses, just be nice. God knows, Selena had put on a smile and endured Beth's cheap, controlling, adulterous ex-husband Jon for the near decade they were married. That was the golden rule of friendship. Be nice. It was a decent rule in general, wasn't it? If more people followed it, the world would be a better place. Also: let your friends keep their secrets. Support them when things go to shit.

As things had gone to shit last night.

All day, she tried not to think about the scene between her and Graham. Her own voice—low because of the sleeping children but sizzling white hot with rage—rang back at her. Shocking. The things she'd said. *His* words like punches to the kidneys. How ugly it had been. When had so much vitriol, so much anger grown between them? It was like toxic mold; they knocked down the drywall and all she could see was black rot.

"Dad didn't call to say good-night," said Oliver now, voice muffled.

"Must have bad service," she said to the ceiling.

"He didn't say goodbye."

Selena felt a pang of guilt—for what had happened, for the lies she'd told. She was lying to her children now. Nice.

"He'll call tomorrow," she said lightly. "Now go to sleep."

"Mom," started Oliver. "I saw—"

"Not now, honey," she said. If they started talking about this thing or that thing he saw in school or on television, or on the computer, it would be twenty minutes of conversation. Of course, Stephen would chime in on whatever it was. Then there would be an argument. "Go to sleep."

"But—"

"Oliver." She summoned her mom voice. "Go to sleep."

She wondered how many times you uttered that phrase over your life as a parent. Because your day as a parent didn't end until your child was sleeping. In the life of the full-time parent, it was the only guilt-free, quiet space when you could just be yourself, you could drop your vigilance for a bit, the endless litany of wants and needs ceased for a few hours. She really needed some time to think—about what had happened, about what she was going to do.

On the commute home, she'd scanned the train for the woman she'd met last night. She simultaneously wanted to see her and fervently hoped they'd never cross paths again. There was something about that moment they'd shared, that confessional space, that was more honest and true than any other place in her life right now. She badly wanted that release, and feared it.

What had the other woman said? *Wouldn't it be nice if your problems just went away?*

Something about the memory, about the sound of the other woman's voice, sent a cold finger down her spine. *Bad things happen all the time.*

Selena closed her eyes, felt sleep tugging at her almost instantly. She wondered how long before she could crawl out of there. She didn't want to sleep on the floor, wake up at 2:00 a.m. with aching bones. She waited, counting her breaths, listening to the boys. She opened her eyes and met Stephen's steady gaze.

"Don't go," he said, reading her mind.

"Close your eyes," she answered.

After a while, their breathing grew deep and even. Stephen, her deep sleeper, sounded congested. Oliver, who like her would wake at any sound, shifted and sighed. She got up quietly and left the room, always a tricky maneuver.

She padded down the hall, and closed the door to her bedroom. She took a breath.

There were certain times when she was *just Selena.* Between her commute and the walk through the front door, where she was alone in the car maybe listening to a podcast, or an audio book, or just driving in silence. She relished it. It was about fourteen minutes. So, twenty-eight minutes a day—on the way to the train, and on the way home—she was just herself.

Or when the kids were asleep and Graham was out, and she could choose what she wanted to do without considering anyone else. When she wasn't the person she was at the office—efficient, reliable, always bright, on point—or the person she was at home—mom, wife, loving, accommodating, understanding. In the dark leather interior of the car, no one needed or wanted anything from her. It wasn't *a thing.* She hadn't been unhappy. She loved her life, didn't she? All those smiling social media posts—#grateful #blessedtobestressed #lovemyboys—that's what she put out there.

Last night there had been screaming, shattering glass, sobbing that miraculously didn't wake the boys. If it wasn't their first blowout, it was certainly their worst. Her headache ratcheted up.

But *had* she been happy?

She and Graham stood on the sidelines at soccer fields and baseball games, smiling, laughing, cheering. They had their foldout event chairs, their cooler filled with water and oranges to share with the team and other parents. There were parties with friends and picnics and lovely family vacations. They had a legion of friends, acquaintances, neighbors. School functions, backyard barbecues, charity auctions, community fun runs. It was a life that they had built—one that seemed to spring up all around them without much thought. And it was a good one. Wasn't it?

But before all that—what had she wanted to do? What had she wanted to be?

A writer.

For the first time since last night, she let herself cry. She turned on the television and buried her face in a big soft pillow and let it rip. All her anger, sorrow, the fatigue of holding it all in, her fear for what came next released into the cotton. When she was done, she felt better, cleansed.

She needed to think, figure out what to do.

Her phone lay dark and silent on the comforter next to her. Who could she call? Who *should* she call? No one. Her sweet mother. Her perfect sister. Her successful friends. Who could she tell what a shambles her life was about to become? The only person she wanted to call was Will, her ex, the man who she'd left for Graham. Improbably, they were still friends. Good friends. She could call him; she knew that. He'd be happy she did. A little too happy. It was a bad idea. She didn't call anyone.

She thought again about the woman from the train. Martha, that was her name. Her confessor. She felt like maybe she would tell Martha what had happened. What would she say? Not that she had any way to reach the other woman.

On the dresser was a photograph of Graham, Oliver, Stephen and Selena, a family portrait taken at a low point in their marriage. It had been sheer chaos getting everyone dressed and out the door to the park to meet the professional photographer. Stephen wailed the whole way there. Graham thought it was a stupid expense, groused about that, about traffic, snapped at the boys. It was miserable. But everyone managed to pull it together for the session, fake smiles plastered on bright.

"Don't worry," said the photographer, an older woman with a wild head of curls and a wise smile. She must have sensed their stress levels, though Selena had tried to hide it. "It will be worth it."

She meant more than the photo session, gave Selena a warm squeeze on the arm.

When the photos came back, they were perfect. All of them looking blissfully happy, she and Graham in love, the boys like little angels. She chose one for their photo Christmas card; everyone raved about it. The photographer was right, Selena thought when the proofs arrived. It's all worth it.

What a fraud, she thought now, holding the portrait. She wanted to smash it. Instead she placed it down again, lay back on the bed, blanked out staring at the screen. *Game of Thrones*—everyone beautiful, draped in leather, smoldering, urgent with the approach of war. She let herself escape into that beautiful, dangerous fantasy world for a while. Dragons. Dirty sex. The Three-Eyed Raven. An army of undead soldiers. All of it *way* more manageable than real life.

Then she heard something, turned down the volume on the TV.

The security alarm was set; she'd done that before they came up.

Walking out into the hallway, she was greeted by quiet.

At the landing, she paused and listened, then went down. She checked the front door—locked. Alarm still armed and active. Back door closed and locked. Selena checked each window on the first floor, moving room to room. There'd never been a break-in in this neighborhood that she knew of.

But what the woman on the train said was true, wasn't it? Bad things happen all the time. Randomly. When you least expect it.

At the top of the stairs, a slim figure hovered. A scream crept up her throat.

For a terrible, reality-altering second, she thought it was the woman from the train.

"Mom." It was Oliver. "I heard something."

Relief flooded her system as she climbed the stairs. At the top, she took his shoulders. "You scared me, buddy."

"I'm sorry."

"Back to bed."

"Stephen's snoring. Can I sleep with you?"

She looked into those wide, dark eyes. Her little old soul. He came out of the womb staring at her. Stephen wailed and fussed, wouldn't nurse, was colicky and a general pain. But Oliver had been her angel baby, her kindred spirit. When she looked at him, sometimes when he wasn't being a troublemaker and a con, she saw all the layers of past, present and future. Who he was before he was born, who she had been, the man he'd become, who they'd be together, and long after they were both gone.

They climbed into the big bed, and she teddy-bear-hugged him, relishing the warmth of his little body, the role of mother that allowed her to back-burner everything else.

"I heard you and Dad fighting last night," he said when she thought he was asleep.

She thought about denying it. Then, "I'm sorry."

She thought the boys had slept through it. But really, how could they have? It was epic.

"It sounded like you hated each other," said Oliver.

She felt a dump of sadness in her middle. "No."

"You said that. You said, 'I hate you, Graham.' You said you wished you'd never married him. That you should have married Uncle Will."

Shit. Had she said that? That was low, and not exactly true.

"Let me ask you a question," she said. "Do you and Stephen fight all the time?"

"Yeah."

"Do you tell him that you hate him?"

"Yeah."

"Do you mean it?"

He didn't answer right away. "I guess not."

"Just sometimes when you get so mad, so frustrated, you say things that you don't mean, right?"

"I guess."

"That's what happened with me and your dad last night. I'm sorry you had to hear that."

She remembered what it felt like to listen to her parents fight. She and her sister used to cling to each other while their parents raged. She remembered—she felt helpless, powerless, afraid. That's how she'd made Oliver feel. God, that was terrible. She hated Graham, she did. And she hated herself.

She stroked her son's silky hair; his forehead felt hot.

He was quiet a moment, his chest rising and falling with his breath.

"Zander's parents are getting a divorce," he said softly. "He says he gets two birthday parties and two Christmases now."

"Okay." She didn't know who Zander was.

"I don't want two birthdays," he said.

"I understand."

"So where is Dad?"

"Boys' weekend. I told you."

The lie hung between them.

"Okay, I think he's at Uncle Joe's," she admitted finally. That's usually where Graham went when they needed a break, to his brother's bachelor pad.

"I think he's outside," said Oliver.

"What?" she asked. "What do you mean?"

"I think he's sitting in his car across the street."

Selena got up and went to the window. Sure enough, there was Graham, sitting in their SUV across the street. She bit back an intense roil of anger, of annoyance. *What the fuck?* She told him that she needed time and space to think. That he should stay away. That she'd make an excuse for the boys and he could call on Saturday to talk to them. But, of course, he was going to do whatever he wanted. Because that was Graham. He didn't respect or even understand that other people had boundaries and only bullies pushed through them.

When she was a young woman, out of college, working, and her mother had finally confessed to Selena and her sister the true scope of their father's many affairs, Selena pretended to understand why her mother had stayed so long.

She said all the right things, offered her mother compassion and sympathy. But, deep down, she *hadn't* really understood. Why had her mother endured the shame, the humiliation, the rage and just let him get away with it for, it turned out, decades? How could she live with it, with him, with herself? Selena had wondered. In this moment, in the dark of her bedroom, talking to her oldest boy, the truth of it came home, hard. You'd endure just about anything to spare your child pain. She pulled on her robe.

"I'll go get him," she said. "Let's get you back into your bed, okay?"

"But—"

She stewarded him to his room and tucked him in again.

"*Do* you hate him?" Oliver asked as she moved away.

The answer was so complicated it backed up in her throat. "No," she said. "Of course not. No more than you hate Stephen."

He nodded, seemed to get the complexity of the statement, her little old man. "And we both love you and your brother more than anything. Never forget that."

No matter what happens next, she thought, but didn't say.

He was already drifting off, exhausted, as she pulled the door to his bedroom closed.

Downstairs, she turned off the alarm and walked out into the dark in her robe and slippers. She knocked hard on the window, startling Graham from his doze. She looked around the neighborhood. She should have just called him on his cell phone; what would people think if they saw? They'd think they were a flawed mess of a family, just like everyone else probably was.

"What the hell are you doing?" she asked when he rolled down the window.

"Joe kicked me out," he said, pathetically. "He had company."

"Have you ever heard of a hotel?"

"I didn't want to spend the money."

He had her there. She'd thought about canceling all his credit cards, moving their money from accounts he had access to into one that he didn't know about. But she hadn't followed through.

He had a bandage over his eye. In her rage, she'd picked up Stephen's robot and hurled it at Graham, hitting him right on the forehead. There had been lots of blood. Not her finest moment. She almost felt sorry for him.

"Just come inside. Do you want the neighbors to see you out here?"

"I don't give a fuck about the neighbors."

"Or anyone else."

He offered her an elaborate eye roll, dropped his head back against the seat.

"Selena."

She walked across the street and up the path to their door, hugging herself against the cold, and he followed.

"Sleep in your office," she said.

"Can we talk?"

"No," she said, walking up the stairs.

She didn't turn to look at him, just returned to her bedroom, closing and locking the door. She sat in the chair a while, heart racing, mind spinning. What was she going to do?

She was surprised to hear her phone ping, half wondered if it was Graham texting her from downstairs.

A text from an unknown number read:

Hey, how's it going? Great meeting you last night.

Who was this now? She was about to delete when her phone pinged again.

I'd love to continue our conversation. I've been thinking about it a lot. Can we get together?

No, thought Selena. It couldn't be.

The woman she'd met, her dark tone, the strange energy of it all, came back to her vividly. Heat came up in her cheeks:

Selena had confessed her most personal secret to a stranger. Of course, the other woman had shared her secret, too. There was something oddly bonding about that, wasn't there?

They hadn't exchanged numbers, had they? She moved to delete the text, but her finger hovered.

Maybe she *should* answer. She felt a powerful desire to hear the other woman's voice, to tell her what she couldn't tell anyone else in her life. She hadn't even told Beth. Yet there was a strong pull to bare all to this stranger.

No. It must be a wrong number. She tapped to delete and block, but the phone chimed again before she could complete the action.

It's Martha, by the way.

From the train.

ELEVEN

Selena

SELENA WOKE MONDAY morning before the alarm went off. It was still dark, and the wind howled, knocking branches against the window. Before she even opened her eyes, her to-do list asserted itself into her consciousness—write an email to Stephen's teacher and schedule a meeting, get a birthday gift for her nephew, Jasper, polish her part of the big client presentation that afternoon, file her expenses, call her mother.

Amazing.

World crumbling, still making lists. Life went on.

Graham pushed in the bedroom door and climbed into bed beside her. He was sleeping in the home office, coming into their bed before the boys woke up. She ignored him, kept her eyes pressed closed. The truth was that, at the moment, she could barely stand the sight of him. The image of Geneva on top of him was on an ugly loop in her mind.

"Are you awake?" he whispered, reaching for her.

"No," she answered, shifting as far away from him as possible while still remaining on the bed. He turned away, lay on his back, gazing at the ceiling.

The truth.

Selena had posted on Instagram three times over the weekend. First, the boys helping with breakfast on Saturday morning. *Every smart mom teaches her boys how to cook!* she wrote. *Their wives will thank me one day!*

Then, the family walk they took at the state park about a half hour from the house. They'd hiked the trails, the boys rambling the rocky paths, she and Graham lagging behind, a dull silence between them. She snapped a picture of them by the river—Graham leaning down to show the kids a rock he thought might be a fossil. *Nothing like a couple hours in nature to center and calm after a busy week!*

On Sunday, she and the boys finally got started on the Lego Death Star, an epic project that would take weeks. She posted a photo of the open box, the stack of instruction manuals, the clear bags filled with tiny pieces. *Oh, boy! This is going to be a major undertaking!*

What didn't make it onto social media: the leaden silence between Graham and her; the boys, clearly picking up on the tension, acting out every chance they got; Oliver and Stephen literally wrestling on the floor over a ladle; how they never got very far on that Lego project because of a fight over who got to open the first bag; Graham checking and checking his phone compulsively while the boys raged and were finally sent to their room. Later, while Selena did the laundry and some of the cooking for the week, the boys vegged in front of the television—for hours. She let them, just to get some quiet time. More laundry. The dishes. Stephen's skinned knee. Selena crying in the shower out of sheer exhaustion and unhappiness.

Was it a lie to only show the glittering moments? What about the dull, the mundane, the ugly? If they weren't posted online, were they less real? Graham wanted to know: Why post at all? What are you trying to prove?

"What's going to happen?" Graham asked now. "What are we doing here?"

Morning light made its debut, leaking milky gray through the blinds. He moved closer to her, pulled her back from the edge of the bed, and draped an arm over her middle. She thought about pushing him away. But the truth was that his warmth comforted her. She stayed still, marveling at how she wanted to throttle and cling to him. Even though the weekend was hard, they still laughed at times, still parented, still cooked and ate. The *truth* was that it was everything—the beautiful and ugly all in one impossible tangle.

"I have no idea," she admitted.

The workweek loomed ahead—though the office was an escape sometimes. She needed some help. Obviously, Geneva would have to be fired. Today. Which meant Graham needed to stay with the kids—*which* meant that she couldn't kick him out permanently. Yet. Maybe she needed to talk to Beth; she'd have ideas on how to navigate next steps.

"We just go through the motions?" said Graham.

"For now."

"Until what?"

"I don't know, Graham," she nearly yelled. Christ, he was like one of the kids. She took a breath, released it. "I'll take the boys to school and then head into the office. You fire Geneva."

He nodded but stayed quiet. They lay like that a moment, then she got up to take a shower before she had to get the boys started.

She liked the water hot, nearly scalding. She let it beat on her skin, fog up the bathroom.

She did her hair, her makeup, dressed in slim black pants and a blush-pink top, heels. By the time she exited the bedroom, Graham had roused the boys from bed. How nice that he chose this morning to finally step up.

"Good morning," she said on her way downstairs.

Stephen and Oliver groaned at her like sleepy zombies, moving slow, dressing in the uniforms that she'd laid out for them last night.

By the time she came downstairs, Graham had set the table, waffles in the toaster, boys' lunches packed. If only he behaved like this when their marriage wasn't imploding. The fact that he was being so on point now only aggravated her more.

She poured herself a cup of coffee while he served the boys.

She hadn't thought much about the text she'd received on Friday. She'd deleted it from her phone and blocked the number. Likewise, she'd purposely pushed it from her thoughts. Martha was going to get ghosted. That was that. She didn't need more complications in her life.

When the doorbell rang, Selena startled, nearly spilling her coffee.

Shit. Geneva was early. She'd hoped to be gone with the boys before she arrived. In fact, as much as she had liked and appreciated Geneva *before*, she'd hoped never to lay eyes on Geneva again. She'd seen far too much of her already.

"Did you forget your key?" she asked, opening the door.

But it wasn't Geneva.

At the door was a broad, clean-cut man, with dark hair. He wasn't wearing a uniform, but there was something official about him even before he held out his detective's shield. A black sedan lurked in their driveway, and another man—older, rumpled, climbed out and approached them. The morning was alive with birdsong, the air warmer than it had been in months. Maybe spring would come early. Selena's heart started to thump for reasons she couldn't name.

"Mrs. Murphy?"

"That's right."

"I'm Detective Grady Crowe, and this is my partner Detective West."

She kept the door partially closed, her body blocking their view into her house. She fought the urge to call for Graham.

"What can I do for you?" she asked.

"Do you employ a woman by the name of Geneva Markson?"

"We do."

"When is the last time you had contact with her?"

Detective Crowe kept a steady stare on Selena, but West's eyes were everywhere else—around the stoop, past her into the foyer, inspecting the potted plants, the shrubbery.

"Why? What's happened?"

"Can we come in?"

Her mouth felt terribly dry. Was it just something about cops that made you feel automatically as if you'd done something wrong?

The boys went tearing up the stairs, not interested in who might be at the door. But Graham came up behind her as she let the detectives inside.

The detectives re-introduced themselves to Graham, who instantly slipped into charm mode. He had that way. He put on this certain expression, a kind of wide-open affability, and took control of the situation. He led the cops into the living room, offering coffee, man of the house. He was showered and dressed, hair combed. A small miracle considering the state he'd been in since he lost his job.

"She left here around four o'clock Friday afternoon," said Selena, sitting on the arm of the couch. "I came home early from work."

Detective Crowe scribbled in a notebook. The other detective stood by the entry, eyes moving over everything.

"You were both here?" asked Crowe.

"No," said Graham, rubbing at his eyes. Something he did when he was about to lie. "I was visiting my brother, helping him with a home project."

Helping with a home project. She nearly laughed. As if. As

if Joe would have a home project. As if Graham would be any help at all.

"Where's that?"

"In Remsen, about fifteen minutes north."

If she didn't know he was lying, she'd never suspect it. No one would.

"Can you tell us what's wrong?" asked Selena.

"Local police had a call from Ms. Markson's sister saying that she was concerned not to have heard from her. Apparently, they were meant to meet for breakfast Saturday, but Ms. Markson did not show up. Her car is not in her parking space at her home. Her apartment is empty—her sister apparently has a key."

"Oh," said Selena. "That's odd. She never mentioned a sister."

Had she?

"What time does she usually show up for work?" asked Detective West.

Selena glanced at the clock. "Right about now."

"Well," said Graham easily. He leaned back on the couch, crossed his legs. "She's young, single. Maybe she took off for the weekend with friends or a boyfriend."

Selena flashed on the image of Geneva on top of Graham, pushed it away. She sank into one of the chairs, looked out the window.

Their neighbors across the street, the Browns, were pulling out of the drive. They left all together in the morning, taking their twins to school, Jill dropping Bobby off at the train so that he could commute into the city. Selena was usually pulling out at the same time, waving across the street. *Have a great day!* As Selena watched them disappear, she felt an odd sinking in her middle. That should be us. Off to start another normal day.

There was some thumping upstairs, a shout. The boys were up there unsupervised; she rose to go check on them.

"Is it usual for her to be late?" asked Detective Crowe.

"No," said Selena quickly. "She has never once been late."

"What happened to your face there?" asked Detective West, pointed to Graham.

While Crowe had seated himself, West had moved over to the bookshelves.

Graham touched the cut on his face. He nodded out the window from where the stone wall, the one he'd been trying to repair, was visible, still in shambles. A year later, he hadn't finished the project. They all turned to look.

"I was trying to fix that wall on Friday, bent over and cut myself. Not exactly a handyman I guess."

Wow, he didn't miss a beat. That self-deprecating smile, the touch of embarrassment. Even Selena almost believed him. He hadn't touched the thing, refused to call in someone who could do the work. The wall had become one of their go-to arguments—how he started things he didn't finish, how he made promises he didn't keep.

Crowe made a note, West nodded, both men smiling in understanding. Home projects could be such a bear.

Of course, Graham had to lie. What else was he going to say?

Oh, during a marriage-ending fight, my wife threw a toy robot at me.

What were you fighting about, sir?

I was caught on camera fucking the nanny. You know, the one you're here asking about.

"What about her phone?" asked Selena, eager to move away from Graham's lies. "Can't you track her that way?"

"Her phone is offline," said Detective West. "She hasn't used a known credit card since early last week."

She thought of Geneva, shuttling the kids back and forth to school, running all the errands—to the grocery store, the dry cleaners, even getting the car serviced. Such intimate work, to run someone's daily life.

"She's here every weekday," said Selena, musing. "She eats her meals at our place and makes a plate to take home for dinner. I give her cash for errands, groceries, whatever. So she probably doesn't use her card much during the week."

"That's what her sister told us," said Crowe, nodding.

Had Geneva ever mentioned a sister? A sister who was close enough to know her habits, to become concerned enough to call the police because of a missed breakfast date, with a key to her house. It seemed like Selena would have known about a sister. That she should have known.

"Did you pay her on Friday?"

"I did," said Selena. "By check. She usually mobile-deposits it, sometimes even before she leaves." Another nod, another scribble.

"Can you check your account and see if it came through?" he asked.

A light sheen of sweat sprung up on Selena's forehead. A glance at the clock told her that the boys would be late for school, that she would miss her train. "Of course."

"Did she mention any plans for the weekend?" he asked.

"No," said Selena. "In fact, she told me to text her if we needed any help over the weekend, that she'd be around."

Not we, *me*, thought Selena. Because she'd said Graham was away on "a boys' weekend." Another lie. This one hers.

"And did you?"

"No," said Graham.

A shift of his weight, a slight leaning forward. "We had a quiet family weekend at home mostly. Oh, and the park. We went to the park."

A family weekend. How idyllic. *You guys are just too cute. Those boys so grown up. Such a good mom! Nothing more important than time with your family!* All the comments on her Instagram posts.

"What about boyfriends?"

Graham looked thoughtful, rubbing at his chin, then shook his head. He looked to Selena in warm inquiry. If anything about this was unsettling to him, it did not show. Even a little. He simply struck the perfect posture of concerned employer.

"Not that she mentioned," said Selena, shaking her head.

Other than my husband?

Who she was fucking while I was working late, supporting my family? Not that she mentioned.

Honestly, she and Geneva didn't talk that much. Their conversations were about the boys, the chores, the errands. Selena left when Geneva arrived, and Geneva left when Selena got home. Shift workers, passing each other by. Did Selena know anything really about Geneva's life? Very little.

Geneva's father lived nearby, Selena thought she'd heard the other woman mention. Or had. Had he passed on? Embarrassingly, she couldn't recall. She didn't remember a sister, friends, stories about how she spent her off time. There was no mention of a boyfriend. In some real sense, Geneva stopped existing for Selena when she was not caring for Oliver and Stephen. But maybe that's because Geneva was so quiet, so deferential with Selena. And Selena was just so busy, caught up in the day-to-day of it all. She tried to remember what they talked about on the playground, before Selena had hired her. The Tucker boys mostly, childcare stuff, routines, and device and television rules, organic eating, allergies.

"She's late now," said Selena, looking at the clock. "She hasn't called. That's never happened."

She walked to the window, half expecting to see Geneva coming up the drive, moving quickly, flustered for being late. *So sorry! I went out of town last minute! Lost my phone!*

No. There was a cold hollow in her middle.

The boys came tearing down the stairs.

"Aren't we late? Where's Geneva?" asked Oliver, always aware of situations. Then to Detective Crowe, a direct, "Who are you?"

"I'm Grady," he said, easily, offering his hand. Oliver took it and shook. "Nice grip, buddy."

Oliver seemed pleased by that.

"Running a bit late for school today, boys," said Graham rising, pushing them back toward the door with a gentle hand on each boy's back. "Go watch television for a bit."

They ran off happily. That was a major departure from the no devices, no television before school rule.

"I'll have to call work," said Selena. "Let them know I'm running behind."

Graham seemed about to object, then pressed his mouth closed.

As she went for her phone, she wondered about the videos of Graham and Geneva, which she'd recorded and were saved on her computer for anyone with the password to see. And weren't they likely in the cloud somewhere, saved by the company that made the camera, designed the app and software?

Even if she deleted them from her computer—weren't there supposedly all kinds of ways these things could be found? Not that it would come to that. They weren't going to be searching her computer, of course! That was ridiculous. She'd watched too many episodes of *Criminal Minds* in her life. Geneva was going to turn up. Of course she was.

She left a message for Beth, called the school. Then she tried Geneva, but the call just went to voice mail.

She logged into their checking account via the app on her phone. Geneva's check hadn't cleared—but if she'd deposited late Friday, it might not have. Sometimes the funds didn't sweep from her account until Tuesday. Back in the living room, she shared this with Detective Crowe. He nodded, then launched into more questions.

"Did she mention anyone she might be having problems with? Someone following her? Calling too often?"

"No," said Selena. "Nothing like that."

But would she have? Beth and some of Selena's other friends were so close with their childcare employees that they seemed more like part of the family. But she didn't have that with Geneva, even—before. Again, an ugly flash on Geneva and Graham. Selena's cheeks went hot, and she wondered if anyone noticed.

"Who employed her before you?"

"The Tuckers," said Selena. "They live a few streets over."

Crowe flipped back through his notebook. "Her sister said that there were some problems there, that she left abruptly."

Selena shook her head. "I don't think so. I think Mrs. Tucker—Eliza—just wanted to stay home with the kids."

But she didn't really know. She didn't *know* the Tuckers per se, though they were Facebook friends, the kids all went to the same school. They'd provided a reference via email. Maybe it had seemed a *bit* terse?

"Something to do with the husband, she thought," said Crowe. "Unwelcome advances."

Was the room spinning? She heard the boys turn on the television in the playroom.

"Geneva never said anything about that," said Selena.

But she wouldn't, would she? She swallowed hard and it seemed like Detective West noticed. She consciously kept her eyes from drifting to Graham.

"What can we do?" asked Graham, the very image of sincere worry. "For you guys? For Geneva?"

Crowe slid a card across the coffee table. "Let us know if you hear from her. Maybe keep trying to call her. It's possible that she doesn't want to talk to her sister, but she'll answer a call from her employer, you know. Call your bank, see if they have any further information on that check."

"Of course," said Graham. "Absolutely."

There was a moment, just a breath, where silence fell between all of them and Selena saw the eyes of both detectives set on Graham.

"Quite the handyman, huh?" said Detective West to Graham.

"How's that?" asked Graham.

"Working on that wall Friday," said West. "Then over to your brother's place for a home repair project."

"Oh," said Graham, with a laugh. He folded his arms across his chest. "I guess? Neither project went very well. But I do try."

"What were you working on with your brother?"

"Cabinets," Graham said, clearing his throat. "A cabinet door falling off its hinges."

"Two-man job, is it?"

"For us, I guess," said Graham with a grin. "Or maybe just an excuse to spend a little time catching up."

Again, manly nodding all around. "What time did you get back?"

"On the later side. What would you say, honey?"

"Nine or ten?" she answered. For a second, she wished she was dreaming, that she'd wake up.

The detective asked for Graham's brother's name, address, and phone number. Graham provided it without hesitation. For all she knew, he *had* helped with the cabinet. She hoped for his sake that he had. Or that Joe would know to lie, which he might. Bro code, Graham liked to call it.

"Where's Geneva?" asked Oliver, slim and small in the doorway, leaning against the wood frame. "What's wrong?"

The detectives both moved toward the door, and Selena, whose whole body had grown tense, jumped liked a spring to tend to Oliver.

"We're not sure, honey," she said, her voice high and way too bright. "Everything's okay."

Oliver didn't look convinced, serious eyes on Selena. She shook her head, just ever so slightly—no one would have noticed but him. And her child knew to be quiet, whatever he was thinking, wanted to ask or say. He knew what his mother wanted him to do, the way all children do without words.

"Go take care of your brother," said Selena. Oliver disappeared down the hallway.

Graham ushered the detectives into the foyer and out the front door.

"I noticed that you have one of those camera doorbells," said West on the porch. "Does it turn on with motion? Is it set to record?"

"No. It's an older one," said Graham with a regretful wince. "It's a bit glitchy because our WiFi needs an upgrade. Doesn't always even work."

"Technology."

Was West going to ask to see the app? Would Graham show it to him? *Was* it set to record? She didn't even know. What about the other cameras? Were *they* set to record? They were all visible on the same app.

She knew that they should say no, if they asked to see it. That was their right. She braced herself. What would she say? If they really wanted to help, had nothing to hide, they'd show them the app without question.

But they *did* want to help. They *didn't* have anything to hide. Did they? An affair, no matter how tawdry, wasn't a crime.

She looked at Graham, who was easily chatting with West now about all the new surveillance technology out there, how it was so cheap, how it made their job a lot easier. *People don't even know. They are eyes everywhere now—these little cameras in their doorbells, in their living rooms, on their phones. They're everywhere. Privacy. It's gone. Not taken. But given away.*

Selena looked up and down the block. Most people had the camera doorbell now. There was even a neighborhood network. She got the little notices on her phone: *Stranger at my door! Package missing! This dog pooping on my lawn!*

"We'll be on the block a while," said Crowe. "Let us know if you hear from her. Or—you know—if you think of anything else."

On the block? Asking questions? Talking to neighbors?

"It's probably nothing, though, right?" asked Selena. "She's just met someone maybe. Lost track of time."

"Hard to say," said Crowe. He looked up at the sky. "It's one thing to stand your sister up. But I don't love that she didn't turn up for work. Someone so responsible."

It was all there on the tip of her tongue. She imagined it all coming out in a tumble. Confession—it was good for the soul or something. Right? Geneva was sleeping with my husband. I threw something at him; it cut his face. I told him to leave but he came back, late at night. I let him in because of the boys, even though I didn't want him to come home. I met a strange woman on the train. There were these weird messages on my phone this weekend. The encounter, it was strange. She said something like: *Maybe she'll just disappear.*

But it was all so crazy, unrelated to Geneva being missing, right? It was just the chaos of her life at the moment. When had things gotten so out of hand?

"Mrs. Murphy," said Detective Crowe. "You okay?"

Crowe glanced over at Graham, then back to Selena. She liked the dark honesty of his gaze, the cool seeing of it. Graham's chuckle rang out over the quiet of the neighborhood, something amusing in his conversation with West. A girl was missing. What the hell was he laughing about? Was her husband really such an accomplished liar?

"I'm just worried," she said softly, offering the detective a wan smile. "About Geneva. She's like part of our family."

TWELVE

Oliver

GROWN-UPS LIED. *A LOT.*

They lied about how things were going to taste. *Just try it! It's yummy.*

They lied about how bad shots were going to hurt. *Just a little sting. Over before you know it!*

Oliver knew he shouldn't be at the door listening. But he did anyway.

"It's probably nothing, though, right?" asked his mom. It was her worried voice. "She's just met someone maybe. Lost track of time."

"Hard to say," said the stranger. "It's one thing to stand your sister up. But I don't love that she didn't turn up for work. Someone so responsible."

Both his mom and dad were frowning. Oliver moved in closer to the door, even though he was supposed to be taking care of Stephen.

"Mrs. Murphy," said the stranger. "You okay?"

Grown-ups told you things were okay when they weren't.

Mom always said she was fine even when he could see she'd been crying. The Easter Bunny, Santa Claus, the Tooth Fairy. All lies. It was Eli at school who'd told him all this. Eli was a year older than everyone else, even Oliver, who'd started kindergarten late. Eli was *left back* everyone knew but didn't dare say because Eli was mean and big, and really good at hurting you fast so that teachers didn't see. And at first, Oliver didn't believe it.

Go ahead, said Eli, *ask your mom about Santa*.

So he did.

People who don't believe in Santa don't get presents. That was his mom's answer. Which even Oliver knew was not an answer.

He pressed. *Do you swear to god there's a Santa?*

His mom just looked away. *We can believe in all sorts of things that we can't see or touch. Santa isn't real or not real. He's magic.*

Magic.

Was magic real?

Why so many questions? his mom wanted to know. He told her about Eli and watched her make the face she made when she was really mad about something and was trying to pretend that she wasn't.

You know what? she said. *There is always going to be someone who will try to take the sparkle out of your life. Don't let him. Okay? Just enjoy the stories, and for now don't worry about what's real and isn't real. Deal?*

He took the deal because he liked getting presents and Easter baskets and money from the Tooth Fairy. But it was clear that Eli, even if he was a bully and sparkle stealer, was right.

They lied.

As Oliver hovered outside the door, Stephen in front of the television, he listened to his parents talking to the strangers. His dad lied about the cut on his head. He lied about the wall. He was probably lying about the cabinets—because his dad was not a handyman. And even the wall project was kind of a joke because he really did suck at things like that. Oliver's pine derby car had been the worst of everyone's, really bad. But he didn't care because they had fun doing it. And Stephen put google eyes on it and it was wobbly and really funny. So, no one would call Dad to help with a home repair project.

Mom lied about everything being all right—her voice all high and her smile fake.

She'd lied about Dad's boys' weekend.

And Dad lied about the doorbell. He told the police that it didn't record. But he told Oliver and Stephen that it did, that all the cameras did. That's how his dad knew every bad thing they were doing—even when he wasn't there. That's what he told Oliver and Stephen, anyway.

I'm always watching! he'd say in a scary voice, then monster-chase them down the hall, everyone screaming.

Was he lying then? Or was he lying now?

Oliver moved closer to the door. If he was quiet and still, his parents forgot he was there. Like now.

Geneva hadn't come to take them to school today. And Mom was still home. And Dad was that way he was when other guys were around—kind of too loud, laughing a lot. And something was wrong.

Oliver had watched Geneva leave the house on Friday, the way he watched her leave every night from his bedroom window. He even recorded it on his iPad, because that's what he and Stephen had been doing that afternoon in their room when they weren't fighting. They were taping each other on this app that played your recording in reverse, so that you flew back up on the bed, or ran backward through the door. Then they were doing slow motion videos to make their stuffed animals look like they were flying. So when he watched Geneva, he hit Record.

He wondered where she went when she left them; he tried to imagine where she lived.

He'd asked her: *Where do you live? In a house?*

In a castle, she told him, *high on a hill.*

No, you don't, he said. *There are no castles around here.*

Aren't there?

Do you have a pet dragon? asked Stephen.

That's a stupid question, Oliver told him. *She doesn't live in a castle. She doesn't have a dragon.*

Geneva laughed. Her eyes were glittery, her lips a glistening pink. She had a lot of freckles and her cheeks were always flushed pink. *I just live in an apartment, silly boys. About twenty minutes from here.*

Are you married?

Do you have children?

A dog?

Nope. Nope. Nope.

Do you get lonely? Living all by yourself?

Geneva was serving them grilled cheese sandwiches with apple slices. She put a plate in front of each of them. Oliver liked the way she cut the sandwich diagonal just like his mom did. Dad cut them in rectangle halves, or not at all. Just a big square on the plate. Sometimes he didn't melt the cheese all the way. Or he burned one side because he got distracted by his phone.

How could I get lonely when I have you? she said.

Stephen was satisfied with this. But Oliver liked to watch faces. He could see that her eyes were sad.

I think you do live in a castle, he said to cheer her up. *Because you're as pretty as a princess.*

She touched a soft hand to his cheek, smiled. *And you're a very sweet boy.*

He didn't remember what happened next, because they were on to something else. But every night when she left, he watched her go, wondering where she went. And why she was sad.

The last time, he'd watched her all the way to her car. When she got to her car, she stopped and turned around, as if something had gotten her attention. She clutched her bag to the front of her body and frowned. Said something—her mouth was moving. Then she walked out of sight, away from her car.

There was someone else on the street, but he couldn't really see; the big oak in his yard mostly blocked his view. He tried to get a better look.

Then Stephen tackled him because he was hiding the remote, and his mom broke it up again, and they were punished for a while. His iPad, which he'd left recording in the windowsill, was shut off and taken away from him. He forgot all about Geneva.

But when he looked out his window later, her car was still there. At bedtime, he'd tried to tell his mom, but she wouldn't let him talk.

The car was there all weekend. Which he thought was strange. But grown-ups did lots of strange things that they didn't always bother to explain. And he forgot about that, too.

Now, he had the uneasy sense that he'd done something wrong, something that would result in having his iPad taken away from him.

As he stood outside the doorway and listened to his parents lie to the strangers, he wondered if maybe he should say something—about how he'd recorded Geneva leaving. But then he just didn't.

Words didn't always come out right. And he'd gotten in trouble for saying things he shouldn't say—like the time he told Mom that Dad slept in his underwear on the couch, in the daytime when she was working. Or that Dad had let them eat toaster waffles for dinner or watch a movie that gave Stephen nightmares. *Hey, buddy*, his dad said. *There's a bro code. Don't rat out your old man to your mom. It's not cool.*

Not cool.

That, according to Eli, was the worst thing you could be.

So he just stayed quiet. And when the strangers were finally gone, he was glad. He hoped that they wouldn't come back. And that tomorrow Geneva would return from her castle and everything would go back to normal.

THIRTEEN

Selena

LIES ARE A VIRUS. They spread, replicate. One lie breeds more. Selena's mother always said that, usually when talking about Selena's father. You have to keep lying to protect the original lie. The idea bounced around Selena's head now as she watched from the walkway, knowing she should go back inside but frozen.

The detectives crossed the street, wind tossing leaves across the lawn, sun dipping behind clouds. Feeling eyes on her, she turned to see Graham standing in the window, his form dark, face in shadows. Once the cops had left, he'd dropped that genial facade he put on so well. He'd turned sullen, wouldn't look at her, returned inside.

Who are you? she thought.

He was a stranger inside her house, her bed, her heart.

And where is Geneva?

There were always little things, Selena's mother said when she came clean about Dad's many affairs. A phone call at a strange hour. Once an earring clasp—something cheap and insubstantial—found while she was cleaning the car. A receipt in his pocket from a restaurant in a city she wasn't aware he'd visited. He traveled for work; there were women in his life—clients and colleagues. Everything was easily pushed away. She *wanted* to push things away; she'd admitted this. If she acknowledged what she knew in her heart to be true, she'd have to do something about it. *Incurious*, that was the word she used. Willfully incurious.

Selena's father became bolder, almost flagrant. Her mother became blinder, developed migraines. Selena remembered the closed door, how she'd push inside to the dark room and see her mother lying on the bed with a cool cloth over her eyes. Selena would slip in beside her and her mother would wrap her up in her slender arms without a word. How unhappy Cora must have been. How had she borne it?

Selena hadn't understood, not really, when her mother finally confided to Marisol and her about the affairs—years after their divorce. She pretended to understand. But secretly she wondered—*how could you, Mom?* How could you let him treat you that way? She understood now, how you turned away until you couldn't. Until the pain of knowing and doing nothing was greater than the fear of what might come next.

She should have turned Graham away on Friday night. She should have told the police he was sleeping with Geneva. But what about the boys?

Now what would happen?

Don't you wish your problems would just go away?

Geneva wasn't the problem. The problem was Graham.

She went inside, closed the door. The house felt hushed, as if everyone were holding their breaths. The boys were quiet; the television droned upstairs.

"I don't have to say it, right?"

She startled. Graham was standing in the arch between the living room and the hallway. "What?"

"That *whatever* this is, it has nothing to do with me."

He stood there watching her. And for a moment it was as if she was seeing him for the first time. Her husband. The adulterer. The liar. What else?

"Selena," he said. His voice was almost stern. "Say something."

The world spun.

Then the doorbell rang, startling them both. When she opened it, Detective Crowe stood waiting there.

"Mrs. Murphy," he said. "I think we've found Geneva Markson's vehicle parked on your street. Did you know she'd left it?"

Selena shook her head, felt something catch in her throat. "No."

She wasn't even sure what kind of car Geneva drove; the other woman never parked in their driveway and she always used their second car, a late-model Subaru, to drive the boys around.

She followed the detective's gaze and saw a white Toyota parked across the street. People had started to gather. A squad car arrived.

"Were you planning on going anywhere today?" he asked.

She shook her head. "I'll work from home."

"Your husband."

Something about the way he said it made her stomach bottom out. "He's—between jobs at the moment."

Between jobs? That sounded shady. But the detective only nodded, polite, neutral.

"So, yeah, he'll be here, I mean." Graham stood in the dark of the hallway, stiff, frozen.

"We may come back with more questions," said the detective. Was there something in his tone? "We'd appreciate it if you could both be around."

"Of course. We'll be here."

She closed the front door as he walked down the path.

"Selena," said Graham.

In the kitchen, her phone was buzzing. She walked away from her husband, slipping instantly into crisis management mode. She'd call her mother and ask her to take the boys for a few days until this all worked itself out. Then, she'd call Beth and tell her what was going on—as little as possible. Will was a lawyer; he would be her next call. Not that they needed a lawyer. But they might. William was famous for saying that if the police show up at your door and you don't call your lawyer, you're basically handing over your rights. It sounded dramatic, very lawyerly. Until it sounded like solid advice.

When she picked up the phone, there were a string of texts from yet another unknown number.

Hey, girl.

How's your day going? Time for a drink after work tonight?

It's Martha, by the way.

From the train.

FOURTEEN

Anne

ANNE LET HER finger drift over the diamond bracelet on her slim wrist. A Tiffany Victoria line bracelet. Small, the lowest carat count. But still. More than ten thousand, for sure. Closer to fifteen. The sun coming in from the windows caught on the gems and cast rainbow shards of light on the walls, on the ceiling. It should have been enough, the payout from Kate. The look on her face. But somehow it just wasn't.

"Do you like it, darling?" said Hugh. She loved that even though he'd been caught, that surely his whole life with Kate hung in the balance now, he still couldn't resist her. The power of that was delicious.

"I love it," she gushed. "It's beautiful."

The grift. The con. It was almost an old-fashioned idea, the stuff of noir novels and black-and-white movies.

The Nigerian prince seeking help from afar: *Give me your bank account and I'll transfer my wealth, pay you handsomely for the favor!* The shell game: *Next time you'll get it!* The pigeon drop: *Hey, buddy! Did you drop your wallet? Whoa—look at all this cash.*

There were a hundred ways to separate a fool from his money. Except it was never about the money. It was about the thrill, the intimacy of being taken into someone's trust, of extracting from them a thing they didn't even know they wanted to give. And they *did* want to give it.

You can't con an honest man. That's what Pop always said.

That was true without being the whole truth. Anne had a bit of revision. You can't con someone who doesn't *want* something, who wasn't willing to wade into a gray area to get it. You can't con someone who is a stranger to desire, to need.

Take Hugh for example. He thought that he'd seduced Anne. But in a way, hadn't she led him to it, gently, delicately? Even though she'd come to the firm, ostensibly, to work, to go straight, as Pop liked to say. Hadn't she seen an opportunity pretty quickly, maybe even subconsciously? She knew immediately what kind of man Hugh was. A flat come-on would not have worked. He needed to think it was his idea.

A little flattery: *I'm learning so much from you!* A little vulnerability; she'd let him catch her crying over a breakup. (Except there wasn't a breakup. And she'd never *actually* cry. Especially not over a man.) Standing a little too close in the elevator. One or two accidental brushes of her hand against his. It was so subtle. She was subtle. Maybe too subtle. After a while, she thought maybe she had him wrong. That he was a faithful husband, in love with his wife.

Then the hand on her knee. Right there, her plan to go straight went right out the window.

See what I'm saying, kitten? A tiger can't change her stripes.

What did Hugh want? He wanted to be wanted. He wanted to be young again. He wanted to have something, anything, that didn't belong to Kate. There was a thrill in knowing that, in giving that—and in taking it away.

Anne and Hugh lay entangled on the king bed, their hotel

room looking out over Central Park. She luxuriated in the exquisite sheets, watched the bubbles in her champagne glass.

She'd let him text her for days.

I'm so sorry, Anne. Forgive me.

I can't leave her. She needs me. She's—not well.

I can't stop thinking about you. Oh, god. Please meet me.

Anne.

I'm desperate.

She rather enjoyed it. In fact, she kind of liked Hugh, which was not always the case. He was an acrobatic lover, in great shape, generous, gentle. He could be funny. Anne could see why Kate held on tight; most men were monsters deep down. Not Hugh. Deep down he was a little boy.

He moved a strand of hair from her eyes, touched her cheek. "I was drowning without this. Without you."

"This is the last time, Hugh," she said, trying to look bravely hurt. "I'm not a mistress. I thought we'd be together someday. *Really* together."

"I know." He sighed, kissed her deeply. "I know. It's not fair to you."

The game. It was so sweet.

It was Pop who taught her that her beauty was a weapon. Her lean, strong body—not too thin. Her flawless olive skin. Her long, (currently) blue-black hair that hung blade-straight down to the middle of her back. She groomed—waxed, plucked, exfoliated, manicured, moisturized, exercised religiously. She took care of herself. Her beauty was a commodity, a thing that people wanted. It could be used to manipulate men *and* women. Men wanted to possess it, control it. Women wanted to believe that it was a thing within their reach, a weapon that they too could wield. *Who does your hair? What's your secret?*

She turned her head away from him, exposing the delicate flesh of her neck, where he promptly placed his lips. She shivered—he thought from pleasure.

What's the game now? Pop wanted to know. *You've gotten all you can from his wife.*

Had she, though?

For Pop it was all about the money. Run the game, get away clean. Anne always wanted a little bit more. She reveled in her role as puppeteer.

And that's where you get into trouble. You don't need to turn the knife every time.

"I have to leave the city," she said softly.

"What? Why?"

"My sister," she said. "She's really sick. There isn't much time."

"I'm so sorry," he said. His hazel eyes glittered with concern. He was earnest, she'd give him that. He really did care about her, as much as someone like Hugh could care about anyone but himself. "What can I do?"

Didn't he know that she was playing him?

The funny thing was that they almost never, ever did. And even after they figured it out, they doubted themselves. Wanted to believe they were wrong. Even when there was no denying that they'd been had, you could almost always go back for a second helping. Like the sweetheart scam. That was her favorite. So many very lonely people in the world. So many of them with money. They trawled online for love, knowing of course how easy it was to be scammed. But there they were, desperate enough to try. And try again.

There was a look. A kind of sweetness around the eyes. A sort of slouch to the aura. Something else. Hope. Without it, things were harder, if not impossible. Hugh was a different category: all ego, easy to flatter.

"I have to give up my place here," she said. "I don't know when I can come back. All the money I have—it'll have to go for caring for her. She—doesn't have anything. She has two small kids, my niece and nephew."

"Husband?"

"Left," she said. She sighed, going for sad, helpless. "Men. They're not all like you."

He kissed her again.

Cash—he had a grand in his wallet. He handed it over to her. The bracelet; the baby-blue box gaped on the nightstand. And his credit card number for flights and hotels. The one Kate didn't know about. *Oh, Hugh, how can I ever thank you?*

She showered with him, pleasured him on her knees in the steamy tile bathroom, the scent of sage and mint heavy in the air.

She loved it when they were exposed, moaning and helpless.

Then Anne watched him dress, late for his afternoon meeting. Where did Kate think he was? If he was Anne's husband, she'd be tailing him every second. But maybe Kate couldn't be bothered. She knew she had him on a short leash. Or maybe she was just another mark, fooled again and again by her handsome, charming, and totally unfaithful husband.

Anne wrapped herself in the big plush robe and got back into bed as Hugh was fixing his tie. He watched her in the mirror.

"Keep the room if you want," he said. "Go to the spa, relax while you can. I'll call you later. Things have a way of working out, Annie."

She nodded, going for uncertain, fragile. Yes, things had a way of working out if you were a wealthy white man.

He moved over to her, sat on the bed, and took her into his arms, then kissed her long. In the space of that kiss, she let herself be the woman he thought she was—someone who loved him, who wanted to marry him, who had to go care for her sick sister. She let herself imagine what it would be like to be tender, loving, someone's mistress waiting for him to leave his wife. How vulnerable she might be, how hopeful. Would she cling? She would. Anne held on to him a second after he tried to pull away.

"I promise," he said before he left. "We'll figure this out."

She walked him to the door, and when it closed there was something final about the click of the latch.

The con is a method actor, Pop always said. *Become the lie.*

And she was good at that, disappearing into the person she was pretending to be. She was Anne Porter—young, ambitious, a mind for numbers, from New Jersey, a Rutgers grad. She had a sister, someone she loved. That part was true-ish, that she had a sister. Kind of. But her sister wasn't dying of some unnamed disease. There was no niece or nephew. There were pieces of her in every character, little handles that helped her keep things authentic. She was authentically uncomfortable with heights; she loved sushi. Her mother was dead. She never really knew her father. These things recurred in all of her characters.

Before Anne, she was Ellie Martin, young widow wondering if she could ever love again. Before that there was Marlie Croft, an orphan looking for her lost family. Before that. Before that. She was a Russian doll, every shell a different face, a different color. Right now, her hair was black—but she'd been a blonde, a redhead, a mousy brunette. She'd gained weight, lost it. She was good at *becoming*. The only problem was that the real person was buried deep, so tiny and formless that Anne could barely remember her.

Who you were is gone. Who you will be—she doesn't exist. The only thing that matters is who are you are right now. Pop. Con artist. Zen master.

Did you get what you wanted? He would surely ask. *Are you done? Not quite.*

She finished the lunch they'd ordered but hadn't touched—a

beautiful lobster Cobb, whole grain bread with truffle butter, cut strawberries. She poured herself another glass of champagne, watched the darkening clouds drift over the treetops, the city streets far below.

When she was done, she walked unhurriedly to the bathroom where earlier she'd propped up her phone and set it to record, turning it off after they were done. Back in bed, she played the video and watched the steamy image of Hugh and her in the shower. It was a little blurry, but there was no mistaking it was him—especially with all the moaning. Her back was to the camera. His groans were guttural, primal. It went on and on. She had to hand it to herself: stamina was her strong suit. Then, as Hugh climaxed clumsily, Anne turned to face the camera and smiled. It was a sweet smile, mischievous as if she expected that Kate would be in on the joke of it all. Because wasn't marriage the ultimate long game?

She imagined that, on some level, Kate would feel a measure of gratitude to Anne for showing her once and for all that her husband was a cad. Kate, who had everything, who could probably take her pick even now from a hundred eligible men, would be well rid of Hugh. He didn't deserve a woman like Kate. She liked the guy, but he was an unrepentant cheater.

Now, comfortably propped on the plush pillows, Anne did a little cropping, a little editing, even filtered just a shade—the skin on her back looked a little pasty in the white bathroom light.

Then, she showered alone, taking her time—relishing the hot water, the thick body wash, the whisper of water on the heavy marble tile. Once dressed, she sat at the desk and opened her laptop. Using the credit card number Hugh had given her, she purchased a slew of things—a pair of Jimmy Choo pumps, a Gucci tote, gleaming Prada sunglasses—she had saved in her Neiman Marcus shopping cart, then had them shipped overnight to an address that couldn't be traced back to her.

She called housekeeping, asking for more of the luxurious toiletries, amber bottles with crisp black-and-white labels. When the maid arrived, Anne tipped the young, wide-faced woman generously. And the girl gave her even more from the cart, giggling and saying something in another language. Czech if Anne had to guess. Anne stuffed the haul into her roller suitcase, along with the unused bathrobe in the closet and some of the fresh towels.

Online again, she sent a few emails, managing a few more of the various personas she had running.

So sorry I've been out of touch, my love! I'm having a bit of a family emergency. Can we talk later?

Can't wait for Saturday! It's so nice to feel like a part of a family.

Then a text.

This one was being stubborn. She hadn't had a response yet.

Was Anne going to get more aggressive about it? Or let it go? The whole thing was—sticky. That was Pop's word. Some people were too smart, too intuitive. Or they were skeptical, slow to trust. Or they didn't want enough. Then suddenly you were the one wanting something from the mark. And that was always a bad place to be. Anne watched her phone. No read receipt. No little dots that indicated the other party was typing.

Also, it was messy. A couple of moving parts that weren't *cooperating.* And she'd already had to do more management than she liked. And the motive…well. For Pop, it was always about the money. Sometimes Anne had a different agenda.

She waited. No answer.

When Anne was ready by the door, bag packed, she took a last look at the gorgeous room, the beautiful view. *Don't forget to breathe. Take in the moments and appreciate them. They pass too quickly.*

She did that.

Before she left, shouldering her tote, and rolling her stuffed suitcase over the plush blue carpet, she did two other things.

She sent the video to Kate. It stalled a moment, the file quite large. Then it was gone with a satisfying swish.

Yep, she thought. All done here, Pop.

Then she fired off another text, an adjunct to the one she'd sent earlier to her stubborn case—just to make sure there wasn't any confusion.

It's Martha, by the way.

From the train.

FIFTEEN

Pearl

"SO—WHO'S YOUR FATHER?"

The storeroom was overwarm, the air conditioning on the fritz again. Pearl and Charlie were both sweating with the effort of packing up books.

"I don't have a father." She used to make up stories about the man she imagined could be her dad. She'd stopped doing that, now that she was older.

"Everyone has a father," said Charlie, not looking at her. He was filling out a shipping label. He had very neat handwriting.

"Not everyone," she said.

He peered at her over his glasses. "Biologically. Yes. Everyone."

"I don't know." Pearl blew out a breath, annoyed. This was not her favorite topic of conversation.

"Your mother never told you."

"She's not sure," she said. "Could be a couple of different people. You know Mom."

He was quiet a minute and she figured he'd let it go.

"Aren't you curious?" he asked.

She finished putting a box together with a swipe of the packing tape gun, then let her arms drop to her sides.

"Curious about a man who doesn't know I exist? Who is basically a sperm donor?"

Charlie lifted his shoulders, still watching her over his glasses.

"Some people are even curious about the sperm donor, you know," he said. "It's normal to want to know where you came from."

"The past doesn't matter. That's what Mom always said. All we have is right now."

"That's very evolved of you."

"I just don't care," she said exasperated. Once he was on a topic, you could not get him off. "You've seen the kind of men she's with. What if I went looking and found him? What if he was just another tattooed muscle head, someone with a man bun? What if he worked in marketing?"

Charlie laughed. They were packing up books for return, filling boxes, sealing them, printing address labels. It was always so hopeful when the new shipment arrived and they stocked the bestsellers, the obscure literary titles, the new nonfiction. Every book crisp, unopened, waiting for its reader. Then, after a certain point, the books went back if they didn't sell. The publisher refunded the money.

It seemed to Pearl that more and more books went back. The store was empty much of the time, despite Charlie's efforts to increase foot traffic. Mom had a new boyfriend; but Charlie stayed. He manned the store, took care of Pearl—drove her home and made sure she had dinner. He even proofread her homework. He, Charlie, who had been in her life for fewer than six months, was more a parent than she'd ever had. She kept this to herself.

"Your mom didn't come in today," said Charlie. The packing tape made a loud hiss as he ran its dispenser over the box, sealing the fate of the books inside. Return to sender.

Pearl had a nightmare last night. Raised voices, some kind of loud bang. A scream. She woke panicked. But when she walked out of her bedroom, the house was quiet. There was a dim light from under the door of her mother's room, music playing. She knew better than to knock, looking for comfort. In the morning, she hadn't seen Stella. But she'd heard the toilet flush, water running for the shower.

Pearl ate a bowl of sugary cereal and left for the bus; she hadn't thought about her mother again.

"Late night, I think."

Charlie, who was smallish, was very strong. Hauling heavy boxes, stacking them.

"The store is not doing so well, Pearl," he said. "I tried to talk to her about it, but she wouldn't listen."

"The store never does well," said Pearl. "It's a bookstore. That's the model."

"Yeah, but it's been operating in the red all year."

Pearl shrugged. The mysteries of how her mother made ends meet did not interest her. *It's your job to be a kid, my job to worry about everything else*, which was a very motherly thing that the nonmotherly Stella often said.

"There's a stack of past due bills," said Charlie. Then he shook his head. "Sorry. I shouldn't be talking to you about this. You're just a kid."

"She owns the building."

It was a big warehouse on the bad side of town, an area that was supposed to gentrify but hadn't. There was someone in Stella's life who had given her money in the past, a large sum. She turned to him when things got tight and he always came through. Who he was, why he'd give Stella money, Pearl had no idea. Stella called him her "benefactor." But she hadn't mentioned him in a while.

"Yeah, but there's a tax bill she hasn't paid," said Charlie.

Pearl shrugged.

"Forget it. I'll talk to her again," said Charlie with an easy wave. "She'll have a plan for how to manage if I know Stella."

Did anyone know Stella?

Pearl held an unread paperback in her hands. On the cover a faceless woman in a flowery dress drifted dreamily past a beach house. She stacked the book in the box with the others.

Pearl watched Charlie pack and seal, lift and carry. She pretended not to watch him, or to notice that he sometimes watched her. She didn't know how old he was; he didn't look much older than the senior boys at school—he was narrow, pretty around the eyes, clean-shaven always. He had a long nose and full mouth that looked very serious until right before he smiled.

"What about your father?" asked Pearl. He rarely talked about himself, his family, where he came from. Just snippets here and there.

"My father," he said, dropping a box, "was a monster."

"Really?"

He turned to her, wiped a forearm across the sweat on his brow. "Yes, really. He was a drunk, an abuser. A con man."

"I'm sorry."

"He's dead now." Another box on the dolly. His face was still; there was no tension to him, as if he was just stating the facts.

"And your mom?"

"She's gone, too." He sealed the final box.

"It's just you."

"Yes. An orphan. The only child of unhappy people."

"That—sucks," she said. Because what else was there to say?

He shrugged. "You get what you get, and you don't get upset, right? What's that book? *Pinkalicious?*"

A book about a spoiled girl who was in a rage over cupcakes.

"But she got very upset."

Charlie smiled in that knowing way he had.

"And how did that work out for her?" he asked.

"I think she made herself sick—or something like that."

"So there you go." He nodded in affirmation and Pearl laughed as he rolled the dolly out to the front door, where the UPS guy would pick the boxes up. The sun was setting, and the store was completely empty. The after-school thing had petered out. The open mic night dried up when they stopped serving free food and wine, which they could ill afford in the first place.

They stopped for Chinese food on the way home, and he parked in front of the house, walking her inside. He carried her heavy backpack and the food. She opened the door.

"I have to talk to your mom. Maybe she'll eat with us."

He was going to leave. She could tell. He had that sad, careful look that grown-ups had right before they were about to disappoint you in some way. Stella had used him up, probably she'd stopped paying him or something. That's what she did. She took everything she could from people and, when they were done, she showed them the door, not caring whether they walked, ran, yelled or cried.

I never asked you for a thing, Pearl had heard Stella say to more than one angry beau, friend, neighbor. And that was true. Stella never had to ask.

But the house was dark and quiet when they went inside. Pearl turned on the lights; Charlie put down her bag, carried the food to the kitchen. Pearl's morning dishes were where she'd left them.

Something. Something made the hair stand up on the back of her neck, made her breath catch.

"Stella?" Charlie called out.

Their eyes met in the dim of the messy kitchen, and something passed quicksilver between them. She couldn't even say what. A kind of knowledge, an awareness of a subtle shift of energy. Over the years, she'd come back to that moment. It would mean something different every single time she recalled it.

He walked past her, brushing close, hurried. She caught the

scent of him—soap and paper. Pearl stayed rooted, listening to his footfalls move from room to room.

When he called out in shock and terror, his voice a vibrato of despair, she stayed stone still, frozen, unable to move, unable to think. Time stopped.

Oh, God. Oh, Stella. No! Oh, nonononono.

Pearl followed the sound of his wailing and stood shaking in the doorway. Charlie was on his knees beside the bed. Stella stared unseeing, eyes red and glassy, her neck black with bruising. Pearl felt part of herself die, too.

SIXTEEN

Selena

SHE PULLED INTO her mother's driveway, the boys both uncharacteristically quiet in the back. In the rearview mirror, she saw that Stephen was dozing, but Oliver stared out the window, frowning.

"Everything's okay," she said. "Just an unexpected visit to Grandma."

Oliver caught her eyes in the mirror, looking older than his years. Stephen was a little Tonka trunk, chunky, rough-and-tumble, oblivious. But Oliver was an observer. His expression, the one he wore when she tried to keep the Santa thing going or convince him that he was going to one day love brussels sprouts, was skeptical, nearing disdain.

"Okay," he said.

She looked up at the house. Her mom, Cora, stood in the doorway, waving. She was a small woman who seemed to be shrinking a little bit every time Selena saw her. Cora and Marisol both got the compact, petite thing. Selena got the tall, athletic thing. Secretly, she always wished she was tiny like her sister.

Paulo, Cora's second husband, was tall behind her, nearly filling the door frame.

"Paulo!" cried Oliver, frown dropping, replaced with a grin. Stephen stirred awake, groggy.

Paulo—a husky, jovial guy—was beloved by the boys. He was a bear hugger, a piggyback ride giver, Lego builder, all day at Extreme Jump kind of grandpa. No kids or grandkids of his own, he was fresh to the fight, as he liked to say. He had lots to give to her, her sister and their kids. Which was nice, because Selena's actual father was an impatient jerk—always annoyed with the kids, their noisemaking, their poor table manners, their fighting. Scolding and frowning was his default setting. He thought they were pampered, hassled Selena and Graham about their lack of discipline, their lack of scheduling, and just made himself generally difficult to be around. Then he wondered why they weren't all closer and complained that they didn't visit enough.

Cora and Paulo came to the car to greet Selena, Paulo giving her a big squeeze and an encouraging pat on the back, then ushering the boys inside with their luggage and big box of toys. Cora took Selena into an embrace.

"I'm sure it will just be a couple of days," said Selena. There was a weight on her shoulders that she couldn't shift off, a deep fatigue tugging at her brain.

"As long as you need us," she said. "We're here."

Inside, they got the boys settled in the room that was just for them, another one adjoined by a jack-and-jill bath for their two cousins, Lily and Jasper. Paulo said that he'd tend to the kids, and Selena and her mother went to the kitchen, where Selena told her everything. The cheating, Geneva not showing up for work. Not the girl on the train.

"This is all just some crazy thing," she heard herself say. "A misunderstanding."

That could still be true, right? She pulled a tissue from the box Cora had produced, dabbed at her eyes.

Cora pulled the folds of her blue cashmere wrap tighter around her. "But he slept with her?"

Selena turned to the door to the kitchen, which her mother had pulled closed. The kids, especially Oliver, had a way of sneaking up.

"Yes," Selena admitted. She felt her face redden, her eyes fill again. "He did."

Her mother reached for her hand.

"But you don't think—"

"That he has anything to do with her disappearing? No," said Selena, a shock moving through her. "Of course not."

But of course everyone was going to think that, if it came out. Which, it still might not. Geneva would turn up. All of this was going to be a big nothing. So what if Geneva's car was there all weekend and she'd missed a date with her sister, hadn't turned up for work? Maybe she'd met someone, went on a bender. It happened, right? Even to nice girls like Geneva. Who wasn't such a nice girl, after all, was she? Sleeping with Graham, and now rumors of issues with her last employer. So, maybe Geneva was somebody else entirely than she pretended to be. That happened all the time.

"No," Selena said again, adamant in her mother's silence. "He's a man-baby, not a monster, Mom."

"No," said her mother gently, patting her hand. "Of course he's not."

She thought of him standing in the shadows, that unreadable expression. Maybe Graham, too, was someone other than he pretended to be. And she, like her mother, was the incurious wife so wrapped up in work and family and the inner hurricane of her own thoughts that she missed what was right in front of her. Like that big ape dancing in the background of a video where the viewer was focused on counting basketballs. Almost no one ever saw the ape at all, so concentrated were they on the bouncing orange orbs.

"Selena," her mother said. "Are you listening?"

"Sorry," she said, snapping back from her thoughts.

"You need a lawyer, sweetie. You should call Will."

"I already did," she said. "He's meeting us in an hour."

Which hurt. It hurt to call him, her kind, handsome, successful criminal defense attorney ex who was a loving, faithful guy. Right. Why would she want to spend her life with someone like that?

Her mother pushed a strand of her gray-blond bob behind her ear, looked down at the table between them.

"When I look back on the mistakes I made in my marriage, I'm ashamed," she said. "I thought I was protecting you girls. I turned away from the truth, made excuses for a man who didn't deserve it."

"I'm not doing that," said Selena. She didn't like how defensive she sounded, felt. "I know who he is."

On the kitchen counter was a framed portrait of all of them—Selena, Graham, Stephen and Oliver, Marisol, her now ex-husband Kent (another cheater), Jasper and Lily. It was last Christmas. They were all relatively intact less than a year ago.

"Those days, you tried to stay together for the children," she said. "But now we know how toxic it can be for children to grow up in such an ugly marriage."

"Mom, please," she said. She didn't really want to talk about her mother's marriage, how maybe it was a poison and even now they were all still feeling its effects. "We've been through this. You did what you thought was right. And I'll do the same."

Cora reached for Selena's hand.

"You girls are strong," Cora said. Her hand felt frail, but her grip was tight. "Stronger than I was."

Was that true? Did it require more strength to stay in a bad marriage, or to walk away?

"What does that mean?"

"That you won't make the same mistakes I did. You don't have to. We're here for you, to support you in making a change."

Selena found that she couldn't meet her mother's eyes. She

didn't want her to see how scared, how uncertain she was. The rest of her life was like a cliff she was about to walk off, hoping she had wings.

"We tell the girls who come to the shelter that our main objective is to give them time, space, safety to find a new way," said Cora. "Many of them have nothing. You have everything."

Cora and Paulo volunteered at the woman's shelter in town, and Paulo took shifts at the suicide hotline. They were the kind of people who helped others, asking nothing in return, both of them. But the reference irked her.

"I'm not a battered woman, Mom."

She thought of how she'd thrown that robot at Graham and he'd just stood there and taken it. It wasn't the first time. Once she'd slapped him hard across the face.

"There are all kinds of abuse," said Cora. "I wish someone had said to me, hey, I'll help you find a way out of this mess. So that's what I'm saying to you."

Selena didn't know how to respond, the words *thank you* were so tangled up with fear and her injured pride that she just couldn't push them out. So she just got to her feet.

She had to go meet Graham and Will at the station where they were scheduled to answer questions for the police. She and Graham had agreed not to talk about his affair with Geneva. Graham had deleted all the videos from her computer and from the web application for the camera.

If the police really come looking, they'll find the files, and know I deleted them, he said.

He was right. She'd researched this. Apparently there was software like Oxygen Forensic that allowed the police to recover deleted files. Or they might access those videos from the camera company, which likely stored them on their cloud. They'd need a warrant, of course. She was praying that it wouldn't come to all that.

Why did she let him do it? Why didn't she make him come clean to the police? Because she couldn't. She didn't believe he would hurt Geneva. But those videos would start a narrative, one that was too familiar, too easy for the police to make dark assumptions about.

Don't give them anything, Will had concurred. *Make them come looking. Don't answer any questions beyond what you've told them already until I'm present. Not a word. Are we clear?*

Won't that make us look like we're hiding something?

It doesn't matter what it looks like. It only matters that you don't say anything that they can use to hurt you and Graham.

Will's cool practicality was one of the things that always annoyed Selena. She was so hot—quick to anger, eager to fight, work it out, make up. He was so measured with his words, calm to the point of being lethargic. That easy tone of his voice was soothing to her now.

We'll get this managed. Don't worry.

Maybe that's what he said to all his clients. Because how could he know? Maybe he just thought he knew them, knew Graham. They'd formed a kind of friendship over the years, accepted each other. Selena, too, had come to enjoy Will's wife—now ex. Bella had left Will for another *woman.* Poor guy. Selena still saw Bella in Saturday morning yoga sometimes. She had a svelte, strong body—so did her new girlfriend.

"Selena," said her mother again, snapping her back. She couldn't seem to keep her focus. "Are you listening?"

"No," she said. "Sorry."

Her mother, who suddenly seemed tired around her gray eyes, a bit washed out, repeated herself.

"See him through this if you must," she said. "But don't stay. It's not worth it. He won't stop. You always think it's going to be the last time. But it's only the last time when you leave him."

Her stomach bottomed out, looking at the grim expression on Cora's lined face. She saw there how bad, how ugly this could be. The cheating was bad enough, a life-rupturing event. But now a girl was missing. She and Graham were hiding things from the police. Something toxic had leaked into their life. Everything they were, everything she'd planned for them to be—it was all cast now in a bruised shade of gray.

She gathered her bag, walked into the living room to kiss the boys. Stephen ran off, oblivious, back to whatever game they were playing with Paulo. But Oliver clung when she kneeled down to him. If Stephen was Graham's soul mate, then Oliver was hers. She took in his scent, felt his warmth.

"How long?" he whispered, his breath hot on her neck.

"Not long," she said. "I promise."

She didn't say that she was thinking of coming back here tonight. She'd make that decision later. There was a room for her, too, in this warm, expansive house. Yes, she was lucky that there was a safe place for her and for her children. Not every woman in trouble could say that.

"I—" he started. But she cut him short before he could say—*I don't want to stay here.* Or *I want to go with you.* Because she already felt bad enough.

"I'll call you before bed."

"Mom," he said.

"Oliver, please, I'm late. I love you, sweetie. The sooner you let me go, the sooner I'll be back, and all of this will be behind us, okay?"

He nodded, eyes down. "Okay."

In the car she pulled away, Oliver and her Mom waving at the window. When the house had disappeared from her rear-view mirror, she let herself cry again. At the stoplight, her phone chimed and she dug it from her bag.

Maybe we should meet for a drink? I'm eager to continue our conversation.

Then another ping.

It's Martha, by the way. From the train.

SEVENTEEN

Selena

THE LIGHTS IN their kitchen were dim. Will and Graham sat at the table—Will leaning back, jacket off, Graham with his head in his hands. For a second, she felt a twinge of compassion for her husband. But it passed quickly.

Selena stared at the corkboard that hung over the workspace tucked into the far corner of the room. It was a riot of the boys' artwork, thank-you cards, photographs, coupons, sticky note reminders—all the detritus of their day-to-day.

Sitting in one of the tall chairs by the island, Selena kept her distance from the men. She had a bottle of cabernet open, was already on her second glass. They had spent three hours at the police station, each of them in separate rooms with the detectives. Her head was swimming, every nerve ending frayed. How did they get here? She kept waiting to wake up.

"The good news is that there's not a whole lot of evidence that *anything* has actually *happened* to Geneva," said Will easily. "And I didn't get the sense that they considered either of you suspects in her disappearance. You are the employers, the people who saw her most often, the people who saw her last. In some ways, you knew her best."

Graham nodded, still silent.

"So it makes sense that they'd want to talk to you both," Will went on. "They're just covering their bases for the moment."

Will looked back and forth between them. He was fine-featured—high cheekbones, long aquiline nose. He sported a wild cloud of golden curls. His eyes—a kind of stormy gray-green—were like laser beams. He had a gift for reading faces, body language. When they were dating, he always knew when something was bothering her, when she was holding something back. He kept his eyes on her, and she looked down at her glass.

"What aren't you guys telling me?" said Will finally, when neither of them said anything.

The wine, dark and fruity, was moving through her veins, creating warmth, easing the terrible tension that had crept into her neck, her shoulders.

"Graham was sleeping with her," said Selena, causing Graham to look up quickly, as shocked as if she'd Tasered him. Will's gaze settled on her husband, cool, unsurprised.

"Really."

"I caught them on the nanny cam," Selena said. She took another big swallow from her glass, poured a little more.

"Okay." Will sat up from his easy slouch. "Where's the video?"

"Deleted," said Graham. "We deleted it from Selena's computer and from the app."

Will lifted his eyebrows. "It's possible that the video still lives somewhere in the cloud."

"I know," said Graham, putting his head back down.

"You slept with the nanny," said Will. "And now she's missing."

The words hung heavy on the air between them, all the implications swirling.

"It was nothing," said Graham. "Stupid. A distraction."

"Stop saying that," Selena snapped. "Why do you think that makes it better than if it *had* meant something to you?"

Her husband looked at her with sad eyes. Once upon a time, that look could melt her. How many times had he used it to get himself out of trouble? Tonight, she saw it for what it had always been, probably. Insincere. Put on. Now it just made her angry.

"I don't," he said. "I'm sorry, Selena."

Selena could feel Will's eyes on her, though she was staring at her husband. Graham was so slouched with misery that it looked like he could just slide out of the chair and puddle up in a pile on the floor.

When she finally turned to look at Will, she could almost read his thoughts.

You left me for this guy?

She'd had the same thought many times over the last few years. When her marriage was in crisis, when Will's fell apart. Their friendship had endured and deepened over the years.

Wouldn't we have been better off together?

Maybe. But then—no Oliver or Stephen. Will didn't have children with his ex, so he didn't know how complicated it could be to regret marrying someone.

"Will, man," said Graham, in his most earnest "bro" voice. "Wherever she is, I had nothing to do with that. We agreed to stop fucking around. It wasn't a thing—seriously. No emotion. No heat. She wasn't making any threats."

"Quite the opposite," said Selena, taking another sip from her glass. "She *couldn't wait* to get away from you."

Will held up a hand to Selena. "Let's all take a breath."

But Selena didn't want to take a breath.

"She probably just left this stupid town, with all its cheating husbands and clueless working wives," she said.

Red wine made her aggressive; this was a known thing. She pushed the glass away. Then pulled it back and took another sip.

"You're referring to the Tucker family," said Will, looking

down at his notes. "Geneva slept with Erik Tucker. Apparently, according to Mr. Tucker, there was some blackmail there. A new car to keep quiet and quit her job."

The so-called "problems" with her former employers the Tuckers included an affair and extortion.

Apparently the other references on Geneva's glowing résumé weren't real. According to Detective Crowe, the phone numbers rang and rang, or were disconnected. Emails bounced.

"Did you call all of these people?" the detective had asked. They hadn't brought her into the same kind of space where they'd apparently grilled Graham. He'd been in an interrogation room with Detective West and Will. Selena had been led to what looked to be Crowe's small, windowless office.

Crowe had offered her a stiff, uncomfortable chair, a bottle of water. She sat, tense and upright, still in the clothes she'd have worn to work, the waistband of the skirt tight and uncomfortable.

"I knew the Tuckers," she told him. "I wrote to them. They confirmed that she'd been a good nanny, that the kids loved her. But I already knew Geneva, from the park."

He looked down at the paper in front of him, then handed it to her.

"And what about the others? Did you ever actually talk to any of these people?"

She glanced at the list he handed her; it had been a while since she'd seen it.

"I sent an email to this family—the Wrens. But I didn't hear back."

He frowned at her. "You didn't think that was odd?"

She hadn't thought it was odd, no. Men didn't get it. They didn't understand what a chaotic rush it all was, how much email flooded your inbox, how many administrative tasks passed by your eyes—work, school, the business of running a home, a family. Doctor appointments, dentist visits, haircuts, this request for a donation, that birthday party invitation. She didn't think it was odd that she didn't get an answer. In fact, she'd probably just forgotten that she'd sent the email at all. Checking references was just a formality. She knew—or thought she knew—the young woman she invited into her home to care for her children.

"Well, I *knew* Geneva. I tend to go on instinct."

"And your instincts have served you well in the past?"

There had been more than a lilt of sarcasm there, an edge. She ignored it.

"Well enough," she said. Well enough. Was that even true? Given her current situation, she guessed not.

That's when Crowe told her about the blackmail. That Geneva had slept with Erik Tucker, and according to the Tuckers, blackmailed Erik to keep it from his wife. She wanted a car; Erik got her one. Recently, Eliza Tucker had discovered the purchase. How, she wondered, did a man think he was going to keep the purchase of a car from his wife? Graham couldn't even go to Starbucks without it popping up on their accounting software.

"That's—terrible," said Selena.

It was really hard to believe. It just didn't jibe with the woman she thought she knew. It meant that Geneva, the girl who was always ready with extra wipes, or a spare bag of Goldfish in the park, was also an extortionist. Then again, Selena had seen the video of Geneva and her husband, and she had trouble reconciling that, too. The lovely person with the ready smile, the one who was an efficient and competent worker, a loving but firm caregiver, a respectful employee, was also someone who was sleeping with the husbands of hardworking moms.

Geneva, it seemed, was a shape-shifter, an actress. Selena wasn't the only one who had been fooled.

"Are the *Tuckers* suspects in Geneva's disappearance?" Selena asked.

Suspects. Disappearance. These were not words she wanted coming out of her mouth.

But Crowe didn't answer. Just went on.

"So, nothing like that going on at your place?"

"No," she lied. "No, she's a fantastic nanny. Reliable, great with the kids, above and beyond with housework, errands—everything."

Her throat felt dry. Didn't cops know when you were lying? Wasn't there some kind of training they received? She caught herself tapping her foot, something she did when she was nervous. She forced herself to stop by crossing her legs. Had he noticed?

"But your husband was home all day, right? Why did you even need a nanny?"

She laughed a little.

"Good question," she said with a light eye roll, looking for a connection. But he remained neutral, watching her. She cleared her throat. "Graham was looking for another job. We didn't plan for him to be home long. And he needed the freedom to interview."

It sounded like bullshit. Because it was, essentially, bullshit. Graham hadn't been caring for the kids, or working, or actively looking for another job, had he?

"He lost his last job. Is that right?"

It sounded really shady, the way he said it.

"He was laid off," said Selena. "His division folded."

"That's rough."

She didn't like the note of pity in his voice.

"It happens," she said stiffly.

He scribbled something, even though he told her the conversation was being recorded.

"You weren't concerned about your husband and the nanny being alone together all day?"

"No," she said. "I wasn't."

"How's your marriage in general?"

"Good," she said, her whole body rigid. A good wind and

she'd snap in two. "As good as any long marriage. We're—happy."

She looked around his office for something personal—a photograph, a child-made piece of pottery, a team pennant. But there was nothing—just stacks of files, a laptop, his phone, an old mug filled with pens. There was a wilting plant on top of the file cabinet.

"No infidelity?" he pressed.

"Is this relevant?"

It felt personal, like he was prodding at her, and maybe he was. Will went in with Graham, but he told her before they separated to give the detective nothing. He offered to call a colleague for Graham and stay with her. But she'd waved him off. She had nothing to hide, she told him. Denial. Stupidity. Desperation. All three maybe.

"I think it's relevant, given the situation," he said, watching her.

"No," she said finally. "No infidelity."

Should she keep track? Of the lies, how many? Yes, a notebook of all the lies she was telling to others and to herself. It could come in handy.

"Isn't it possible," she said, "that Geneva just took off? Maybe she met someone? Got tired of the childcare gig? I mean, there's no indication that anything *happened* to her, per se."

"At this point," said the detective, "anything is possible. The car is worrisome, though. Why would she leave her car?"

She supposed there were a hundred reasons people did things, reasons that might never occur to people who were grounded in their lives. People who locked their doors and protected their identities, who worked to pay bills, who saved for their children's educations—who didn't sleep with other people's husbands, then blackmailed those men into buying them cars.

Seems like the police should be more interested in the Tucker family than they were in the Murphy family, but she wasn't going to say that. She wasn't going to throw another family under the bus to deflect attention from her own. Or *would* she? If it came to that.

"From what I'm getting," said Will now, bringing Selena back to the present, "they really don't have anything to go on. Geneva is missing, but there's no evidence of foul play. At this point, she might just be your run-of-the-mill con artist. Working her way into families, taking what she can get from them and moving on. Maybe the Tucker woman found out about the car, confronted her. Maybe Geneva figured she might not get much from Graham. It was time to move on."

The three of them sat there—Graham staring off into space, Will and Selena locking eyes.

"Is anything missing from your place? Jewelry? Cash? Pills?"

Selena shrugged. "I don't think so. I'll check."

Will shifted in his seat, tapped his finger on the wood surface of the table.

"My guess is that if no further evidence of foul play falls into their laps, her body doesn't turn up, they'll have to move on."

"Her *body* turns up?" said Selena, shocked. "What kind of thing is that to say? She's a *person*."

He lifted his palms.

"I'm just saying," he defended. "Unless that happens, there's not a whole lot they can do. It's not a crime to walk away from your life. And as for the blackmail, the car, all that—it's Tucker's word against hers. She could say it was a gift."

"What if they come with a warrant—want to search our computers, or the camera app?" said Graham.

"They likely won't do that unless we're talking about a murder investigation—which we're not at the moment. If that happens, we'll have to revisit, decide whether we want to come clean about the affair rather than let them discover it in a search and seizure."

"So then—what?" asked Selena.

"The hardest thing," said Will. "Go about your business and wait to see what happens next. Unless the sister keeps applying pressure, or the media becomes a factor, or there's a further development, I'm betting this just goes away."

She felt a little burst of hope.

Don't you wish your problems would just go away?

Maybe they did sometimes.

Graham looked like he was going to be sick. Finally, he got up and left the room. Selena heard him flop onto the couch. A second later, the television came on. She looked at Will, those stormy eyes unreadable. He opened his mouth as if to speak, then closed it again.

"I should go," he said finally.

"I'll walk you out."

"Thank you for this," she said at his car. "And I'm sorry. Sorry to drag you into the mess of my life."

The air was cool and the wind blustery, the tall oaks up and down the street whispering. Lights in neighborhood houses glowed, the picture of warmth and security.

"I'm sorry this is happening to you," he said, leaning on the hood of his sleek black late-model BMW. "You deserve better than this, Selena. So do the boys."

She shook her head, wrapped her arms around her middle, not trusting her voice. She looked back at her own house—empty of her children, her cheating husband lying on the couch inside. What had she wanted when she was younger? What had she imagined? Nothing like this.

"What are you going to do?" he asked. His voice was soft and deep.

"I don't know."

He put a hand on her shoulder.

"I'm here for you," he said. "You know that. We've been friends a long time and that hasn't changed. It won't."

"Thank you," she whispered.

There was still a pull to him; that connection, that attraction, it never went away. She just chose someone else. And that's all life was—a series of choices and their consequences. What was it about Graham? He was wild, where Will was staid. He connected her to the part of herself that wanted to take risks—like skydiving, and zip-lining. Will had his feet planted firmly on the ground and wanted her to stay there, too. Will had always been the one who pushed her—to do better in school, to get a good night's sleep, to work out. Graham would party all night—they'd go to clubs, get home in time for a catnap and a shower before heading to work. Life with Graham was fun—last-minute trips to Vegas, lavish dinners, shopping sprees that neither of them could afford. Will was predictable, always did the right thing. He saved, hated debt, only bought what he could afford.

She chose Graham, for reasons that seemed right at the time. Reasons that seemed childish now. She wanted to live on the edge, push the boundaries, walk on the wild side while she was young. She hadn't been ready to settle into a life where she already knew the beginning, the middle and the end. Graham lit her up. She'd loved him wildly. She'd loved Will, too. It was just—different.

"I met someone the other night," she said. Will's expression made her clarify.

"No," she said. "Not like that. On the train the other night, I met a woman."

He issued a little laugh. "I've heard that one before, too."

"Stop," she said with a smile. "She's been—texting me."

A frown. "What about?"

She tried to explain the encounter to him, the odd energy, why she felt compelled to tell this stranger about her life, what the woman had revealed to her. How she'd been ignoring the texts that arrived.

"Did you give her your number?"

"No," she said. "I didn't. I don't even remember giving her my last name."

Will's frown deepened. "That's odd."

"I'm just telling you because—there is someone out there who knows about Graham. Or knows that I suspected him of being unfaithful."

He nodded carefully. "What was her name?"

"Martha. I didn't get her last name. I blocked her the first time. But the later texts came from a different number. It was almost like she knew I blocked her."

She handed Will her phone and he scrolled through the texts. After a moment, he shrugged.

"Ghost her. Certainly don't engage."

"What do you think she wants?"

"Maybe nothing," said Will. "Maybe she's just looking for a friend."

Selena shrugged. There *was* a connection there, wasn't there? Maybe the other woman felt it, too. Maybe she was lonely. "Seems like an odd way to try to connect."

"These days, the world is full of people with bad ideas on how to connect with others."

"If this becomes *a thing*," she said, reaching for his hand, "she knows that Graham had an affair with the nanny. Or that I thought he might be."

"But it's *not* a thing yet," Will said, taking her hand in both of his. "The media is not involved—all we have is a girl who missed a breakfast date with her sister, then didn't show up for work. There's no evidence of more. Geneva could return at any point. You're always ten steps ahead. Just stay here now."

"Right," she said. But the world, the swirling possibilities, seemed so manic, out of control.

"And the next time you need to confide in someone, call a real friend. Like me."

He pulled her into an embrace and held on tight. She felt

herself sink into him—the expensive material of his suit, the subtle scent of his cologne. When she was younger, why had the safe and predictable life seemed like a straightjacket? Now it was all she wanted.

When she saw Graham watching from the window, his dark form dominating the frame, she didn't pull away from Will.

EIGHTEEN

Pearl

"PEARL S. BUCK?"

Charlie trying to make conversation. His words leaked through the thick fog surrounding her awareness.

"No," she said, after a long pause where the road was black and the tires hummed, and the wind roared around the vehicle. "*The Pearl* by John Steinbeck."

Her voice was thick in her throat, her arms and legs leaden with fatigue.

"That's pretty grim reading."

It was—a difficult, sad story with a hard ending. Still, Stella had loved it for its stark beauty.

There it lay. The great pearl. Perfect as the moon, her mother used to whisper to Pearl when she was small.

"Stella wasn't exactly a ray of sunshine," said Pearl. But, Pearl thought, she loved me, I think. In her broken-down way. And now she's gone.

"She had her moments," said Charlie. He wore a sad smile, eyes straight ahead.

"A few, I guess. Here and there."

They drove and drove; they'd been driving for days.

Pearl had never been out of the northeast—the gray ceiling winters and fecund green summers, the smell of leaves in autumn, the gray slush of late February. The tentative burst of color in March. It was all she knew. From the highway every place looked more or less the same until they got to Texas, where things got dusty and flat. Then the southwest exploded in bold clay reds, and towering browns and evergreen. Diners got kitschy and full of themselves. Big cerulean-blue sky, towering cumulous clouds. And a night filled with so many stars it didn't seem real. The painted desert at sunset. Low adobe structures surrounded by scrub and silence. The hustle of the modern came to a dusky stillness.

"I feel like we're on the moon," she said.

They mostly rode in silence. She'd slept for days, not sure what was real and what was a dream. The diner where an old woman dressed in black stared and stared. Charlie's wail of despair. Stella's dead stare. A dust storm outside a run-down restaurant where a cowboy walked out of the murk. A motel where she slept on the bed and Charlie on the floor beside her. Kneeling in the roadside, vomiting.

"That's good. That's where we need to be for now."

Charlie said he had a place in a town called Pecos, outside of Santa Fe, and that's where they were headed. When they arrived, she barely noticed the town before they'd passed through it completely. It consisted of a general store and a bar, a gas station turned art gallery, a diner, a consignment store. It took them less than five minutes to pass through it in its entirety.

They wound along clay roads, past houses that were hidden in the trees, wind chimes on porches, birdsong, until finally they arrived. A small adobe structure waited, surrounded by trees, mountains, and sky. The other properties they'd passed were miles back.

"We'll stay here a while," he said, coming to a stop in the squat drive.

"Whose place is this?" she asked. It looked oddly familiar, though she'd never been anywhere like it.

"Ours for now."

There was a mailbox crafted from the same clay as the house, a collection of pots on the stoop in front of a wooden door, wind chimes hanging.

Pearl opened the car door and stepped outside, kicking up red dust. The smell of juniper and sage was fresh and broad, filling her senses. Something inside her that was tight loosened. And the quiet—no traffic noise, no voices—it expanded.

"What about school?" she asked. Her voice seemed to disappear, swallowed by the wind.

Charlie closed his car door, the sound of it echoing off the mesa behind them. "You can go online."

He had an easy answer for everything since she'd come back to herself. She nodded, unquestioning. Yes, of course. She could go to school online. Why not?

Something happened to Pearl when she saw Stella—broken, her body left bleeding and twisted in her bed. Blood on the floor, on the sheets. Her eyes open, staring with confused rage. Pearl must have blacked out when she came in to find Charlie on his knees before the mess. His wailing. It was a siren. She'd hit her head on the floor when she fell; there was still a knot. The next thing she remembered she was in the back of Charlie's car, lying across the rear seat under a blanket, head on the pillow from her bed.

Woman murdered. Child missing.

That's what the headlines said, all the newscasts they'd caught in roadside diners, what they'd read online.

True and not true.

Pearl wasn't missing, she thought, looking at the world around her. She was found.

They unloaded the groceries they'd picked up in Albuquerque. He had a key, unlocked the front door as if it was a place well-known to him, flipped on the inside lights. The place was all windows—the living room, dining area and kitchen just one big room—vaulted ceilings that gave the impression of height. The walls dominated by glass inviting in views of the mesa behind them, the Santa Fe National Forest, the valley below.

He settled her in a simple room with a queen bed, a wood dresser. Placing her suitcase by the door. The walls were eggshell, no art. A blank slate. A big window. The bed was a white cloud, clean cotton sheets, comforter, pillows.

"You're going to be okay," he said. He'd said this a number of times like a mantra, wearing a worried frown. "I'm going to take care of you."

They hadn't spoken much about what happened; she'd barely uttered a word about anything. He panicked, he said, when they'd discovered Stella. Packed Pearl's things—her bedding, her books, clothing, toiletries, her stuffed bear—and put them in his car. Pearl walked with him; he didn't carry her. He'd repeated that a couple of times, like it was important that she'd walked under her own steam. Stunned, nonresponsive, Pearl let herself be led away from home.

"They'd have taken you, right? Into child protective services? Stella wouldn't have wanted that. She'd have wanted me to take care of you. That's why we ran," he said the second day. He'd repeated this as well, a couple times. A narrative he was running. She supposed it was true. There was no one else to take care of her; she was a minor. Charlie wasn't her father, not even her stepfather. Charlie wasn't even her mother's boyfriend, technically. Her biological father—she had no idea who he was. Pearl would have gone to foster care or something.

"You're going to be okay," he said again. "I promise."

Now, she sat on the bed, nodded.

"I'm going to make some dinner," he said. "We'll talk more. When you're ready."

There was a mirror over the dresser. She didn't recognize the girl she saw there. In Texas, they'd cut her hair in a short bob, dyed it black. Charlie shaved his dark mane down to a crew cut. He grew a goatee. They weren't the same people they were when they were packing up boxes in the bookstore. It hadn't even been a week. Could life change so fast? Could you be one person on Monday, and someone else by Sunday? She touched the necklace she wore, Stella's locket. Charlie had taken it for her. That and a picture album, some journals that Pearl didn't even know her mother kept. She hadn't opened them. There was a shoebox of cash; he'd given that to Pearl, too. He'd grabbed files—her birth certificate, Social Security card. Everything she owned was in a single large suitcase.

She took a shower. The water was tepid, the flow flaccid. But she felt more alert, more focused when she was done. She got dressed, listening to Charlie move about the kitchen. Finally, she joined him. He'd already set the table, was serving the food.

"Sit," he said.

Grilled chicken breast with a fresh green salad, mashed potatoes with butter. They ate and ate. It had been all burgers and fries, sodas, microwave burritos, chips for days. The food on her plate now was fresh and clean, healthy. They drank about a gallon of water. Neither of them spoke until they were both done.

"I'm sorry this happened to you," said Charlie. "I can only imagine how you must be feeling."

But she wasn't feeling anything. That was the strange thing. She wanted to feel something—grief, fear, rage. But there was just a floating numbness inside, an awareness of the present that wasn't impacted by the past.

"But here we are," he said. She saw it in him, too, that strange coolness, that ability to only look ahead. "If they don't find us soon, their case will go cold. You have no family or connections that will put pressure on them to keep looking. No one's going to hire a private investigator or anything like that."

Pearl figured that was true.

"So, if no one spotted us, recognized us from the news, called in a tip—and we were careful…" He paused here, maybe thinking back to all the places they'd been, the precautions taken or not. "Then we should be okay here until we figure out what comes next."

Even though he was much changed—thinner, cropped hair, goatee—those eyes were the same.

"Did you?" she asked.

"Did I what?"

"Did you kill her?"

His mouth dropped open, hand flying to the center of his chest. "No. Whoa, Pearl, no. You were there. You were with me all afternoon."

That was true. But she'd been at school all day. She'd heard something in the night. Hadn't seen Stella in the morning, though she'd heard movement. Was Stella dead in her room while Pearl was eating breakfast? Was her killer still there?

"Then who?"

"I-I-I don't know," he stammered. He leaned forward across the table. "Did you think that all this time? That I—killed your mother?"

"It crossed my mind."

Charlie looked stricken, which was not what she expected from him. He was cool, slow in his speech, not reactionary. She'd expected him to calmly offer her a yes or a no.

"I—cared about Stella," he said, his voice soft. "I wanted to be with her, but she didn't want me like that. While I was with her, I grew to care about you. I've made mistakes in my life, done things I'm not proud of, yeah. But I'd never hurt anyone—not like that."

She flashed again on Stella's broken body. She did feel something, a twist in her gut. But the feeling didn't have a name. She watched his face; he didn't break her gaze. Finally, she looked away.

"So, if the police find who killed her, they'll think that he did something to me, right?" she said. "They'll assume I'm dead, too."

Charlie watched her, some of the color returning to his cheeks. "Maybe."

The sun was setting outside the picture window, the sky turning a painted pink, purple, and orange. She was still hungry. She felt like she could eat another full meal, and then keep eating until she'd devoured the whole world. And then she'd still be hungry.

"So far, they have no leads, except for the fact that I'm missing, too," said Charlie. "That's made me a person of interest. My DNA is not in the system; I don't have a record. So even if they find it at the scene—and they will because I was there—it won't matter."

"Okay." She wasn't sure what he meant for a moment. Because they already knew who he was. The police wouldn't need his DNA to identify him. Then it struck her. Charles Finch wasn't his real name. What was it? Did it matter?

"So, we stay here for a while, lay low," he went on. "We'll keep track of what's happening. Figure it out day by day."

She tried to imagine Stella's house sitting empty, Pearl's locker at school deserted. The store unopened. The books collecting dust. What happened to all of that when you just walked away? She thought of the boxes of books, waiting for shipment. Who would dismantle their life? She had no friends to wonder what had happened to her; the neighbors were distant and unfriendly. There was no family—no worried grandparents, or gaggle of loving cousins.

The truth was, no one would miss them. She would just disappear and be forgotten.

"They'll forget about me," she said. "I barely exist."

He drew in a breath, put down his fork.

"You exist here," he said. "With me."

"Yes," she said. There was an essential truth to that, but she didn't feel real. She felt like a ghost about to be absorbed into the ether.

"What about the bookstore?"

Charlie pushed his glasses up. "It's bankrupt. Stella was about to go under, and she knew it. She had a pile of debt, hadn't paid the property taxes in two years. She was about to lose the building."

"Logistically, what will happen?"

She thought about all the beautiful books, crisp and fresh, waiting hopefully for their readers. The story nook, the counter cluttered with pretty pens, funny buttons, bookmarks, the shelves she and Stella had built together, the big prints with quotes from famous works.

"I imagine the items inside—books, furniture, computers—will get sold off to pay the taxes, and the building will go to a seizure auction."

"And what about her bank accounts?"

Charlie shrugged. "Honestly, Pearl, she was living on credit. There was nothing except the cash in that shoebox. A little under three grand. It's yours; save it for a rainy day."

If rainier days were coming, she didn't want to know about it.

Outside, something hooted, low and mournful.

"So now, the good part," he said, standing with his plate. "This is where we recreate ourselves."

"How's that?"

She cleared hers as well, moved over to stand beside him at the sink.

"My father, I told you, was a monster," said Charlie. "But he was a master con artist—until it got him killed."

"How?" she asked.

"That's a story for another night. But he taught me everything I know about making the most out of people, situations, and life."

"You thought she had more, didn't you?"

He rinsed the plate, washed it with the sponge and soap. The scent of lilac was strong and soothing.

"I did think she had more. When I first met her, she presented like someone with money. Expensive bag and shoes, a store that looked successful, a nice house."

"You were going to con her?"

"No," he said quickly. He rinsed the dish and put it in the rack. "Maybe. I don't know. But it was clear pretty fast that Stella was no mark. She intrigued me. Then, I broke a few of my own rules. I stayed too long. I got—distracted from the game."

"Distracted by what?"

But she already knew the answer.

"Distracted by you."

Pearl was fifteen but she looked older, she felt older. She knew more than people twice her age. Some of the men Stella brought home, they stared. If her mother noticed, the offender got kicked right out. It wasn't like that with Charlie. There was something there, something between them. But it wasn't weird. Not weird like that.

He washed her dish, too. She dried them and placed them back in the cabinet, wiped down the counter. It already felt like home.

"I cared about Stella," he said. "I wanted to help her—and you. But she wouldn't let me. She was already too far gone."

Pearl knew what he meant. Her mother, always in a rush, seemed like she was either arriving or leaving too late. It never seemed as if she was there, present. She was always looking to make her escape. And now that she was gone, Pearl wasn't sure what she'd left behind, what there was to remember her by. Even her more recent memories were blurred, fading fast.

"So, first, we'll get you enrolled to finish school online. I'll figure out the whole identity thing."

The whole identity thing, as if who she had been was an outfit they could change.

"How? How does that work?"

"I have contacts, people who can help."

"I don't understand."

"It's not important now," he said. "But if you want to learn, I'll teach you sometime. Things are harder than they used to be. But there are ways to live off the grid."

It would be a while before he told her about his work, about the network of people he knew and how they all operated. She kept quiet now; she was tired. The world was something other than she imagined it to be, and it was exhausting to find her way.

"And, hey," he said. "It's okay to grieve for your mother. It's okay to be sad or scared. We're going to get through this."

She searched inside herself for feeling, and, as usual, she came up empty.

"I guess we all grieve differently."

Or not at all. *What if there's nothing inside me?* she wanted to ask. She felt like she could ask Charlie that, like he wouldn't judge her. *What if there's just a sucking black emptiness where my soul should be? If that's true, then what does that make me?* Even those thoughts, those questions, didn't frighten her—though she knew that they probably should. But, still, she kept quiet.

"But if you need to talk about it—"

He let the sentence trail.

"Yeah," she said. "I get it."

They finished cleaning in silence.

In the living room, Charlie made a fire with the small amount of wood he found outside the back door. She sat on the floor and held her hands up to the warmth, felt the heat on her face. He stayed on the couch behind her, reclining there with his eyes closed. The furniture was plush, comfortable, the place decorated tastefully, simply with a Southwestern flair—cow skull on the wall, oil paintings of deserts and sunset skies, starry nights and howling coyotes. Where were they? What was this place? How did they get here?

Maybe I'm dead, she thought. *Maybe this is what comes next.*

"You're going to need a new name, okay?" he said into the quiet. "I will, too."

A new name. A new self. That was interesting, an idea she liked. The girl in the mirror with the unfamiliar haircut and haunted eyes. Yes, she needed a new name.

"Portia? Delilah? Cleopatra? Scheherazade?" she offered to the flames, then turned to check his reaction.

He gave her a lift of his eyebrows, a wry smile.

"Something simple, nondescript. Something that doesn't call attention."

"How about Anne?"

He nodded. "That works. Like *Anne of Green Gables*. Not like Ayn Rand, right?"

"Right," she said. "Sweet, innocent, good-hearted Anne. What about you?"

"I'll give it some thought."

"Othello? Humbert? Mr. Knightly? Svengali?"

That earned her a guffaw.

"You're officially off the name committee," he said.

"How about Bob?" she offered.

"Closer," he said. "For our purposes, though, as we move into whatever the next game is, it's best if people think I'm your father."

She didn't know what he meant by "the next game," but she had an inkling. She'd already learned to play along with him.

"So, you're Bob the widower?"

"Widower is a bit high-profile—engendering too much sympathy attention; it can be an attractor for a certain type of woman. I think she left me, your mom. Maybe she left us. She remarried, isn't much of a mother to you. But she's in and out of the picture."

"So you want me to call you Dad?"

"Are you okay with that?"

"It sounds a little normie, doesn't it?"

"That's what we're going for," he said with another chuckle. She liked the sound of his laughter; it was big and full-bodied. "What do you want to call me?"

"I think," she said, moving over to lean against the couch where he was lying. "I think I'll call you Pop."

He dropped a hand on the crown of her head, let it travel over her hair to her shoulder. She took his silence as assent. They sat a while like that, and then she rose, her fatigue so heavy now she could barely keep her eyes open.

"Good night, Anne," he said, his voice soft, the fire crackling.

"Good night, Pop."

NINETEEN

Anne

ANNE ALWAYS THOUGHT of herself in the name she was currently using the most. She was Anne most of the time, or had been recently. Now that she was no longer working in Hugh's office, and she was done with Hugh, that self would start to fade. Who would she be next? There had been so many names, so many selves, all of them lies, all of them true. Maybe it would be Martha. Sometimes inside, she still heard her true name, Pearl. But rarely. More rarely all the time.

Whoever she was, she settled in before the crackling fireplace as darkness fell outside. She had her laptop open, a steaming cup of tea on the table beside the couch. Outside, the temperature had dropped, and the wind howled.

She lifted the computer onto her lap, started scrolling through her emails. Since she arrived home, she'd closed down a couple of the games she was running—deleted email accounts, ditched burner phones, erased a fake Facebook profile.

Pop wasn't a fan of multitasking. And truly, as she got older, she was starting to see why. It was draining to keep track of so many different lies, so many selves, so many people wanting. She needed to focus.

Now that she was done with Hugh and Kate, she only had two things going. One that wasn't progressing as planned. One that was humming along nicely.

People didn't fall in love with other people. They fell in love with how other people made them feel about themselves. And so, it was easy to get someone to love you—if you knew how they wanted to feel.

Take Ben, for example, a childless fifty-five-year-old widower in Ottawa. Bespectacled, roundish, but sweet-faced, not unattractive. A pediatrician. He fostered rescued greyhounds until he could find them good homes. He wanted, she knew almost right away from his dating profile, to come in for the rescue. He wanted to be a hero. He had a soft spot for the creature in need.

After a blazing online romance, she and Ben were supposed to meet for the first time this weekend—a romantic Montreal rendezvous. But then Anne (who was known to Ben as Gywneth—he had a preference according to his profile for willowy blondes so no point in being subtle) became so worried about her bipolar sister. A strange late-night phone call was her first warning that something was amiss. Then, her sister didn't turn up for work. All sure signs that sis was off her meds, devolving. Gwyneth might not be able to make their getaway. How could she take a romantic vacation? When her sister might need her?

She logged on to her messages and saw that he'd texted a while ago: Thinking about you. Here to help if you need me.

I'm so sorry, Ben. I have no choice, she typed. I'm going to have to cancel. There's still no word. I have to go see if she's all right.

She waited. Would he become angry in his disappointment? If so, she'd have to cut him loose. Then his reply:

I'll meet you.

Of course, he'd meet her and help both Gwen and her fictional sister. The nicest, kindest people made the best marks because they believed that everyone was as goodhearted as they were. Sad, really.

No. She wouldn't be able to handle a stranger in the mix. I'll call you when I get there.

Again, she waited, the little reply dots pulsing. No response. She dashed off another sentence.

She's all I have. I'm so sorry, Ben.

Then:

Don't be silly. I understand. She's lucky to have a sister like you.

I'm so worried.

When's your flight?

Early tomorrow.

Can you talk?

Maybe later.

Okay. Don't worry too much. I can be there if you need me.

Poor Gwyneth; she was down on her luck, too. Just lost her job, but no, she wouldn't accept an airline ticket from Ben. She always made her own way. She'd made that clear to Ben. Since their parents died in a car crash, she and her sister Esme had taken care of each other. They'd never accepted any help. She was eighteen at the time of the accident, Esme sixteen. She took care of her sister, made sure she graduated from high school. Gwen worked as a waitress to put herself through community college. They had some money, though, a small inheritance. It had helped them survive, evened out some of the rough patches.

Things just seem so much easier since I met you, she typed. Thank you for being you.

That's what friends are for.

Friends...

You know what I mean.

I do, she typed. I know exactly what you mean. And I can't wait to hold you in my arms and show you how much your friendship means.

She could almost feel his passion pumping in those little pulsing dots.

I never thought I'd care about anyone again.

Neither did I. We're so lucky to have found each other.

He hadn't said the *L* word. But he was close. Very close. They'd talked on the phone. He'd demurred from FaceTime—which probably meant he was a lot heavier than his profile photo. And it was fine, because it was better if they never saw her face. Not just because they wouldn't be able to identify her. They wouldn't; she looked different all the time. It was just better if they created a fantasy woman, someone who perfectly matched their deepest inner desires. She kept her texts simple, even avoided emojis. That way they could imbue her words with any imagined tone they needed or wanted.

His response took longer than usual.

I'll call you tomorrow.

She used to wonder about those silences when they first started chatting. But after talking to him, she realized that he was the kind of guy who got jammed up by emotion, fell silent in conversation, even virtual conversation.

The dots pulsed. Was he going to say it? No. He was waiting until they saw each other, she suspected. Until they made love—in the flesh. Which was never going to happen. Of course, she was never going to meet him in Montreal or anywhere. But no doubt he had run the fantasy a thousand times. He wasn't one to sext, send photos, or talk dirty. He was a nice man, looking for someone to care for, someone to love. Poor orphan Gwen, beautiful and brave, was his dream girl.

I'll be thinking about you.

Oh, I know you will, Ben, she thought but didn't type.

Good night.

"The con," Pop always said. "Isn't violence. Isn't a smash and grab. It's a dance. It's a seduction. You always have to give something first. And then they'll give you everything."

She'd taken her time with Ben. They had a relationship, nearly three months of texts and long emails, phone calls where she kept her voice breathy and low. She told him about her scars from the car wreck. One on her leg, one across her chest, how self-conscious she was, how she didn't like to bare her skin.

He didn't talk about his wife much, far less than most men

talked about their ex-wives, or girlfriends who had left them. Those guys couldn't wait to rattle off their list of complaints and criticisms, catalog the many wrongs they'd suffered, painting unflattering portraits of the unfaithful, the controlling, the addicted women in their pasts. But Ben mentioned her only a couple times, briefly, warm memories, or funny anecdotes. He never talked about her illness or death. She didn't pry; she really didn't want to know. In fact, she liked him a bit more than was smart.

She closed the lid on the laptop, stared at the flames in the fireplace.

"Are you going soft on me?"

Pop sat in the chair, just a shadow tonight. She was never sure what form he was going to take. Sometimes she could hear his voice, clear and strong. Sometimes it was just an echo on the wind. He was a reflection in a mirror, a creak on the stairs. She turned away from his dark shape; she didn't want to see him. But he was always with her.

"Of course not."

When she looked back at him, he was gone.

The closed laptop. The silence of the house. The howling wind. She tried to sit with it, to go blank. Sometimes she tried to go back and back and back to the girl she was before, her true self. What was that girl like? What was her favorite food, color, flower? What had she wanted to be once upon a time? She loved animals. She remembered that about herself, how easy it was to be with a cat or a dog; how present they were. Occasionally, she caught a glimpse of herself, like a shade slipping into darkness.

She picked up her phone. Nothing back from Selena.

She flipped on the television, scrolled through the news channels. Nothing at all about a missing girl. Opening her laptop again, she did a search. Nothing.

"I'm not sure I'm with you on this one."

Pop again, this time standing in the corner. He'd bought this house for them. *This is going to be our forever home*, he'd told her. *The place where we can really be who we are.* And that had been true for a time. But the wolves were already at their heels then, though neither of them knew it. And forever isn't forever.

"I don't see what you have to gain here. They probably don't have that much money. And that Selena, she's not biting."

She felt herself bristle; she didn't like having to defend herself to Pop. She shouldn't have to. The student had far surpassed the teacher.

"This one is not about the money," she said.

"Ah. One of those."

She opened the laptop again, visited Selena's social media pages, which had no security settings whatsoever. Her life out there for everyone to see—her friends, where she worked, where her kids went to school. Where she spent her time, where she shopped. The entirety of her life, just out there like chum in the water for any shark that happened to swim by. Stupid.

Selena hadn't posted anything since her happy pictures from the weekend. What a bunch of liars everyone in the world had become with their inane social media feeds; Selena's husband was fucking the nanny and she took the time to make everyone in her life jealous of her pretend-perfect little family.

Selena Murphy, formerly Selena Knowles, was nothing special. Not the school homecoming queen. Not the valedictorian of her class. Just a pretty, upper-middle-class girl, with a traditional upbringing. Smart. Good grades. NYU graduate. Successful in her chosen profession—marketing and publicity, of all things. Lots of friends. Happy marriage (or so she'd like everyone to believe). She was a mother of two adorable boys. No, she was nothing special, a normie as Pop liked to call them—except that she had everything.

"You're *not* jealous. Of *her*."

Pop was over by the fireplace now. He was as she had last seen him, eyes glassy, a hole blown though the middle of his chest.

She heard the echo of her own voice, carrying over years. *Please don't leave me here. Pop, please.*

"I'm not sure it's jealousy, exactly," she said. "It's just that it doesn't seem fair, does it? That some people have everything. That things are handed to them. That they walk through life not even knowing what it's like to want and struggle, to live without a safety net. You can see it on her face, can't you? That blank entitlement, that ignorance to critical truths of the world."

"So, this is about social justice?"

They both knew it wasn't. That it ran so much deeper. That it was personal. "Maybe," she said anyway.

He laughed. "I got bad news for you, kid. You can't con a con."

She threw a throw pillow at him and it landed softly by the hearth. She could still hear the echo of his laughter.

Pearl and Charlie slipped right into it. It only took her a couple of days to forget Pearl, to become Anne. And Charlie with his new glasses, his crew cut growing out into its natural salt-and-pepper color, became Pop, the father she never had, never even knew she wanted. Somehow, he'd managed to age himself ten years. Or maybe with his other look, the round specs, the baseball hat, the black hair dye, he'd been able to capture a youthful essence for Charlie. Charlie, the young hipster Stella had brought home, the bookstore marketing whiz, he was someone else, too. A man she used to know, one she remembered fondly but knew she wouldn't see again.

"Think of your discarded selves as other people, distant family members. You know them; they're part of your life. They're characters, you can take pieces from them, use those pieces to flesh out your current self. But keep it simple. The more lies you tell, the more you have to remember."

Pearl enrolled in an online high school. In the tiny isolated house, she got up and made breakfast for them. She took her online classes in the morning, while Pop went out to look for a "job." When her schoolwork was done, she'd wander down the dirt road, finding the trailhead. And she'd walk and walk through the towering pinyon-juniper, aspen, spruce, cottonwood, her head filled with silence, her senses alive—the smell of sagebrush, the cerulean blue of the big sky, the whisper of wind. The sun hot and the air dry.

Everything inside her felt more alive as she became Anne, and left Pearl and Stella behind—distant figures in a life that seemed more like a dream. She rarely thought of Stella, which she knew was odd—but it was as if everything that came before had ceased to be real, even her mother. Who someone had murdered. Who? But even the urgency of that question had faded.

The case around Stella's murder and Pearl's disappearance quickly went cold. It fell out of the news within a matter of weeks. Charles Finch, Stella's lover, the bookstore manager, also missing, was a person of interest in the murder and Pearl's disappearance. The pictures that were circulating of her and Charlie—it didn't even look like them anymore. She felt reborn.

About a month into their new life, Anne was online, searching for news stories, and she came across a feature article about their case. With no suspects, no sightings of the missing Pearl, local police were frustrated. A cold case investigator had been hired by the department, a man named Hunter Ross.

"We know that Stella Behr was murdered in cold blood, strangled in her own home. Her fifteen-year-old daughter Pearl is missing. Charles Finch, Ms. Behr's lover and the manager of her failing book store, also disappeared that night," he was quoted as saying.

"We have come to learn that the man known as Charles Finch was a fiction. None of the information on the job application we found is accurate. Name, address, Social Security number were all falsified."

There were pictures, of Pearl, of Stella, of the storefront. They apparently only had one picture of Charlie. It must have been from Stella's phone; he was smiling devilishly at the camera. There was a bit about Pearl—how she was a star student, but a loner with few friends. Teachers described her as polite, intelligent, always distant.

Her heart thumped as she scrolled through the article. The pictures there looked fake; the story sounded like a catalog of lies.

There was a timeline of the night of Stella's murder, including a neighbor sighting of Pearl and Charlie leaving the house, bags packed, Pearl apparently acting of her own free will. Another man, not matching Charlie's description—this one tall, muscular, with long blond hair and a full beard—had been seen arriving and leaving quickly a short time later earlier that day.

"A woman is dead. A young girl is missing. And the man at the center of this mystery is a ghost. My guess is that Charles Finch is a con, and that he's moved on to his next mark. Maybe Pearl is with him—likely in the thrall of whatever con he might be running on her."

She stared at the picture of Charlie. In the photo, he was in character, whatever character he was playing for Stella—the attentive lover. He played another character for Pearl, the caring friend. She looked deep into the eyes, and recognized something there, something from her own inner self—a vast emptiness, an icescape frozen and barren.

"We have a couple of leads that I'll be following up," said Ross. "Some of these are out of state, which means that the FBI could get involved. And there are some clues as to the true identity of Charlie Finch due to tips from the photos we ran nationally. He may be the wanted perpetrator of a number of high-level cons, rip-offs, and scams across the country. So this investigation is far from over. However long it takes, we'll find answers. We won't stop looking for Pearl Behr."

The front door opened and closed with a bang, the sound

moving through her like a gunshot. It hadn't occurred to Pearl-now-Anne that Charlie-now-Pop might be running a con on her.

She walked out of her room to greet him. Pop was whistling in the kitchen, putting away groceries. A bouquet of fresh flowers lay on the counter.

"Hey," he said. He stopped mid-action to give her a concerned smile. "What's up? You look like you've seen a ghost."

"They're still looking for us," she said. She was shaking and she didn't even know why. "There's a hired cold case detective. He said that there are leads."

Pop nodded, went back to taking the milk from the reusable sack and putting it in the fridge. "I know."

He was his constant, easy self. If what she said unsettled him, he didn't show it.

"You said that they'd stop eventually."

"They will."

"The article said that there are leads, that the FBI is involved."

"They always say that," he answered, stopping to walk over to her. He put strong hands on her shoulders.

"In the article," she pressed, "the detective said that they had leads on your identity, from other cons you've run, that they won't stop looking."

He had told her some about his past, his childhood, how he lived. Not everything. But she was starting to get the picture.

Now he bowed his head, tightened his grip on her. "Do you trust me?" he asked finally.

She looked into his face—the kaleidoscope of his eyes, the set line of his mouth.

"Yes," she said. It was true and it wasn't. You couldn't really trust anyone, could you? Not even yourself.

"Then don't worry about the article, or the detective, or the FBI. They're looking for people who don't exist anymore. Pearl and Charlie—they're long gone."

"I don't want to go back."

He put a warm palm to her cheek.

"As long as I'm alive, you're safe. I promise you that."

She couldn't find her voice, but let him pull her close. She usually shrank from physical affection, didn't like people near, or touching her. But she could tolerate his closeness, even craved it sometimes.

"Now, go put on something nice—you know, like, sweet. And come help me with dinner. We're having company."

"What do you mean?"

"I found a job."

A job. The word had a very different meaning to Pop than it did to most people. He had his own language. "New friend" was someone he met who might or might not be a mark. "Girlfriend" meant he had one on the hook. "Venture" meant that it was bigger than a personal con, something that might take longer, be more complicated. "Breakup" meant that it was time to get out of town. A "job" meant that it was showtime.

Now, Anne looked for him in the shadows of the firelit room. But he was gone.

"Good night, Pop," she said. A log tumbled in the fire, sending sparks up the chimney.

She was about to turn in for the night when her phone pinged. She expected something from Hugh, something desperate or ragey, accusations, or begging to meet—depending on whether Kate had kicked him out or not. But no.

Well, well. How about that?

I had a late meeting. Free for a drink?

This is Selena, by the way.

From the train.

TWENTY

Selena

THE SOUND OF her footfalls on the pavement echoed in the rainy hush, nerve endings pulsing. What was she doing? Acting against all logic and good sense, clearly.

After Will left her house, and she'd returned inside, she found Graham passed out on the couch, snoring. That was Graham's escape hatch, sleep. Stressed or depressed, the guy just passed out cold. She stood over him, thought about waking him up, grilling him about his time with the police. Questioning him about Geneva, if there was more she needed to know.

But the truth was, she couldn't even stand the sound of his voice, didn't want to hear all his excuses, heartfelt pleas, apologies. She didn't believe he would ever hurt anyone, didn't think he had anything to do with whatever had happened to Geneva. If anything had happened at all.

But looking down at his prone form, something had switched off inside her. They'd had everything. Whatever doubts she'd had before the wedding, she'd loved her husband. They'd created a family; she'd been a faithful and loving wife. He'd set fire to everything they'd built. Not once, but three times—that she knew of. She couldn't forgive him, not now. She wasn't sure she even loved him anymore.

Alone in the kitchen, she'd tried Geneva another time. No answer. "It's Selena. Please call us," she pleaded with the voice mail. "Let someone know that everything is okay so that we can all go on with our lives."

Then, she'd scrolled through the texts from Martha. The only person other than Graham and Will who knew that her husband had been sleeping with the nanny.

One thing she knew from her work in PR was that a little preemptive damage control could go a long way. Sometimes, if you could get out in front of something, you could divert disaster altogether.

So she sent a text.

I had a late meeting. Free for a drink?

Now, as she made her way up West Broadway, beneath the thrum of anxiety, wasn't there something else? Something dark and glittering. Why did doing the wrong thing sometimes feel right? There was a tingle to breaking the rules, to doing the thing you shouldn't do—like driving too fast, going home with a stranger, fighting when you should back down. There was an energy in that space, an electricity, an aliveness she didn't feel when she was doing all the things she did as a good mom, a good wife, a good daughter.

She passed a couple that leaned into each other, the woman laughing. A man sped by on his bicycle, jacket glistening with rainwater, moving too fast for the wet road. A homeless man sat beneath an overhang, buried under garbage bags piled against the weather. She took the five she had in her pocket and dropped it in his bucket. They locked eyes for a moment.

"God bless you," he said.

"You, too."

Though, at the moment, she didn't feel very blessed, and she didn't imagine he did either. How did she wind up here? How did *he*? How did anyone wind up where they were?

In Tribeca the city seemed to lower its voice. There was the mania of midtown, the quaint chic of the West Village, the too-cool grit of the Lower East Side. Every neighborhood had its energy and personality, a character in the story of the city. But this neighborhood with its stratospherically expensive lofts and artfully curated shops, dim restaurants owned by this celebrity or that, seemed apart somehow, unattainable. Selena always thought of Tribeca as a place that was keeping a secret. You only knew if you knew.

She shook out her hair, damp from the drizzle since she didn't have an umbrella. She was cold, chilled to her core. This was a mistake. She needed to go home and put back the pieces of her life.

But then she found herself in front of the address she was looking for and paused at the door. Last chance to be smart, to do the right and careful thing. Go home and wait for what comes next, the solid advice from a staid and reliable friend. To be the good girl that she'd been raised to be.

A motorcycle gunned up the street. Beneath her feet, she felt the subtle rumble of a subway train.

Almost. She *almost* turned around.

Just like she *almost* broke up with Graham right before their wedding. Because didn't she know that beneath the pulse of excitement that came with doing the wrong thing, there was an abyss? Hadn't she observed his eyes linger on other women, wondered who he was talking to on the phone with a very particular tone? There'd been a lie or two, said he was somewhere when it was later revealed he hadn't been.

The week before she'd married, she'd had a drink with Will. He'd been dapper, as always, put together and cool, but she could see the fatigue under his eyes, knew that he chewed on his thumbnail when he was stressed. It was bitten to the quick.

"I couldn't let this week pass without telling you that I love you as much as I did the day we met," he said over glasses of prosecco. "That I'll never stop loving you."

"Will," she said. The pull to him was still strong; her guilt for hurting him, disappointing him, was heavy on her heart. They'd been together so long—through college, and his time at law school, their first jobs. Everyone thought they'd get married. Everyone *knew* they would. It was like she was breaking a promise she'd made to all their family and friends.

"There isn't *more*, you know." He took her hand. "That's what you said, right? That you want *more* than safe, *more* than predictable. You want to experiment, explore, discover. And that's okay. Do that. Just don't marry Graham. Come back to me when you've done what you need to do."

His eyes gleamed, and she bowed her head, kept hold of his hand.

"You know," he went on into her silence. "Quit your job. Travel. See where the road takes you. At the end of the day, when you close your eyes before sleep, think about it. What do we all want? We want to love and be loved. We want to belong. We want to see the world, but we want to go home to the embrace of people who care. That's all there is. There isn't *more*."

Her sadness dissipated as he spoke, replaced by a bristling annoyance. Will made her feel like a child. Like he was the wise and knowing one, and Selena was the misbehaved bad girl, the one making the big mistake. She hated that feeling, and she had it a lot with Will. She didn't want a daddy; she wanted a partner.

She'd taken back her hand, shifted away.

"I'm a grown woman, Will," she said. "I know who I am, where I am going. And I don't need you to explain to me the true nature of what we all want."

He looked down at his glass, and when he looked at her again, she saw how much she'd hurt him. Something welled in her and she moved over to his side of the table, slid into the booth beside him. She reached for him then, on impulse, and kissed him long and slow on the mouth.

"I'm sorry," she whispered, her lips against his neck. "I'll always love you. But not the way I love him."

She left him at the bar that night but thought about him endlessly all that week. She had an inkling that he might be right, woke up at night remembering that last kiss, his eyes, his words. But the wedding, it was a runaway train—costing a fortune, friends and family coming from all over the country, a dress from Paris, the stunning invitations, the forest of flowers. There had been no stopping it.

Now, nearly ten years later, she pushed through the fashionably distressed metal door and stepped into the warmth of the low-lit wine bar.

She spotted Martha right away; she'd grabbed a booth in the far corner of the space. Conversation was a hum, a current run under by a strain of soft piano music, as Selena made her way past the bar.

There it was again, that feeling of knowing her, the tingle of recognition.

Martha's dark hair was twisted into a thick plait that draped over her shoulder like a snake, a contrast against the light gray of her tasteful silk blouse; she was as erect and slim as a dancer. Martha smiled when she caught sight of Selena—it was genuine and sweet, the expression of a woman happy to see a friend. Selena had been carrying a tension, a sense of foreboding. It all faded.

Had she misread this?

She shouldn't be here. She knew that. Will had expressly told her not to engage.

What had led her to reach out to this stranger? And why was Selena so pleased to see her, as if they were old friends?

After that late-night text, she drove into the city. She hadn't been out of her house after 11:00 p.m. since Stephen was born. Nobody told you that when you became a parent, you became a child again; it was early bedtimes and grilled cheese sandwiches for all. Every date night was a negotiation, every invitation that you actually had the desire or energy to accept became a strategic maneuver that may or may not work out after all. It was back to park playgrounds, soccer fields, and Chuck E. Cheese's.

So, in spite of the odd nature of her outing, the chaos of her life, Selena felt a little thrill at being out, alone, close to midnight, in the city.

She slid in across from Martha.

"So glad you could make it out," said Martha. "I wouldn't have pegged you for a night owl."

"Not usually, but that meeting ran late, and I decided to stay in the city. My husband's away; my kids are at my mom's. So—why not?" She offered a conspiratorial wink.

"Live dangerously, right?"

"Right!"

Selena shifted off her coat, looked at the wine list and, when the waiter who was also the bartender arrived, ordered a cabernet.

"I was surprised to hear from you," Selena said. Light, chatty. "How did you get my number?"

Martha tilted her head a little, smiled. "You gave me your card."

"Did I?"

Martha dug through her bag and came out with the blue-and-white card, handing it over to Selena. The other woman's nails, bloodred, glittered in the candlelight.

"Oh," she said, staring at it. She had no memory at all of the exchange. "That vodka must have hit me harder than I thought."

"Me, too," said Martha, rolling her eyes. "Look. The reason I reached out—"

The bartender came with Selena's wine and Martha paused, thanking him. A moment passed between the two, a lingering look, a smile. Oh, right—that. People flirted, hooked up when they were free and single. Martha was a stunning beauty; she could probably have any man she wanted.

"I shouldn't have said what I said," Martha went on when he'd left them. "Any of it. I'm embarrassed."

Selena sipped from her glass, feeling its warmth, and allowing the liquid to wash away any lingering tension. Now that she knew she'd given Martha her card, the texts seemed way less unsettling. More like just someone looking to connect, like Will said. But—when? She did not remember at all.

And then there was Martha—light, warm, like any of Selena's friends. She'd liked Martha on sight; she remembered that now. Right away there had been a connection. She still felt it.

Selena lifted a palm. "It's totally fine. It's in the vault. Just between us."

Martha smiled gratefully. Selena twisted the stem of her glass, the red sloshing inside.

"I'd had such a bad day—and you have such a warm energy," Martha went on. "And I just felt like I wanted to spill my guts to you."

"I get it," said Selena, leaning forward, lowering her voice. "I'm embarrassed, too. And after all of that, it turned out that my situation was a false alarm."

Martha blinked. Was there a little flash of surprise on her face? "Oh?"

"I was just being paranoid," Selena said, going for a self-deprecating smile. "My husband and I have hit some rough patches in the past. And I have trust issues to begin with. But there was nothing going on at all."

More lies.

"Well, that's a relief, right?" Martha took a sip of her wine, a sparkling rosé. "Here's to problems just going away."

They clinked glasses over the candle between them.

"What about you?" asked Selena.

"I broke it off with my boss." Martha sat up a little straighter. "He took it like a gentleman, and it's business as usual—for now. I do think I need to find another job."

Was the other woman lying, too? Did she reach out over and over because she too regretted what she had said to a stranger? Well, that was fine. They could each tell their lies and keep their little secrets.

"That's great," said Selena, touching the other woman's hand. "You did the right thing."

"After we met, I wondered what you must have thought of me. A woman sleeping with a married man."

"Hey," Selena said with a wave of her hand. "We all make mistakes, errors in judgment, right?"

A couple nestled at the table behind Martha—young and in love. *Just wait*, thought Selena, surprised at her own bitterness. At another table, two women leaned in close, talking in whispers. The bartender dried glasses, most of the seats in front of him empty on a rainy Monday night. He kept glancing at Martha, and Selena noticed his powerful build, how defined were the muscles on his arms. On almost every table, smartphones glowed.

"So, what happened with your husband?" asked Martha, looking down at the table. "How did the conversation go?"

What she wanted to say: *I confronted him. We had a huge blowout. I threw a toy robot at him. My son heard everything. I kicked Graham out and only let him come home because Oliver saw him sitting outside in the car, stalking the house. Oh, and now the nanny's missing. I have no idea what's going to happen next.*

"I confronted him," she said instead, keeping her tone light and measured. "And he assured me that there wasn't anything going on."

Martha kept an intense gaze on Selena. "Okay. And you believe him."

"I do," Selena said with a shrug. "I have to. He's my husband."

Martha lifted her eyebrows. "Is that how it works?"

Selena regarded the other woman. "More or less. If you don't have trust, you don't have much."

God, she was so full of shit. But Martha lifted her glass as if in cheers to the truth.

"I've never been married, not even close," said Martha. "So what do I know?"

Martha looked down at an emerald ring she wore on her right hand, turned it, its brilliance catching the candlelight. A beautiful cushion cut in a white gold band.

"In fact, I'm not sure I'm the marrying type," Martha went on.

"No?"

Selena couldn't help but take in the details of the other woman—her perfect manicure, the expensive drape of her clothes, her dewy flawless skin. This was a woman who spent a lot of time on her appearance—one who had a lot of time to spend. And money.

"My parents—they weren't happy," the other woman said. "There was violence. Infidelity. I guess I carry that with me."

There was something about the way she said it and Selena felt a jolt. Did they really have that thing in common? Of course, lots of people grew up caught in the crossfire of a bad marriage. Or was it some kind of dig? Did this woman know more about Selena than she should? No. That was crazy. How could she?

Her phone pinged. Graham: What the hell are you doing in Tribeca? Did you leave with Will?

He was obviously tracking her. She ignored his text. He didn't have a right to get weird about where she was and who she was with. He could fuck right off.

"That's hard," Selena said, keeping her voice lightly sympathetic.

"Did your parents have a happy marriage?" asked Martha.

What was it about Martha? This uncomfortable insta-intimacy. She wanted to tell Martha that her father had been chronically unfaithful, that her mother had endured for the sake of her children. That Selena believed it had scarred her, the way it had Martha. But she didn't. She was here for damage control, not to reveal *more* personal things about herself to this woman. She wanted to extract herself gracefully from this mess, not become more entangled.

"No," said Selena. "Not really. But my mother's second marriage is happy. So maybe it's just about finding the right person."

"Well," said Martha, draining her rosé and lifting her hand to the waiter for another. He practically raced over to take her empty glass. "You seem like someone who really has her life together."

Selena laughed, feeling a rush of pleasure that at least she was putting up a good front. "I hope that's true. I wonder if anyone ever feels like she has her life totally together."

Martha smiled. "Maybe not."

"Most of the people I know are just making it up as they go along. Good days. Bad days. That's how it goes, I think, maybe for everyone."

Another text from Graham: I know you never stopped caring about him. There are all kinds of infidelity, you know, Selena.

Oh, really. He was going to try to pull that crap? Selena picked up the phone, ignoring his second text, and stowed it in her bag.

Martha nodded toward where Selena's phone had rested. "Hubby wondering where you are?"

"He is," she said. "I should probably head out after this one."

The waiter brought another glass for each of them. She hadn't even realized that hers was nearly empty.

"I thought he was away."

Shit. "He is. But he still wants to say good-night."

"Sweet."

Selena took another sip of her wine. She felt the fatigue of this awful day pull on her eyelids, settle like an ache in her head. That sense of freedom she felt when she first left the house and headed into the city now felt more like an unmooring, like she could just float away into space.

"So what about the nanny?" Martha asked. "Are you keeping her on? Even after your suspicions?"

She had managed to push Geneva completely out of her mind. She'd always been good at that, putting unpleasant things away to focus on something else. Maybe she got it from her mother.

"Well, that might not be an issue," she said. "She didn't show up for work today. That's why the kids went to my mom's place."

"Oh, wow," said Martha. "That's weird, huh?"

"People can be unreliable," said Selena. Again, the urge to tell all was strong. Selena took another sip of her wine instead.

"Kind of a coincidence, though, right? You confront your husband and the nanny disappears."

Something cold moved up Selena's spine. She thought of that moment when she felt Graham staring at her from the bay window. How strange he seemed.

He'd never hurt anyone. Not like that. Why did she feel the need to keep reassuring herself? Maybe because a part of her, something buried deep, knew it wasn't exactly true. That, in fact, he had hurt someone once.

"I'm not sure one thing has to do with the other." She knew it sounded stiff.

"Oh," said Martha, waving her hand. She issued a little laugh. "Don't mind me. I just have a dark imagination. Of course, you know your husband, you trust him. And there must be a million good nannies out there. Probably for the best."

A heartbeat, a sip of wine. Martha made a quick glance at her own phone.

"Things always happen for a reason," said Selena.

"Exactly."

They chatted a while—about restaurants they liked, plays

they'd seen, married life, single life. It was easy, enjoyable, and for a while she forgot all about the ugliness waiting outside the door and it just felt like one of those stolen hours with a friend, where everything was easy. The dark reason for her errand seemed distant, almost incidental.

"It's really nice getting to know you," said Martha. She motioned for the check, and when it came, insisted on footing the bill. "I don't have many female friends."

All the worst women said that, those who vamped for male attention, as they gossiped, sabotaged and backstabbed, then acted confused when other women didn't "like" them. She supposed it tracked; Martha *had* slept with her married boss.

"Do you have any family?"

A quick shake of her head. "My parents are both gone."

"I'm sorry," Selena said. The other woman wore an easy expression, a slight smile. But Selena could almost feel her disconnection, her loneliness. All of this made more sense; maybe she *was* someone just looking for a friend.

"And no one serious?"

"No," she said. "Like I said, trust issues, I guess. I can't seem to find 'the one,' you know?"

Selena nodded, looked down at her glass. *And you might not even recognize him when you do find him.* "It's not easy."

"You're lucky."

"Well," said Selena. She felt a twist of guilt, thought about her social media posts. What a fraud she was. "A long marriage takes work, compromise, all these little negotiations. It's not all champagne and roses."

"No," said Martha smiling. "I'm sure not. But someone like you—smart, attractive, a loving mom and wife—you deserve a good man. Someone who takes care of you, protects you, loves you well. Someone who's faithful."

Selena cast her eyes down again to her now empty glass, feeling the weight of the words.

"I have that," she whispered. "I'm blessed."

"Some women accept far less," Martha said. "They shouldn't."

There it was again, that dark tone. Martha held Selena's eyes when she lifted them again, and Selena felt a chill move through her.

"Like my mother," said Martha. "She thought my father was one kind of man. It turned out that he was something so different. She just—put up with it for so long. Why do women stay?"

"Inertia," said Selena. Her throat felt dry. "For the kids. Maybe fear. There's a psychology to abuse. My mother works at a shelter now. Sometimes people just don't know how to get away."

The other woman's gaze was an abyss, dark, unreadable. It was oddly hypnotic.

"Like I said. You have a good man who treats you like you deserve. Lucky girl."

The blood rushed in Selena's ears. "Yes. Very lucky."

"And if you ever found out that your husband was not the man you thought he was, would you leave him?"

"I'd like to think so," she said. "Marriage—it's complicated."

Martha drained the rest of her glass. "Another?"

"This has been—*so great*," Selena said. She sat up, took a deep breath, breaking the spell. "But I should get going."

"Thanks for reaching out," said Martha with a warm smile. "I'm glad we connected."

"Me, too. At a certain point in your life you think that maybe you're too old to make new friends," said Selena. "But that's obviously not true."

"Aw, I love that. Thank you," said Martha. She seemed genuinely pleased, her smile warm.

Whatever darkness Selena sensed was gone, replaced by friendliness and warmth. Was it her imagination? Her own fears? The darkness in her own life?

Now, Selena inwardly congratulated herself on a job well done. She'd sealed the relationship, made sense of their encounter on the train—they both had secrets they wanted kept—and enlisted Martha as a friend. It would have been better if Selena had never opened her mouth, of course, but at least she felt like the situation was in hand. Of course, if something had happened to Geneva, if her disappearance became a news story, would she be able to trust Martha? Probably not. She was still hoping that it wouldn't come to that.

"Let's do this again soon," said Selena.

"Definitely. And, hey, you know, if you ever need to talk to someone—about anything—let me know. I'm a good listener. No judgments. I like to think of myself as a solution architect."

"A solution architect."

"There's always a solution for any problem. And I like to find it." There it was again, that sort of dark glint Selena had intuited on the train. Something slithering beneath the surface.

"That's an important skill," Selena said with a wink, as if she was in on the joke.

"Because problems don't always just go away."

"That's very true."

They embraced, and Martha held on just a second longer than Selena, pulling her back a little then finally releasing her. For reasons she couldn't explain, Selena felt a rush of heat to her cheeks, a strong urge to get away.

"Well, same here," said Selena. "Call any time."

"I'm going to stick around for a while," said Martha, subtly shifting her gaze to the bartender. She took her seat again.

"Oh," said Selena. She'd almost never been single—a serious high school boyfriend, then Will, then Graham. But her friends talked about it—the excitement of random hookups, also the loneliness, the frustration of never finding the right guy, the dating apps, and failed encounters. The dangerous moments when someone got too aggressive, wouldn't take no for an answer. The nice guys who suddenly turned creepy after too much alcohol.

The bartender was watching Martha in the reflection of the

mirror behind the bar, a slight smile on his full lips. He ran a hand through his thick, dark hair, and Selena noticed a tribal tattoo on his wrist.

"Well," she said. "Be careful, okay?"

Martha smiled sweetly, reached out to squeeze Selena's arm. "You're a good friend."

On the street, instead of walking back to the parking garage in the rain, Selena caught a cab and climbed inside.

"Where to?" asked the cabbie.

She thought about it a moment. Back to the car, then the long ride home? Back to a confrontation with Graham, another sleepless night. No. She gave the cab driver Will's address, then dropped him a text.

He answered right away: The doorman will let you up.

On the way uptown, she scrolled through the pictures in a text from her mom. The boys were asleep in their beds.

Everything is okay, her mother had written with the photographs. This too shall pass.

TWENTY-ONE
Anne

ONE OF HER gifts was following people. There was a skill to it, a craft. Most people didn't imagine that they were being followed, so that was a built-in advantage.

Beyond that, these days, most people weren't present at all; they weren't paying attention. If they weren't lost in the storm of their own inner lives, they were numbing themselves with their devices. They were either obsessed with their wants, needs, grudges, aspirations, insecurities, watching a movie of themselves on the inside of their brains, or they were playing Candy Crush, trolling through social media, sending or receiving inane texts about the minutiae of their lives.

So these days, it was easy to observe, to move unseen through the world, to sneak up behind, easier than it had ever been.

Anne let Selena leave, let the other woman think that her new slutty friend was hanging around to hook up with the bartender. Which she could, of course. She could have him, or really almost anyone. But why? He was hot enough, but what was the point? She'd had Hugh that very afternoon; she could still feel him.

She waited a beat, then gathered up her things, and followed Selena. The other woman was still on the curb, hand in the air. Anne stayed inside the door, watching. A cab pulled up and Selena ducked inside; Anne grabbed the cab that pulled up right behind.

"Follow the taxi in front of you," she said to the driver.

He didn't respond, which she took as an assent. His phone rang, and he started talking in a language she didn't understand. West Slavic? Russian? Polish?

Selena's cab raced uptown, Anne close behind.

"Where are you going?" she whispered, though she had an inkling.

Prediction. That was her other gift. Where would Selena go if she found herself suddenly free from the things that held her to her life? When things got rocky, the ground shifting, to whom would Selena turn?

Up Tenth Avenue, across town through the park via Seventy-Ninth, then up Madison. The Upper East Side. The streets were slick; had it rained?

It was so easy to infiltrate a life these days between social media and everyone's insatiable desire to broadcast their day-to-day, the show they put on of themselves. It only took Anne a couple of hours to piece together a picture of almost anyone's life, where they lived and worked, where they shopped, ate, partied, where their kids went to school. It had never been easier to gain private information and access. People just gave it all away now, often without even realizing it.

Of course, she'd devoted more than a few hours to Selena, much more. Their encounter on the train was anything but chance. There was very little she didn't know about Selena Murphy. She even knew things about Selena that the other woman didn't know about herself.

When Selena's cab came to a stop, Anne's driver pulled over, too. Still talking, meter running. He seemed to know to sit and wait. Anne watched as her slim and elegant friend exited the cab and quickly ducked into a fancy doorman building with a maroon awning.

Anne snapped a picture quickly with her phone.

Well, she thought, that didn't take long.

She watched as Selena had a quick, smiling exchange with the doorman, then disappeared into the luxe lobby. The lawyer, the ex. The first and last safe place Selena had known. She should have married him.

As much as she knew about Selena Murphy, the woman she met tonight had surprised her. Anne had expected her to be frazzled, confessional, insecure. But the woman who'd sat across from her at the bar was put together, intelligent and in control. She lied, easily and with purpose. She was calculating.

She was both stronger and smarter than Anne would have imagined. Not good traits in a mark.

"This plan is flawed." Pop. "And it's flawed because it's personal. I taught you better. You chose her for the wrong reasons. Pull the plug."

"I know, I know," she said out loud, startling at the sound of her own voice.

But the taxi driver, if he heard Anne at all, probably assumed that she, too, was talking on the phone. She felt a buzz of anxiety, which quickly turned to a simmering anger. No, it wasn't anger. It was something darker, meaner.

"Rage," Pop never failed to mention. "It makes us sloppy. And in our business sloppiness kills. Remember that?"

"What?" asked the driver, glancing at her in the rearview mirror. "Where to next? Just sit? The meter is running."

She ticked through her options. She had already broken a hundred rules for Selena. Time to retreat. Regroup. Time to turn up the heat on this enterprise and make something happen.

"Grand Central," she said.

The cab started to move, the driver still talking and talking. Who was on the other line? she wondered.

"Remember Bridget?" asked Pop beside her. She jumped. Lately, he'd been more of a shade, a shadow, fading in and out. But now he was there, flesh and bone. She reached for him, but then he was gone.

"How could I forget?" she said, looking out the window as they dipped into the park.

TWENTY-TWO

Pearl

SHE AND POP were on the move again. That sweet little house in Pecos was a distant memory. Since then, there had been an isolated cabin outside of Boulder, a run-down ranch in Amarillo, a two-story in Phoenix. She'd been Mary, Beth, Sarah. Pop had been Jim, Chris, Bill.

Pop was at the wheel of their used Volvo, but he had gone dark—as she liked to think of it.

When things went badly or not as he anticipated, or if something made him angry, he kind of checked out. He got this blank look, stopped talking. It was unsettling at first; once he was nearly catatonic for an afternoon, sitting on the couch, staring at the dark fireplace. She tried everything to get him to respond. Talking. Yelling. Crying. She shook him. Hit him. Finally, she just lay on the floor at his feet and waited. When he came back to himself, he didn't remember anything about the last few hours.

"I'm sorry," he told her. He held her that day, and she let him, though physical affection between them was rare. "It happens sometimes. Just ride it out."

He'd come home to the Phoenix house—which she'd really liked—and started packing without a word to her. She'd followed suit without asking why. Maybe it was her years with Stella; she was accustomed to following nonverbal cues quickly and without question. All of her and Pop's belongings fit into a roller suitcase each. They made sure to take everything. They cleaned the place vigorously, leaving no trace of themselves behind. Or, anyway, that was the plan.

That had been Phoenix—hot, flat, red. Friendly people, lots of smiling faces, a definite Southwest hipster vibe. Pop's "girlfriend" had been a middle-aged accountant that Pop had met via a dating app—Bridget.

What did they want? That was the first thing to find out.

And they will always tell. All you have to do is watch and listen.

Maybe they won't tell you with their words. They may not even truly know themselves. But they will tell you with the way they wear their hair, how they do their makeup, how they dress. They'll tell you by their favorite song, book, movie. What they say about their parents, how they hold their bodies, whether they look you in the eye, whether they look at themselves in the mirror when they walk by.

An unmarried woman of a certain age—that was easy. She wanted the fairy tale, the one that had been promised all her life. She wanted that long-awaited prince, the one who made all those frogs worthwhile, if there had been any frogs at all. She ached for romance, attention, the love that made up for all those lonely nights, that closet full of bridesmaid dresses, the Christmases she spent alone. After all that time, she wanted to be able to say, *I was just waiting for you.*

And Pop was good. He was very, very good at giving women what they wanted.

He was loving, attentive, respectful. A listener. A doer. He was handy, someone who could fix broken things and wanted to. He cooked.

And Anne—or Mary, or Beth, or whoever she was at the time. She was the sweet icing on the cake. The latchkey child raised by her single father. The one looking for a mother, a friend—but old enough to take care of herself. Together they offered the insta-family. This might send a young woman with good prospects running. But not the woman who worried that she missed out on everything—true love, children, grandchildren. For that woman, Anne was part of the prize package.

And she played her role to perfection. Rarely she had to play the role in person; most often it all happened online—email and the occasional FaceTime conversation. She'd be shy at first, slow to warm. Eventually, she'd come around. Start calling Pop's new lady friend of her own accord—asking for advice on this or that. She'd send a funny text or two. A meme. An adorable cat video.

"You're a natural," Pop said. "But don't overdo it. Don't reveal too much, don't give too much. And, whatever you do, don't fall in love." She never did, of course. But Anne made sure they fell in love with her.

Then, after the mark—which was a cold word and didn't convey the whole truth of it—was in love, baited and hooked, just days before they were all supposed to meet for the first time, Anne or Beth or Mary would suddenly fall ill. Usually while she and Pop were away "on vacation" ostensibly in the location, maybe, where they were all to meet. Of course, they were nowhere near that place, nor would they ever be. Or maybe they'd been robbed, Pop's wallet stolen, his beautiful daughter clinging to life after the attack. The mark rarely hesitated to wire the money he needed. Five thousand, ten thousand, sometimes more. These were short games, usually a couple of months at most.

Once the money had been wired—or if the mark got suspicious, tried to fly in for a rescue—then poof—they disappeared. Online profiles deleted, burner phones discarded, email accounts canceled. Most women would never even report the crime. Shame kept them quiet. These were wealthy, accomplished women. How, they'd ask themselves, could they have been so easily duped?

But Bridget? Anne had sensed that she was not the typical mark—she had an edge, there was a distant coldness. She wasn't as enamored of Anne as the others had been. Anne said something to Pop about it, but he wasn't hearing it. She was a big fish, lots of money. But when he tried to reel it in, Bridget didn't wire the cash. First, she offered to fly in to help. Then she offered to send a lawyer. She called and called Pop's burner phone. Finally, she sent an email threatening to call the police. Pop had to shut everything down fast—the online profile, the email account, the Skype ID, the phone. Even though there was no way Bridget could know where they physically lived, they left the Phoenix house.

They were miles away, nearly to El Paso, when Pop finally spoke.

"How did you know?"

They were on a dark desert highway, city lights blinking off in the distance, sky rattling with stars. She watched them through the moon roof. They gave her a kind of comfort, reminding her that nothing mattered very much. There was stardust in her bones. Not so long ago, she hadn't been here at all. One day she'd be gone for good. And she was okay with that.

"I just didn't get the warm fuzzies. She didn't have smiley eyes when she looked at me. I think she had trust issues."

"I didn't see it," he said, gripping the wheel.

She'd noticed that his knuckles were raw, that he had a slight bruise on his cheekbone. She knew better than to ask him about it. Sometimes he went out at night, drank too much. He didn't always remember what happened.

"You can't win them all," she said.

It was something Stella used to say. She should know. Anne remembered random things about her mother—the smell of her perfume—Chanel No. 5—the sandpaper of her laughter, how cold her feet and hands always were—how she'd bury her toes under Pearl as they lay on the couch together. Sometimes details like that came back, and she almost felt something then. A tugging at her heart.

"Maybe I'm losing my touch," said Pop. "They say it happens. Your instincts dull."

"Maybe you should retire." It was kind of a dig. She was mad. She'd liked the Phoenix house; she'd made a friend, a boy in the neighborhood.

She thought he'd go dark again. She almost wanted him to; that way she could be mad in quiet.

"Not just yet," he said. "I'm not ready to retire yet."

"Can she find us?"

"No," he said quickly. "No way. We're ghosts."

But he didn't sound entirely sure. And it would turn out that he was wrong.

TWENTY-THREE

Hunter

HUNTER ROSS ENTERED the diner, the little bell jingling to announce his arrival. Not that anyone would hear it over the din. The waitress at the counter waved to him, then nodded with a knowing smile over toward the rowdy group of older men in the back. Hunter issued a sigh and made his way toward them.

Retirement didn't appeal to Hunter Ross. In fact, he had actively started to dread his Tuesday morning breakfast group, a bunch of old guys out to pasture from various gritty professions. On any given Tuesday, there might be a cop, a lawyer, a firefighter, an EMT, and an FBI agent. Men who had strongly identified with their work, and who now used all that pent-up energy to complain about the state of the nation and the world.

They were out of shape. They watched too much television. And, frankly, the way they ate—giant chili cheese omelets and piles of hash browns, sides of bacon, thick sausage links, pints of juice, gallons of coffee—made Hunter nervous.

Some Tuesday soon, one of these old guys was just going to stroke out right in front of him. Not if. When.

They called him "son." Because Hunter was in his late fifties, and they were all pushing seventy. He wasn't *technically* retired, because since leaving the job, he'd hung out a shingle and investigated cold cases for families, understaffed police departments, whoever had a case that had run short of leads, time, money, energy. Sometimes he did it for free.

The group chided him for working when he could just be taking it easy. But they were jealous, too, he could tell. When you did the kind of jobs these guys did, it was never easy to just let it go. There was always a fire, a crime, a victim, the need for a first responder. Other, younger people were running to the rescue now.

Hunter had three cases going right now—a missing teenager who was probably a runaway, a couple—doomsday preppers, who had gone off the grid and not been heard from since—and something that was personal, a case he hadn't been able to solve that was nearing its ten-year anniversary. Because of that milestone, the old case had been on his mind lately, making him cranky. Maybe if he got some closure on that, he could think about that European riverboat trip his wife was pushing for.

He took his seat at the table.

"You're late, son," said Phil, retired beat cop, tall and skinny-fat—a naturally lean guy who never met a vegetable he could stand, who would only run if chased, who hydrated primarily with bourbon. His belly hung over his belt, tenuously kept in place by his golf shirt. "We ordered for you."

"Great," Hunter said, settling in next to Andrew. "Because my cholesterol isn't high enough."

"He's *busy*, can't always *get here*, you know," said Ray the firefighter, expansive with sarcasm. He had a heart attack last year but bounced back; now he had egg whites—smothered in cheese, with a side of bacon. "This one still thinks he's going to save the world. One cold case at a time."

"What are you working on, champ?" asked Andrew, the retired lawyer who now did pro bono work for at-risk kids in the system. He was another one who couldn't let go.

"I got a lead on my runaway," he said. "I'm on my way to check it out. Just gonna grab a coffee and go."

"She *ran away*. Why not just let her go?" Jay, the other cop. Bitter as hell. Divorced. Estranged from his kids. The job had chewed him and spit him out.

Hunter shrugged. "Family's still looking."

Jennie had been missing more than a year. She was sixteen years old but looked much older. There was abuse from her biological father, though her mother and stepfather were good people, trying to help her. Jennie fell in with a group that was taking oxy. Her mother quickly lost control of the situation. And then she was gone.

Jay rubbed at his full salt-and-pepper beard. "They did a better job, maybe she'd still be at home."

The other guys made affirming noises, like they were all parents of the year.

"Maybe," said Hunter.

That was his way, easy deflection, allow other people's negativity to roll over him and pass by. Hunter didn't argue. It used to drive his wife crazy until she took up yoga and meditation. Now she got it. Hunter couldn't touch his own toes, but he knew that you couldn't win an argument. Anything you fight against gets stronger.

"He's one of those *everybody counts* cops," said Andrew. Andrew gave him a hearty pat on the back. "Reads too many Michael Connelly novels. Thinks he's Bosch."

"Everybody does count," said Hunter. "Everybody counts to me."

Mavis brought the food, stacked plates of eggs, pancakes, waffles, breakfast meats, donuts, and was greeted with enthusiasm from the group. They were like a bunch of kids at a birthday party when the cake came, lighting up and shouting.

She put a black coffee and an egg white and avocado on rye in front of Hunter.

"Hey, that's not what I ordered for him," said Bill in mock annoyance.

"But that's what he gets every week," said Mavis with a knowing smile.

He shot her a grateful look, because god knew if someone put a chili cheese omelet in front of him, he was going to eat it. He was only human.

"Thanks, Mavis."

They all started to eat—and talk. As the conversation veered from politics to health care to reverse mortgages to sports, they got loud—shouting, laughing, ribbing each other. Hunter mostly just listened. This is why he came. He liked these guys, in spite of all their bad habits and rough edges. All of them had spent their lives on the front lines of humanity. Their combined knowledge, experience and earned wisdom were incalculable. He brought his cases here and "workshopped" them. They always had ideas—some of them wrong, some of them right, almost all of them leading him down a road he might not have found on his own.

It had been Phil who suggested that he Facebook-stalk Jennie Murray, his runaway. If he hadn't done that, he might have missed the post from her ex. *Hey, I thought I saw you at Tommy's Cove the other night. Was that you?*

Jennie hadn't answered, but Hunter searched the place out online and discovered it was a bar a couple of towns over, a dive frequented by bikers. This was Hunter's first lead in a month.

In a brief lull, he spoke up. "Anyone hear of Tommy's Cove?"

"Tommy's Cove?" said Phil, with a knowing nod. "Lots of truckers, bikers through there. Drugs. If she's there, she's probably turning tricks for oxy or meth."

Hunter had figured as much. There weren't that many ways for a drug-addled girl to get by.

"Even if you bring her back and get her into rehab," said Jay, "she'll be back out there within six months. They don't get clean. Not from that."

That was a typical cop's attitude. Bad stayed bad. But it wasn't always true.

"Everyone deserves a chance to straighten her life out," said Andrew.

Hunter's thoughts turned to Stella and Pearl Behr, his grudge match, as he'd come to think of it. The case he'd never solved, the girl who was still out there either living a life or buried deep. The woman who'd been murdered and forgotten by everyone but Hunter—whom she'd never met. A struggling single mother with a teenage daughter and a failing business, a string of loser boyfriends. She was strangled in her own bed, her child taken.

Everyone deserves a chance to straighten her life out. Some people never got it.

"Want some company?" asked Andrew. The conversation had gone on without Hunter, who was staring into the muddy circle of his coffee.

"Sure thing," said Hunter. It was always good to have a partner.

He drained his cup, polished off his sandwich, grabbing a single piece of bacon from Phil's plate. Then he left to jeers and shouted goodbyes. No doubt the other restaurant patrons would be happy when they all left.

They were walking out the door when something on the television screen mounted in the corner of the restaurant caught his eye.

The tagline across the bottom of the screen read: Missing Nanny.

He walked over to the set, reached for the remote that sat on the counter and turned it up a little. "Twenty-five-year-old

Geneva Markson didn't turn up for work yesterday," said the newscaster, "after her sister reported her missing this weekend. On Monday, police discovered her abandoned car in the well-heeled neighborhood of her employers. And so far, there are no clues as to her whereabouts, no immediate indication of foul play. If anyone knows the location of this young woman, police are asking that they please call this tip line."

The face swam before his eyes, oddly familiar. He knew her. He'd seen her before. And he never forgot a face. There was a tingle in the back of his skull as he dug through the recesses of his memory. Where? When?

"What's up?" asked Andrew, who had come to stand behind him. "You know her?"

"Maybe," said Hunter.

After they'd followed up this lead, he'd go back home and scour his old files. He'd make some calls from the car. He wasn't as sharp as he used to be. But he'd remember eventually.

Everybody counts. Of all the faces of all the missing kids he'd searched for, the murder victims for whom he'd sought some justice, the rape victims whom he'd promised would someday feel safe again when their attacker was caught, he'd never forgotten a single one.

TWENTY-FOUR

Selena

"HOW DID YOU SLEEP?" she asked Oliver, phone on speaker.

Will's bed was as enormous and soft as a cumulous cloud. She let herself sink in. In spite of everything, she'd had the best night's sleep she'd had in a while.

"Okay." Oliver had his pouty voice on, sleepy. He must have called her the second he opened his eyes.

"What's Paulo making for breakfast?" she asked, trying to keep it light.

"He said pancakes. I can hear him in the kitchen."

"Your favorite!" Her bright tone sank into the silence.

"When can I come home?"

"I"—not "we." He couldn't care less about Stephen; would leave him there if he could, wouldn't he? Was that normal?

"Really soon," she said.

"That's not an answer, Mom."

"Just," she said, took a breath. "Just go to school today. And by the time you get home this afternoon, I'll have an answer."

It might not be the answer you want, she thought but didn't say. At any rate, tonight she would stay at her mother's. She wasn't going home to Graham. Staying at Cora's might be the answer for now. For her and the boys.

"Okay," he said. She listened to the rasp of his breath.

The sheets were divine, crisp and silky all at once. Cost a fortune, she was sure. Will had taught her everything she knew about wine and art, about expensive fabrics, design. The sun was just peeking through the drawn dove-gray drapes. She pushed the button on the remote by the bed and watched as they glided silently open, revealing the milky gray of a city view.

"Where's Dad?"

"Still sleeping." She felt a pang of guilt. But it wasn't a lie. He probably was still sleeping, even if she wasn't there to say for sure.

"Did he sleep in his office again?"

You really couldn't fool your children, no matter how smart you thought you were.

"How did *you* sleep?" she asked, changing the subject.

"Stephen snored. All night."

Selena heard Will get up from the couch in the living room, where he'd slept. She listened to his footfalls as he headed down the hall to the bathroom.

They'd talked late into the night, she in a pair of his sweatpants and college T-shirt. He made a fire and they talked about Graham—how things had been hard since the kids were born. She didn't tell him everything. They talked about Geneva, about what might have happened to her, about the woman from the train, what she wanted. She had another glass of wine with him, was sleepy and relaxed in his company, in the dim light of the room.

"I hate that it's like this," he said. "But it's good having you here. Nice talking to you like this again. I've missed it—missed you. All these years."

She didn't know what to say. Had she missed him? Sometimes. Maybe. Missed what she imagined might have been. But life didn't work that way. You didn't know what lay on the road not traveled.

"You don't have to say anything," he said. "I know—it's complicated."

"I'm sorry I hurt you," she said. "I've always been sorry about that."

He shrugged. "Love is a lightning bolt. Sometimes there's no avoiding it. We don't always choose who we love or why. We can't make ourselves love someone we don't."

I do love you, she wanted to say. *I did. Maybe I didn't even know what love was then.* But she didn't say that, just stared at the fire. Then, "And Bella? Was that a lightning bolt?"

He smiled a little. "Bella? I think we were just really great friends and confused that for love."

"There are worse things to base a marriage on."

She should know.

"Yeah," he said. "But ultimately it's not enough. You need the heat first, the passion. If it cools and leaves friendship, that can work. But if it's never there, there's always something missing. And—you know—she really liked girls. Always had, just couldn't come to terms with it. Until she did."

"I'm sorry," she said, releasing a breath. "I know how it feels to discover someone you love is not who you think."

"I guess you do."

He kept his distance, giving her the couch, sitting in the big chair across from her. The room was filled with the electricity of mistakes about to be made. It would have been so easy. But. No. She was faithful and so was he. No matter what Graham had done, she wouldn't cheat.

Will rose after a few moments of silence. "I'm going to change the sheets on my bed," he said. "I'll take the couch."

"I'll take the couch."

"No way," he said. "No arguing."

In bed after Will had fallen asleep in the living room, she

didn't answer Graham's calls, but it didn't stop him from texting her until nearly 3:00 a.m.

Please come home. I'm so sorry.

I just need space and time to think, Graham. You have to give me that.

Can you ever forgive me?

Could she? Could she ever forgive him? She didn't have an answer.

"Paulo's calling for breakfast," said Oliver now.

"Okay," she said. "We'll call as soon as school's over. I love you, buddy."

"I love you, too."

"It's okay," she said. How many times did you say that as a parent? "Everything is okay."

The silence was heavy on the line; she sensed he wanted to say something else and she waited.

Then: "Mom, you hang up first."

"Love you," she said again. "Give Stephen a hug for me."

"Love you, Mom."

She ended the call with a weight on her heart. What a mess her life was. Just a year ago, if anyone had asked, she'd have said it was close to perfect. She thought Graham's issues were behind them. She was home with the boys, her husband happy at work.

This too shall pass. Even the good times.

Her phone pinged. Graham.

So how was your night with Will? Everything you remembered?

He slept on the couch, of course.

Really.

I've never cheated on you. Not about to start now.

I know that. I'm sorry. You never answered me. Can you ever forgive me? Is there a way forward for us?

Another question without an answer.

She saw herself moving on…selling the house, moving back to Manhattan. Working, forging ahead into the unknown of the future. Then, she thought of Oliver and Stephen, the devastation of their happy lives, and she was kneecapped. She was her mother, enduring the abuse, the bleak humiliation of it, for the sake of her children, withering under the pressure of maintaining a facade.

Her phone pinged again. Graham *again*.

Oh, shit.

What?

The cops are here.

If it was a ploy, which he was not above, it worked. She dialed his number but the call went to voice mail. Her throat was dry, belly clenched.

Why would the cops be there so early?

She put the phone down and walked into Will's beautifully appointed kitchen—where coffee had already been brewed in a gleaming machine that cost about as much as a used Volkswagen. Grabbing the remote, she flipped on the television, then felt the room spin and pitch as the bottom dropped out of her world.

On the screen was a picture of Geneva—smiling and lovely,

her wheat hair whipping around her face. The pretty image was made ominous by the red type beneath it reading: Missing Nanny.

"Twenty-five-year-old Geneva Markson didn't turn up for work yesterday, after her sister reported her missing this weekend," said the svelte, heavily coiffed newscaster. "On Monday, police discovered her abandoned car in the well-heeled neighborhood of her employers. Though there is no immediate indication of foul play, neither is there any clue as to her whereabouts. Two local men are being brought in for questioning, police say.

"If anyone knows the location of this young woman, police are asking that they please call this tip line."

Will came up behind Selena. "Oh, shit. Someone called the media."

"The police are at the house now," she managed, though she felt like she was sucking air through a straw. "Graham just texted."

"I'll get dressed and get over there."

She heard his voice, felt his presence—just before she passed out cold, knocking her head on the marble countertop on her way to the tile floor.

"Three may keep a secret, if two of them are dead."

—Benjamin Franklin,
Poor Richard's Almanac

PART 2

ALL OUR LITTLE LIES

TWENTY-FIVE

Selena

THERE WAS A kind of midafternoon light that Selena associated with illness. The way the sun had filtered through the gauzy pink drapes in her childhood bedroom when she was home sick from school. There was a special rosy hue to it, a hush to a house kept quiet so that she could rest. Maybe she'd hear her mother in the kitchen. Her father would be at work, her sister at school, and in that special glow it was as if time had slowed.

Today, in the living room of her own home, the light that came in through the drapes was a cruel white. There was a sickness, to be sure. The world outside was waiting, a wolf at the door, huffing and puffing.

Geneva was officially missing. Her husband, Graham, and Erik Tucker, her former employer, had both been brought in for questioning.

Selena sat on her couch with Detective Crowe across from her. His hair was wild, suit rumpled, purple fatigue shadowing his eyes. She was numb, head throbbing. She held an ice pack to the lump on the back of her skull. She'd just passed out cold.

Who did that? What if there was something seriously wrong with her?

Her husband was going to prison.

Her children would be all alone.

Reign it in, she told herself. *Pull yourself together.*

It was almost one, and her mother would be picking up the boys from school soon. She'd promised Oliver answers by the time he got home. She didn't have any. Not one. And now there were only more questions.

Where was Geneva?

What had Graham done?

How was she going to hold their life together for the boys?

She was shaking from deep in her core. She sat on her free hand, so that Detective Crowe wouldn't see how scared she was.

Detective Crowe had questions, too. She knew she shouldn't answer any of them. But here he was. There was something safe and upright about him, in the way he leaned toward her, gaze steady. Something comforting about his presence.

"How long did you know that Geneva Markson and your husband were having an affair?" he asked, voice gentle.

There was no point in lying now. The police apparently knew everything.

On the table in front of her, she stared at a printout of texts between Graham and Geneva. Somehow these had also been leaked to the media. Who would do that?

Graham: I'm still raw from fucking you. Hurts so good.

Geneva: I can still taste you in my mouth.

God. How disgusting. There were two full pages. She'd barely read any of it. But she'd read enough.

"About a week," she said. She sank back into the plush of the sofa. "I caught them on the nanny cam."

"So—you lied." He seemed tired with the knowledge. She was just another liar sitting before him, one of many probably.

"Yes," she said with a nod.

She almost apologized and then didn't. Because why should she? Why should her husband have fucked the nanny, and then that woman disappear?

And then, as if that wasn't bad enough, why should Graham and Geneva's disgusting, raunchy texts—revealed when police accessed Geneva's phone logs—have been leaked to the media this morning?

And then, after all of that, why should Selena have to apologize for trying to protect her children—her *life*—from the shameful actions of her husband?

"Why?" asked Detective Crowe. "Why did you lie to me?"

"Hmm," she said, putting a hand to her chin in mock wondering. "I don't *know.* Shame. Fear. A fervent hope that I could hold my life together until this was all revealed to be a silly mistake. Denial, maybe."

"Okay," he said, lifting a hand. "I get it. I do."

He'd come alone, without his partner—who was no doubt interrogating Graham. Will was at the station with them. She'd watched enough police procedure shows to know that this was probably by design. Separate the husband and wife. Catch Selena at home when she was weak and afraid, when the lawyer had bigger fish to fry.

She should have turned him away when he came to the door. That would have been the right and smart thing. *I can't talk to you without my lawyer present*, she should have said. But she hadn't. And now here they sat.

Maybe if she hadn't been alone reading those texts online, and all the comments about them on Twitter, on Reddit, she wouldn't have been so desperate for any kind of company. She was actually happy when she saw him standing there on the porch, an honest person looking for answers. Just like Selena.

"Can we agree to move forward with the truth?" he asked.

The truth. What a slippery concept.

"Yes."

"Did you know about the texts?"

"No." Heat rose from her neck to her cheeks.

The raunchy, dirty, humiliating missives added a new layer to Geneva's disappearance. There was some violence to the exchange—threats of bondage, punishment.

I want to spank you till you scream.

I'm going to tie you up and take you from behind.

Really? Not Graham's thing, Selena wouldn't have thought. But what did she know? Also leaked: Geneva's affair with Erik Tucker. There was apparently a text chain associated with that relationship, as well. Equally vile.

On Twitter there was already a trending hashtag: #TheNaughtyNanny.

Selena's phone was ringing and pinging every few minutes. She kept checking it to make sure it wasn't her mother or the school. The last text from Beth: I'm coming to your house.

Her house—which she thought was made of bricks, was made of straw.

There were other texts, too, between Graham and someone else. Apparently now they had access to his phone. More nastiness. Words used that Selena had never known to cross her husband's mind, let alone his lips. Those communications, too, were borderline violent, dark. Even more unsettling:

I know who you are. And I know what you did.

You won't get away with it. I promise.

She imagined they must have taken Graham's phone. But she didn't know. She didn't know how things like this worked. Would they want *her* phone? Was she required to give it to them if they didn't have a warrant?

Detective Crowe nodded toward the printouts on the table between them. Selena felt vulnerable suddenly. She shouldn't have let him in, should have waited for Will. Another mistake.

"Any idea who this might be?" he asked. "What this person might have seen? What Graham wasn't going to get away with?"

Amazingly, there was a part of her that still wanted to lie. *It was me*, she wanted to say. *Just a little role-playing game.*

Partially to protect her children, by protecting their father.

But mostly to protect herself, or the image of herself that she wanted people to hold. Selena—good mom, happily married, successful career woman. Perfect. Instagrammable. Better than her sister. Better than her friends. But you know, in a humble, generous way.

Humiliation had a taste, a thickness at the back of her throat.

Fear had a sound, a ringing in her ears.

"Mrs. Murphy."

"I don't know," she snapped. "How should I know?"

"Has he cheated before?"

"Yes," she said. She stared down at her wedding ring, the big diamond, the platinum band.

"More than once?" His voice was gentle.

She ran it down for him. The sexting with his ex-girlfriend, which he said was nothing more. The counseling. Then the incident in Vegas.

Crowe looked at his notes. "A stripper," he said. "Is that right? There was an assault."

"Yes."

"He propositioned a stripper after a lap dance, and when she declined, he assaulted her. A fight ensued between the club bouncers and Graham and his friends," he said.

"That's right," she said stiffly. Only her mother knew about this incident. Maybe her sister knew too. Selena always suspected them of gossiping about her behind her back.

"More counseling after that, I'm guessing," Detective Crowe said.

When she looked up at him, she expected to see mockery or judgment on his face. But instead she saw kindness, compassion.

"My wife," he said. "She cheated on me a couple of times before I got the message that she was always going to cheat. That it wasn't about me but about her."

He wasn't wearing a wedding ring.

"I'm sorry," she said.

He nodded. "I am, too."

Outside, she thought she heard voices, but it went quiet again. Would the media gather? she wondered. Probably. Wasn't that the way it worked now? A circus of news vans, true crime bloggers posting theories and pictures, endless phone calls, emails.

"It's obstruction, you know, that you didn't tell me any of this."

She was quiet a moment. Then, "I didn't think it was relevant. Truly."

He nodded. "I get it. There's a disconnect between those things and this thing for you. Those things—the texting was virtual, right? The woman in Vegas, almost an abstraction, far from his life with you. You didn't want to believe that he could have anything to do with Geneva's disappearance."

The words hung on the air, ominous. You didn't want to believe that your husband would hurt a young woman. Even though you *knew* he had already hurt another young woman.

"What about your husband's job?"

There was a dump of dread in her belly.

She knew, didn't she? On some level, she knew that he hadn't told her the real reason why he'd lost his job. Jaden, his boss, their friend, hadn't returned her calls. The last email Selena had received had been friendly, but brief. We miss seeing you! Sorry we've been so busy. Maybe we can plan something for the warmer months?

A clear blowoff.

Selena had ignored those instincts, too. She didn't want to know.

She was just like her mother.

"What about it?" she asked quietly.

"There were allegations from a junior member of his department."

She shook her head, not trusting her voice.

"You weren't aware."

Another shake. She didn't want to cry. If she started, it was going to get ugly.

"A coworker accused him of making advances, not taking rejection well. She said he became aggressive, threatening."

Again, the urge to defend. He said, she said. Wasn't this the minefield of the workplace these days? But no, she wouldn't do that. Wouldn't even think it. She wouldn't be another woman hiding the bad behavior of men.

Who was he? Who was her husband?

She remembered the bruised face of the Vegas stripper—her black eye, swollen purple mouth. A lap dance gone wrong. He wanted more; she declined. So he beat her. That was her husband; there was no disputing it. Even *he* didn't try to deny it. She'd flown to Vegas, bailed him out. He got a drunk and disorderly summons, paid a fine, flew home with her the next day.

But Selena still thought about that girl, a young woman he'd hurt because she didn't give him what he wanted. His infant son and wife asleep across the country, waiting for him.

Who was he? Who was *she* for staying with him? For burying that incident so deep in her subconscious so that it only surfaced when she was angry, or on sleepless nights when all her worries and fears danced and spun in the dim of her bedroom.

"Has he ever been violent with you?"

"No," she said quickly. "Never."

He pointed to her eyebrow, which was bruised from her fall.

"I fainted, hit my head on the way down."

They locked eyes and his were dark and deep, probing.

"Look," he said. "If you know more, if you have suspicions about what might have happened to Geneva, now is the time to help her. I know you want to protect your family, but a woman is missing."

She shook her head. "My husband, he's been unfaithful. He's lied to me. And, you know, in the best case, our marriage is probably over. But I don't believe he's capable of hurting anyone."

He raised his eyebrows at her. When he spoke, his voice was gentle.

"How can you say that? He *has* hurt someone."

"Acting violently when drunk is different than—whatever it is you're implying. Abducting, killing."

She hated the way she sounded, like an apologist. But it *was* different, wasn't it? "It's like a different profile, right?"

God, she was pathetic. Crowe's expression reflected a version of herself she didn't want to acknowledge.

"Violence escalates, Mrs. Murphy," he said. "In my experience violent men get more and more violent. When life stressors like job loss or problems in the marriage start to ramp up, those dark tendencies rise to the surface."

Dark tendencies.

Fear, panic constricted her breathing. Everything was slipping from her grasp. She reached for the frayed edges of her life and felt them slip through her fingers.

"She wasn't sleeping just with Graham," Selena said. Desperate. She sounded desperate. "What about Erik Tucker? Isn't he a suspect?"

So much for not throwing people under the bus. He didn't answer her, just looked down at his notes.

"Do you or your husband have access to any isolated property anywhere—a lake house, a hunting cabin? Anything like that."

"No."

Did he, though? His friend Sean had a place somewhere—was it in the Adirondacks? She didn't know if Graham had access, or how isolated it was. She told him as much; Crowe scribbled in his notebook.

"Why do you want to know that?"

He tilted his head. "Because a woman is *missing*, Mrs. Murphy. I want to know if there's someplace he might be keeping her."

Another blow to the gut. She picked up the ice pack again, but it had grown warm. The pounding in her head was reaching a crescendo. She wished she would just pass out again. Unconsciousness would be a blessed break from this nightmare.

"So, if you knew for a week that Geneva was sleeping with your husband—*why* didn't you at least fire her right away?"

Good question. It was an impossible thing to explain to anyone who was living outside of her head. Anyway, she was about to fire Geneva but then she disappeared.

"It's really hard to find a good nanny," she said stupidly.

He gave her a look. She slumped back into the couch.

"I don't know," she breathed. The truth. "Denial. I just felt numb, unsure of what to do. Graham was unemployed. I needed to work and make sure the kids were taken care of. She *was* a good nanny; I trusted her with the boys—just not my husband. And, I guess, I was biding my time, deciding what to do next."

She didn't expect him to understand. She didn't even understand herself. She was just chicken; that was the truth of it. She was afraid to blow up her life.

Her phone kept up its manic pinging and ringing.

"When I caught my wife the last time," he said, "it was almost like I didn't even care. The trust was already broken, and

I wasn't even sure why we were still married. It was a couple of weeks before I moved out, but in the meantime, we still went through the motions—got movies on Netflix, went out to dinner. We didn't have any kids, so there wasn't that complication."

She nodded. So maybe it wasn't so hard to understand.

"But I was angry," he said. "Deep inside, you know. Man, I had some dark thoughts about her, about the guy she was with."

She could see where he was going with this, stayed quiet. She pushed farther back into the cushions of the couch, just to put some distance between them.

"Did you think about hurting Geneva?" he asked when she didn't say anything.

Even though she was kind of expecting it, the world still stuttered.

"You're kidding, right?"

There had been a folder on the coffee table between them. He'd taken the printed pages of texts from it at the beginning of their conversation. Now, he retrieved a slim stack of photos and handed them to her. She flipped through a series of grainy images of her block. A fish-eye lens, obviously captured from personal doorbell cameras from the neighbor's devices, showed Geneva's progress from the front door, down the street, to her car.

She looked so small, young like a teenager. Her shoulders were slouched, her face set and sad. There she was in front of the house. Then walking past the neighbor's place. She reached for her car door, paused and she turned around as if something caught her attention. Most of the images were obscured by shrubs and trees, the cameras really only designed to capture the stoop. The late afternoon light was low.

In the final image, a second figure was captured, coming from up the block along the middle of the street. A black jacket, a baseball cap, jeans, boots. A slow dawning crept on Selena.

Though the face was obscured, something about the figure's carriage was familiar.

No, she thought. *Not possible.*

"Any idea who that might be?"

She leaned in closer, heart thumping. But the image was so grainy and indistinct, it was hard to identify gender. There were no other images capturing a front view.

She flipped through all the pictures again.

"After that, we don't have any other photos. They just disappear."

"Is it—a woman?" asked Selena.

"Small, slim, could be," he said.

Hands in pockets, an easy approach, casual.

"Awfully laid-back for a kidnapping, right? Not the kind of approach you'd expect."

"Kidnapping?" he asked, as if surprised.

"Well, that's the implication, right? That someone took Geneva, *has* her? You're asking about isolated properties. She didn't just run off with some other working mom's husband?"

"You're angry," he said.

She put the pictures down on the coffee table.

There was a woman I met on the train, she almost said. We talked. I told her about my husband, though I'm not even sure why I did. It got weird. She said something that has stayed with me. Didn't I ever just wish my problems would go away? Then, she texted me. I went to see her—I don't know why. Maybe because she knew too much about me. She called herself a solution architect.

Could this be her?

But she didn't say any of that.

Because—it was suspicious, wasn't it? Wasn't there a dark undercurrent to each of their encounters—the train, the bar? Wasn't there some tacit understanding that Selena should say nothing, and if she stayed quiet, then so would Martha? Even though there were no more secrets to keep. The affair, the disappearance, her shattered life would become the main news event of the moment, if it wasn't already. It would be the number one topic of conversation at school, at the tennis club, on the soccer field. It was one of those stories, salacious and bizarre, that captured the attention. The nanny you let into your home seduces your husband, sets fire to your life. And all because you wanted to work *and* be a mother.

And if that was Martha on the street with Geneva, then what did that mean?

"Do you recognize that person?" asked Detective Crowe.

She leaned in closer. Really, it could be anyone. A smaller young man, a large teenager. Eliza Tucker was petite, athletic, a runner. She, too, had reason to be enraged. But it was hard to imagine a preppy mom of two confronting Geneva on the street.

"No," said Selena. "I don't."

"Did Geneva mention anyone to you? Anyone bothering her, following her?"

He'd asked that before. "No. But if she was in the habit of sleeping with her employers, then blackmailing them, she probably had one or two people who didn't wish her well."

Her phone started ringing. She could see that it was her mother, told the detective so. Crowe gave her a nod.

"Mom," she said, answering.

"It's me." Oliver sounding pouty and tired.

"Hi, honey," she said releasing a breath. "How was school?"

"You said you'd have an answer for me, Mom. Can I come home?"

"Sweetie, I have to call you back, okay? In fact, just sit tight. I'll be there in a bit."

She heard him start to protest. "I love you, Oliver. Just sit tight."

She hung up with a twinge of guilt. Another text came through, pinging several times, but she stuffed the phone in her pocket. She only had to answer calls from her mom and her kids. Everyone else would have to wait.

"As you know, Geneva Markson was allegedly blackmailing Erik Tucker," said Detective Crowe, snapping Selena back to the moment. "He bought Geneva a car to keep her quiet about the affair."

"Okay." Selena knew this but still couldn't process it. Sweet, helpful Geneva. Now, the Naughty Nanny.

"What about you?" asked Detective Crowe. "Are there any large sums of money missing from your accounts? Any purchases your husband made that you didn't understand?"

Selena almost laughed. *She* had always been the one to manage all their finances, set the budgets, meet with the advisors, schedule all their savings for college and retirement. Graham never wanted anything to do with it. All their various purchases popped up in their accounting program. That was a lesson she'd learned from her mother: never be the woman who doesn't understand money.

If Geneva wanted to blackmail Graham, she'd have been out of luck. "No. Nothing like that."

"You have knowledge of and access to all accounts."

"Yes," she said. But what other secrets was he keeping? What other lies had he told? "If Graham has other money, or other cards, I'm not aware."

Crowe had his eyes on her, watchful but not unkind.

"Are we done here?" she asked.

"I have to be honest," he said. "I'm getting the feeling that there's still something you're not telling me."

"And I have the feeling there's something you're not telling me," she shot back.

"See, that's the difference between us," he said. "I don't have to tell you everything."

She wished that she could just sink into the soft folds of the couch, just disappear into chenille oblivion.

"I didn't hurt Geneva, if that's what you're getting at," she said. "I've never hurt anyone. I've never even *been rude* to anyone. And that's not Graham in the photo, or anyone else I recognize. So maybe you should be looking elsewhere for what happened to Geneva. Obviously there were a number of people who wished her harm."

He stared at her a moment, and she held his gaze. She remembered something about herself in that moment, something that it was easy to forget. She was a fighter; she didn't back down—not from bullies on the playground, not from mean girls in college, not from backstabbers at work. Marisol used to cry when people picked on her. Selena got mad—or she got even. She wasn't afraid of Detective Crowe. He lowered his eyes to the floor, then rose.

"We're not done, Mrs. Murphy," he said. "But we're done for now. Stay easy to find."

She nodded but didn't get up. *Fuck you, Detective*, she thought but didn't say. She didn't rise to show him out, just listened to his footfalls on the hardwood, the door open and close.

She felt her phone buzz and pulled it from her pocket, stared at the screen.

Great seeing you last night.

I think we need to talk, don't you?

It's Martha, by the way.

From the train.

Now it read like a dare, like a taunt. Selena felt the cold finger of dread press into her belly. Selena's truth was all over the news. And Martha likely knew everything, and knew that

Selena had lied about Graham. But everyone knew that now, even the police.

Those images, that person on the street with Geneva. Was that Martha? What had she said during that first encounter on the 7:45?

Maybe she'll disappear. And you can just pretend it never happened.

And now Geneva had disappeared.

Bad things happen all the time.

One thing was certain, the woman from the train wanted something from Selena. What was it? Who was this woman? And did she know something about what had happened to Geneva?

Was it just last night that she'd called herself a solution architect?

Beneath the dread was a current of hope. Who was she? What did she want?

Selena sent her response.

TWENTY-SIX

Pearl

SHE'D BEEN SLEEPING. She didn't know for how long. This drive. It seemed like they had been on the road for months. They'd changed cars twice, and now they were in an old Dodge minivan that smelled of stale cigarette smoke and something else—something sickly sweet like spilled soda. She'd been vaguely ill since they'd left Indianapolis, nauseated and weak. She couldn't remember the last time she'd eaten anything but saltines and ginger ale.

Pearl stayed still even after she opened her eyes, listening. She could tell what kind of mood Pop was in before he even opened his mouth, just by the way he breathed. He'd been in a bad place the last couple of days, quiet and moody, snappish. They were on the run. The Bridget thing.

"Did I ever tell you about my father?" he asked. He must have sensed that she was awake.

"Some," she said. She shifted out of the awkward position she was in, head at a weird angle against the car door. Rubbing at her sore shoulders, she cracked her neck. Pop reached over and put a hand on her back.

"I'm sorry," he said. "About everything."

"It's okay," she said.

"The place we're going now," he said. "It's ours. It's home. And we'll be safe there. We'll settle down."

They had been driving east to this promised place. A pretty house in the woods, not some ticky-tacky suburb home that they would have to leave again. It had been two years since she had become Anne and started calling Charlie Pop. She had graduated online high school. She was about to turn eighteen. What's next for you? he wanted to know. What will you do now that you're nearly of age? She thought maybe college. Pop thought that was the biggest con of all. You're already smarter and have read more, know more, than most people with advanced degrees.

Stella was always big on college. It wasn't a question of if Pearl would go, but where. Pearl had the grades, the brain, the work ethic, the test scores. She had some money, since Pop had split all of his scores with her. She wondered: Could you just show up at the bursar's office with a big bag of cash?

They'd closed out all of their accounts. Pop was anxious about how much they were holding. All of it. All of their money was in two suitcases in the back seat.

"Tell me about your dad," she said. "You said he was a drunk and a con. That he died in prison."

Pearl had seen a picture. Pop had a single photo album among his few belongings. She'd flipped through it a couple of times. Her favorite was a picture of his parents on their wedding day running down the steps of a church, the air full of rose petals—everyone smiling. And there was a black and white of Pop in his father's arms in front of a Brooklyn brownstone. Pop's face looked the same—earnest with big blue eyes. His father, balding, with eyebrows like caterpillars, wiry in a wifebeater T-shirt, looked away. He wore a scowl, had a blurry tattoo on his arm that Pop said was a mermaid.

There were other pictures—women, some girls. All of the women had a particular look—a kind of forgotten starlet angst, big eyes, buxom, thick, wavy hair. Like Stella. And the girls, all willowy, fair—like Pearl had been, though these days she was sporting a jet-black fade, with long bangs that hung over her eyes.

"All true," he said. "But he taught me a lot."

"And beat you, right?" she said, though she knew it was borderline goading. Lately, as she approached her eighteenth birthday, there was an edge to him that there hadn't been. They squabbled some. He got terse with her, and she had the urge to push at his boundaries. "I've seen the scars."

"Maybe that's the best lesson of all," he said, staring at the road. "That you can't trust anyone, even the people who are supposed to love you."

They were on a dark, rural road that wound through thick forest. They hadn't seen another car for—she wasn't sure how long, since she'd been sleeping. But it seemed like they were someplace other, an enchanted wood, another planet. And it was only them forever, just the beam of their headlights, a blade splitting the night ahead.

"Take your father, for example," he said.

"I don't know who my father is."

"Exactly," said Pop. "Your father is supposed to be the person who protects you from everything dark and scary in this world. But he didn't, did he?"

"No."

When she was small, she used to make up stories about her father. He was a spy on a secret mission in Russia (where else?), and one day he was going to come home a hero, and take care of her and Stella, bringing money and toys. He was an astronaut on a seven-year journey to Mars. When people asked, she told them he'd died in a motorcycle crash. Or that he was in Afghanistan, which she'd heard people say. Thank you for your sacrifice, one woman had said to her, touching her cheek. And Pearl had no idea what that meant. She told her teachers so many different things, that the lies caught up and Stella was called.

"Don't fantasize about your father," Stella told her. "He wasn't anything special."

When Pearl grew older, Stella told her the truth. That she'd had an affair with a married man, and when she got pregnant, he wouldn't leave his wife. But he paid support and promised that he'd take care of them financially until Pearl graduated college—which was more than most men would do, according to Stella. He had a family, other children. But he didn't want contact with Pearl and Stella. He just—couldn't handle it.

"I want to meet him," Pearl had said.

"Why would you want to meet someone who doesn't want to meet you?" she said. "Let it go."

But there was money—for food, clothes, education, braces. Later, Pearl figured that was how the store stayed in business. Money from her mystery father. Who was nothing special. Who didn't want to meet her.

"What else did he teach you?" Pearl asked Pop now.

"Never stop looking over your shoulder."

"Nice one."

"Don't ever let them take you alive."

"Wow," said Pearl. "This conversation has gone really dark."

Pop smiled at her, and then he laughed, some of his light coming back. He hadn't been himself since Phoenix.

"What if I told you that I know who your father is?"

Pearl shrugged, but something tingled inside her. "What if?"

"I found some paperwork in Stella's bedroom. I know who he is. There's a name and an address."

"Okay."

"I think you should reach out to him."

Pearl felt a notch in her throat. "He doesn't want me."

"That may or may not be true. But I think he owes you."

Pearl could see where he was going with this. The con always needed a mark. Even when the wolf was at his heels. Even though there was enough money to be quiet, comfortable, lay low for a good long time. He was the shark that couldn't stop swimming.

"And he'll pay," said Pop. "Because you're his little secret."

She nodded. She'd do what he wanted her to do. Because as much as she could love anyone, she loved him.

The car slowed and they pulled off onto a dirt drive that seemed to go on and on, tires crunching, darkness piling onto darkness. Once a pair of yellow eyes as something darted across the road. Finally, a house rose out of the distance—a low, late-century modern with a flat roof and big windows. It was dark, but there was something welcoming about it, as if it had its arms open wide to them. She felt something release, and Pop heaved a sigh.

"This is it," he said. "We're home."

TWENTY-SEVEN

Hunter

IF PEOPLE KNEW the truth about investigative work, there wouldn't be so many books and television shows about it. There was a crushing heaviness to the work, an emptiness that wasn't apparent at first but later took its toll on a person. It could be a terrible slog—long hours sitting and waiting, watching, eating bad food, maybe with a partner who you couldn't stand. Mountains of paperwork. Bad leads, dead ends.

The people you chased, those you caught, often they were no criminal masterminds, no born bad thugs. Sometimes they were kids. Sometimes they were intellectually impaired, just folks not smart enough to make good choices. Often, they were victims themselves. He left the job after twenty-five years, and he never told anyone—not even his wife, Claire, who he thought knew on some level—that he had wasted his life.

People were so hung up on the concept of justice, of wrongs punished, streets safe, criminals put where they belonged. But the system was broken, like so many systems. And the world was so impossibly vast, even now with technology tightening the net, that some people just stayed lost.

"Don't take it so hard," said Andrew from the passenger seat.

They sat in Andrew's driveway with the sun dipping low. The search for Hunter's runaway had yielded nothing, except a foray into the dregs that had left them both wondering what had happened to the world. The tattoos, the piercings, the blank-faced young people staring into screens. Tommy's Cove used to be a biker bar, a wild place, lots of brawls and gang violence. That seemed tame, old-fashioned compared to what had become of the place. Permanent midnight with windows blacked out. Blaring music, weird strobes. And everyone—so blank. Hopped up on pills, or that new thing, kratom—opium's legal cousin. Lots of lost kids looking like zombies, stumbling, dead-eyed. No Jennie.

Hunter didn't want to face Jennie's mother with more bad news.

"Do you ever think about retiring?" said Andrew. The gloaming had settled on the pretty manicured lawns of his street. Somewhere a lawnmower buzzed. "Like really retiring."

"And do what? Work on my backhand?"

Andrew shrugged. He was a big guy who had lost a lot of weight. Now he was a skinny guy who looked like he was waiting to get big again. He hadn't updated his wardrobe, so his clothes hung off of him. "That's what people do. You could take a class. Woodworking. You used to do that, right?"

Claire wanted him to fully retire, as well. She wanted to travel. Take ballroom dancing classes. "Maybe."

"I'm just saying. You look tired."

He *was* tired.

But. But. How did you stop being the sheepdog? There were sheep in this life. And there were wolves. He'd heard it in a movie, and it struck him as true. And then there were the men and women on the job—the ones in the squad cars and the ambulances, the firetrucks, those fighting on the front lines at home and overseas. They were guarding the perimeter between bad and good. The sheepdogs, on the lookout for the predators, and bringing the lost lambs back into the fold.

Andrew climbed out of the car, rubbed shyly at his balding head. "Call me if you ever want company again."

Hunter drove home, through the quiet of Andrew's middle-class neighborhood, up a rural road to his own house. Claire was always the high earner working in medical sales; that's why they could afford the big house they had, set back on five acres of land—idyllic with big trees and a stream at the edge of the property. He parked in the garage and killed the engine, checked the mail—all catalogs and fliers—walked inside.

He expected to find his wife at home, in the kitchen with the television on, cooking something or another. Instead there was a note reminding him that she had book club and that there were leftovers in the fridge. He was guiltily glad for it.

He wanted to pull out his old files on the Behr case and didn't want to do it under the disapproving stare of his wife.

Some of this stuff, Hunt, you just have to let go.

Everyone was all about *letting go* these days. But, in this world, it seemed to Hunter that way too much was just *let go.* Pearl—there was no one to hold on to her. And she—a teenage girl, flesh and bone, heart and soul, just disappeared. Hunter prided himself on being the only one holding on to her.

Missing people. Missing children. There was always a big fuss at first. A media feeding frenzy, search parties and helpful volunteers, endless news loops, press conferences with tearful parents. Then, as the days and weeks wore on, leads ran cold, people went back to their lives. They had to. Because the ugly truth was that some things—even people—got lost and were never found. There was a special kind of hell to that for folks. An always waiting, always wondering, end to life as they knew it.

In the spotlessly clean kitchen, he nuked the lasagna Claire had left for him and ate way more than he would have if she'd been there. After he'd finished, going back for seconds and even thirds—Claire would have called him out on his stress eating. He always had a huge appetite after a bad day. After the lasagna, he inhaled a half a box of Girl Scout cookies—Tagalongs—then cleaned up the mess like a good husband.

Upstairs in his office, he climbed the shaky stepladder to reach the high shelf where he kept cold case files and reached for the heavy box, nearly losing his balance. That would be all he needed, to take a fall. That was always the beginning of the end for old guys, wasn't it? Not that he was so old.

He put the box on the desk that had belonged to his father, a career cop who'd gone all the way to chief before he retired. Hunter was never into politics. He liked the work, wanted to do the job, not sit behind the desk in a fancy uniform, sending other people out into the streets. He and his dad, they didn't see eye to eye on most things, never really had the chemistry that Hunter had effortlessly with his own children. That was the way of it sometimes. He knew the old man did his best.

The box, beige and sagging, was covered in a thin layer of dust. The particles lifted into the light as he removed the lid, causing him to sneeze. He hadn't put any attention on Pearl and Stella in a while. He sat in his leather chair and started sifting through the files.

A photo, grainy and fading, of a strawberry-blonde woman smiling tentatively at the camera. High cheekbones, a full mouth, inviting eyes.

Stella Behr, single mother, bookstore owner, was thirty-five years old when she was strangled in her own bed. Hunter didn't love how, in death, a few details came to define you. But so it was. Young, a bombshell beauty with a string of boyfriends, on the brink of financial ruin. Several of the men in her life questioned and released.

Another photo, a girl with Stella's eyes but dark, a stillness to her face, a sadness there. Her smile seemed strained. There was a cool prettiness, something reserved.

Stella's daughter, Pearl, was fifteen. A very smart young woman, according to teachers, grades and test scores. A loner, though. Odd, said more than one of her instructors. A flat affect to her, unemotional. Quiet. Never in trouble, but no teacher's pet. There was no information about who Pearl's father might be—nothing in the public records or in the house.

The neighbor, an older woman who was nearly a recluse, saw Pearl leave with Charles Finch, the bookstore manager, the night Stella was murdered. It appeared that she left of her own free will, quietly, neither of them appearing rushed or upset.

Charles Finch was a ghost. That was not his real name; all his employment records had been falsified. Even the car he'd been driving, a restored GTO, was registered to a man who'd been dead for ten years. Stella had apparently been paying him in cash. All her bank accounts were empty. She had a pile of personal debt, owed taxes on the store and on the house. She was months from losing everything.

When the department called in Hunter as part of an initiative to clear cold cases, there was very little—nothing really—to go on. They had a DNA sample and some prints that did not match anything in the system. The neighbor who saw Charles Finch and Pearl leave that night, she couldn't provide many details, except that Finch was a regular at the house. That he was one of a string of men who came and went. That Pearl was a nice girl, who took out the trash, didn't run around, and could be seen at her desk doing her homework most nights.

In the movies, there is always one thing that leads the detective to the truth. Even the documentaries and podcasts usually focus on crimes that were somehow, against all odds, solved. A witness comes forward. Technology catches up with evidence left behind. The DNA sample finally hits a match in the system because of another crime.

But the real world was impossibly vast with lots of back alleys and unexplored places. Some crimes went unsolved forever; some people disappeared without a trace.

Almost.

Hunter found the file he was looking for and opened it.

About two years after Stella was killed, and Pearl went missing, another woman was murdered, her teenage daughter disappeared. This was about fifty miles from the Behr home.

Maggie Stevenson, thirty-six, a nurse and a single mother, was strangled in her home, her teenage daughter disappearing the same night. An ex-boyfriend was questioned and released. Very little physical evidence at the scene. A coworker said there was a new man in her life, someone she was excited about. She'd been using a dating site, but there was no evidence that she'd ever met with anyone.

There was a single text on her phone, from a number that was traced to a burner phone.

Can't wait to finally meet you.

He stared at the pictures in the file. Maggie was another bombshell beauty—same thick, wavy hair and bedroom eyes, darker than Stella but with the same wild vulnerability to her gaze. Her daughter, Grace, cool and slim, long tresses of golden hair, a doll-like sweetness to her face. Another hardworking single mother, murdered, her child disappearing. Maggie had no family, loose friend connections. She had, on the day of her murder, cashed out the meager contents of her accounts—a grand total of about $5000. There were several large unusual charges on her credit card—from Best Buy. From Macy's. Their case went colder faster than even Stella and Pearl's.

There were patterns, things that matched.

And then a piece of luck. DNA evidence at the Stevenson home matched evidence at the Behr home. Unfortunately, that

DNA evidence did not match anything in the database of known criminals. Another dead end.

But new data was added every day; every six months or so, Hunter would request a new search to find a match. He was past due for a request to the department. He'd have to call in a favor; he wasn't on the payroll for this case. There was no budget for a ten-year-old case. It had become his personal thing, a grudge match that he could not let go.

He opened his computer and searched out the news story he'd seen earlier today and pulled up the picture of the missing woman.

Looking back and forth between the image of Grace Stevenson from his file and his screen, he couldn't be sure. People change—especially kids. Especially people who want to change. So many years. The young woman on the screen had a narrower face, her hair was darker. Some of the sweetness was gone. But around the mouth and the eyes, it could be. It might be Grace.

The Naughty Nanny.

He opened his file on Charles Finch. It held a single photograph, taken from among Stella Behr's possessions. Heavily lashed blue eyes, defined cheekbones, clean-shaven, a wide, smiling mouth. Not just handsome. Beautiful in that way that some men were. Even other men saw it. A pretty boy, they'd call him on the playground or in the joint. Smallish, angular. Even the photograph radiated charm. The number one most important quality every con must have—the ability to charm and disarm. And this man was a con if Hunter ever saw one.

Hunter had his theory. That he was a guy who worked his way into the lives of vulnerable women. Maybe he wanted their money; and maybe sometimes that's all he took. But sometimes maybe he wanted something more. And sometimes he took that, too.

He opened another file, this one filled with articles printed from the internet. He regularly scoured the web for cold cases that matched the pattern. There was a case in Tucson, where a woman was dating a man who tried to strangle her, but she was saved by a neighbor who heard her screams. She had a teenage daughter who was out for the evening. Her assailant got away. She only had a single picture of him. It might have been the man Hunter knew as Finch, but the picture was grainy and indistinct. The man looked heavier, wore glasses and a full beard. There was a slew of sweetheart scams, online predators convincing wealthy widows and widowers to wire money for this emergency or that. It happened a lot. There were a lot of grifters out there, lots of victims. More than anyone knew.

There was one in Phoenix, a woman named Bridget Pine who said she was nearly scammed by a man and his daughter. She and the man—who she knew as Bill Jackson—had been having an online relationship when he claimed his daughter had been in an accident and he needed money. She'd been suspicious, she said. Then she ran a few checks, checking up on details like where he supposedly lived and worked, quickly realizing almost everything he told her was a lie. She reported him to the authorities—local police and the FBI. She alerted the media. But, like Charles Finch, he was a ghost; disappeared without a trace. The picture she had of him from his online profile did not resemble Finch; there was no image of the girl.

Most people who were victims of the sweetheart scam just slunk away; it was a humiliation, the death of a dream. But Bridget Pine raised a fuss and when Hunter called her, she detailed for him everything that had transpired. The passionate emails, the late-night phone calls, the delicious tension of awaiting their first meeting. She wasn't a beautiful woman; so, the ability to get to really know someone before meeting—she thought that it was a truer connection.

"The physical shell doesn't matter," she told him. "It's what's inside that counts, isn't it?"

"Of course," said Hunter. But intimacy was about more than

late-night conversations and promises. He thought of his own marriage—imperfect, enduring, how you had to accept every facet of each other, even the things you didn't like.

"On some level," she said, "I guess I knew. I'd given up on love and romance. But something about the online dating. It felt safer. I didn't think it would hurt as much if it didn't work out."

"I'm sorry," he told her. "This happens a lot. More than you know."

"How do I find him?" she asked. "Can you help me? I can pay you."

"I've been looking for him—or someone like him—for years. You don't have to pay me. If I find him, you'll be my first call."

"How have you been looking for him?" she asked.

He told her his techniques of scanning news sites, following up with similar stories, cold calling. Sometimes taking a road trip.

"All it takes is one detail that leads you somewhere new," he said. "But my advice? Just let it go, move on."

She laughed a little. "I don't have anything to move on to. Bill—I think he was my last chance for love."

Bill. Charlie. Whoever. He wasn't even real.

"If you get a lead," he said, "don't follow it up on your own, call me. Let me help. No charge."

She promised that she would. This was a couple of months before Maggie Stevenson was murdered, her daughter Grace disappeared.

Later, Bridget Pine walked off the face of the earth. She bought a new car, quit her job, cashed out some accounts, packed a bag and slipped away from her life. When he couldn't reach her—email bounced, phone disconnected—Hunter called around, finally finding a former coworker who knew her a little.

"She was an odd duck," he said. "She kept to herself. Then, one day, she just quit. She said she'd made enough money to retire and she wanted to travel. It was—odd."

No one had ever heard from her again.

Hunter kept reading through his old notes. Then scanned the various news sources for all the information he could get on the Naughty Nanny, and then he scanned through the cold case websites he liked. He was looking for it, the one thing, that connected all of them. The one piece of information that would lead him on a fresh trail.

The sun set and the lamps came on outside. Hunter knew there was about an hour before his wife came home. Until she did, he'd spend a little time on Stella and Pearl Behr, Maggie and Grace Stevenson. He'd keep looking. Because everybody counts.

TWENTY-EIGHT

Selena

SHE PULLED THE blinds and pretended there was no one out on her lawn, on her driveway, on the street. As the detective left, a handful of reporters, a couple of news vans, a few other unmarked vehicles had come to gather around her house. Neighbors were at their windows and on their porches. It wasn't a mob. But the sight of the strangers filled her with dread. Now, Selena was one of those people, the ones you saw on the news, their lives in a shamble because of scandal or a crime.

She sank onto the couch, not sure of what to do. Pack. That was it. She needed to gather her things and more clothes and toys for the boys. She needed to leave this house and go home to her mother. Because—what else? Where else?

When there was an aggressive knocking on the door, she sat frozen. The detective again? The police coming to take her in? Her heart thumped. She waited. Maybe they'd go away.

"It's me." A familiar voice through the door. "Selena, it's Beth. Let me in."

Relief was a flood as she ran for the door, let her friend inside. There were shouts from the lawn.

What happened to Geneva Markson, Selena?

Did you know your husband was sleeping with the nanny?

Beth, blond hair tousled, clutching her tote tight to her body, moved inside quickly and pressed her back against the closed door.

"Is this happening?" she asked Selena, eyes wide. "Is this really happening?"

"It is," said Selena. "This is my life right now."

They stared at each other. They'd been in dark places together before, watching their dear friend die. Her grim funeral. The implosion of Beth's marriage, the ugly, contentious divorce—luckily or unluckily without kids. A miscarriage Selena had before Oliver was born. The time Beth broke her leg while they were hiking, and Selena had to practically drag her five miles because they'd both decided to "unplug" and left their phones in the car.

"Shit," said Beth. "Shit. What time is it? Can we drink?"

It was after three. "I have a bottle of cab."

Selena didn't want to drink, but Beth made her way to the kitchen, dropping her bag at the table. She poured them each a glass from the bottle on the counter, and Selena took a tentative sip, then another. She felt that familiar warmth, a softening of edges. Her shoulders relaxed a bit.

"Tell me everything, Selena," said Beth. They sat at the kitchen table, the heart of any house. "Start from the beginning. All of it."

She told her friend about the first time, the sexting, the Vegas incident, then how she'd moved the camera and caught Graham with Geneva. She told her about the woman on the train, about the late-night meeting, the texts she'd been receiving, all the things Detective Crowe had told her about why Graham really lost his job, about Geneva blackmailing the Tuckers. The dirty texts. About Will coming in for the rescue, her spending the night at his place. It all came out in a stream, Beth nodding, making all the right noises, reaching for her hand, giving Selena her unbroken attention.

"So, yeah," said Selena when she was done. "That's what's been going on with me."

"Why am I just hearing about all of this?" she said, incredulous. "Where were you keeping it?"

"Deep, deep inside," she said. "Where we keep everything ugly, all the things we don't want to broadcast, don't want to deal with."

Beth drained her wine, refilled both their glasses, gave a knowing nod. "I've been there. I know how much energy it takes to keep up a facade. How many years did I keep waiting for things to get better, rather than do what I needed to do? Get away from someone who was hurting me."

Selena never once suspected that Beth and Scott weren't happy—or happy enough. You learn pretty early in your adult life that few marriages are perfect. There are almost always secrets, negotiations between couples that no one outside the marriage would understand. Her sister, Marisol, endured her husband's porn addiction, until he also developed a gambling addiction that almost ruined them financially. Only after she'd asked him to leave did she reveal the truth to Selena and their mother, Cora. Selena always thought the Tuckers looked so perfect, so happy and in love.

"Is it them or is it us?"

Selena looked at her friend, who was rubbing at her temples. She cocked her head in question.

"I mean—are some men just flawed by nature? Or do we enable their bad behavior, make it worse in a way because we hide it, and don't demand better from them?"

"Maybe it's some combination of both."

"Because the women I know, they're not creating damage

in the lives of the people they're supposed to love and protect. They're not cheating, abusing, lying. Or worse."

Or worse. Was it worse than she imagined? Was her husband a monster?

The wine was going down too fast. She couldn't afford to get drunk, to not have a clear head going into the rest of the night. Selena pushed the glass away.

"What happened with you and Will?" asked Beth.

"Nothing," she said. "He slept on the couch. The perfect gentleman."

Beth circled a manicured fingertip around the rim of her glass.

"He still loves you."

"No," said Selena. "That's ancient history."

Beth gave her a look, and Selena offered an assenting nod. "Well, then, it's ancient history for me."

"But you went to him last night," said Beth. "You could have come to my place."

She shrugged. "I didn't have to tell him why I was there. He already knew everything."

"He must have loved it. Being the one to ride in to the rescue."

Beth hadn't much liked Will either.

"Remind me why you left him?"

That was a thing Beth did, made you say the thing she was thinking. But Selena wasn't going to give it to her, though she knew what Beth was driving at.

"Because I met Graham, realized that I wanted different things from life than Will did."

"So, you were perfectly happy until the night you met Graham."

"No one's perfectly happy."

Beth leaned forward, tapped a finger on the table.

"He was possessive. Controlling," she reminded Selena. "He

always wanted to know where you were, who you were with. He monitored you, didn't he? Bedtime. Exercise."

"He helped me to be more disciplined. He—pushed me to be my best self."

Beth smiled, shook her head. "He wanted to be your *daddy*."

"He wanted to take care of me," said Selena. "Maybe I should have let him. It would be better than this."

She swept her hand around her dream kitchen, which now felt like a sound stage, propped up from behind, fake, one good push and it would all fall down.

"I'm just saying. Don't go backward because you're scared now, honey. Don't rush into Will's arms to get away from Graham."

Few friends would dare to say something so bold, so nakedly true. Because that's exactly what she wanted to do. And, even though she'd just denied it, she knew he was there waiting. It was a comfort to know that.

"We'll get through this like all the other ugly," Beth went on. "And when you come out the other side, you'll be stronger."

"*If* I come out the other side."

"I'm here." Beth leaned forward, laced her fingers through Selena's, blue eyes blazing. "I'll drag you through if I have to. Just like you dragged me out of the woods."

They looked at each other for a moment, then both started laughing, remembering, though it had been far from funny at the time—Beth in so much pain, the afternoon waning into darkness, the fatigue, the struggle of it.

"You were Iron Woman. All mettle and determination," said Beth. "That's who you are. Don't forget it."

Selena wasn't that. She wasn't as strong as Beth, who'd been alone since she'd left her husband. Her friend had a few lackluster dates, but nothing ever developed into more. Her stance lately was very anti-male. She owned her own business, often traveled alone, or with her single friends. She seemed to like being alone, making her own way and living by her own rules. If she was lonely, she never said so. But would she? Would she admit that to her allegedly happily married friends?

Selena had never been single, wasn't even sure what it would be like.

"And this woman?" said Beth. Another pour. "What's that all about? You tell some stranger about Graham, but you don't tell me?"

"It was just this weird moment in time," she said with a wave. "Believe me, I regret it."

"Well, cut that woman off," said Beth. "Don't talk to her again. That's creepy, Selena. Is she like some stalker type?"

"No," she said. "I don't know."

"Don't answer her. If she texts you again, have Will step in. And, you know what, tell the cops about her."

"How will it look now? Another thing I've kept from them."

"Have Will do it," she said. It made sense. That was exactly what she should do. Why did she feel a stubborn hesitation?

"Is Will *your* lawyer or is he Graham's lawyer?" asked Beth.

She hadn't considered that. The question opened up a hollow in her center. "I guess he's *our* lawyer."

Beth shook her head. "Girl, you need *your own* lawyer. Someone who represents your interests alone. Things are going to get ugly and you don't want to be the one twisting."

She nodded. What a mess. She felt tears come, but she pushed them back.

"You're Iron Woman," said Beth. "Don't forget it."

She wasn't made from iron, far from it. She had never felt weaker and more vulnerable in her life. But she smiled at her friend, remembering the day in the woods. How scared they'd been, how she was sure she didn't have the strength to get them through, how Beth had walked the last mile gritting her teeth against the pain. They'd made it then, through sheer force of will. Sometimes that was all you had and all you needed, just the mettle to take the next step.

"What now?" asked Beth.

"Pack up—my stuff, and some more things for the boys."

"You're leaving," said Beth.

"What choice do I have?" she said. "I can't stay here. No matter what happens next. I have to go."

Beth nodded. "I'll help you."

When they were done, moving from room to room, gathering clothes, stuffed animals, paperwork Selena might need, they put the suitcases by the door.

"I'm here for you," Beth said again as she held on tight to Selena in farewell.

But they both knew that all she could be was a voice, a loving face over a glass of wine. On the dark road ahead, Selena would have to find her own way.

Selena watched Beth duck her head and rush to her car, ignoring the reporters who followed. There seemed to be fewer of them. The news vans were gone. She felt a glimmer of hope. Maybe this wasn't such a big story, with no body, as Will said, nothing solid except some dirty texts. Maybe it could still all just go away.

Beth waved from the car, and Selena waved back.

They'd agreed that Selena should take some time off work. Beth offered to keep her at half salary, but Selena declined. Her friend ran a successful small business. She wasn't going to be a burden when she'd come on to be an asset. They had savings; she had her parents. She couldn't work anyway, not with the boys and everything that might come next. Life was on hold. Maybe her job would be waiting for her when this was over. Maybe she'd do something else.

She sat again, knowing she had to call Oliver but looking into the dark fireplace instead, her limbs full of sand. She'd used up all her energy to pack. Should she turn on the television, see what they were reporting on the news? No. She couldn't stand it. She breathed in the quiet a moment. Then, as she headed upstairs to make one last pass of the rooms, there was another knock on the door.

A muffled voice thought the door: "Selena, it's Will."

She let him in, closing the door quickly behind him.

"What happened?" she asked.

"They questioned Graham rigorously," said Will. "He was consistent. They slept together. The dirty texts were just in *fun*, according to him. They'd agreed that sleeping together was a mistake, that they should stop. And he has no idea where she is."

"Do you believe him?"

Will seemed to consider. "It's not my job to believe or disbelieve. It's my job to protect his rights and defend him if it comes to that."

"Will," said Selena. "Do you think he hurt Geneva?"

Will released a long breath, his gaze slipping away. "I don't know, Selena. That Vegas thing, those texts—it changes how I see him."

It wasn't what she expected him to say, and the words landed heavily on her shoulders. He didn't know what Graham was capable of doing to another person. Neither, it seemed, did she.

"I'll take you to your Mom's?"

"I need my car."

"So, we'll drive your car and I'll Uber back to get mine."

She wanted to drive alone, but she let him help her load the car with the suitcases, the small bins of books and toys she'd taken from the boys' room.

Their room—*Star Wars* sheets, airplanes hanging from the ceilings, soccer trophies, action figures, shelves of toys and games—which she had decorated so carefully—seemed abandoned. The house, lovingly decorated—every drape and pillow, every hue of paint and placed object, curated by Selena. Without the energy of their bustling life, it all seemed cheap, empty, a body without a soul.

"Have everything you need?" Will asked.

She nodded, hefting a box, which he took from her. They walked into the garage.

The police had impounded the SUV that Graham drove Friday night. So there was only their Subaru in the garage. They loaded the car, and then they climbed in.

"Ready?"

"Let's go."

She pressed the button on the remote and the door opened. The growing crowd of journalists parted as the car pulled out. They were shouting, snapping pictures.

Will had coached her to keep her expression neutral and her eyes forward, betraying nothing of the roil within. She did that.

Where's Geneva? What's happened to the Naughty Nanny? Did your husband kill her?

They sounded like seagulls, clamoring and calling, their words nonsense. She was grateful for the dark tinted windows of the car. She was so tired, so numb. She could sleep for a thousand years.

"They can't hold him much longer," Will was saying. "There's no physical evidence. They let Erik Tucker go. There's no body or really any indication of foul play."

"They can keep him there for the rest of his life for all I care."

"Selena."

The ride was smooth and quiet. She felt ensconced, isolated from other cars on the road, as they drifted down her street and away from the mob. No one followed them. They took the little-known back roads that wound and twisted to her mother's house.

"Detective Crowe asked if I was angry, if I'd thought about hurting Geneva," she told Will. "Like he thought maybe I had something to do with this."

Will shook his head in disapproval. "You should never have talked to him."

"I know."

"What did you say?"

"Nothing. He knows my schedule for that day. The weekend is documented on social media. I'm sure he can discern where I was and what I did via my smartphone data. They have video of Geneva leaving our house unharmed on Friday. I think he was just goading me. Trying to get me to react."

She stopped short of telling Will she wanted to come clean with the police about the woman from the train. Something inside kept her from uttering the words. Why?

Maybe because more than anything, Selena wanted this to just go away. Was that still possible?

She spent the rest of the ride turning back the clock. If she'd left after the sexting. Or after the Vegas incident. How would things be different? But you couldn't do that, could you? Not when there were children, people formed from your love for someone. There was no undoing the bad without losing the good. That was the trick of it all. The tangle of life. Just move forward, recalculate, recalibrate, find a new path.

There were no reporters at her mother's place, and they pulled into the garage that had been left open in anticipation of their arrival. They sat a moment after Will killed the engine. It ticked in the silence that fell. She didn't want to go inside; she couldn't go home. She let herself sit a moment, collect her resources to deal with the boys.

"I wish…" Will started, putting his hand over hers.

Beth's warning rang in her ears. It was solid advice from a good friend. What she needed was space and time, to find her footing.

"Don't," she said. He kept his eyes on her. She felt the heat of his gaze, though she didn't return it.

"That I went to that party with you."

It wasn't what she expected him to say. She turned to look at him. He ran a hand through those wild honey curls.

"What *party*?" she asked.

"The night you met Graham. Remember?"

She remembered. Of course she did.

Cora and Paulo's garage was meticulously organized—tools hung, bicycles on racks, kids' gear from scooters to roller skates mounted or in clear bins. A stupid thing to notice, except that it struck a stark contrast to the disorder in her own life.

Will's voice was soft when he spoke again. "I was supposed to go with you. But I had to work late."

"Don't do this," she whispered.

He lifted his palms. "I'm just saying. How would things be different?"

"You don't have kids," she said. "It's easy to say you regret how things went. But I have Stephen and Oliver."

"I know. Just—"

"Don't."

He nodded slowly, dipped his head. She flashed on the younger version of him, a day at the beach when he was tan and laughing, their toes buried in the sand. The girl who loved him was so free; she didn't even know what freedom was then. Was he controlling? He used to buy clothes for her. She remembered liking that, that he knew her size, what looked good on her. But, yeah, sometimes she wore things she didn't like to please him.

"I'm—here for you. And for Graham."

With his hand still on hers, she felt the warmth of him, but also something else.

He still loves you, Graham always complained. They'd all tried to be friends. So evolved, weren't they? But dinners were always awkward, conversations stilted. Then Will and his wife divorced. *It's like he's just waiting for you to find your way back to him.*

She disagreed. Will's wife, Bella, was beautiful and sweet; they'd seemed happy. Together—in that way that people were or weren't, loving looks, casual touches. But obviously she'd been wrong. So many marriages imploded before her eyes—her parents', her sister's, more than half of her friends', her own. Maybe you just weren't supposed to be together forever. Maybe it was too much to ask.

She pulled her hand away gently, touched him on the leg. He watched her for a moment, then lowered his eyes.

Whatever there was still between them, this wasn't the time. She wasn't the girl she was with Will, the woman she was with Graham. She wasn't sure who she was right now. Maybe she was just a mother; that was all she had energy for as her life fell to pieces.

He pressed his lips together, gave a tight nod of understanding, then helped her unload the car. Or maybe, she found herself thinking, as she hefted her suitcase from the car, maybe this was the moment where she found herself—not her parents' daughter, Will's girlfriend, Graham's wife, Stephen and Oliver's mom. She was all those things, or had been, would always be a mother. But now that her life was cracked, fractured beyond repair, maybe this is where Selena emerged, more *herself* than she had ever been.

Inside the house, Stephen clung. But Oliver kept his distance, dark eyes on Will.

"Where's Dad?" he asked.

"Boys," said Paulo. "Come help me with dinner. Real men know how to cook."

He marshaled the boys into the kitchen.

Selena let her mother take her into her arms and hold on tight.

"Mom, is it okay if we stay here for a while?" she asked, though she already knew the answer. But could you find yourself when you were sleeping in your mother's guest room? At least it wasn't her old room from childhood; her father still lived in that house. She rarely visited.

"This is your home," her mother said. "Wherever I am, that's where you belong."

You were always a mother, she guessed. No matter how old your children were. Her mom ushered her to the living room. Selena heard Paulo's baritone, then the boys' laughter.

"Are you hungry?" Cora asked. That was always the first rule of mothering: make sure no one's hungry.

"Starving," she admitted.

"I have some soup." Cora patted Selena's arm. "I'll heat it up. Just sit here, try to rest."

Will's phone rang and he went into the other room to take the call. She tried not to listen. But she tensed just listening to the sound of his voice, even though she couldn't understand the words. She knew that voice, quiet but dark. When he came back, his face was grim.

She let the moment expand with her breath. The last moment, she thought for no reason. The last moment where things could still turn out okay.

"Police have found the body of a young woman," he said. "About five miles from the house. Joggers found the body off trail, back in the state park."

The trails Graham ran, regularly, when he used to run.

Selena's mother gasped, and Selena felt the world tip, sank into the couch.

"Is it—*Geneva*?"

Will looked behind him for the boys, she guessed, then lowered his voice a bit.

"The body is so disfigured that it will take some time to identify."

Cora released a helpless, frightened noise. It was soft, but Paulo must have heard because he emerged from the kitchen.

Selena dipped her face into her hands and started to cry—for Geneva, for herself, for her boys, and for the dark road ahead of them—which just got darker.

TWENTY-NINE

Pearl

POP HAD BEEN busy. Gone a lot, leaving Pearl to set up house. She presumed he'd found another lonely woman. This time, Pearl had her mission, separate from his. But she wasn't making much progress. After all, she wondered, how could it work? Wouldn't her father, if she found him, want to know where she'd been all these years? Would he want to know what had happened to Stella?

Pearl had enrolled in community college, an institution that she knew was far beneath her intellectually. But she believed that your education was what you made of it. You could learn what you needed to learn anywhere. Fancy degrees from fancy schools, that was just another con—selling you the illusion of status. That's what Pop said.

Anyway, Pop wasn't sure that her identity would hold up to very much scrutiny. And those fancy schools, they did tend to check into your pedigree. So some of the bigger institutions, the better ones, to which she aspired, were out of reach. She'd have to settle.

"Do you imagine he cares?" asked Pop, when she brought up her concerns about her father and what questions he'd have for her if they connected. He wasn't being cruel, just practical. An analysis of the mark—who was he? What did he want?

It was one of the rare nights that she and Pop were home together. Things had changed between them somewhat. She wasn't an asset to the game anymore. Now that she was an adult, and looked like one, she wasn't a lure for that vulnerable older woman looking to mother. She was a threat—someone younger, more beautiful, in the way. They lay on the couch, her head on his thigh as he twirled at the length of her hair.

"If he did, don't you think he'd have—I don't know—maybe hired someone to find you? Or kept on top of the police."

She wondered if the police had questioned him when Stella was killed. After all, if Pop could figure out who her father was, couldn't they? She'd never read anything about him in the news accounts.

"Maybe he did," she offered, looking up at him. In the firelight, his features were licked by darkness, eyes hollow, valleys on his cheeks.

Pop had a way of creating a silence that made her question her own statements without his saying a word.

"But he probably didn't," she said finally, looking toward the flames.

"When Stella died and you disappeared, it was one less bill to pay, one less problem to manage. The guy is obviously emotionally bankrupt."

Like father, like daughter? Maybe that's where she got it, the emptiness inside, the absence of feeling.

They'd done their research. Her father was on LinkedIn but not Facebook or Twitter, not Instagram. But from the posts of his daughters, and some family friends, they had a picture of him. A profile they'd developed.

Pop went on. "He has family. A wife. Two daughters. A big

job as a bank executive. If you turn up, start making noise, he'll pay to make you go away. That's my guess."

In the few pictures they'd found online, he was stiff, unsmiling. A family portrait where his lovely dark-haired girls sat before him and he draped a possessive arm around his petite, fake-smiling wife—who looked a little like Stella. He was tall, severe with a large forehead and dark eyes, thick eyebrows that formed a perpetual frown. He had the aura of judge, warden, strict principal, someone who could wither with only a glance. The one picture they'd found of him smiling had been with his dog. A Rottweiler who resembled him not a little.

He was certainly not the father of her imagination. The spy. The soldier. She'd always thought of him as svelte, with sandy hair and a ready smile. Someone funny, adventurous, in on the joke of it all. Someone like Pop.

"What if he killed Stella?" Pearl asked.

Pop considered this with a lift of his eyebrows, as if maybe it hadn't occurred to him.

Which she was certain it had; because he always thought of everything. Or so she believed at the time.

"Unlikely," he said after a moment. "But if he did, he'll be even more motivated to make you go away. Maybe he'll pay up even more."

"Or."

"Or?"

"Or he'll kill me."

Pop pulled her up and into him. She let him hold her, her arms at her sides. He released her and took her cheeks in his palms. "As long as I'm alive, no one is going to hurt you."

She smiled; he kissed her on the head. "Don't make promises you can't keep," she said.

"I always keep my promises. You know that."

They were quiet a moment.

Then he went on. "I think since he's made a habit of paying

people off, he'll continue doing that. The best predictor of future behavior—"

"—is past behavior."

But something about what she said hung between them. The silence swelled.

"Make a soft approach," he said finally. "Nice and easy. Don't startle him."

So she'd sent him an email to the address she'd found on LinkedIn. The subject line read: This is Pearl. In the body, she wrote: Do you know who I am?

She waited. One day. Two days. No response. She went through all the gyrations—wondering if she had the wrong email, if an assistant went through his inbox, maybe it went to the junk folder. Three days. Four. She felt an uncomfortable wanting. But what she wanted precisely she couldn't say for sure. She didn't want a father. She didn't care about the score, not the way Pop did. But still, there was an ache inside her that she couldn't name.

She took the train to the city, left a note for him at the front desk of his office.

I am Pearl. Do you know who I am?

She left the number of a burner phone she'd picked up. It had been a pretty stupid move, considering the network of security cameras that existed now, a web all over the city. But she didn't know about that, then. She knew that Pop didn't like smartphones, said that they were practically tethers. But she didn't know about the network of home cameras, security cameras, and police-owned surveillance that was just starting to crisscross the world.

She waited. No email. No phone call. Five days. Six.

"Maybe he didn't get my email," she agonized to Pop. "Maybe

the woman at the desk trashed my note. She looked at me like I was something she wanted to scrape off her shoe."

"Or maybe he's just hoping you'll go away."

She thought about giving up. There was a pile of homework for her major in psychology—useful in any profession. Her professor was interesting, someone who pushed and challenged. Pearl had even started dating a guy who made her laugh. When she looked back on that moment in her life later, she thought that maybe the doorway to "normal" was open just a crack. She could have walked through possibly. But Pop.

"Time to turn up the heat a little," he said. "Just a little."

Her father's house. It was so—beautiful. It wasn't that it was so grand. Certainly, there were grander. But the brilliant green of the lawn, the crawl of bougainvillea around the pergola that hugged the garage, the brick stoop, red door, black shutters, white siding. How his BMW glided from the driveway when he left for work, sometimes with his younger daughter (the older already away at college) in the passenger seat. Her glossy black hair, slim body, pretty clothes.

She was lovely. But it was more than that. She was oblivious to the darkness in her life; she only knew the light. Pearl could tell by the smooth innocence on her face, the careless way she walked, and tossed her backpack into the trunk, stared at the phone in her hand. Life for her was easy. Nothing ever broken that couldn't be fixed. Nothing ever lost that couldn't be replaced. Her life was so easy that she didn't even know there was another kind of life—hardscrabble and unpredictable.

That ache. It was a black hole inside Pearl, swallowing light and time.

For a week, she just watched, burning with feelings she could barely understand.

She parked just up the street in the mornings, watching as they left for work and school. Then she'd leave after his wife departed for her morning errands.

Pearl then returned around 3:30 to watch the girl come home on the bus, usually with a gaggle of friends. Designer clothes and styled hair, lip gloss, and bubbling laughter—teasing, pushing, chasing. They'd disappear behind that red door and to Pearl it seemed like they had entrée to a world from which she'd always been, always would be, excluded. A world not of privilege, but of belonging.

Then one night in the gloaming, she climbed out of her car and began slowly walking up the street. She knew he'd be pulling into the driveway at 6:10, so she made sure she stood behind the big oak—out of view of the house, but visible from the driveway. She stood listening to the birdsong and the wind kicking leaves up the street.

When he pulled in, he turned his head and saw her.

She lifted her hand, and they locked eyes. Did he know her?

Then, he turned his head and the garage door opened. He pulled inside. She waited, heart thumping, thoughts wild. Did he see me? Recognize me? Maybe it's too dark. Maybe this is too bold.

The garage door closed heavily behind him, rumbling and squeaking, quieting the evening birdsong. He never even exited the car.

She walked back to her vehicle. Her inner life was usually cool, but that night it roiled with a storm of anger she didn't know was possible.

It was something deep, something that maybe had always been there, lying neglected, silent. She got in her car and drove, gripping the wheel, until she came to an empty parking lot across from a deserted sports field. Pearl pulled in there, found a far spot, stopped the car.

A long wail, like a siren, escaped her throat. A sound she didn't even know she could make. It rocketed through her; and then she did it again and again, pounding on the steering wheel. She screamed for herself, for Stella, in rage at the man who was her father, his pretty, clueless daughter—her sister?—the normal life she'd never had. Even Pop—who was what? Her father? Her captor? The man who probably killed her mother? And yet she was hooked into him in a way she had never been to anyone else.

Then a flood of tears, as if a whole lifetime of pent-up emotion was released in a single moment.

When it was over, she was spent, exhausted, rested her head on the wheel, her breathing ragged. The sun set, casting the field in gold. Then streetlamps came on. Finally, she was in darkness. After a while, she took the long drive home. Home. Back to the house she shared with Pop.

But when she got there, the house was empty, as it often was lately. Pop was busy. He had a new job, something that was taking a lot of time and energy. She was often alone with her schoolwork, with her books. She read and read, just as she had always done—disappearing into other worlds, other lives.

When she checked her email on returning to her laptop, there was a note from her father. Her biological father. The man who was nothing special.

Yes, it read, I know you. Should we meet?

THIRTY
Anne

ON THE KITCHEN counter, there were three phones, all charging. Two burners, both flip phones, and a smartphone. Anne currently managed four email addresses, five post office boxes. And she held two properties, condos, owned by a shell corporation. Thanks to Pop's crooked old lawyer, Merle, her assets were managed, and she had a single legal identity that was utterly clean—passport, Social Security number, driver's license.

That identity was her escape hatch. She'd finish up what she was working on, and then she was going to go clean.

"This is my final—act," she said out loud.

She didn't like the word "con." It had such a base connotation—a scam, rip-off; there was something ugly about the word that didn't reflect all the careful nuances of the game. What she did, what they did, it was so much more than theft. It was a science and an art, a delicate give and take. Pop believed that he gave as much as they took, which she always thought was bullshit. But later she saw that there was a truth to it, without it being the whole truth.

Pop was quiet, which meant he disapproved or disagreed. He was just a ghost in the corner today, barely a shadow. That's what he was. A ghost. A shadow. Long gone but still with her.

"And then what?" he said finally.

That was Pop. He was always accusing her of going in too deep, getting too personal, giving too much. But Pop? He didn't even know who he was when he wasn't running a game. He'd become edgy, restless. He'd sit blank for hours, as if he'd been powered down. He was nothing without it.

But it wasn't like that for her.

She could become anyone, go anywhere, shift off one self, pick up another. She could give it up anytime. And when she did, she'd spend some energy getting to know herself finally—the real girl behind all the masks she'd worn.

"I'm tired," she said. "I want to just 'be' for a while. Travel. Take some cooking classes in exotic places. Learn how to ski. Whatever. Whatever it is people do."

He laughed a little—gently, not unkind. Never unkind. He loved her, in the way that he was able. "Life's not like that for people like us, kitten."

"I'm not like you." It came out edgy, defensive. Softer, "I'm not."

"Oh, no?"

"I can live without it."

"Are you sure?"

One of the burner phones jumped and danced. Ben.

She'd been out of contact since their last chat. He'd called several times, texted, emailed. Then he'd gone silent for a while. She could imagine him sweetly worried, but also desperate. She'd given him something—hope that he could love someone again, that he could *be* loved. She fed his broken ego with her words, her need for him, their talks when she'd asked his advice, the photos they'd exchanged. She'd given him the free flight of fancy. What might be.

Pop always said that you couldn't con an honest man, but that wasn't the whole truth. You couldn't con someone who didn't need something, who didn't want something badly enough to believe it was possible.

"You like him," said Pop. "Is that it?"

She didn't answer him.

"Big mistake."

She picked up the burner phone, scrolled through Ben's texts.

"What?" goaded Pop. "You think you'll get married. Settle down. Leave this life behind?"

She could just let Ben off the hook right now. Never answer him again, close down her profile, cancel the email she used for him, trash the phone. He'd be sad that he'd lost "Gwyneth." He'd get over it. Eventually. But she didn't want to let him go.

I'm so sorry, she typed. I'm okay.

I've been so worried.

My sister, she overdosed. She's in the hospital. Just dealing with all of this. I'll call you later.

Her phone rang. It was Ben but she didn't answer.

"He's ripe," said Pop. "He's hooked. Right now, he'll give you anything. He's desperate to keep you in his life. Don't give that desperation time to turn to anger. You know how men get when something gets taken away from them."

Sorry, she typed. I can't talk. I didn't want to say it like this.

?

But this situation with my sister. Life is short.

What are you saying?

I love you, Ben.

It almost felt true. Even though she wondered if she would recognize a true feeling within herself. She waited, a little breathless.

I love you, too. I wanted to tell you in person.

Soon. I promise.

Looking at the words on the screen, she felt the utter disconnection of the text message. How it floated in space, no touch, no tone, no expression. It was perfect for the con, a blank slate that others could fill with meaning. But so flawed for true connection. And, yet, she felt a connection to Ben. Didn't she? She wanted to tell him her real name. Her real story. But how could she now?

"Wow," said Pop. "I stand corrected. You're the master. Keeping him on the line, driving that hook in as deep as it can go."

Her other phone pinged. She picked it up. It was from Selena.

Who are you? it read. What do you want?

Good questions. Truly.

"Too many balls in the air," said Pop. "Didn't I teach you never more than one? How many do you have going—three?"

It was just two now. Ben and Selena. She'd let the others go—the family who thought she was a long-lost cousin, the guy who thought she'd hacked his camera and caught him watching porn.

"This is it, Pop. Just this one last thing. And I'm done."

"Yeah. That's what they all say."

The silence expanded between them. She almost killed Ben's burner phone, but then didn't. He was her escape hatch. She could easily become the woman he thought she was. She could disappear into that life if she wanted to, couldn't she? Maybe she could even stay there. Maybe she even wanted to.

"So, *who* are you, kitten?" said Pop. "What *do* you want?"

She caught a reflection of herself in the window over the kitchen sink. Just a dark form, lit from behind.

"Maybe it's time for me to find out."

He issued a soft chuckle.

"Start peeling back those layers, you might not like who you find."

THIRTY-ONE

Oliver

STEPHEN WAS STUPID. He was snoring, mouth wide open, arms flung over his head, cheeks flushed. Oliver watched him, wished he was sleeping, too. But he couldn't. Because his mom was in the room next to them, and after an evening of closed doors, and lowered voices, he heard her crying through the wall. She'd come in to read to them, give them kisses. She lay with them a while, as long as they promised not to talk. He knew when his mom was upset—when she was sad, when she was tired and cranky, when she was mad at Dad. When she was mad at them. He knew. Stephen never noticed anything because he was stupid.

Oliver wished that he was stupid, too.

He knew that something was wrong, and no one would say what. He'd talked to his dad earlier that day. *Take care of your mom*, he'd said, his voice on the phone sounding strange and far away.

Where are you, Dad?

Don't worry. Everything's okay. You'll see. A couple of days and things will be back to normal.

But he'd never heard his dad sound like that. There were unfamiliar noises in the background of the call—a ringing phone, voices he didn't recognize.

Everything's okay. Just hang tight.

His mom had said that, too. But Oliver was old enough to know that when grown-ups kept saying that, then it wasn't true. Things were not okay.

And, then, after Mom left their bedroom, went back to the room next door where Jasper and Lily slept when they were all visiting together, after they'd been quiet for a long time, he heard his mom crying. Not just getting teary, the way she sometimes did. Not yelling-crying the way she sometimes did when they were really being "little assholes," as their dad liked to say. Just crying. Stuttering breaths, little sighs. Crying the ways girls did, long and sad. She cried for a while, probably didn't think anyone could hear her, and then she was quiet.

He got out of bed and walked through the jack-and-jill bath (why did they call it that?), pushed the door open. He walked over to the bed. He was going to ask to climb in with her. But the bed was empty. Mom was gone.

Maybe she went downstairs the way Grandma did sometimes. Sometimes Grandma went down and made warm milk. A couple times he'd followed her. And they sat and talked, about whatever—school or comic books, things his mom and Aunt Marisol did when they were younger. The tree house that used to be out back of what was now Grandpa's house, what trip Grandma and Paulo were taking. Why Grandma and his real grandpa weren't married anymore. *Sometimes people fall out of love, and they're just better off apart. Sometimes that happens. And it's hard at first but then, after a while, everyone adjusts.* It sounded like another lie that grown-ups told. Zander said that it sucked, even with two birthdays, two Christmases. But Oliver's mom wasn't a kid when Grandma and Grandpa got divorced. And his real grandpa was way less nice than Paulo.

He figured that his mom and his dad were splitting up. And somehow it had something to do with Geneva, who didn't come back to work.

He walked back through the bathroom and got his iPad.

He heard sounds from downstairs, so he left his snoring brother and sneaked down, creeping on the stairs. He figured maybe he should show his mother the pictures he took when Geneva left. He had so many pictures—pictures of Geneva, pictures of the neighbor's dog, a picture of Stephen's naked butt, his own butt. He had pictures of his mom in the kitchen. His dad in his study, staring at his computer, which is where he usually was. He had a picture of his dad's butt crack as he bent over to try to fix the wall. *Cut that out, you little stinker,* he'd yelled. *Delete that picture.* But Oliver had laughed so hard that Dad started laughing, too. His mom always held up her hand. *I'm a wreck! Stop, Oliver! Ugh, that's the worst angle for me.* He had a whole catalog of backward slow-motion footage of Stephen jumping off the bed, the couch, the front stoop—one where he fell and started to cry. That one always cracked him up, how fast Stephen's face changed—happy one second, then wailing at the camera in pain and misery.

Oliver crept down the stairs, past the gallery of photographs on the wall—pictures of his mom and aunt as kids, Oliver, his brother, his cousins, Grandma and Paulo on trips, the time they all went to Disney. He liked looking at them; he didn't remember a lot of the moments. But the photographs were like a memory, he could *almost* remember being there because he saw the picture so many times, heard the stories told again and again. There was one picture of his mom holding a puppy—their old dog Chewie. She was ten, Grandma said—which seemed impossible. How could his mom ever have been a kid like him?

At the bottom step, he saw the light on in the kitchen. Oliver thought he'd find his mom, bent over her phone, or staring off into space the way she sometimes did, the expression on her face unreadable. But instead it was his grandmother. She was at the stove, wearing the same pink robe she did most nights, the smell of warm milk meeting him at the door frame. She would put honey in it, some other spices—weird things like pepper and something else he couldn't pronounce. She called it golden milk; it was maybe his favorite thing ever. He took his seat at the table. Grandma never got mad at him for getting up.

"Mom's not in her bed," he said, moving toward the table, pulling up a chair. More pictures everywhere, on the walls, on surfaces. At his house, all their pictures were on the television screens, the computers, iPads, phones. There were hardly any paper photographs in frames. One from Mom and Dad's wedding, where Mom looked like a princess and Dad was *a lot* thinner.

Grandma turned to face him; she always smiled when she looked at him and Stephen, Lily and Jasper. Her eyes got all crinkly. But tonight, she looked a little worried.

"I heard her leave," she said with a nod. "It woke me."

"Where did she go?"

"Sometimes when she was younger, she'd go running at night. When she was stressed, or upset about something, she'd just get out of bed and go jogging."

"You let her?" Oliver wondered what it would be like to just leave a place without permission, alone. It didn't even seem possible, even for his mom, who was always home, or with them, or with Dad. Dad could go out alone; he could be gone for days and it didn't matter that much. Like now. But Mom? That was different. *Take care of your mom*, Dad had said on the phone earlier. How was Oliver supposed to do that? He hadn't asked; it was one of those things you were already supposed to know. Like the "bro code."

Grandma shrugged, turned back to stirring the pot with a wooden spoon. "Your mom's an adult. And I'm a firm believer in letting people be who they are. Right or wrong."

He looked out the window; all he saw was black. "Is it safe?"

"Selena—your mom—is smart and strong, as able to take care of herself as anyone I've known. Even when she was your age, she used to go out back by herself without asking."

"I've never been outside by myself."

She looked over her shoulder at him, gave him a smile. "Things are different now. Parents—do things differently. Maybe better."

She came over with two mugs, sat across from him. "Be careful. It's hot."

"Are Mom and Dad getting a divorce?"

She reached for him, put her hand on his hair. His grandma always smelled like flowers, her skin soft. He waited for her to lie. *Of course not!* she might say. Or: *Don't say things like that*. "Look," she said instead. "There are some grown-up things going on right now. But we're all going to get through it together."

Not a lie. But—

"That's not an answer, Grandma."

She nodded. "I know it. But it's the only one I have for you. Not even grown-ups have all the answers. Unfortunately."

He already knew that.

He took a sip of the milk. It was spicy and sweet, but it burned his tongue a little. Not too bad. He didn't say anything—she'd just told him it was hot. Stephen would be jealous if he knew about Oliver's special time with Grandma. Their special drink. Oliver loved having something that Stephen didn't have, and he would never complain about it.

"Is it because of Geneva?" he asked. "Because she didn't come to work?"

Grandma sighed, rubbed at her temples. She was quiet a minute, and he thought maybe she wasn't going to answer him. That was another thing they did. Just change the subject.

She took a sip from her milk. Then, "Look, honey. When your mom comes back, we'll all sit down and talk about it. But all you need to know right now is that you and Stephen are safe. And your parents love you as much as ever. Can that be enough for right now?"

He nodded, because he knew that's what she wanted him to do, to understand more than he did.

He pushed his iPad across the table.

"The night she left," he said. "I recorded her."

"Who?"

"Geneva."

Grandma looked at him, frowning, then down at the iPad. "On this?"

"Yeah." He turned it to her and pressed Play.

"Did you tell anyone about this?" she asked.

He shook his head, and her frown deepened. She leaned in and watched. He watched, too. Geneva crossed the street, stood at her car digging through her purse. Then she turned around.

Oliver had gotten distracted here, ran off after Stephen who was being a jerk about the remote. But he'd left the iPad in the window, recording.

Geneva walked into the street. Another person approached. He wore a jacket with a hood. It looked like a "he." Or did it? Maybe a kid? An older kid.

Geneva looked angry, brow wrinkled, body stiff. She was saying something—Oliver wished he could read lips. Geneva pointed toward their house, and the other person, taller than Geneva, turned quickly, then back to Geneva.

For just a second, they'd seen a face.

"Oh," said his grandmother.

"Who is that?" Oliver asked aloud, even though of course his grandma didn't know. But when he looked at her, Grandma had her hand over her mouth. She looked—scared. Which scared Oliver a little. He got a funny feeling in his stomach.

Then, Geneva and the other person walked out of view, leaves blowing around them. A ginger cat walked up the sidewalk on the other side. Oliver had seen it before but he wasn't sure where it belonged. There was just the empty street, cars passing by intermittently—for a while. Mom stopped the recording finally. There was a flash of her annoyed face as she turned it off before taking it away as punishment for fighting with his brother.

"Oh, my goodness," said his grandma, still staring at the screen even though there was nothing else to see.

"Mom?" The voice startled them both.

Oliver looked up to see his mother standing in the door. She was wearing her running clothes, cheeks flushed, her shirt damp with sweat.

"What are you guys looking at?" she asked. But Grandma just shook her head. A tear fell from her eye and Oliver felt awful, looked at his mom. He'd made his grandma cry. He felt the heat of his own tears coming. He fought it back, because he already knew that boys weren't supposed to cry. *Man up, Oliver,* his dad would say if Mom couldn't hear.

"You guys," said his mom, moving in, sounding scared herself now. "What *is it*?"

THIRTY-TWO

Pearl

THE GIRL POP brought home was mousy and pale. She had a strange, glassy look to her, as if she might shatter into a million glittering pieces. As Pearl drew tentatively closer, she could see that the girl was shaking a little. Quaking really, a kind of full body vibration. There had never been anyone in their house before. And Pearl didn't love it. In fact, she hated it. It felt like a terrible invasion, a broken promise.

"Gracie here," said Pop, as Pearl put down her things. "She's in a dark place. We're going to take care of her for a while."

"Oh?" said Pearl.

The girl looked at her, then quickly looked away. A single tear trailed down her face from an eye as vague as a morning sky—a kind of palest blue. Barely a color at all. She wasn't beautiful, not in the way Pearl knew herself to be. But then again, she was just a girl, doughy, small-breasted. Unformed. Maybe Pearl herself had been so, before Pop taught her how to be what she'd become.

"She's a diamond in the rough," said Pop, as if reading Pearl's mind. He glanced worriedly over at the girl. There was an untouched cup of tea steaming in front of her.

"I see that."

"Don't be unkind," he whispered. "She's just lost her mother."

There'd been another girl, one who'd interested Pop. Where had they been that time? She couldn't even remember—someplace bland and humid. But it hadn't worked out. Pearl wondered if there had been girls before even her. If there had been, they were gone without a trace.

"Once upon a time," said Pop, directing himself to Gracie, "when tragedy struck, I took Pearl in. I cared for her and helped her to move forward. Now we'll both take care of you, okay, sweet girl?"

That was a lovely little narrative, if not quite the whole truth. But what is the truth after all? Just a story we all agree upon.

Gracie nodded, seemed to straighten a bit. She ran a hand over her thin hair, cleared her throat. Pearl thought she might say something. But after a moment of them all staring at each other, Gracie leaned over and threw up on the kitchen floor. This was followed by a coughing fit, one that turned into terrible, uncontrollable it seemed, sobbing.

Pearl looked on in horror—something churning in her middle. Disgust.

"Okay, okay," said Pop, going to Gracie tenderly. "You're okay. Let's get you some rest."

He wrapped the girl up in his arms. The sobbing subsided some, replaced by whimpering. The girl, already tiny, seemed to shrink and disappear into Pop as he ushered her from the kitchen. He glanced back as they left.

"Pearl? Get that—will you, honey?"

He still called her Pearl when they were at home, though he never ever slipped when they were out, or on a job. And when she was home with him, she still thought of herself by that name. Even though she called herself Elizabeth at that time. Not Liz.

Not Beth. Elizabeth, common but still regal, elegant. She had a boyfriend at school; someone she'd kept from Pop. He wasn't a mark. They went to the movies, and he took her to dinner. They studied together. They'd fooled around, heavily, but not made love. He called her Elizabeth, and it had a nice sound when he whispered it in the dark. Maybe he was a mark, in a way. Her con was that she was a normal girl, a student, his girlfriend. She had a waitressing job, a cash situation at a pizza place. She didn't want anything but to be the girl he saw when he looked at her.

"I can't get close enough to you," he'd said the other night, kissing her. She wasn't sure what he meant—physically, emotionally, maybe both. She liked him—Jason. He was smart, could play the guitar. He was a doorway to the kind of life other people had. She thought about packing her bags now, taking her very few things, and leaving Pop with his new project. She could go. She had her games, her own money now. She didn't think he'd try to stop her.

"Sure," said Pearl loudly. "Why not? I'll clean up the puke. Like I'm the maid."

But he had already left her behind to take care of Gracie.

There wasn't much vomit, just a small puddle of nearly clear bile. She might have felt bad for the girl, if she didn't hate her.

She was aware of a bubbling anger, something mean and small. What kind of bullshit was this? Some stranger in the house that was supposed to be their forever home. Their place safe from the world.

She heard a wail from upstairs, followed by Pop's soothing tones. Another wail.

Had she been such a wreck at first? she wondered as she mopped up, threw away the paper towels, scrubbed with a little bleach. She washed her hands in hot water.

No, she hadn't been.

"There aren't many girls like you, Pearl," Pop had said—more than once. "You might be one of a kind."

Looking back, she saw Gracie joining them was the first dark omen. After that, bad things started happening. Wasn't that always how it worked? One mistake leading inexorably to the next, like a trip down a steep flight of stairs. But maybe it started back in Phoenix. The Bridget thing.

"Don't be mad," said Pop, returning to the kitchen alone. Pearl was still washing her hands, scrubbing them raw in hot water. They hurt when she turned off the faucet.

"Why would I be mad?" she said, sharper than she'd intended.

"She's for you," he said, staying by the door. "A sister."

Did he even hear himself? She almost laughed but then she looked at him—dark circles under his eyes, a fatigued sag to his eyelids. She knew he hadn't been sleeping. She heard him at night, moving around his room. He'd aged since the problem in Phoenix—deep lines had settled around his mouth and on his brow; he'd grown thinner, taking on a hard, wiry quality. Something about it had rattled him hard. He hadn't regained his footing.

He came to the table and she sat across from him. She could still smell the vomit, mingling unpleasantly with the bleach.

"You don't just bring home a sister," she said. "It's not like getting a puppy."

He bowed his head, looking down at his cuticles, which were gnawed and rough. "You *are* mad."

"No."

Yes. She was mad. Not just about the stranger in their home; there were a thousand things. Nothing she could name—just that, lately, she felt like an animal in a cage, pacing. That she was bound to him somehow, without wanting to be. That she could leave him, should leave him. But she couldn't. She didn't say any of it.

"You haven't been yourself," he said into the silence. "What's going on?"

"I could say the same to you."

She got up, put on a kettle for tea—just to get away from him. That stare, those intensely staring eyes and how they saw everything about everyone and knew just how to exploit whatever want, need, fear was lurking beneath the surface.

"It's your father," he went on, not turning around to face her. "That whole thing."

She shrugged, glad he couldn't see her. She wasn't sure she could keep the rush of emotion off her face.

"It went well," she said, her voice going higher than she liked. "Big payout. Just like you said."

Yes, a big payout. She had a pile of cash, delivered with the promise to never communicate with him again. Then, when she could have gone far from him, never thought about him again, let it all go once and for all—

"You burned him down," Pop said.

She heard the note of disapproval in his voice. It bothered her, more than it should.

She looked at her watch. She was late for Jason. She was late for Elizabeth; her normie self. Student. Waitress. Ordinary small-town girl. Nothing special. The teakettle started to whistle, and she took it from the stove, poured the hot water into the two mugs she'd retrieved from the cupboard. World's Best Dad, one of them read. The world was full of little ironies, wasn't it?

"What if I did?" she said, walking back. She put a cup in front of him, but he didn't reach for it.

Yes. She'd left her father's life in ashes. He'd moved out of that beautiful house. A messy, public divorce had commenced. His daughters wouldn't speak to him. Stella hadn't been his only affair, not by a long shot. There was a whole other family, apparently, another woman, other children. Women he worked with, when the news hit, came forward to tell of his aggression in the work place, his unwelcome advances. A wealthy philanthropist, bastion of the community, revealed as a serial adulterer, a workplace predator. It wasn't big news. But it was news enough. He'd been removed as CEO of his company, last she heard.

"That's not how it works," Pop said softly. "Not how it's supposed to work."

"Maybe that's how it works for me." She didn't sit, started gathering her things. "Maybe sometimes it's about more than money. Sometimes it's about making people pay for the things they've done."

"Never leave them with nothing left to lose. Didn't I teach you that much?"

"I have my own way of doing things," she said. "You've never had a bigger score than that. Have you?"

He offered a deferential nod. "The student surpasses the teacher."

"Is that what we're talking about? You think I've surpassed you. Is that what she is?" She pointed upstairs. "Your new student?"

"Of course not. She's just someone who needs us right now. In this world, you make a family where you can find it."

"You just need someone to worship you."

He shook his head, looked down again, this time at the grain of the wood on the table. "I've taken care of you, Pearl. Haven't I? Good care of you? I've loved you like my own child."

That anger, it boiled over, was a siren. But she stood stock still. She almost never lost her temper.

"Children grow up," she said quietly.

Pop looked at her as if she'd slapped him.

She went upstairs. She could pack her things, everything that meant anything to her in twenty minutes. She did so. Through the wall, she could hear the stranger still weeping. The sound was low and despairing, toxic sadness, leaking in through her pores.

Fuck. This.

When she got back downstairs, Pop was waiting by the door.

"You don't have to do this," he said. "We can be a family."

"I need space," she said. "I need to figure out who I am."

He smiled, expansive, understanding, took her into his arms and held her tight. She found herself sinking into him, almost changing her mind. But then she hardened inside again. He seemed to feel it, released her with a kiss on the forehead.

"Come for Sunday dinner," he said. "Children may grow up. But they can always come home."

She walked out the door, opened the trunk of the car she'd bought with her own money and put everything she owned inside. A glance in the rearview showed Pop in the doorway, waving, and the shadow of a girl in an upstairs window.

Her anger subsided; Pearl, Anne, Elizabeth, or whatever her name was now, felt nothing at all.

THIRTY-THREE

Cora

"WHAT IS IT, MOM?" demanded Selena.

Cora clutched the iPad, still staring in disbelief. Her daughter's face was a mask of confused anger. "This woman on the street with Geneva—" Cora still couldn't quite believe her eyes.

"Oliver," said Selena, looking at her son. A tear trailed down his cheek. "Go to bed, sweetie. This is a grown-up conversation."

"But—" the boy said, staring back and forth between them. "I'm sorry."

"Now," said Selena, too sharply. She shut her eyes, as if summoning patience, then softened her voice. "Please, honey. Please."

Oliver opened, then closed his mouth, finally storming off, the door swinging behind him. Cora heard him stomping on the stairs, had the urge to chase after him, to comfort him. He'd be upset because he was a sensitive child.

Selena took the iPad from Cora's hands and touched the screen, the glow lighting her face as she watched the video.

After a second she gasped, sank into the seat behind her with a thud. She shook her head, seemed to be puzzling.

"Do you *know her*?" Selena asked finally.

"Do *you*?" asked Cora.

"I—met her on the train," Selena said, sounding a little dazed, incredulous. "She's been—texting me. I saw her again for a drink in the city."

The revelation pulsed through Cora. "Oh my god."

"Who is she? Mom?"

The words jammed up in Cora's throat. There were so many things that she'd never told her daughters about their father, the things he'd done. She'd kept his secrets, to spare her girls.

Cora reached for Oliver's iPad again, clicked on the image. Yes, it was her. Cora had immediately recognized the girl in the video.

"Mom!" said Selena. *"Who is she?"*

The first time Cora laid eyes on her, the girl was young, in her late teens. She was hovering outside the grocery store. Dark, with strong features like Cora's husband, slim like their daughters—there was something feral about her, something that awakened Cora's mothering instincts. She saw the girl in produce, inspecting apples. What was it about her, she always wondered, that caught Cora's eye that afternoon? Then she was by the newspapers.

Cora almost approached her. *Do you need help?* She wanted to ask, even though there wasn't any overt indication that anything was wrong. Just a sense she had. But when Cora was finished with checkout, the girl was gone.

The next time, the girl was walking up their block, trying to look like she belonged there. But she wouldn't belong anywhere, Cora thought. She had the energy of an outsider, eyes searching, shoulders hiked. Her clothes were shabby, but she was leggy and buxom, a bombshell beauty. She kept walking.

Then, a few days later, she was hovering by the oak tree. Cora watched her from the kitchen window, then sauntered out onto the porch to water some plants, wondering if she'd approach the house. Finally, Cora walked down the flagstone path. *I'll invite her in. See what she wants*, thought Cora. But the girl scurried off.

Cora knew who she was. The resemblance was so strong.

Marisol was off to college. Selena was a senior, would be leaving for NYU in the fall. It was spring, a time of new beginning, rebirth.

That girl. The girl on the street outside her house. The one on the video now.

She was the final straw for Cora.

Not because she was angry that her husband had clearly fathered another child outside the marriage; that was bad enough. But that he had *abandoned* that child and now she was so lost, so alone that she hovered on the street, waiting—for what, Cora didn't yet know. What kind of man was he? How could she have ever loved someone so utterly morally and emotionally bankrupt?

Cora summoned her courage. It was so much easier to talk to her older daughter.

Marisol. Marisol *talked*—she might cry, or yell—but they talked and talked, worked it out. For Selena, everything was always black-and-white, good or bad—she was like her father that way. Marisol understood the shades of gray that comprised most of life—that sometimes what seemed right was wrong, that what was wrong might feel right. She wasn't as hard on Cora as Selena had been and still was. Cora knew that Selena thought she was weak for staying with Doug so many years, for keeping his secrets. But she'd done what she knew how to do. She'd endured her own unhappiness because she thought an intact home was best for her children. Or maybe she was just afraid.

And now Selena found herself in the same mess—even worse. As a mother, how could Cora not take some responsibility for that? She'd been a poor role model.

The words, when they came, were little more than a whisper.

"She's—your father's daughter by another woman. A child from one of his affairs," she said.

Selena blanched, mouth opening.

"She's your half sister," Cora went on. "Her name is Pearl."

THIRTY-FOUR

Pearl

THE CALL CAME LATE. The ringing of her phone leaked deep into her dream, where she ran down the stairs of an underground turret that bored into the earth. Her footfalls echoed and a shadowy figure was behind her. She could feel its chill breath. Down, down. Deeper, deeper. The sunlight above faded, and the stairway let out into a system of low caves. She felt her way toward the ringing of the phone, a lifeline, a way out. When it finally pulled her from sleep, she saw her phone glowing on her bedside. Jason had an arm and a leg draped over her; he slept like a child, deeply, nearly impossible to wake.

The phone stopped ringing. She didn't reach for it. Nothing good; she was sure of that. It was 3:00 a.m. She hadn't been back to Pop's since the night she left. She figured it was him calling. Something was wrong.

She lay in the dark, her heart thumping, the tendrils of the dream pulling her back toward sleep. She nestled in closer to Jason. His body was a furnace.

Pearl had all but disappeared into her life as Elizabeth. She'd moved in with Jason, sharing his simple one-bedroom apartment near campus. They went to class together. She worked at the pizza place; he worked as a mechanic at a local shop, fixing vintage cars as an apprentice. They went to the movies, whatever he wanted to see—art films, and obscure documentaries. They hung out with his friends at house parties and barbecues. They ate out, inexpensive dinners at casual restaurants. They made love finally. It was easy. So easy. A normie life, as Pop would call it. It washed over her, like a cleansing rain. Every day, Pearl got a little fainter, and Elizabeth got a little stronger.

She remembered her life with Stella—all the drama of her many boyfriends, constant stress over the store, Stella's moods, her distance. Little Pearl lived in her chaotic mess of a life, burying herself in stories, in books. She escaped into other worlds, other lives. In the pages of her books, she became. Jane Eyre always running from one bad situation to the next. The new Mrs. DeWinter withering under the hateful gaze of Mrs. Danvers. Laura Fairlie in the evil clutches of Sir Percival Glyde. This wasn't so very different. She'd disappeared into the story of Elizabeth and Jason.

Jason wanted to know about her life before, her parents, how she grew up. Pearl-Elizabeth wove a story of half truths. Her mother died; she never knew her father. Her uncle had taken her in. She traveled around with him for a while, but they'd had a falling out. Jason said he had a big family back in Minnesota; they planned to visit over the summer. He loved her; she could see that. She could pretend to love him and enjoy doing that. Maybe he sensed it, her distance.

Sometimes, I wonder where you are, he said one night. *It's like you're always just drifting away from me.*

I'm right here, she said. She went down on him, making him go helpless with pleasure. And that seemed to settle the matter.

Sometimes in the night, she looked at the objects around the room cast in shadows. Her clothes over the chair, her books and laptop, flowers in a vase, the television they bought and rarely watched. What would I take with me if I had to run? she thought.

Maybe some of her books. A few items of clothing. The bag in the closet that contained money, passport, Social Security card. She'd never been out of the country, then. But if she had to run, she thought, she'd go to London. She didn't know why. There was something about the gauzy idea of it, the gray skies, the persistent chilly drizzle she imagined, that appealed. It was a place where you could disappear into the fog.

The phone rang again, and this time Pearl reached for it. A number she didn't recognize. She should just send it to voice mail. But she answered. There was weeping on the other line, a voice she recognized. A girl.

"Pearl?"

"What is it?" She could barely contain her annoyance.

"Please come."

She felt a jolt, a shock of fear through her system. She extracted herself from Jason, who rolled over oblivious, still deeply asleep.

"What's happened?"

"Please," she said. "Please come. I—don't know what to do."

She ended the call and lay quiet for a moment, then she got up and packed her few things. She took her duffel from the closet, stuffed in her clothes, her books, her laptop.

She didn't know why. Something about the dream, the call, the sound of the girl's voice. Some strange energy on the air. She suspected that once she walked out the door, the way back to Jason, to Elizabeth, would be closed to her. A closed book, a story ended.

When she had everything, she lingered a moment, her bag heavy on her shoulder, and stared at Jason sleeping. She searched herself for feeling—sadness, regret, longing. And, as usual, she felt nearly nothing. Maybe a twinge of something, a faint wish that things were another way.

She gave herself a moment with the story—he proposed, they got married, maybe they moved back to Minnesota to be closer to his family. They bought a pretty house, nothing fancy, lived a quiet life—maybe had children, raised them in safety and comfort. Elizabeth took over. The story became the truth; Pearl faded to nothing, just a ghost from the past, a girl who barely ever was. She could almost see it. She could almost go there.

Jason never stirred as she left without a sound.

She drove nearly an hour back to the house, leaving the little college town behind, taking the winding roads into the country. She hadn't been there since the day she left, though Pop kept calling, inviting her to dinner. He left messages that were more like letters with updates, little snippets of news, mentions about the house, things that needed fixing. He had stories about his new little pet who he referred to annoyingly as her sister. *Your sister—don't get me wrong, she's nothing like you—is a quick study. I think she'll adjust to the life just fine.* She kept sending him to voice mail.

Just come home, little girl, he said in his final message. *Nothing's changed. We're family. Family is never perfect. There are always problems, but we're always here.*

Family.

Pop was obviously losing his mind. The distance she'd achieved from him allowed her to see what he was more clearly. A con at best. Maybe something worse. Maybe her abductor. A killer. Stella's murder—it remained unsolved all these years later. And where had Gracie come from? Who was she? Where was her mother?

When Pearl brought the car to a stop, she saw the girl sitting on the porch, a slouched rag doll against the railing. She was curled up over her knees, fetal. Pearl felt a dump of dread;

she sat with it. Listening to the ticking engine of her car, she thought, *I should go. Far from here.* But she didn't. Because she knew it wasn't what he wanted her to do.

She exited and walked to Gracie, footfalls crunching on the drive.

"What's happened?" she asked. Her voice rang back harsh; she sounded like Stella, who never had any patience for weakness. *Pull yourself together, Pearl.*

But the girl just shook her head, expression blank. Pearl moved in closer and saw that there was a dark skein of blood down the front of her shirt, on her hands, under her nails. Those pale blue eyes were staring at something a million miles away.

"Are you hurt?" Pearl asked. Her voice calm, softer now. It seemed to disappear in the heaviness of the air.

Another slow shake of her mousy head.

The door stood ajar, light casting a yellow rectangle onto the boards. Silence. The night held its chilly breath. Pearl climbed the steps to the porch, the wood creaking beneath her weight. Slowly. She paused at the top, trying to quiet her beating heart. Then she pushed inside.

There were two bodies, lying side by side, blood pooling. An unpleasant odor, something metallic and sharp in her nose. She took a step back, time freezing solid. Pop, faceup—a hole in his head, in his chest. He lay on his back, palms up. Eyes calm, mouth frozen in surprise, as if he died trying to believe what was happening.

Was it another nightmare? Would she wake up? Down, down the turret that bored into the earth, a shadow behind her. But no. The details were too sharp, the odors too strong.

"Pop," she whispered. But he just stared back at her, knowing.

There was no justice in the system for a con. When the tables turned, when the mark got wise, when the bill for your deeds came due, there was no one to call. There was an order to the universe, and you could only run your scam for so long.

Beside him, a woman lay prone, the back of her head a messy pulp. Even so, Pearl recognized her. Pearl felt bile rise in her throat but she forced it back. Something about the thickness of the woman's shoulders, her style of dress—tacky top and too-tight jeans. The dyed red of her hair. Bridget. The woman who'd rattled Pop in Phoenix.

Never leave them with nothing left to lose. Pop hadn't taken his own advice. He'd hurt her and she'd hunted him down.

She stared, a siren in her head. Then, tears. They seemed to spring from her eyes of their own volition, not propelled by any feeling. Inside, she was quiet as a tomb.

Footsteps behind her. Soft, shuffling.

"I killed her," said Gracie. It was just a whisper.

Pearl surveyed the scene. The gun Bridget clearly used to kill Pop lay near her hand, some kind of semiautomatic, she thought—but Pearl didn't know anything about guns. Also on the ground, covered with blood and gore, a heavy jade bookend Pearl recognized from a set in the study. A Fu Lion, something Pop had taken from the bookstore. Stella had picked them up at an estate sale; Pearl remembered her elation at the find. Supposedly they protected their owners from harm. Another one of life's little ironies.

"I hit her from behind," Gracie said, voice more solid. "She just—crumbled. But I was too late. She'd already shot him. He died—so fast. We were just cooking dinner."

Pearl could smell onions on the air.

She couldn't find her voice, so she turned to look at the girl. Gracie was thinner, her features more angular. A kind of common prettiness had started to emerge. Her eyes were steely, revealing a strength that Pearl wouldn't have imagined from their few encounters where she'd largely been weeping, puking, hunched into a fetal position.

"What do we do?" the girl asked. She gulped back a sob.

We? thought Pearl.

Yes, we, Pop would have said. *She's your sister. She's all you have now.*

The shock of it started to lift. There was a problem here to be solved and she was good at that. Her brain started to work again—calculate, strategize. A solution architect.

The property was isolated; chances were that no one heard the gunfire. Pop was a ghost. He barely existed. The only people who would ever come looking for him were already there. All good things.

She knelt down, hesitated a moment. Careful of the pooling blood, Pearl then started looking on the woman's body for her phone, finding it in the back pocket of her jeans. A smartphone. She pressed the home button, quickly determined that it wasn't password-protected.

Bridget. When Pop first found her, she'd been the perfect mark. No family, few friends. An isolated loner, desperate for connection.

"Where's her car?" asked Pearl. She rose and walked to the door, checking what she could see of the long, isolated drive. Maybe she'd passed it, not seeing it in the dark. But no. There was no car other than her own. "How did she get here?"

Gracie lifted slim shoulders in a helpless shrug.

Pearl checked for a ride-sharing app on the phone and didn't find one. That would be a wrinkle, if there was a record of Bridget coming here. Pearl would go through her phone, her email, her social media feeds. Then she'd use the phone to create a digital trail away from the house.

"Her car," said Pearl. "It must be nearby. We have to find it."

She looked up at Gracie, who was staring at her, eyes wide.

"And," she went on, "we have to get rid of the bodies."

"Bodies," Gracie echoed. She got a little glassy, slipping away again.

"Gracie," said Pearl, her voice sharp. The sound of her name seemed to wake the girl up. She stood a little taller, looking at Pearl as if awaiting instruction. Pearl went on.

"I'm going to need you to plug in and help me handle this. Pop wouldn't want us to curl up and die here. He'd want us to work together."

Something passed between them, a knowing. Pearl had no idea what Pop had done to Gracie, or how he came to take her and why. But he was right, they were sisters. Sisters of circumstance, bound now by this ugly moment in time, by Pop and whatever he had been to each of them, for each of them.

Gracie looked down at the bodies, and then back to Pearl. This was the moment. Was she going to pass out? Collapse? Start screaming? Run? This was the moment when Gracie would decide who she was. For Pearl, the moment had been in Pecos, years earlier when she became Anne. She chose Pop; she chose the life, even if she didn't understand then what the consequences would be later. Because of all the things Pearl was, most of all she was a survivor. She chose the path that kept her fighting another day.

But what about Gracie, this mousy little girl that Pop had chosen to be her sister. At her core, what was she?

Seconds ticked by and Gracie looked around. The confusion dropped from her face and her jaw seemed to settle, eyes clear. In the moment, Pearl saw in Gracie what Pop must have seen. She was one of them.

"Okay," Gracie said. She looked square at Pearl. "What do we need to do?"

THIRTY-FIVE

Cora

"WHY DIDN'T YOU ever tell us about this, Mom?" asked Selena. Her eyes were dark with recrimination. "Don't you think we had a right to know?"

Cora felt a lash of anger. Selena just wasn't getting it. Her younger daughter was angry at Cora for a hundred things, had been since her teens. Cora was too strict, didn't understand the "modern" world, worried too much about nothing. They were at loggerheads from age thirteen until she left for college. On the other hand, Selena had worshipped her father; his fall from grace was brutal for Selena. Marisol was always a momma's girl, tender and attached. Even now, they were closer than Cora was with Selena. Not that she loved her younger any less. It was just a chemistry thing.

"No," said Cora, sharper than she intended. "I *didn't* think you had a right to know. It was your father's responsibility to tell you what he'd done. If you're going to recriminate anyone, let it be him."

Selena drew in and released a rush of breath. The look on

her face—bewilderment, disappointment—put a squeeze on Cora's heart.

"Mom," she said. Selena put a hand to her forehead. "This woman—Pearl. She approached me on the train. I don't know why, but I told her—things about my life."

"What things?"

"About Graham. And since then—she's been texting me. Now Geneva is missing."

"Oh," said Cora, feeling the weight of it. What was the girl capable of? She'd done so much damage already.

A few weeks after she saw the girl, Cora noticed a large sum of money disappear from one of the accounts Doug thought he had hidden from her. But Cora, for all her many failings, wasn't one of those women who didn't pay attention to money. Doug wanted to control everything, but she always had access to accounts. She made sure of it, snooping if she had to for account numbers and passwords. She kept records; she was biding her time, hoping to launch the girls, at least to college, before she left.

On a night when Selena was off sleeping over at a girlfriend's house, Cora confronted Doug—about the money, about the strange, hovering girl. Cora had expected the usual denials, accusations of instability, a furious exit—that was the usual way of things. This time, though, she'd already called a lawyer. She was done.

But he didn't deny. Instead he started weeping. All his little secrets and lies, they all came out. Pearl. Another family, a woman and two children in Atlanta. A third girlfriend. It was a sickness, he said. He was seeking help.

Could she forgive him?

No. She could not. Not again. Not anymore.

Dominoes. Tip one and they all fall down. That was what happened to their life when Pearl entered. Doug's daughter from one of his many affairs. Selena and Marisol's half sister.

She didn't just want money. She wanted revenge. She ruined Doug—it all came out.

Now, Cora told Selena everything that she had tried to hide. All of it.

And when she was done, they sat in silence. There was only the ticking of the grandfather clock in the foyer, Selena's breath.

"I'm sorry," Cora said when Selena said nothing, her eyes glassy, foot bouncing. "I'm sorry I kept so many secrets from you. I thought it was for the best."

Her words sounded weak, watery on the air.

"So," said Selena. "Has she been watching us—watching *me*—all these years?"

The thought made Cora go cold. *Had* she?

Cora had let that part of her life fall away. In her new world, the one she built with Paulo, she'd let the past retreat into memory. Doug—his affairs, his nasty controlling ways—they faded into the distance. She rarely thought about him—or about Pearl, the lost girl who wanted to hurt her father and did.

"What does she want?" asked Selena.

"More money maybe," said Cora. "Your father; I'm not sure he's managed his assets well. I don't know what he has left. If he's been giving her money. I just don't know."

But even as she said it, she knew that money wasn't what Pearl wanted. It was never what she wanted. She was a pain giver. She wanted to hurt people, acting from whatever psychic wound she carried inside. Cora saw that in the girl in the grocery store, the one hovering by the yard. And now, years later, the one on the street in front of Selena's house. An injured animal, desperate, in pain, dangerous.

Was she stalking Selena? Had she orchestrated the encounter on the train? What did she want from Selena now?

Selena was staring at the picture on Oliver's iPad.

"She looks like him," Selena said. "I don't know why I didn't see it. Or I guess on some level, I did. Maybe that's why I subconsciously hooked in to her. There's a connection."

A connection. Yes, Cora had felt it. A pull to that lost girl. Maybe she wanted money. Maybe she wanted to cause harm. But beneath it all, there was something more. She wanted to connect, and this was the only way she knew how.

"We should call the police," said Cora. "Whatever game she's running, for whatever reason, it needs to be stopped."

"No," said Selena, leaning forward. "Who knows what she'll do if we call the police?"

"She's a destroyer," said Cora. "What if she killed Geneva? What if she wants to hurt you?"

"No," said Selena again, grabbing at Cora's hand. "We can't call the police, not yet."

"Sweetie," said Cora. "What do you think you're going to do, then?"

There was a look her daughter got, a stubborn set to her face.

"I'm going to find out what she wants," her daughter said, tone cool and practical. "And then I'm going to give it to her and get our life back."

Her daughter was delusional.

The clock chimed one. Selena wasn't going to "get her life back." Surely, she knew that. Her marriage was over at least. The body of a young girl had been discovered. Things weren't going to go back to the way they were a week ago, even a day ago. And in some ways, Cora was responsible. If she'd told Selena about Pearl, she wouldn't have been vulnerable to whatever plan the other woman had.

"How?" Cora asked.

"I—I don't know. But what if I can give this woman what she wants—and this nightmare just goes away? Maybe that's what she's been trying to tell me. All of this—maybe it's just extortion."

Cora shook her head. Nightmares rarely went away. In Cora's experience they usually got worse.

"She's playing with you," said Cora.

Selena shook her head. "I think it's more than that."

Cora didn't say anything, just watched as Selena rose and took her bag from the back of the chair, still in her running clothes. She was tall, like her father, with his athleticism and strength. Cora and Marisol were petite. Maybe it was something to do with size, it made Selena bolder.

Selena picked up her phone and started to text. Cora walked behind her to see what she was doing.

I know who you are, Pearl.

So just tell me what you want.

They both waited. But no answer came.

Cora's heart started to thump; she reached for Selena. Selena took her hand. Cora had always felt powerless against the wills of the stronger people in her life. Her throat was dry with anxiety, palms tingling.

"Don't do this," said Cora.

"I have to, Mom," she said. "If you don't hear from me in two hours, call Will, call the police. Tell them everything."

She let go of her daughter's hand and followed her to the door, then watched as the car glided from the drive and disappeared up the road.

THIRTY-SIX

Selena

SELENA PULLED INTO the driveway of her childhood home, where her father Doug now lived alone. She remembered once thinking the house was so big, so grand—with its white pillars and big door. But tonight, it seemed smaller. The yard, which her mother had carefully tended, was neglected, grass brown, shrubs anemic, weeds pushing up through the paving stones of the walkway. It was dark, shabby, whereas the other big houses on the block were bright with elaborate landscape lighting, meticulously maintained. Her father, getting older, must be having a hard time keeping things up. Marisol—who was closer to him—had said as much. But Selena had barely listened. Her sister forgave their father for his transgressions. Selena couldn't—wouldn't.

Now this. His sins come back to haunt, not *him* but Selena and her family.

She exited the car and marched up the path. She paused at the door a moment, the adrenaline of anger pulsing, then started aggressively ringing the doorbell. Once, twice, three times.

After a moment, lights started to come on—upstairs, then on the stairway she could see through the side window. Finally, she saw her father making his way down, a frail old man in a robe and slippers.

When was the last time she'd seen him?

He peered through the window with a scowl. Then surprise softened his features. He swung the door open.

"Selena," he said, peering behind her into the night. "What's going on?"

God. What was she doing here? Why had this seemed like the right thing to do?

"I need to talk, Dad."

He rubbed at his thinning hair. "Selena, it's the middle of the night."

She pushed her way into the towering foyer. A pile of mail sat by the door, a stack of newspapers tilted near the table where everyone used to put their keys and pile book bags, purses. The air smelled musty and still, making the inside of her nose tickle. She heard Marisol's voice: *He's letting the place go. He's letting himself go. Don't you care about him at all? I mean, I get it, he's made some huge mistakes. But none of us is perfect.*

She spun to look at him. "This can't wait, Dad."

Her father, too, seemed smaller. Always a big man, athletic, powerful, he was suddenly shrunken and gray. His striped pajamas hung off of him. The pocket of his robe was ripped.

Some of the anger she held against him dissipated. Some. Before her was an old man, not the powerhouse he had been. But someone frail and suffering. She told her own boys, *Parents are just people. We make mistakes.*

Selena often forgot about that when it came to Doug and even Cora.

She softened, put a hand on his arm. "I need to talk to you about Pearl."

He drew in a breath, closed his eyes a moment. Then he

waved her toward the kitchen. She followed him over floors that needed cleaning, into the kitchen, where dishes were piled in the sink, potted plants wilted on the windowsill. Marisol said that the woman he was seeing had moved out a few months ago. *I think he's clinically depressed*, Marisol had said. Selena hadn't even cared enough to call.

"Everything okay here, Dad?" she asked now. There was a smell, something in the garbage.

He looked around at the mess. "The cleaning lady comes tomorrow," he said.

"The yard's kind of a wreck, too."

"I fired the service," he said gruffly. "They were ripping me off."

"I can call around for you," she said. "Find someone else."

His thinning hair was a wild tangle; he seemed to catch sight of it in the reflection of the window over the sink, moved to smooth it out.

"Did you come here in the wee hours to discuss my home maintenance skills, Selena? Because that can wait until morning."

"No," she said. "That's not why I'm here."

"So, tell me about Pearl," he said. "What's she done?"

She pulled out a stool at the island and her father put on a pot of coffee, while she told him everything that had happened. When she was done, they were both silent. The coffee he brewed and put in front of her was strong. She drank it gratefully, felt the caffeine pulse through her veins.

"I've made mistakes in my life, Selena," he said. "Big ones. I know that won't come as news to you."

He'd taken a seat beside her.

"Pearl is my daughter," he said. "By a woman named Stella Behr. Stella—was a fling, an affair I had when I was married to your mother."

His candor surprised her. They'd never talked about the things he'd done, or why. She never wanted to hear his side or understand why he'd been the kind of husband and father he'd been. She just wanted to put as much distance between herself and the mess her parents had made as possible.

"I supported the child financially," he said. "But then Stella was murdered, and Pearl went missing. And it was years before I heard from her again."

He delivered the information so flatly that she wondered if she misheard him. His indifference now was chilling; Selena shifted away from him.

"I'm sorry—you said her mother *was murdered*?" she breathed.

"That's right," he said, looking into his cup. If he felt anything at all about this, he didn't show it.

"Who—who killed her?" Selena asked.

He shrugged. "Stella was, you know, a loose woman. There were a lot of men in and out of her life. It could have been any one of those."

"Did you ever look for Pearl? Or try to find out what happened to her mother?"

"No," he said. He looked down into his cup. "I was concerned that the police would find out I was her father and come looking for *me*. But that never happened. My name wasn't on her birth certificate. And Stella, for a price, promised she'd never tell Pearl who I was."

Selena thought of Stephen and Oliver, how loved they were, how wanted. She tried to imagine turning away from one of her children. She couldn't. The silence between Selena and her father expanded. The distance that had grown between them increased. Who were these men in her life?

"When Pearl turned up years later," he said finally, "I figured she just wanted money."

"And did you give it to her?"

"I did," he said. "I paid her a large sum of money with the agreement that she leave me alone for good."

He paid his daughter to go away—forever. Did that hurt Pearl? Selena called up the memory of Pearl's face—Martha's face. Was there pain there, longing? A desire to belong? Is that what drew her to Selena? Was this whole thing just her twisted way of trying to connect, to be part of a family?

"But she was your *daughter*," said Selena. "Didn't you want to know her?"

He offered a bitter laugh. "I had enough problems at that point."

Problems? Did he mean his *children*? His other family? The wife he betrayed. Something hollow and sad opened inside her. She always wanted to feel close to her father, envied women who had warm and loving relationships with their dads. Even when she was younger and worshiped him, he always seemed just out of reach. A stiff hug, a peck on the cheek, money from his wallet—but never time, never affection. Maybe, she thought now, he simply had nothing inside to give.

"So, what happened?" she asked.

"I paid her off," he said. "But she didn't go away. It took me a while to figure out that it wasn't money she was after."

"What did she want?"

"She wanted revenge. I paid her, but it wasn't enough. She filed a complaint with my office anonymously—but of course it was her—claiming I was harassing employees. A few women came forward, too, with claims as well, encouraged, I think, by Pearl. She contacted the local gossip columnist, revealing that I had another family. Your mother left me."

The end of his marriage, the loss of his job, his reputation decimated. Selena had been away at school, watched from a distance somewhat. She'd almost experienced a kind of denial about it, blocked it out. Neither her mother nor father ever talked about it.

"Pearl didn't just want money. She burned my life to the ground."

She's a destroyer, Cora had said.

But was that the whole truth?

"When did you last speak to her? Has she reached out to you for more?"

"I haven't spoken to her since I paid her," he said. "Years ago now. I thought she got what she wanted—a big payday, my life destroyed."

Selena didn't know what else to say. She was about to rise and leave when her father put a hand on her arm.

"Whatever she wants now," he said. "Don't give it to her. It will never be enough. She's dangerous. If she's back, it's because, for whatever reason, she has decided that she wants to hurt you. And she won't stop until your whole life is in ashes."

THIRTY-SEVEN

Pearl

IT DIDN'T TAKE Pearl and Gracie long to find the car Bridget had driven to the house. They'd set out in Pearl's Toyota and found the vehicle about halfway down the isolated drive.

Bridget must have pulled it off to the side, into a path that led through the trees, then approached the house on foot. That's why Pearl hadn't seen the car when she'd arrived. She hadn't been looking, focused on whatever might be going on at the house.

Pearl brought her car to a stop and climbed out, the night around her silent and cool, the drive beneath her boots soft. She was numb, head spinning. The other girl was practically catatonic again. Pearl wanted to slap her; her hand practically ached with the urge.

Pop was dead. What did Pearl feel? Predictably, nothing. Just a siren in her head. A vague nausea. That sucking emptiness. She found herself thinking about Jason, who was probably still asleep. In the morning, he'd wake up, start looking for her. The girl she was with him. But she'd never see him again; she knew that. And Elizabeth, that self, was already fading. She felt a rush of anger toward Pop. He never wanted her to have a normal life and now he'd made sure of it.

Pearl approached the slick late-model silver Mercedes, the key she'd lifted from Bridget's body in her pocket. As she neared, the doors unlocked, headlights and interiors coming on. Chimes dinged softly. She slid into the spotless buttery leather interior and started the car; it hummed to life, the dash a glow of colored lights and gleaming screens.

The GPS showed their location, just a blip off the main road. Pearl scrolled through the recent navigation history. Pop's address was the only entry listed. Pearl deleted it. There were fewer than three thousand miles on the odometer—practically brand-new. She ran her hands across the dash, the center console. It was a sweet ride, an S-Class. 100K to start. Of course. Bridget had money, lots of it. Earned, inherited, hoarded. A Gucci tote sat in the well in front of the passenger seat. Pearl grabbed it; she'd go through it later.

Pearl had a million questions.

First, how had Bridget found Pop? That was the big question. He was so careful, always so sure that he could not be traced, followed, found. Obviously, there was a failure in his planning. The house was vulnerable.

Next, who else knew that Bridget had come here? Would others follow when Bridget failed to return home? Police? A private detective, maybe?

That seemed right. That Bridget had hired someone to help her. Someone who had been able to follow Pop's trail from Phoenix to this house in the woods—over years and miles. Pop was sure that he was a ghost, that he was safe, that they were safe in this house. Where had he gone wrong?

She sat a moment, wondering if there was a way she could keep the car. Probably not. Was it a lease? she wondered. If it was, it probably had a LoJack, which would allow the leasing company and thereby the police to find it when Bridget was reported missing.

How long would that be? Was there a ticking clock?

When Pearl knew Bridget, however briefly, the other woman had no family, a smattering of loose tie acquaintances, mainly connected to work. She was a lonely woman, with a prickly personality. An accountant, someone more interested in numbers than in people. A loner. Exactly Pop's type. She'd opened to him like a flower. He lit her up with his attentions.

She said I made her believe in love, he'd told Pearl proudly.

If Bridget had held a grudge this long, gone to such lengths to find Pop, the chances were she hadn't improved her social life much. She was probably lonelier and more disconnected than ever. Decisions like the one Bridget had made—to hunt and kill someone who had wronged her—were made in a vacuum, where there were no dissenting voices. No one who cared enough to lead her down another path.

Pearl climbed out of the car, left it running, and walked back to hers—which had seemed like a perfectly fine car this morning and now, compared to the Mercedes, looked like a piece of junk. She knocked on the window and the girl lowered it. Her eyes were glassy. She was going to cry again. Or maybe that's how she always looked.

"How old are you?" she asked Gracie. "Can you drive?"

The girl nodded. "I'm fifteen."

"Follow me back to the house."

Gracie slid into the driver's seat, and Pearl climbed back into the Mercedes. She pulled out, Gracie following behind as they headed back to the house.

For Pop, it was never just about the score, but about how well you played the game. He was like one of those vampires who tried not to drink human blood. He believed you could scam a person, take their money, but leave them with something they didn't have before. He believed you could run your con with kindness, with respect. You could give a lonely woman love, romance, pleasure—for a time. You could give a family the joy of believing they'd found someone they'd lost. You could make a person believe they were going to receive an unexpected windfall, a big win after a life of failed enterprises.

He didn't view himself as just a con. He saw himself as a dream weaver.

He wove a dream for Bridget. When he yanked it away, she got mad. Mad enough, apparently, to tirelessly look for him for years, find him, and eventually kill him.

"You screwed up, Pop," she said to no one.

In the garage, she found some tarps, two shovels. There was an unopened container of lye. Why would he have that in his garage? But she already knew there were lots of things she didn't know about Pop. Things she didn't even want to know.

The lye would certainly come in handy now. When mixed with water, it aided in the decomposition of tissue. There were shelves of gallon jugs of water; Pop was a bit of a hoarder when it came to supplies. He liked to know there was enough—enough food, water, cash to get them through hard times. She took five jugs, loaded them in the car.

When she got back to the Toyota, the girl was still sitting there, immobile and pale as a statue, staring ahead. God, she was useless.

"I'm going to need your help," Pearl said. "I can't do this alone."

The job ahead of them was big and physical. It would take hours and probably more strength than either of them possessed.

"Shouldn't we call the police?" said Gracie, turning to look at Pearl. "She killed him."

"The police?" said Pearl softly. "What do you think will happen to you if we call the police?"

Gracie shook her head, her wheat locks shimmering. She

gazed at Pearl with wide eyes. "That's exactly what he said. When we found my mother."

Pearl stayed quiet.

"Someone killed her," Gracie went on. "Pop brought me here. He said if he didn't that they'd take me away, put me in foster care or someplace worse."

Pearl was back there again, that night they found Stella. She did feel something, something sharp and tight in her heart.

Pearl didn't know what to say to the girl. *What's done is done*, Stella would surely say. There was nothing to do but manage the situation and try to move forward.

"Are you going to help me or not?" she asked the girl. The night expanded all around them.

Gracie nodded finally.

Four hours later, the sun was rising, painting the sky a milky gray.

Bridget and Pop lay in the same shallow grave, back in the woods on the ten-acre property. The grave—it needed to be deeper, a lot deeper—Pearl knew this. But neither one of them were strong enough to do more.

No trails crossed this land. It was private; they'd be safe out here. Bridget and Pop, together forever just like Bridget wanted. Well, maybe not just like she wanted.

Pearl and Gracie were both covered in grime, hands raw and blistered. Pearl emptied the container of lye over the bodies—a blizzard covering them in white. She dumped the water into the grave. There was a sizzling sound as the water reacted with the chemical.

She should say something, shouldn't she?

"I'm sorry, Pop," she said. "I'm sorry it ended like this."

Gracie wept, lying on her side on the ground. Anyone could see she was spent, finished. She'd vomited twice—once back at the house when they were moving the bodies; once when they'd dropped Pop carrying him from the car. Pearl didn't even bother to try to make her finish shoveling the dirt back into the grave.

Pearl worked, her shoulders and back aching until Bridget and Pop were covered with earth. Then she used the shovels to scrape leaves, sticks, other forest floor debris over the site. In the dim light, it looked like all the rest of the forest around them. Pop would be pleased with the job she'd done, Pearl thought. She'd thought clearly, acted fast. All she had to do was deal with Bridget's digital footprint and the car.

"Did he kill your mother, too?" Gracie asked from the ground.

The question took Pearl by surprise. She almost didn't answer.

"I don't know," said Pearl finally. "Maybe."

"She loved me," said Gracie. "She was a good mom."

Her voice had a faint and faraway quality, as if she was talking to someone Pearl couldn't see. "She, you know, did her best. She used to tell me stories. About owls."

"That's nice," said Pearl, keeping her voice gentle.

Gracie was wobbly, unstable. Pearl knew that she couldn't be trusted. She was going to have some kind of breakdown, if she wasn't having one already. If Pearl was smart, she'd kill the girl, too, and throw her in the grave they'd dug together. What was it that Pop always said? Three can keep a secret if two of us are dead. One down, one to go.

But Pearl wasn't that. She was a lot of things. There was ice water in her veins. She wasn't sure she'd ever felt the things that other people seemed to. But she was not a killer.

Instead, she helped the girl up to her feet.

She'd picked this spot for a reason.

There was an old root cellar out here. It was one of the main features that had attracted Pop. He called it the safe room. After they'd moved out to the house, they'd spent a couple of weeks stocking it with supplies, water, canned and other nonperishable foods, sleeping bags, battery-operated lights, shelves and shelves of books, games. A hoarder's paradise.

If the shit hits the fan, this is where we go, okay? We can ride out any storm here. It's totally off the grid, not on the property survey.

He'd marked the door in the ground with a piece of wood, a red flag tied at its tip.

Pearl found it now. She unlocked the latch while Gracie sat, rocking, and pulled open the door with a haunted house squeal.

"I'm going to take care of you, okay, Gracie?" she said softly as she helped the girl to her feet. "I don't know what happened to your mom. And Pop is gone. But we'll be okay. I promise."

Gracie leaned heavily against Pearl, and allowed herself to be led down the stairs, and hardly made a peep when Pearl laid her down on the ground, covered her with a sleeping bag.

"Just rest, okay?" she said. "I'll be back after a while, Gracie."

"Okay," she said. Her voice was a child's whisper. She was a child. Just like Pearl had been once.

The girl didn't move an inch as Pearl climbed the steps, then locked the door behind her. She'd go back for Gracie, after she'd taken care of Bridget's digital footprint and her car.

The social media was easy. A Facebook post, using a selfie she found on Bridget's phone: "All my life, I've done the right and careful thing. Now, I'm off on a grand adventure, going off the grid to discover the real world and myself. Wish me luck!"

The poor woman had fifteen friends, loose tie connections—coworkers, a distant cousin. She posted infrequently, had little engagement on her few entries—a stew she'd made one Sunday, a picture of her new car, a selfie after a new hairstyle. A smattering of likes and wan comments. Poor Bridget, she barely existed at all. This was good news for Pearl. No one knew where she was. No one cared enough to come looking.

Then, the car. She knew a guy. A friend of Pop's, a guy named Les who they'd used before. She called him from Pop's phone and he told her where to park the vehicle. She drove it there, then jogged the five miles home. The car, she knew, that beautiful shiny new thing, would be taken apart until there was nothing left. How, where the parts went, to whom they were sold, Pearl had no idea. It was a specialized skill, one that was best hired out.

By the time she got back to the house, it was midmorning. She briefly thought about school—right now she'd be in world economics. Jason had probably called her about five times. But Elizabeth, the student, the girlfriend, the normie—she was gone.

You think you can just lead a normal life? Pop had wanted to know. *It doesn't work like that. Not for people like us.*

He was right, of course.

She'd known it all along.

Finally, she retrieved a nearly catatonic Gracie from the root cellar and brought her back to the house. Pearl had made Gracie strip down and throw all her clothes into the wash. Then, Pearl stood outside the door while Gracie took a scalding hot shower. Through the door, she could hear the girl sobbing.

What had Pop seen in her? Pearl might have caught a glimpse of it when they were carrying the bodies, digging the graves. There was a mettle there, some will to survive despite the circumstance.

"Scrub," Pearl said. "Don't forget to clean under your nails."

She'd given the girl clean clothes from a laundry basket Pearl had found in her room. A pair of underpants with hearts on them, faded leggings, an oversize NYU sweatshirt.

Then she'd showered herself, dumped all her clothes in the wash, put the cycle on as hot and as long as it would go, dumping in more detergent than was needed. Next, she'd have to clean the foyer. The blood would seep into the wood; it would be nearly impossible to remove all traces. Pop had taught her that about blood. Never shed it, if possible. Not that anyone was going to come looking today. But that was Pop's number one rule: when the shit hits the fan, clean up and go. The act of washing it all away, the self that needed to be abandoned. It helped you to move on.

Down in the kitchen, Pearl made tea while Gracie sat quietly at the kitchen table. Now, she just had a glassy look again, her shoulders hunched in, her arms wrapped around her middle. She'd stopped crying, at least.

She brought the tea, sweet with honey, over to the table and then sat across from Gracie. Pearl stared at the other girl's wheat-colored hair, her too-blue eyes, the delicate turn of her neck, the full pink of her lips. Yes, there was an ethereal kind of prettiness, the unformed beauty of a child. Maybe Pop liked that. A lump of clay he could mold. Pearl knew that she'd never been as malleable as Gracie, but mold her he had. How much of what she was now was because of the things that Pop had done, taught her, showed her?

"What happens now?" asked Gracie.

"How old are you?" She'd asked before. But she'd forgotten the answer.

"Fifteen."

The answer sent a little jolt through Pearl. A child. Why had Pearl thought she was older? Maybe in her twenties, at least eighteen. An adult, someone with agency. Not a child as she had been when Stella died and she went with Charlie.

"I think maybe," Gracie said when Pearl was quiet. Apparently she wasn't going to be able to let this part go. "I think he killed my mother."

I think he killed mine, too, Pearl wanted to say but didn't. Maybe he did. Maybe he didn't. Maybe she would have left with him anyway, if he had asked. Maybe Stella would have let her go. There was no way to know any of this now. Pop was dead. And the past was gone.

"Why do you think that?" asked Pearl.

"We found her," she said, voice shaking. "Someone strangled her. I don't know—who else could have done it."

Pearl flashed again on the moment they found Stella, how the world faded out and went wobbly. How the ground felt like air beneath her. Pop—Charlie, as she knew him then—leading her away.

"He said that they'd take me," said Gracie. "With my mother gone, no relatives, I'd go to foster care."

Did he know before he chose? Did he pick women and girls with no safety net beneath them, no one who cared, no one to ask questions? Of course he did. He was the king of recon. A predator, patient and careful. He chose the ones that couldn't get away, who in some real sense didn't even want to.

"He said he'd take care of me," said Gracie sadly.

And he would have, in his way. Like he took care of Pearl.

"Did he kill your mother, too?" Gracie asked. She held Pearl in a watery gaze that managed a surprising intensity.

"I don't know," said Pearl. "Maybe. There were other men."

Gracie seemed to take this in with a slow blink of her eyes.

"Why did you go with him?"

"Because there was no place else, no one else." That was the truth without being the whole truth.

A slow nod of understanding.

"Did you love him?"

"Yes," said Pearl. And it was true. Whatever he was, Pearl loved Pop as much as she'd loved anyone. He was father, friend, partner in crime.

"I loved him, too," said Gracie. "I don't know why. He was the first person other than my mom to ever see anything special in me. He took care of her, of us. For a while."

That was true for Pearl, too. She allowed a feeling of sadness to expand. Who were you really, Pop? But there was no answer for that because he was a changeling, something different to everyone who encountered him, someone different in every place they traveled. What was at the core? Maybe nothing, just a gaping black maw.

The house was utterly silent except for a ticking from the refrigerator, the hum of air through the vents.

"So, what happens now?" asked Gracie.

And for that matter, who was Pearl? At her core, was there the same emptiness?

"What do you want to happen?" she asked.

There was a moment where they could call the police, report the crime. Here they might tell their stories, what had happened, what Pop had done. It hovered between them, a possibility they both considered.

The whole ugly truth.

But then what? Then, they became defined by what had happened to them, instead of creating themselves. Gracie would go to foster care. Pearl would become a news media curiosity, her true identity outed. She'd belong to the world, instead of to herself.

They held each other's eyes for a long moment.

No. It would never do. It was safer in the shadows of life.

"I want to stay here with you," said Gracie.

The girl didn't know what she was saying. She was a mouse. And the mouse was so afraid that she was looking to the cat for love.

Pop would want them to leave. It was the safe choice. After all, if Bridget had found them, anyone would be able to. She'd worked her magic with Bridget's social media, disposed of the car. But they could never be sure they were safe. There were too many loose ends, Pop would say.

"He said we'd be sisters," said Gracie. "He knew you were mad at him, but he was sure you'd come home again. That we'd be a family."

Maybe that's what he really wanted, deep down. A family. So in his own twisted way, he cobbled one together from the broken girls he found along his path.

The girl reached her hand across the table, and Pearl surprised herself by taking it in her own. The world didn't always give you the things you wanted. You couldn't choose your family, your circumstances, the unfolding of life. Often, things you loved were cruelly wrested away. But Pop was a master of creating a reality, for himself, for others. And he'd given that gift to Pearl.

Pearl and Gracie.

They would stay in the house that Pop promised her was home. And they would be sisters, just as Pop had wanted. Pearl would teach Gracie everything she knew about the game. And they'd play it together. Best of all, Gracie was malleable. She would do what Pearl told her to do. And Pearl liked that about her new sister. It would come in handy in all sorts of ways.

"Okay, Gracie. If that's what you want," said Pearl.

The girl nodded. Her posture softened a bit, shoulders relaxing, arms unwrapping from her middle.

"But Pop doesn't want me to call myself that anymore."

Present tense. Maybe he'd always be alive for each of them. A voice in their heads. A shadow, a trick of light.

"What does he want to call you?" Pearl asked.

"He wants to call me Gennie," she said. "Short for Geneva."

THIRTY-EIGHT

Selena

SELENA DROVE TOO FAST, taking the winding back roads toward home.

A glance at her phone. No answer from Pearl. Selena's text hung on the screen. The stranger on the train. A woman shadowing her life for who knows how long. Someone who might have been a friend, an ally, was a destroyer wanting to do damage. But there was more to it than that, wasn't there? Selena reached for something that kept slipping away—a feeling, a thought.

"What do you want, Pearl?" she asked the empty car.

Her shoulders felt like they were cast from concrete, she was so tense, leaning forward toward the wheel as if that might get her there faster.

Her father's voice, the things he told her, kept echoing back. She felt a twist of sadness, of compassion for Pearl, for the things she'd endured. Abandoned by her father, her mother murdered. No wonder she was a pain giver.

Selena pushed the pedal down. The night was thick and

moonless, no streetlights. Selena knew that a deer could bound out of the darkness at any second. But she pressed her foot down harder still. The speed, the sound of the engine, the squeal of the tires as she took the turns; it felt good. *What if I die on this road tonight?* she thought. A spectacular crash, a blaze of glory. How would the headlines read? Jilted Wife Dies in Fiery Crash. Something about it appealed, like an escape hatch from the ugly mess of her life. Better than: Jilted Wife Struggles to Start Over as a Single Mom after her Husband Goes to Prison for Murdering his Mistress.

It was easier to die than to live, wasn't it?

But no. Her boys. She couldn't stand the thought of them alone in the world, broken by the reckless, terrible actions of their parents. She slowed her speed, drew in a breath.

Pull yourself together, Selena, she chided. *Fix this. End this. Write a better headline.*

Her headlights split the night, the world black around the unfurling ribbon of road. As her speed slowed, so did the racing of her heart, the adrenaline pulse. In the quiet, she wondered how much of her marriage—of any marriage—was built on a foundation of pretty stories, a narrative that you stitched together based on delusion and hope and wishful thinking.

Little lies like the curated, filtered posts on social media that make your life together look so wonderful, just after you've had a big fight, the months of marriage counseling not doing much good. Faked orgasms—guilty. Sometimes, really, she just wanted to get it over with. After parenthood, sleep was the new sex.

Little things like telling him she liked his cooking. She didn't. *It's just nice that he cooks at all*, said Beth, when Selena dared to complain.

God, women's standards were so fucking low. But Selena bought in, always praised Graham's efforts in the kitchen. Because, yeah, it was better than nothing. In her lifetime, she never saw her father prepare a single meal, run the dishwasher, sweep a floor.

So, sure, she praised Graham because he was present in the home—good with the boys, helped with the housework more than most, did the dishes after she cooked dinner. But his efforts were fractional compared to hers; and her praise was equal in measure to the encouragement she doled out to the children for their drawings that showed little talent, their stilted piano playing, or middling efforts on the soccer field. Not lies, exactly.

Then there were the big lies like Graham's, like her father's.

Infidelity. Secrets. Sins of omission.

But worst of all were the lies she told herself.

She knew what her husband was, didn't she, even before they got married? His eyes followed other women. Once, even very early in their relationship, she'd seen him talking to another girl outside the bathroom in a club. He'd leaned in to her in a way that wasn't appropriate when you'd come with someone else.

If she was honest with herself, the challenge of Graham excited her at first. She amped up her fitness routine, wore the sexiest underwear she could find. She made him chase. Blocked his calls sometimes, even stood him up once. Once upon a time, *she'd* been the woman sending dirty texts.

His excitement excited her.

That's why she thought she'd left Will for Graham. Because Graham excited her. Because life with him, what it would be, could be, seemed like a mystery, an adventure.

But maybe, she thought now, pulling into her own driveway, maybe, it was the lies.

Her dad was a liar, a cheater. He was a vacant father, a man-baby always looking for his own pleasure. And Graham, apparently, was just like him.

So, on some twisted, subconscious level, maybe that's why Selena had chosen him. Because that's what she knew about the love of a man, that's what she craved. It was sick. But maybe they were all sick, acting from impulses that were barely conscious.

She killed the engine, drew in another breath and released it.

The house sat dark, deserted. It was funny how an empty house could radiate a kind of loneliness. The energy of their life, their family, their love was gone. It was a body without a soul. She felt the threat of tears, the wobble of a breakdown. But she fought it back.

Not here. Not now.

She needed to change, get a coat. She needed money; she kept a stash of cash in a lockbox in the closet. In that box, there was also a gun, a small off-duty revolver with five shots. She knew how to use it. When Detective Crowe asked her if anything was missing, she'd thought of that box. But when she checked, it was back deep on the top of the closet, buried beneath clothes. It hadn't been touched since the last time she put some money in there—more than a year ago, she thought.

The gun had been a gift from Graham after they bought the house, along with lessons at the range. She'd been uncomfortable with it at first, but found she'd enjoyed the target practice, the instructor who taught her how to aim, breathe, fire. It felt good to know that she could defend herself if she needed to. But she never thought she'd use it; the whole thing was more of a novelty, a very Graham type of gift.

Once she had those things, she would meet Martha—or Pearl, or whatever her name was—and figure out what the woman wanted. She hadn't texted back, and Selena had no idea how to find her, but she knew the other woman was waiting. That she wanted something and that she'd come after it. It was only a matter of when.

One more text: I'm waiting, Pearl. Just tell me what you want.

No answer.

Finally, Selena exited the car, the air around her cold on her skin. She was going to take control of the situation and do what was necessary to salvage what was left of her boys' lives. Maybe it would be easy; maybe Pearl just wanted money. Selena would give it to her. Whatever she had to, she was going to do that. There was a surge of power in the decision.

As she walked toward the house, the trees whispered their little secrets, all the things they knew and had seen. Other homes were warm with landscape lighting, glowing windows. Safe, normal lives being lived in relative peace. Or at least that was the facade. That's how it seemed from the outside looking in.

Her house was quiet, and she didn't bother flipping on lights as she jogged up the stairs. In the master bath, she mopped off, then quickly changed. A pair of jeans, a black T-shirt, her wool peacoat, black running shoes. She had to get the bench at the foot of the bed and climb up on it to reach far in the back of the top shelf of the closet.

When she retrieved the box, it felt light as she sank with it to the floor. She punched in the code and the lid popped open with a snap. Her heart sank. The gun was gone. Maybe half the cash had been removed.

"Goddammit," she whispered, counting the cash.

There had been five thousand dollars. Now there was less than two. Her money, cash she'd saved over the years from birthday gifts from her parents, work bonuses, anytime there was extra from the monthly budget. It was her security fund. She didn't even think Graham knew about it. They never touched the gun. Or so she thought.

What if Geneva had taken it? But, no, only Selena and Graham knew the code. He might have told Geneva, or given her the money, the way Erik Tucker had bought her a car. When Detective Crowe had asked her about their finances, she'd been so sure she was in control of that at least.

She pocketed what was left of the cash.

More secrets and hidden things. Her husband a thief as well as a liar, an adulterer, an abuser of woman. Where was the gun? It was hers, registered to her name, had her fingerprints on it. Her heart thudded as she remembered Detective Crowe's questions, his pointed stare. Did she ever think about hurting Geneva? No, she never did. But who would believe that now?

The room around her seemed to spin. Fear and self-doubt crept up behind her and whispered in her ear. *What are you doing? You're out of your league here.* It took her a moment to register the ringing of her phone, which she'd left on the bed.

She rose and walked over to glance at the caller ID. Will.

Her mother probably called him. She hesitated before answering.

"Selena." His voice was taut with tension. "Where are you? Your mom's freaking out. She said you took off."

She was about to answer, but he interrupted her. "Look, it doesn't matter. The body—police were able to identify it. It's not Geneva Markson."

Relief crashed over her like a wave. Thank god—for Geneva, for her family. She nearly wept with gratitude. Graham—whatever he was, he wasn't that.

"How?" she asked. "I thought you said it could take weeks."

"There was another missing woman. Her family was able to identify the body by a tattoo on her shoulder."

Another missing woman.

"Her name was Jacqueline Carson. Do you know her?"

It had a familiar ring, but she couldn't place it. "No."

"She worked with Graham. She was the woman who accused him of harassing her, the reason he was fired from his job."

The news knocked the wind out of her. A crushing fatigue followed, like someone drained all her energy from her. She sank onto the mattress.

"Have you seen Graham?" asked Will.

She struggled for breath, for words. "Isn't he—still with the police?"

Will blew out a sigh. She could tell that he was driving by

the echo of his voice. "They had to let him go, just about an hour before they identified the body. They're looking for him now. Where are you?"

"I'm home," she said. "At our house."

"Just—get out of there, Selena. Go home to your mom. I'll meet you there."

Yes, that was right. She had to go home to her mom. Her father and her husband were monsters. She was being stalked by some woman she thought was a stranger on a train, but who was really her sister. She had to go with Will to Detective Crowe and tell him everything. That was the only way out. The truth. Whatever hard consequences might follow. Problems didn't just go away. You had to face them down and solve them. Every grown-up knew that.

There was a sound from downstairs, the familiar creak from the hallway floorboard. The noise moved through her body like electricity.

"Will," she whispered into the phone.

But the cell had gone dead in her hand. She hadn't charged it since—she didn't even know when. She moved over to the bedside and rifled around in the drawer for her charger. Found it. She plugged it into a wall socket. The red battery icon appeared on the screen. It would take a while to come back to life.

More noise from downstairs, footfalls, something dropping, the squeak of the door into the kitchen. Graham. It must be.

She should run; she knew that. She should do exactly what Will said she should do—go home to her mom. Right now, with him in the kitchen, she could race down the stairs and get to her car and drive. Even if he tried, he'd never be able to catch her.

Some clanging in the kitchen, the opening and closing of cabinets. He was hungry, rifling like a bear through cupboards looking for food. Or booze.

She could get out of there and never look back. Go to Will,

go to the police, come clean about everything. But she didn't. She couldn't.

Because even through all the lies, there was something there. Her husband—he'd loved her, she'd loved him. Graham was a better father than her father had been. He wasn't perfect, but he loved the boys and they loved him.

And maybe, just maybe, he *wasn't* a monster. It was possible, wasn't it, that this whole thing had been orchestrated by Pearl—that she'd kidnapped Geneva, that she'd killed Jacqueline Carson? She was a destroyer. She was doing what she did best, taking a wrecking ball to Selena's life. Why? Because Pearl hated Selena for being a happy, normal person, when life had treated her so unfairly.

Selena took her phone and charger with her. Downstairs, she plugged it into the wall by the hallway console table. Then she pushed through the door into the kitchen to confront her husband.

THIRTY-NINE

Selena

GRAHAM WAS SITTING at the table, an open bottle of bourbon before him, an empty glass in his hand. Another on the table, as if he knew she was there and he was waiting for her. In the dim light, he was just a shadow.

She drew closer and saw the darkness of his gaze.

"What have you done?" she asked him.

"Nothing," he said, looking up at her. "I swear to god. I never hurt her. I never hurt anyone."

The refrigerator dropped ice cubes into the tray, causing her to jump.

"That's a lie," she hissed. "The woman in Vegas."

"The *stripper*." He poured more bourbon in his glass, and in the other. He took a deep swallow.

She tried to remember the man she met and fell in love with. He made her laugh with his charm, connected her to the wild, adventurous side of herself. But that guy, the one she married, he was a con. This man before her someone blank, someone dangerous, he was always inside, waiting to get out. Bait and switch.

"I was drunk." He looked into his now empty glass, then up at her. "I lost control."

"She's a *person*—someone's daughter," she said. "And drunk is not a free pass."

"I have a—"

"I know." She raised a hand, cutting him off. She felt the heat of anger rising. "You have a problem. You're getting help. Guess what, Graham? Obviously it's not working."

He sank his head into his hands. When he spoke again, his voice was muffled. "I never hurt Geneva."

She wanted to believe that, desperately.

"And what about Jaqueline?"

She saw his body stiffen, but he didn't say anything.

"Detective Crowe told me the real reason you were fired, Graham."

Still no words, but his shoulders were shaking. Yes, he'd start to cry. He always did when he ran out of excuses.

She should stop talking, leave, get as far away from him as she could. But she just couldn't do it. There was that burning rage, something volcanic, that thing she pressed down and pressed down. After her father's lies, she pressed it down, blamed her mother because it was just easier to do that somehow. After Graham's sexting, she pressed it down. After Vegas. After she watched him fuck Geneva in the boys' playroom, she pressed it back.

All these women—her mother, herself, the girl in Vegas, Geneva, Jacqueline, even Pearl—fucked over by terrible men. They were lied to, cheated on, beaten, *killed* because of male *whims*, male *problems*, their *loss of control*. Her father, her husband.

Why were they so broken?

"The body they found," she said, her voice shaking. "It wasn't Geneva. It was Jacqueline Carson."

He looked up at her quickly, his face a mask of pure shock. She almost believed he was surprised.

"Wh-wh-what?" he stammered. "No."

She *almost* believed him.

An object on the counter caught her eye. The gun from the lockbox upstairs. The sight of it sent chills down her arms.

"Who are you?" she asked him.

The expression that crossed his face—some twist of sadness and rage. She didn't even know him.

They'd flown home from Vegas together, she taking the points upgrade to first class and letting him languish in a middle seat back in coach. For weeks, she couldn't even stand to look at him, the image of the young woman he'd hit flashing over and over again in her memory. It was that more than the fact that he was in a strip club to begin with. She could live with that; turn a blind eye to boyish indulgences. But the violence. It made him something else. Something that was vile, frightening.

But she'd let him and the therapist convince her that there was a path forward.

A marriage is a negotiation, the therapist told her. *You both have to decide what you can live with, what you can forgive, how you cope with various behaviors.* It all sounded so reasonable. She could forgive him—for the boys. If not for the children, she'd have been long gone, years ago. At least that's what she told herself. But there was no other self, no Selena without Oliver and Stephen. How could she know what that other imagined woman would do? The unencumbered Selena—she was long gone.

"Who are you?" she asked again of the stranger who used to be her husband. "We had everything. What have you done?"

"Selena." Now the pleading. "Please believe me. I've made mistakes. I've hurt you. That girl in Vegas, I hurt her. But not this. What's happening now. I promise, I didn't hurt either of these women."

He was so earnest. Like the boys, eyes wide and searching, the picture of innocence wronged. The smell of bourbon reached her, turned her stomach.

He rose, and she started backing toward the door.

"You're afraid of me?"

Was she?

When Detective Crowe had asked if Graham ever hurt her, she'd felt a jolt of indignation. Of course not. In fact, her husband currently bore a gash on his head from her last angry outburst. And it wasn't the first time. She'd slapped him during a Vegas argument they'd had after a particularly brutal therapy session where they'd dug in deep about how his father didn't respect women, was verbally abusive to Graham's mom. How it used to anger him when his father mistreated his mother, but he could still hear that voice—women were liars, they teased, couldn't be trusted, they were manipulators. That was the voice Graham heard when he lost control.

After the session they'd had a terrible fight. He'd called her a castrating bitch. She'd slapped him hard enough to leave a red mark on his face into the next day.

Now, he moved closer. His face was dark with anger. A hollow of dread opened, her mouth going dry. She backed away, her hands shaking in anger.

"What are you going to do, Selena?" His voice was a tease, a goad.

"Let me guess," he went on when she didn't answer.

No, he had never hurt her. But would he? Could he?

Selena leaned her weight against the door and felt it give way behind her. She backed up as he kept moving forward, a tense dance.

"You're going to leave me. Take the boys. Ruin our lives."

His breathing was heavy, eyes shining.

In the hallway, she kept moving, slowly. His shaking hands formed into fists at his sides. He was a big man, over six feet. She'd always loved that about him. Graham's size always made her feel small. His strength made her feel safe. Until it didn't.

"It won't be six months before you're back with Will, right?"

"Stop it," she said.

She passed the console table, a glance at the phone revealing that it had come back online. It started pinging and vibrating with texts and calls. Every nerve ending in her body was sizzling. *Grab it. Run.*

"Don't touch it," he said, following her gaze. "We need to talk. There are things I need you to understand."

She thought about the boys asleep at home with her mother. She had to get back to them, away from him.

But she was aware of something else, too, something that had risen in her when she watched Graham and Geneva through the nanny cam. Maybe she felt it for the first time after the sexting. Then, after the woman in Vegas, it grew. Finally, as she watched him with Geneva, it reached another level. But maybe it was there before all that—her father who cheated on her mother, who had another family, other children. Women weren't supposed to feel rage, were they? It was ugly. But that's what it was. Pure and white-hot, a siren. She'd been tamping it down, pushing it back, swallowing it. Her whole body was shaking with it now.

"I've been a good husband," Graham said. "Mostly. Haven't I taken care of our family? I need you to believe me. Selena, I need you to have a little faith in me."

She laughed at that; she couldn't help it. It rose up from her like a wave, a hysterical burst that shifted suddenly to tears.

"Faith?" she said. The word felt like fire in her throat. Then it was scream. *"Faith?"*

There was an explosion inside of her, like a crowd cheering in her veins, adrenaline pumping hot and fast, giving her strength and driving her forward.

She ran at her husband, pushing him back with the weight of her own body and landing on top of him, knocking the wind from him, leaving him struggling for air. Then she lifted her fist and punched him hard in the jaw. He raised his arms to ward her off.

"Selena," he managed. "Stop."

But she kept punching him, with everything she had, sobbing with the depth of her rage and her sorrow—not just for herself.

For her mother, for Geneva, for Jacqueline, even for Pearl. Yes, Pearl. Who'd brought them all to this somehow, but only because she was formed in pain. Only because the fissures were there to exploit.

Exhaustion slowed her blows, and Graham just lay there, bleeding, arms covering his head. Her fists, her arms, were on fire with effort and impact, her breathing animalistic.

It was an easy thing for him to flip her. In one effortless motion, he was on top of her, looking down. The blood from his face dripped onto hers; she felt it on her face, trailing down her throat. He pinned her arms to the ground, his full weight on her middle. She was immobilized, powerless against his vastly superior strength. It was a surprise to feel so weak. She was breathless, arms and hands aching.

"Those times you hit me, Selena," he said. He was breathing hard. "It was only because I let you. I deserved it. Hey, who knows, maybe I even liked it a little. You *are* super-hot when you're angry. But that's enough."

She tried to get away from him, squirming and writhing beneath him. She was a doll, a child, her strength minuscule compared to his.

"Let go of me." Her voice was a ragged shriek, unfamiliar.

Something dark crossed his face and in the next moment, he slapped her, openhanded across the face. Her jaw rattled; she saw stars as the pain radiated—the back of her head, her neck. The world seemed to halt. His face was twisted into an expression she'd never seen before. Was this the man the Vegas stripper saw? Geneva? Jacqueline?

There's something inside me, he told her once. *And when it breaks loose, I'm not the same person.* She thought he was just making excuses for his bad behavior. But now she saw it. She tasted blood in her mouth.

"The boys," she said.

She flashed on Stephen clinging. Oliver sulking at the table with her mother. Oh, god. Was she ever going to see them again? Who would care for them when she was gone? She started screaming, more like a roar of anger and sadness, rage at her own powerlessness.

"Shut the fuck up, Selena," the stranger who used to be her husband hissed. "Don't make me hit you again."

He shifted his weight. And in one swift, direct movement, she brought her knee up hard into his groin. She watched his face freeze, go white. A kind of strangled cry escaped him, then he fell off of her, curling himself up into the fetal position, moaning.

"You fucker," she managed. "I hate you."

All he could do was groan.

She struggled to her feet, grabbed her phone and her charger and was about to run for the door. But then his hand was strong around her ankle, fingers digging into her flesh, tripping her. She fell hard, the phone cracking against the hard wood, then skittering away out of reach.

The wind knocked out of her, she struggled for breath, crawling toward the door. Then he was on top of her. He flipped her again, her head knocking against the wood, and then put strong hands on her neck and started to squeeze.

She couldn't breathe, couldn't scream. She clawed at his hands, kicked her legs.

Her husband. She tried to say his name but couldn't. No air, no sound.

"I gave you everything," he said through gritted teeth. "You spoiled, ungrateful bitch."

Her husband, eyes black with rage, was trying to kill her.

He was killing her.

FORTY

Selena

AROUND HER THINGS started to go gray, her vision a fish-eye lens. Her mind raced, gaze scanning the room for a weapon, a way out, a solution.

Finally, energy waning fast, her glance landed on the family portrait hanging on the wall over the console table. *It's all worth it*, the photographer had said. *I promise.* Her babies. A kaleidoscope of memories played out in her mind—their laughing faces, the day Stephen dumped a bowl of mashed peas on his head, Oliver's first steps, Stephen watching her as she fell asleep, his eyes slowly closing, the feel of their bodies against hers. They were slipping away from her. As hard as she'd tried, she'd failed them completely. Who would they be now without her, after *this*?

Selena felt herself go slack, the darkness encroaching, her limbs heavy and useless. She kept her eyes on the picture of the boys. She wanted their faces to be the last thing she saw.

Then, in a rush of air, Graham's grip loosened, and blessed oxygen flowed back into her lungs.

Selena rasped, drawing it in, hands flying to her brutalized throat. She coughed, great retching bursts, bile rising. Graham still sat on top of her, frozen, stunned, his expression gone slack. His hands loose at his sides.

"Let me go." Her voice was just a whisper.

He looked at her, eyes red and watering—from effort, from sadness, she didn't know. There was a moment when she glimpsed him, the man she thought he was. Then he fell off to the side, landing heavily on the ground, head knocking hard.

She skittered away from him, moving again for the door, coughing. That's when she saw the blood trailing down the side of his face from a wound on his head.

Standing behind him was a woman she knew.

She held their gun in her slender, manicured hand—the weapon she'd obviously just used to hit Graham in the head. She must have hit him hard, a spray of blood across her blouse. She, too, wore a stunned expression, her breath ragged, hair wild.

Martha. Pearl. Her half sister. The stranger on the train.

FORTY-ONE

Selena

PEARL WAS SAYING something that Selena couldn't make out over the roaring in her head. The unreality of the moment spun and pulled. Was she dreaming? She struggled to hold on to consciousness, the lack of oxygen making her loopy and heavy with a strange fatigue.

Pearl moved in close to her, pushed back a strand of Selena's hair. Her face—the pale of her skin, the abyss of her eyes. It was so familiar, like they'd always known each other. Selena almost reached for her, and Pearl helped her climb to her feet, the other woman far stronger than she looked. Together, they staggered to the couch. Selena sat heavily, sinking into the softness of the cushion. She could still feel Graham's hands on her throat, a terrible burning pain, sharp, acidic.

Pearl put the throw blanket on Selena's lap, staying close.

"Is he dead?" Selena whispered, glancing over at Graham, who lay still on the floor of the hallway.

"No," said Pearl, but she didn't seem sure.

Selena kept her eyes on Graham. Pearl still held the gun.

"Why did you do this to me?" she asked Pearl. Her voice sounded faint, breathless. "To us?"

Pearl stayed quiet.

"We would have welcomed you in," said Selena. She didn't know if it was true, that she and Marisol would have brought Pearl into their family. If Cora might have accepted her. But she wanted to believe that about herself. That she could have found room in her heart, in her family, for someone who had been so badly wounded.

"No," said Pearl. She was level. There was no emotion. No heat. A coolness that Selena had sensed in their last two encounters. "You wouldn't have."

"How can you say that? You don't know us."

"Because I know people," she said easily. "I would just be a reminder of your father's flaws, his mistakes, his betrayals. Our father."

Selena regarded the other woman, still aware of Graham, of the pain that was starting to radiate in her body.

"So then you decided to hurt us," said Selena. "You didn't believe you could be a part of this family, so you sought to destroy it. Or what? Is there something else? Do you want more money?"

She took the money from her pocket—a meager couple of thousand—and held it out. Pearl looked at it, a small smile on her face.

"I know it's not enough," said Selena. "But I have more. What's your price? What do I need to do to make all my problems just go away?"

She let the cash drop to the floor and it fell like leaves. It was too late for Selena's problems to just go away. They were, of course, just beginning. Graham issued a groan from the floor. She fought the urge to go over and kick him hard in the gut. She didn't have the strength anyway.

Distantly, Selena heard sirens. She wondered if Pearl heard them, too.

"Maybe it was about money, at first," said Pearl. She sat on the chair across from Selena. "Maybe it was about revenge. Or both. I looked for a way into your life. And I found it."

Selena pushed herself up, pain rocketing up her neck, down her arms, her back.

"I thought your life was perfect," Pearl went on. "But it's not."

"Far from it," Selena said.

"Your husband is a bad man, Selena. I didn't know how bad he was until I started following him. He's a monster."

Selena's head started to clear, the situation coming back into focus. She had so many questions. How had she found her way in? When? Was it Pearl who had been texting Graham? What did Pearl know about Graham that even Selena didn't know? It all came out in a tumble.

But the sirens were growing louder, and Pearl didn't answer. She rose and started backing toward the door.

Selena wanted to reach for her, ask her to stay. But she couldn't. They weren't friends; they couldn't be now. Maybe Pearl was right, maybe they never could have been anything to each other but reminders of how flawed life was, how imperfect, how painful.

"Did he kill Jacqueline Carson? Or did you?" Selena managed.

"I've never hurt anyone," said Pearl. "Not like that."

It was an echo of what Graham had said, both of them qualifying how much pain they were willing to inflict upon others.

"I saw him," Pearl said. Selena didn't know who to believe, what to believe. Who hurt who? Who killed who? These were not questions she wanted to be having about her life. "I know what he did."

"No." The word came out weak and breathy. It was a single syllable of protest—to all of it.

So many questions. She wanted to know what the other

woman had seen, how. She wanted to know everything that Pearl knew. But she barely had a voice. Or maybe, really, she didn't want to know.

The sirens grew louder. Selena's phone rang and rang. Graham was still and silent on the ground. Maybe he *was* dead.

Pearl seemed small, sad, apart from Selena, apart from the world. A butterfly. Beautiful, but elusive. A flap of her wings and the world shook. A black butterfly.

"My mother," said Selena. The edges of the world felt fuzzy and gray. And Pearl was backing away. "My father. They told me everything that happened to you. Everything you did. I know you. I see you. All of it."

Pearl looked at her, a smile on her lips, something like kindness—or was it pity—in her eyes. There was a connection there. She'd felt it the moment they met on the train. It was true; it ran deep. But it was also dark, flawed, not sustainable in the real world.

Pearl looked over her shoulder toward the sound of the sirens, then back to Selena.

"Whatever happens next," Pearl whispered, "the worst of your problems is about to go away. For good."

Selena closed her eyes. She thought for just a moment.

"What about Geneva?"

But when she opened her eyes again, the room was filling with light and shouting voices.

And Pearl was gone.

FORTY-TWO

Selena

SHE LAY IN the back of the ambulance, her house alit in flashing red. She counted—two other ambulances, four police cars, two unmarked sedans. There were twenty men and women, at least, cops and paramedics, moving about her lawn and house, calm in their work. Outside the cordoned area, neighbors collected in their pajamas—arms folded, faces worried. A crowd gathered around her house in the middle of the night, a chorus, an audience to the destruction of everything she'd built and thought was hers. But she felt lifted out, apart from it all. Maybe it was the meds they gave her.

Detective Grady Crowe sat across from her, quiet, gaze intense.

Her body ached. Her jaw, where he'd hit her so mercilessly. Her throat, where Graham tried to strangle her and nearly succeeded. Her shoulders, her back, her hips. Her heart. She pulled the blanket they'd given her tight around her shoulders.

She watched as Graham was wheeled out in a stretcher, flanked by two police officers. She couldn't see his face; she leaned back so she wouldn't have to see him at all. Will, she thought, was still in the house, managing the situation. As much as a situation like this might be managed. It was a runaway train, decimating everything in its path.

She'd told Detective Crowe everything—from the moment she met Pearl to the moment her sister had saved her life. She told him everything that Cora told her, too. How Pearl had been shadowing their lives for years, and Selena never knew she existed. She let it all go. Every secret and lie. He'd scribbled it all in his little book.

"I had a visitor today," said Crowe. "A man named Hunter Ross, a private detective."

The world was fuzzy and unreal, his voice sounded far away. But she listened.

"He was the cold case investigator hired when a woman named Stella Behr was murdered and her fifteen-year-old daughter, Pearl, went missing, more than ten years ago now. A man in her mother's life was suspected of the murder, and of Pearl's abduction. Their case went unsolved and the department brought Ross in to keep following up leads."

Selena let the information sink in. She thought of the girl her mother described, thin and feral, following Cora in the grocery store. Someone on the outside, looking for a way in. Or maybe Cora was right about Pearl. That she was just a destroyer. Someone in pain, looking to give pain to others. She could be either. Or both.

"Our father abandoned her," said Selena. "Then her mother was murdered, and she was abducted?"

Cora had never said anything about Stella, or Pearl's suspected abduction. Maybe she didn't know. Or maybe it was just another thing she hid. So many layers, so many secrets buried deep. Pearl was a child. Who took her? Where was she all those years before she showed up in their lives?

"Ross was never able to find them," said Crowe. "A man

named Charles Finch, a con artist, had apparently worked his way into Stella Behr's life in the months before her murder. But he was a ghost. Hunter Ross believes that Finch killed Behr, and abducted Pearl, raised her as his own."

Selena thought about Pearl, that darkness in her. No wonder.

"But, believe it or not, that's not who he came to see me about today," said Detective Crowe.

He took a picture out of the file he gripped in his hand. There was a picture of a young girl with golden curls and sad eyes. She was many years younger, but Selena recognized her right away. The paper shook a little in Selena's hand.

"This is Gracie Stevenson," said Crowe. "Her mother was also murdered, and she, too, has been missing since that night."

"It's Geneva," said Selena.

Crowe nodded.

"Same scenario, a man worked his way into the life of Gracie's mother, Maggie. Maggie was strangled in her bed, just like Stella. And Gracie disappeared. When Hunter Ross saw Geneva's picture on the news, he recognized her. All these years, he's kept investigating both cases, following stories he heard in the news, pinging the system for any new DNA evidence. Nothing until now."

Selena struggled with it, how the pieces fit together.

"So, they were connected," said Selena. "You think the same man abducted them both?"

"This woman," said Detective Crowe, holding up a picture of a young Pearl, "is the *sister* that reported Geneva missing in the first place."

"They were working together," said Selena. How could that be? Selena met Geneva on the playground. She alone had invited Geneva into their lives. But maybe that was the plan all along. Maybe that was all part of a long game that started years ago.

Crowe went on. "Maggie Stevenson's murder was never solved. Gracie was never found. And the man who was part of their lives, they knew him as James Parker, another ghost. Not even a picture of him left behind. They all disappeared."

"I don't understand."

Outside, the volume was coming up, voices raised a little, news vans arriving.

"Charles Finch, Pearl, Grace—they're con artists," said Crowe. "Working their way into people's lives and taking what they can get."

Con artists. It seemed like such an old-fashioned idea, something almost amusing, harmless, a minor scam like a shell game or three-card monte. An email that you might get from a Nigerian prince. Not this. Not lives destroyed, women hurt and killed.

"So, Geneva works her way into my home, becomes our nanny, then seduces Graham with the intent to blackmail him. And Pearl? What's her role in this? And why?"

"That I can't answer," he said. "Only she knows what kind of game she was running, what she wanted. Maybe she was just trying to hurt you."

There was more to it than that, wasn't there? Selena thought. *More than a game with my life?*

"My guess is that they didn't know what your husband, Graham, was capable of. They misjudged him. Geneva tried to blackmail him like she did Erik Tucker. And he killed her."

A jolt of sadness, a rush of tears to her eyes. She moved to wipe them away.

"You think she's dead," said Selena.

Crowe rubbed a hand over the crown of his head.

"We have some footage of Graham disposing of something in a dumpster a few miles from his brother's apartment the night Geneva went missing. We have the body of another young woman connected to your husband. He has a history of violence against women. And tonight you barely escaped him."

Her husband was a monster. She heard Pearl's whisper: *The*

worst of your problems is about to go away. Was there compassion and tenderness in Pearl's voice when she said it? Had Pearl, on some level, thought she was helping Selena?

The ambulance Graham was in pulled from the drive, sirens whooping to clear people and other vehicles, then going silent as it proceeded out of view. A police car and an unmarked sedan followed. Crowe's gaze traced the vehicles.

"Do you have anything else you need to tell me, Selena? About Graham, about Pearl Behr, about Geneva?"

"No," she said. But there *were* things she wanted to say. Things he probably wouldn't understand.

Geneva was a blackmailer and a home wrecker, but she was a good nanny; she took great care of Oliver and Stephen. She tended to them, played with them, and cared for them as well as Selena could have. The boys loved her; and they were going to miss her. Under other circumstances, Pearl might have been a good friend, a good sister; and she'd saved Selena's life, even as she'd essentially destroyed it. Graham had been a good husband much of the time, a decent father. She'd loved him, forgiven him, believed in him. Then, he'd tried to kill her, take her from her children.

They were bad people who had done unconscionable things. But there was more to them than that. Detective Crowe could never understand all the layers, all the facets, all the glittering good folded in with the bad. How complicated we all are; even the worst among us might still be worthy of love.

"No," she said again. "You know everything I know."

FORTY-THREE

Geneva

THE FOOTSTEPS GREW CLOSER, and Geneva held her breath. She'd had a lot of time to think, about the Murphys, the Tuckers, all the things she'd done. She'd made some decisions.

Closer, louder. Then she heard the outer door unlatch. It swung open with a squeal and then someone was coming down the stairs to the cellar. She roused herself from the cot, sat up.

Pearl turned on lights and came into view, stood slim in the doorway.

"You can't just lock me in here every time you don't know how to handle me," said Geneva.

The truth was, she didn't hate it down here in the root cellar. At least it was quiet. There was time and space to think about all of your mistakes, how you wanted to change, what you would do if you ever got out. She'd made some decisions.

"You were getting squirrely," said Pearl. "You had to be managed. Be happy you were in here. Things got ugly."

"Are the boys okay?" she asked, feeling a stutter in her heart. "Selena?"

A shrug, a wrinkled brow. "They will be."

Pearl approached, boots knocking on the floor, the sound echoing off the concrete walls. She carried a heavy black duffel bag on her shoulder.

"I'm done," Geneva said. "I'm done with this. For real."

Probably she should have just kept it to herself. She couldn't best Pearl in a fight; that had been proven time and again. What was to keep her from locking Geneva in here forever?

"You know what?" said Pearl. "So am I."

Geneva rubbed at her eyes. She was exhausted. How long had she been in the root cellar? Maybe not more than a day or two. It felt like a month.

"Yeah, right," she said. "You're worse than he was. He never locked me up."

There was a catalog of things that Pop had done to each of them. But the truth was, he was the closest thing to a father either of them had ever had. A terrible, manipulative, murderous, con artist father, who had loved them each in his way.

"It's not so bad down here," said Pearl. She wore that smile she had, sphinxlike, always laughing at a joke no one else got.

"It's a dungeon, bitch," said Geneva. "You locked me in the dungeon to keep me quiet and run your little game. That's fucked. You know that."

"You always had a flair for drama."

Pearl dropped the big duffel on the floor.

"What's that?" asked Geneva, eyeing it suspiciously. God only knew what was in there.

"Half," she said. "Half of everything I made with Pop and since. There's a clean identity from Merle—driver's license, passport, and Social."

Geneva dropped to her knees from the cot and opened the

bag. It was stuffed with cash. How much? A lot. Enough. She opened the envelope that lay on top.

Alice Grace Miller. Nice and simple, just like Pop would have wanted it, with a nod to her past self. A girl that was so long gone, Geneva didn't even remember her anymore.

"You can go anywhere now," said Pearl. "You can be anyone. You're free."

Geneva looked up at Pearl—who were they to each other? Sisters of circumstance, Pearl had said once. Geneva figured that was right. She searched herself for feeling, found something that was like a grudging affection, a kind of pact they'd sworn without words. They'd suffered together, knew each other. It bound them somewhat. They'd keep each other's secrets, take them to the grave.

"What about you?" she asked.

"Don't worry about me," Pearl said. "I'll find my way."

"I don't doubt it."

"Come on," said Pearl. "I'll give you a ride. We're a long way from anywhere."

There was something about the root cellar. It was cold and dark, but it was safe, predictable. Light shone in from outside from the door Pearl had opened, bright licking at the dark shadows. The whole big world was out there. Every place. All the possibilities of what her life could be, and damn if there wasn't part of her that just wanted to stay hidden.

Instead, she stood and found her shoes, her jacket. She shouldered the bag and followed Pearl outside, shielding her eyes against the blinding sun. Pearl closed and locked the door behind them. It was all but invisible in the brush.

"If the shit ever hits the fan," said Pearl, "just come back here, to the cellar. Text me."

She nodded. But she was never coming back here. She was never going to text Pearl.

Just a few feet away, they'd buried Pop and the woman who

killed him. Years ago. Five minutes ago. The grave site wasn't visible to the eye, lost, grown over by time and forest detritus. Geneva wasn't even sure where it was until Pearl stopped there for a moment, staring at the ground.

"I'm all done here, Pop," she said.

There was something small about her voice when she said his name, something young and soft. But her face was set in the hard lines of determination. And after a moment, she kept walking.

Geneva—Alice—climbed into the car. As they drove from the property, she looked in the rearview mirror to see billowing clouds of black smoke where the house would be. The place Pop had brought her that night so long ago. Where she lived with Pearl after Pop was gone. It was their home, in a weird way.

She was about to say something, to ask Pearl what she had done.

But, of course, she'd burn it all to the ground.

That was her way.

FORTY-FOUR

Pearl

THE DIVINE NOWHERE of airports. The ultimate liminal space, neither here nor there. Not truly in the place you're leaving, nor in the place you're going. A bardo. Here there might be a breath, a pause between selves, between worlds.

Her last burner phone. She found a section of seats in an empty gate and dialed. The other line rang and rang again. It was early. She always took the earliest flight. Outside the sky was still dark, other travelers were dazed and groggy, with their smartphones and coffees taking up all available bandwidth. Not Pearl. She was wide awake.

In the reflection of the big window looking down on the tarmac, there was a slim woman with a honey-colored bob wearing black leggings, turtleneck, a bomber jacket, black running shoes. Her makeup was light and natural; her belongings, like her outfit, all basic black. She amped down her beauty for this last journey—no lipstick, no perfume, just a light brown eyeshadow. Not much skin exposed, glasses she didn't really need.

Emily Pearl Miller. Her final identity.

She'd have to explain to Ben that her name wasn't really Gwyneth. He'd understand why she felt she needed to protect herself. You can never be too careful with a man you meet over the internet. There were cons and criminals, bad men, lying in wait everywhere.

She was about to hang up when the call engaged.

"Hunter Ross."

If he'd been sleeping, he didn't sound it.

"It's Pearl," she said, "Pearl Behr."

The name sounded off, felt awkward and stiff in her mouth like a lie. But it was the truest thing she'd said in a while.

There was a drawn breath, a moment of surprised silence. Then, "Hi, Pearl. I've been looking for you for a very long time."

"I know," she said. "Thank you. I think."

He cleared his throat. "What can I do for you?"

There were things she wanted to know, and things she wanted to tell. Hunter Ross was the only person she trusted.

"Did you ever find out who he really was? Charles Finch?"

"I never did," he said. "Don't *you* know?"

"No," she said truthfully. "He had so many identities even before I knew him. I'm not sure he remembered himself. And after he died, I looked through all his belongings. I never found a single authentic document."

"When did he die?"

"About five years ago," she said. "A woman he conned or tried to. She hunted him down and killed him, then killed herself." That was not the whole truth, of course. But she had to protect her little sister.

"Who was that?" he asked. She wondered if he was recording the call.

"Her name was Bridget." She didn't remember the last name. She felt oddly embarrassed by that. She didn't remember many of the names of the people she conned. They weren't people. They were marks.

"Okay," he said. "Where are their bodies?"

She flashed on that night. Digging the graves. Grace weeping.

"If I tell you, what will you do?"

There was a moment of quiet, where she figured he considered lying. But Hunter Ross was an honest man.

"Call it in," he said finally. "Someone will go and dig them up."

Did she want that? Did she want them dug up? What would happen to Pop's remains, some government grave?

"Did he kill my mother?" she asked. "Did you ever suspect anyone else?"

A breath drawn and released. "What do you think, Pearl?"

"She had a lot of boyfriends." Stella was a tease, a user. She hurt people just for fun. Any one of the men in Stella's life might have turned angry and violent. That's what men did, wasn't it, when they didn't get what they wanted from a woman? Some men.

"Men that came and went," he said. "No one who stayed on. No one who really, in his heart of hearts, wanted *you*."

She let that sink in, the truth of it.

"He took care of me," she said finally. She didn't want to think that Pop killed Stella. But probably he did. "He never hurt me. Never—touched me."

"It sounds like you loved him."

"Maybe I did. In a way."

"And Gracie Stevenson."

"He loved her, too."

She heard him clear his throat again in that way old men always do. There was a woman's voice in the background. *Who is that, Hunt? It's so early.*

"Her mother was also murdered," said Ross. His tone was gently leading.

"Yes."

"I'm seeing a pattern here. Aren't you?"

She didn't answer him. Just a few more minutes and she'd end the call and trash the phone.

"Where is she? Where's Gracie—or should I call her Geneva?"

"She's somewhere safe," she said, hoping that was true. She was pretty sure they'd never see each other again. "Starting fresh. We're both done."

"With all the games you've been playing."

"That's right."

"I've been trying to figure the two of you out. How you worked together."

"I wouldn't say we *worked* together."

"No?"

"She had her things," said Pearl. "I had mine. We had different styles."

This wasn't the whole truth. Pearl was always the puppeteer, pulling Gracie's strings, whether she knew it or not.

"So the Tuckers, that was *her* thing? Get a job as a nanny, sleep with the husband, then blackmail him to stay quiet."

"Something like that," said Pearl. "I think it was just her twisted way of trying to be a part of a family." Also not really true. Gracie hated breaking up families. But she was *very* good at it. The scores were smallish but consistent.

But it was, in fact, Pearl who brought the Tuckers' need for a nanny to Gracie's attention; they were part of Selena's network of social media friends. And it was Pearl who encouraged Grace to meet Selena in the park, having seen also on social media that Selena was about to go back to work. Then, things just fell together the way they do when you're *in the flow.*

"But Selena, she was *your* thing, *your* half sister. You'd been watching her for years, right? Must have been."

Yes, that was true.

Pearl had hovered on the edge of Selena's life for years—online stalking Selena and her friends, Selena's sister (Pearl's other half sister) Marisol, who for some reason interested Pearl less. She watched from afar as Selena got married, had children, bought a new house, built brick-by-brick her Instagram-perfect life.

Pearl had also watched Graham on social media, though he was far less active and had a smaller network. Occasionally, she followed him. When, a couple of years into their marriage, Pearl realized he was unfaithful, she watched him more closely.

A strange thing happened. She started to feel sorry for Selena.

"So what was it? Revenge? Just another way to hurt the father who abandoned you?" asked Hunter. "What was the game with the Murphy family? More money? To destroy their family?"

The question surprised Pearl, causing her a rare moment of self-reflection.

What was the reason? Was there just one?

At first maybe yes, revenge; she was just on a program of causing the most amount of pain.

There would have been a score most likely—if Selena hadn't moved the camera and caught Gracie and Graham fucking. If Gracie hadn't grown a conscience and kept threatening to pull the plug.

But it was so much more than that. When Pearl realized what Graham was—not just a cheater, but a monster—she wanted him punished. She wanted to liberate Selena, just like so many years ago she had liberated Cora. This was the ultimate long game, one that started over a decade earlier. She'd hovered, waiting for the perfect point of entry. The score? It wasn't about money. It wasn't really about revenge. She wasn't like Pop.

It was about the truth. The truth like a wildfire that burned everything in its path. One that destroyed but also cleansed. And then from the ash, new life.

But Pearl didn't have the patience to explain this to Hunter Ross. She suspected that he was the type of man who only saw things in black-and-white. What she did was wrong. He would never understand that it was right, too.

"Yes," she said just to keep it simple. The call was going on too long. "That's it. Revenge."

And maybe deep down, it was *that* simple. That she didn't want justice for Jaqueline Carson. Or punishment for Graham, the man who used and killed her. Or to free her half sister from the illusions of her life. That she didn't care about anyone but herself, about anything but the games she was playing with people's lives.

"I'd say you did what you set out to do," he said. His voice sounded heavy with fatigue.

"I suppose I did." She had a hollow feeling in her stomach, a familiar empty sadness. She breathed through it.

"So what's next?"

"I disappear. Like I said, I'm done."

"Until?"

"Until."

Another leaden silence where she considered hanging up.

"So—may I ask the reason for your call?" he said finally.

Good question, whispered Pop. He was always just over her shoulder. *What kind of a game are you running here?*

"Closure," she said. "For you, for me. You're a rare breed. A good man who doesn't give up until he finds the truth. One who cares and puts other people first. I like that about you."

He issued a little chuckle. "Thank you for saying so."

She told him where Pop and Bridget were buried. She'd moved the flag that marked the root cellar to mark the grave. It would be relatively easy to find. Pop, Charles, Bill, Jim, Chris, an abused child, a con, a grifter, a killer—he was a wanted man. Pearl wanted Hunter Ross to catch him, finally. So maybe then they both could rest.

She didn't know if anyone was still looking for Bridget, but maybe now she could rest, too.

There was nothing left to say. He had all the answers she had to give.

"Goodbye, Mr. Ross. Thanks for never giving up on us."

"Goodbye, Pearl."

If she had her way, that was the last time anybody would call her that.

She ended the call, took the SIM card from the phone. In the bathroom, she flushed the card down the toilet, put the broken pieces of the phone in the trash.

Her flight was boarding. She stood on line and filed in the early group getting on the plane, finally settling into her first-class seat.

When she stepped off, she'd be someone else. Ben would be waiting for her. A good man, a faithful and loving one. Maybe she could never truly love him, or anyone. But she could try.

She'd told Ben that, now that her sister had died (overdose, of course—so sad), she wanted to travel, to see the world she had never been able to explore. He agreed. He was ready to take some time off of work, as well. He would leave his practice with his partner for a time. Later, they'd decide what to do, where to settle.

What a perfect way to start our new life together, he said. *A fresh start, a clean slate for both of us.*

Emily's thoughts exactly.

FORTY-FIVE

Selena

I DID YOU A FAVOR. *One day, you'll see that.*

A month after Pearl set fire to her father's life, Cora saw the girl hovering again on the sidewalk by the oak where she'd seen her before. This time, instead of hesitating, Cora opened the door and went outside to meet her.

There was a moving van in the driveway, most of Cora's possessions and the girls' in boxes. They were moving out of the big house, into something smaller on the other side of town. Cora let Doug have the house; she couldn't live in a place that was alive with memories, where the ghosts of every one of her broken dreams was hiding around each corner. Selena and Marisol were both off at school and Cora was alone for the first time in her adult life.

What do you want, Pearl? Cora asked when the girl approached. She looked older than the last time Cora saw her, more confident and poised, more polished.

I wanted to say I'm sorry.

This came as some surprise to Cora. *You're sorry.*

I'm sorry you were hurt.

Cora didn't know what to say. She, too, felt like she should apologize. Because Pearl had also been hurt. Cora could see that in her. Unlike Cora, who had absorbed blows, and kept quiet all these years, Pearl had struck out in her anger. She'd aimed at her target and hit a bull's-eye.

You got what you wanted, right? said Cora. *Whatever your price was, he paid it. Now leave us alone.*

Cora remembered that Pearl looked disappointed. *It wasn't just about that.*

No?

I did you a favor, she said, cool and pretty, aloof. *One day, you'll see that.*

Now, in her attic office, Selena sought to capture that final encounter between Cora and Pearl on paper. How could Selena describe what that street was like in early fall, her mother's despair, the beautiful and mysterious Pearl hovering on the street? She remembered how the air always smelled like cut grass, and the blue jays squawked in the trees. She knew what it was like to find yourself face to face with Pearl Behr, who somehow seemed to know more about you than you knew about yourself.

And you know what, Cora told Selena when they talked about that final encounter, *Pearl was right. Ending my life with your father was the best thing that ever happened to me, even though it felt like the worst time of my life. I lost everything, but I found myself. I went to work at the shelter, found Paulo.*

Black Butterfly. It was Beth who encouraged her to write the story of Pearl Behr and Grace Stevenson, and how their lives intersected with her own. After two years of research, with the help of Hunter Ross, Selena was nearing the final editorial draft. Beth had brokered a book contract with a major house, and the book was slated to publish next year. What had she been before she met Will, Graham, had children? She was a writer, a dream she let languish and die. Now, through the ashes of her life, she rose.

Write it, said Beth. *When we narrate our experience, we take control of it. And in controlling the story of our past, we can create a better future.*

Graham's trial and conviction for the murder of Jaqueline Carson, his imprisonment, the boys' therapy, their crushing pain, her own. It had been a long, dark night of the soul where no light was visible at the end of the tunnel. Through it all, she wrote and wrote.

She kept writing as the truth about her husband—all of it—came out.

After years of affairs with coworkers, women he'd met in bars, strippers, and a pattern of escalating violence toward women—the girl in Vegas was just the beginning—the night Selena threw Graham out of the house, he'd killed Jaqueline Carson.

Graham had been harassing Jacqueline via text since she'd gotten him fired from his job. The night Selena hit him with the toy robot, Graham was desperate and enraged, and he'd waited for Jacqueline outside her apartment, forced her inside when she came home, raped and killed her.

He still claimed he didn't remember the deed, that he couldn't remember, either, how he tried to kill Selena, his wife and the mother of his children. He'd wept on the stand. And, truly, Selena could see how his rage turned him into a monster, someone she never met until that final night. When he said that he couldn't remember, she believed him.

But there was video of Graham struggling to put a rolled up rug into his SUV outside Jacqueline's apartment, captured by a security camera. Later, a picture of him passing through a toll booth on the way to dispose of the body. Finally, a photo of Graham throwing what turned out to be his bloody clothes in a dumpster, apparently taken by Pearl, who was following him.

It still wasn't clear to Selena how much Pearl had seen—that night or other nights. Why, if she'd followed Graham and knew he was waiting for Jaqueline outside her apartment, she did nothing to stop it.

But this was something that had come up in therapy. Her doctor had said: "You cannot explain or come to understand the actions of deranged people. You can only accept what has happened and try to move forward, grateful that you have survived them."

And if not for Cora, Paulo, and Marisol, Beth and Will, as well as the resilient strength of her children, she wouldn't have. And for all her failings, without Pearl, Selena might not have survived Graham.

But she was still writing, still trying to understand, piecing together what she learned from the trial, from the stories of the women who came forward to testify against Graham. She would keep writing until she had told the whole story, the whole truth and all its many facets.

The clock read nearly two, just another hour before she had to pick up the boys from their new school, a tiny private place where they were coddled and sheltered from the ugliness in their world. She answered their questions the best she could, brought to therapy what she couldn't, promised herself she'd always be honest with them, no matter how much it hurt.

Oliver and Stephen talked to Graham every Sunday. Weirdly, it had taken on a kind of normalcy—they talked to him about school, their friends, soccer. He moderated their arguments, praised them, soothed them when they begged him to come home. Selena had not brought them to see him, though they'd asked. Neither she nor Graham wanted that, not yet. When they were older. Maybe. Selena didn't think about Graham. Didn't talk to him. He was more dead to her than if he had died.

Sometimes she dreamed about him, as he loomed over her, crushing her throat and taking the air from her lungs.

The house she'd found for herself and the boys was isolated on five acres of property, not too far from Cora and Paulo, who helped her in every way possible, and closer to her sister's house.

Their relationship had grown stronger, her sister helping with the kids, Selena doing the same for her. As a result, Oliver and Stephen were closer to their cousins. Family gatherings were more peaceful. No more secrets. No more lies.

Selena had severed ties with her father. She had no room in her life for someone who'd invited so much darkness into his family.

Their other house languished on the market for a time—no one wanted to live where a killer had lived. But people had short memories, and a few months after Graham's conviction, the story seemed to fade from the public consciousness. The house sold for a bit less than market value. But it was worth it to move on from a place where, as her mother put it, the ghosts of broken dreams lived around every corner.

The house they lived in now, an 1880 farmhouse in an upstate New York town called The Hollows, was a project. It needed work, and it occupied much of Selena's time and attention when she wasn't writing or caring for the boys. Which is exactly why she bought it. The last thing she needed was free time.

Outside, she heard tires crunching on the drive. She saved her work and headed downstairs in time to watch Will come through the front door, holding a large bouquet of tiger lilies, her favorite.

He'd recused himself as Graham's lawyer to become hers after the attack. Another lawyer defended Graham when he went to trial.

Now, Selena and Will were—friends. She knew he wanted more. He knew she was nowhere near ready. She needed space to find herself. Finally.

"What's this?" she asked, taking the flowers. She gave him a squeeze and a kiss on the cheek.

"It's—you know," he started. "Just something to brighten the day."

"Thank you," she said. "You're good to me, Will."

It was Friday. Will came over most Friday afternoons to play with the boys in the yard, then for pizza and movies. Sometimes, Marisol and her kids joined, as well. It was something they'd set up to create a sense of normalcy for Oliver and Stephen—and it seemed to work. Their therapist said that she was doing all the right things, that the boys were dealing with things in a healthy, normal way. Only time would tell.

But did Oliver seem more sullen and dark? Was the pitch of Stephen's tantrums more desperate? Would any of them ever be whole again? Would the darkness from their father, from her own father, infect them? Was it wound into their DNA?

These were the things that kept her up at night, worrying about the contagion of secrets and lies, dark impulses, violent tendencies.

At the kitchen table, she and Will chatted a while—about her book, about a case he was working on, what movies they should watch tonight. When he offered to pick up the kids so that she could get a workout, she agreed. The boys were always happy to see Will; he filled a space that was empty in each of them now. And she was grateful for his friendship, to all of them. A good man, if flawed in some ways, if not a perfect match for Selena, an honest and respectful one. Paulo, too, was a strong and positive influence. Her boys had men to look to, role models of the kind of quiet strength that comes from integrity and a heart that can love women well.

When he left, she went upstairs and put on her running shoes, her workout clothes. Then she hit the rural road that led away from the house. The air was warm, and the sky clear. It took her a while to find her stride after sitting at her computer all day. But the music pumping in her headphones—Nirvana today, Kurt Cobain's ghostly voice raw and wild—brought her energy up. She'd gone a mile when her phone pinged. She slowed to check it, in case Will had run into issues at the school.

Instead there was a text from an unfamiliar number. It wasn't the first time. She hadn't told anyone, but Pearl reached out to her every few months—usually coinciding with a news cycle that included something about Graham. There was a connection there, something strange but true.

I've been thinking of you. I'm happy-ish. Hope you are, too.

Selena never answered. She knew she wasn't expected to. There wasn't going to be more to the relationship than there was. Pearl had disappeared completely, gone without a trace. She was a wanted woman, charges pending for fraud, extortion, blackmail. Apparently, the list of people she and Geneva had scammed and conned was long—most of them men, most of those men guilty of something themselves. Selena was supposed to report contact to the police, but she wasn't going to do that. In her heart, there was a painful kind of gratitude. She'd destroyed Selena's life. She'd saved Selena's life. She'd taken something. Given something. It was complicated.

I saw a picture of Graham in the joint. He really looks like shit. What did you ever see in him?

Selena laughed a little; sometimes Pearl was funny. Sometimes her texts sounded sad, lonely. Other times they were inane—a comment on the price of gasoline or some news event. Occasionally, she sounded angry. The day Graham was convicted: I'm glad he got what he deserved. Now you're free. If she knew about the book Selena was writing, she hadn't said. Selena imagined that Pearl would have a comment or two about that. But whatever the missive, Pearl always ended her communications the same way, a kind of inside joke.

Selena waited, watching the little gray dots pulse.

It's Martha, by the way.

From the train.

★★★★★

ACKNOWLEDGMENTS

EVERY NOVEL IS a journey. It starts with a germ, a thought, a moment. And even though the writing of it is a solitary thing, a quiet and daily evolution from idea to finished novel, there's a whole universe of people who help in all kinds of ways bring it out into the world.

For me, everything begins and ends with my husband, Jeffrey, and our daughter, Ocean. They fill my life with love and laughter and keep me grounded in the things that are important, offering endless support and encouragement. I would be a lesser person and a lesser writer without them.

My agent, Amy Berkower, her assistant, Meridith Viguet, and the stellar team at Writers House offer all manner of support, helping me navigate the big waters of the writing life. I am so grateful for their wisdom, organization, passion and dedication. I feel very fortunate to have such exemplary representation.

My deep and heartfelt thanks to my editor, Erika Imranyi. Her patience, wisdom, intelligence and loving editorial guidance took this book from the best I could make it to the best it could be. I am so grateful for her skills as an editor and her sterling friendship. The rest of the team at Park Row Books—from powerhouse VP of editorial Margaret Marbury to publicist extraordinaire Roxanne Jones to eagle-eyed copy editor Jennifer Stimson—could not be more thoughtful, engaged and dedicated. I am grateful for the vision of the art department, the tireless and often overlooked efforts of the production team and the intrepid spirit of the sales force.

I am blessed with a vast network of family and friends, who tirelessly brag about me and promote my books. My parents, Joseph and Virginia Miscione, and my brother, Joe, are out there endlessly spreading the word and facing books out on shelves across the country. Erin Mitchell is an early reader, voice of reason, champion and wonderful friend. Heather Mikesell has been one of the first readers of almost everything I have written. Nothing feels done until she has read it.

A writer is nothing without her readers. And I am blessed beyond measure to have such a warm, loving and supportive group of family, friends and faithful longtime fans who read, promote and turn up at events locally and around the country. Thank you for showing up, for spreading the word and for reading. It means more than you can know.

This is a work of fiction, but all fiction is rooted in truth, and research is a big part of my process. *The Confidence Game* by Maria Konnikova brought me deep inside the mind of the con artist. *Liespotting: Proven Techniques to Detect Deception* by Pamela Meyer, and the author's fascinating TED Talk, informed my understanding of why and how people lie. That said, all mistakes and liberties taken for the sake of fiction are mine.